OVERTONES

BY
PAUL ABRAHAMS

www.overtonesnovel.com

Paul Abrahams grew up in London's 'East End' and left school at sixteen for a day job as a tax officer. But by night he was playing keyboards round the pubs and clubs, and by 1967 he turned professional, backing acts such as P J Proby, Joe Brown and Percy Sledge. His first writing experiences were as a songwriter for various bands, and later as a composer for the theatre. He is best known now for his teaching and books on learning jazz piano. *Overtones* is his first work of fiction.

In memory of David Worth:
artist and saxophone player.

Cover by Alex Kirby.

This edition is printed by CreateSpace, an Amazon.company

OVERTONES

CONTENTS

PART 1 BULLS
7 November 1977 – 1 January 1978   *Page 9*

PART 2 DARTS
13 January 1978 – 6 February 1978   *Page 105*

PART 3 ARROWS
28 April 1978 – 11 December 1978   *Page 139*

PART 4 OVERTONES
15 October 1987 – 12 December 1987   *Page 233*

PART 1
BULLS

7 November 1977 – 1 January 1978

Monday, 7 November 1977

7.25 p.m. I am perfectly content, thank you very much. Friendless and loveless are two positive words, the opposites of which denote dependency and insanity. I prefer to watch such goings-on from the safe vantage point of my dead aunt's sofa. The fun starts in five minutes.

7.30 p.m. To validate this luxuriating sense of self-reliance, I have chosen to break from the national zeitgeist. Away with *Coronation Street*! I will forge my own path via BBC1.

7.45 p.m. My mood has been blighted, no thanks to Eamonn O'Brien. After fifteen minutes of tedium, this wisecracking buffoon of a host has now resorted to frantically overworking his audience. His upbeat efforts to compensate for an array of lacklustre guests appearing on his mediocre variety show are already wearing thin. I resist the impulse to switch to *Coronation Street*, only because I now lie comatose with one arm dangling towards my can of Fosters. Moving would only precipitate an unwanted change of temperature, a quickening of the heart rate.

A comedy double act by the name of Cannon and Ball bewilders me, but the dumb stooge who behaves as though he has mental problems goes down well with the audience. My mood lightens with the certain knowledge that I will never have to interface with such individuals.

O'Brien bounces back on, delivers a vacuous gag about Jeremy Thorpe and a dog, and then promises us that we are now in for a real treat. We are about to meet a young man from Huddersfield, West Yorkshire: a newcomer who is currently causing a sensation in the darts world. Can such a world truly exist? Apparently, in three months from now, this lad is odds-on to become the undisputed world darts champion. This show must be on a severely limited budget.

I'm just about to switch over to see if Charlie has decided to stay on at 'The Rovers', when I notice that something has gone badly wrong. The house band has completed a chorus of 'Cupid' to bring on the guest. But after an uneasy pause, the tune begins to repeat, as our future darts champion is yet to move from the top step. O'Brien flaps his arms in a bid to maintain the applause while the young man remains rooted to the spot, his watery, light blue eyes staring wildly into the camera.

He wears an oversized cream suit that went out of fashion twenty years ago and what looks like a grammar school tie. Facially, he is a slightly ruddy, podgy, farmer's boy version of David Bowie. His straw-coloured hair is carefully parted to the left. Had he by now been gliding confidently down the steps, egotistically soaking up the applause, one might have taken him for the new David Soul or a glamorous rock singer. But he is petrified.

This promising turn of events coaxes me into a half recline. I take a swig of my now tepid Fosters.

Only a few hands continue to clap as our host finally makes his way up the steps and takes the lad's arm. He starts, as though woken from a trance, then allows himself to be slowly led to the interviewee's chair. Something is whispered to him, perhaps words of reassurance. His hand is shaken.

'Ladies and gentlemen, James Kelly.'

There is another smattering of applause as they eye each other, both looking for clues as to how to proceed.

Almost a year ago, stretched out on this very sofa, I recall holding my breath as Bill Grundy delivered his infamous career-ending provocation to the Sex Pistols: 'Go on, you've got another five seconds. Say something outrageous!' Although James Kelly seems unlikely to say very much at all, I haul myself up to a sitting position, feeling that same thrill of anticipation.

'So James, although you're fast approaching the grand old age of twenty, I believe your interest in darts began as a young teenager.' As though hypnotised, James stares blankly at his interrogator. 'You would have been a bit young to go *tut poob*. So what happened?' The mock Yorkshire accent elicits a mild titter from the audience. James, however, is now craning his neck towards the laughter. 'Are you looking for your mum?' quips O'Brien.

James' head slowly turns back. His face is solemn. 'She'll be watching *Coronation Street*.' This gets the first genuine laugh, and our host visibly relaxes back into his chair. But James is now on his feet. 'Uncle Ken's out there.'

'Now then, ladies and gentleman ...' O'Brien has risen to his feet and I also find myself sitting upright, now transfixed.

O'Brien has wrapped an arm around the boy's shoulder. He flinches. So do I. 'Now then, this isn't just any old Uncle Ken from *oop north*. We're talking about former Yorkshire champion, and winner of the 1969 *News of the World* championships: Kenneth Bell! Where are you Uncle Kenneth? Give us a wave.'

A spotlight falls on a dishevelled, middle-aged man with tufts of ginger hair sprouting from a balding head. His beer gut pokes through a hand-knitted, grey cardigan. Surely no former world champion could degenerate to this extent?

The light applause suggests that no one has ever heard of him, nor do they have the faintest interest in darts.

James points at his uncle. 'He gave me a dartboard when I was thirteen.'

Kenneth Bell forces a grin to mask his obvious discomfort. He beckons James to sit, then sinks back into the darkness, allowing O'Brien to continue.

'And that's one present that wasn't destined for the bottom

drawer. In fact, earlier this year, you followed in your Uncle Ken's footsteps. I believe you came within a hair's breadth of winning the *News of the World* championship. But sadly, you were just pipped at the post by a young cockney lad a trifle less shy than your good self, by the name of …'

'Eric Bristow.'

The host raises his eyebrows to the audience, summoning a forced response from those who recognise the name. 'I bet you two could barely understand a word each other said.'

'We didn't speak.'

'Now, what do we have here? Am I detecting just a touch of rivalry? But that would be hardly surprising, because, ladies and gentleman, for the first time on TV – it's BBC2 so I can mention it – we are soon to witness the very first televised world professional darts championship, sponsored by Embassy cigarettes. Am I allowed to say that?'

The fool might consider allowing his show to rise from the dead by saying nothing for five seconds, but ploughs on.

'So where's it being held, James?'

Silence.

A voice from the darkness comes to the rescue. 'Nottingham.'

'Thanks Uncle Ken – where would we be without Uncle Ken, ladies and gentlemen! So, my boy, who's it to be this time? Who'll be holding up that trophy on February the 10th?'

'John Lowe.'

'The boy's a joker! He should be on the stage; it leaves in half an hour.'

But James Kelly is not making a joke. His words are delivered flatly and without a hint of irony. He then leans slightly forward. 'Would you like to ask me more questions?'

During the agonising moments that O'Brien searches his brain for a question, I hurriedly draw the curtains and drag a chair up to within a yard of the TV.

O'Brien's desperation to curtail the interview has gained momentum. He is clearly rattled. 'I'm sure we could chat all night son, but the clock's almost beaten us.'

James' right arm suddenly lurches forward. I'm willing a bead of sweat to drip from Eamonn's brow as he instinctively raises an arm to protect himself. The lad has produced a dart from his jacket pocket and is poised to press its point into the palm of his left hand. O'Brien has regained some composure, although his wink to the audience looks more like a wince. 'Ah, so you've brought along your ammunition! That's a lucky coincidence, as we have a little surprise in store. Behind that curtain, the lovely Angela can now reveal a dartboard – sadly, that's *all* she's going to reveal tonight, boys – and she'll set a mark, precisely seven feet six inches from the board. Now, I've done my homework and have been reliably informed that this measurement is soon to be lengthened to bring us in line with the game overseas. Any thoughts on this, my son?'

My hope is that James' watery blue eyes will just continue to stare, but he goes one better. 'It makes no difference. I aim at myself.'

O'Brien sidesteps this response by launching into a corny routine.

'Oo, painful! I won't be trying that technique just yet, but to prove that I'm no slouch with the arrows, just you watch this!'

Angela hands a dart to the host, who takes aim and wiggles his behind. To the accompaniment of a swanee whistle, the missile veers wildly to the right of the dartboard and heads towards the piano. I'm now craning forward in the chair, my nose within a foot of the screen, willing the dart to sink deep into the pianist's jet-black toupee.

'Sorry about that Colin – lucky you've got another nine fingers,' quips O'Brien. Well, after that debacle, I'd say it's time to bring in the expert.'

PART 1: BULLS

With feigned nonchalance, Colin attempts to reassert his authority by summoning a roll from the smirking drummer.

James shuffles into position and adopts an ungainly stance. Then, in an instant, it is as though he has stepped on to his own planet. Facing the board, his eyes defocus, forehead muscles relax, and his face drains of any expression. His right arm is raised, but there seems no outward sign of preparation. I am not fooled by the expectant hush: the type of person that attends these shows secretly revels in the failure of others. But I perceive something in his transformed physicality that fills me with an undefined hope. The initial backwards pivoting action of his upper arm is somehow reminiscent of a swan's neck. Then, with a flick of the wrist, the dart, rather than hurtling towards its target, describes a slight upward arc and descends into the bull's eye. Seemingly unaware of the predictable roar of approval, James methodically retrieves his dart and returns to the spot. The hole left by the first dart is instantly refilled, to the accompaniment of a marginally less enthusiastic cheer. I, alone, urge him on. Again, he collects the dart, retraces his steps and throws it a third time into the bull's eye. Now, apart from a solitary heckler calling out 'One hundred and eighty,' the audience is virtually silent. But I've kicked aside my chair and am on my feet with both fists clenched above my head.

Back on his spot, James dreamily raises an arm in preparation for a fourth throw.

'I think you'll find that's one hundred and fifty,' interjects our host, as he gently lowers James' arm and ushers him back to his seat.

I am shrieking at O'Brien: 'No, you idiot, don't stop him!' But he has regained his composure and is back in control.

'Well, ladies and gentlemen, that was quite something! By the looks of it, the lad could go on hitting that bull's eye all evening. And what a warning shot to the other competitors! So

James, any final message to Eric Bristow or ... what's that other chap's name?' O'Brien now knows better than to wait for a response. He claps his hands. 'Well *my* money's on *this* lad. So, ladies and gentlemen, I give you the young man who's currently setting the darts world alight: the phenomenal ... James Kelly! And now, by a spooky coincidence, we have with us an exciting new group from Bristol. You've probably seen them on *Top of the Pops*, they have a top ten hit with "Daddy Cool" and they're called – yes, you've guessed it: Darts!'

8.15 p.m. Although the TV has been off for fifteen minutes, James Kelly continues to gaze from the screen. But now his eyes are full of caring and understanding. He observes me without judgement as I distractedly pace around my room, emitting intermittent high-pitched sobs usually reserved for Abba ballads.

8.45 p.m. Back on the sofa and with a clearer head, I attempt to assimilate what I, and thousands around the country, have just witnessed.

On a damp Monday evening, while most folks were having their tea, a strange, beautiful youth from Huddersfield did one of two things on BBC1: he either made a complete fool of himself or performed a miracle that we could all achieve ourselves ... I'm not sure which.

Whenever I dream that I am levitating, I perform a perfectly ordinary miracle. I simply lift off from the ground with a heel to toe movement that levers me up vertically. I rise a few feet, and casually hover until I'm ready to descend. Then, as I awake, it's as though the knack is only just beyond my grasp. But James Kelly was not asleep while executing his ordinary miracle; he was live on TV. Moreover, it was the total lack of drama that bestowed his performance with such majesty. It was as though he was demonstrating that we are all capable of achieving the seemingly impossible. James Kelly was reminding us how to levitate.

9.30 p.m. I am calm and resolved. Tomorrow morning I will buy a dartboard and a set of darts. Perhaps others will have the same idea, so I'll set out early for Argos in Brixton. This is a catalogue store, where you merely have to look up the item number, fill in a slip, and exchange it for the goods with no questions asked.

Tuesday, 8 November 1977

9.30 a.m. Argos, Brixton. I take a casual walk through the store to ascertain whether any other customers are already studying the darts equipment page. Satisfied that I am alone in my mission, I select my catalogue, locate the sports section and leaf past exercise equipment, tennis rackets, bicycles and fishing rods. The darts page, thankfully, offers me the choice between just two dartboards: the Winmau Bristle at £8.70 and the Nodor, described as 'the world's first and finest bristle dartboard' at £9.25. To save fifty-five pence and miss out on 'the world's finest' does not seem cost-effective; so the Nodor it is. This product also comes with a self-adhesive 'oche' strip, whatever that may be. In the light of this decision, it seems fitting to complement my dartboard with a £12 set of Durro, tungsten nickel-alloy darts, 'complete with flights, stems, wallet and dart holders'. I had been expecting to spend no more than a fiver but there's no turning back. I fill out the paperwork and am handed my goods in exchange for £21.25. I'm surprised by the dartboard's weight, but at least it comes in a box with a handle.

I commandeer a back seat on the number 45 bus and balance the package between my knees. The mild fever of anticipation over a purchase that one cannot wait to get home and unwrap is clearly lacking in this case. In fact, I'm feeling a little ashamed that passengers might notice what I've bought, and so have already rehearsed a reply that it's for my nephew. Not that people usually strike up conversations on South London buses. At least it will be straightforward to set up, with no leads, plugs or incomprehensible manuals to deal with.

It is *not* easy to set up. I had hoped to find just one hook, rather than a bag of screws and a wall bracket. I've never drilled a hole in my life. I will buy a drill.

3.15 p.m I now own a Black & Decker drill, various sizes of Rawlplugs and a pack of thirty-two spare 'drill bits'. This has cost me twice the amount I spent on the dartboard equipment and I only need to drill two holes.

4.20 p.m. My dartboard is hanging up over the disused fireplace in the spare room, its centre precisely sixty-eight inches from the floor. I am positioned seven feet, nine and a quarter inches from the wall, clutching three darts in my right hand. Below my feet is the aforementioned self-adhesive strip, which is already curling up at each end due to my having chosen not to stick it to the carpet. But I do know now what an oche is (although I've no idea how to pronounce it), and that I am not allowed to step beyond it.

I transfer the first dart to my left hand, take aim – and freeze. I'm still tightly gripping the dart with two fingers and a thumb, as I gaze into the far distance. Surely I have done this before sometime in my life, as a child, perhaps, or in a pub in my late teens. But I doubt it. I throw and hit 18; the second dart sticks in the wall; the third hits the bull's eye! I am elated. I leave a triumphant message on June's answer machine and return for a second look. I would take a photo if I owned a camera. I'll not throw another dart this afternoon, but will periodically visit the spare room to witness this extraordinary achievement.

8 p.m. June from upstairs folds her arms over her bulging stomach and observes me as though she knows a thing or two about darts. She may be pregnant again, but it's a wonder how she manages to stuff her legs into those tight jeans. She's counting up my score while spouting off some of the rules.

Apparently she plays darts with her son Stephen.

'Twenty-six … you can only improve.'

'Actually, I threw a bull's eye on my third dart.'

'So you said. But it's really not about bull's eyes, you know. The aim is to work down from either 501 or 301, then to *check out* – that means finish – with a double.' With much irritation, I yank out my darts and hand them over as she continues to pontificate in this schoolmistress-like manner. 'It's good practice to go for doubles, perhaps going *round the clock* – that's numerical order. Anyway, I'm complete rubbish at this, as I will now demonstrate.'

And indeed she *is* rubbish, although marginally less so than I turn out to be. All her darts at least land in the board. She flicks back her unruly hair, tots up her score and hands back the darts. When she suggests that we start a 'proper game', I choose not to reply, but instead throw my three darts in quick succession as though it were my style. She calculates my score and deducts the 11. I am now paying her little attention until she embarks on an explanation of the scoring system. I interrupt.

'June: The only reason I bought this dartboard was to hit the bull's eye. I really haven't the faintest interest in match play. Even if I did, all that subtraction would be beyond me.'

I am feeling wretched, but not because I'm a dunce at maths. Of *course* I realise that darts has a scoring system, and that in order to win, more skill is required than merely aiming for the centre. And yet, as I watched James Kelly ramming home bull's eyes, I was convinced that he had attained the highest of spiritual goals. Perhaps I was getting confused with archery. 'One hundred and eighty,' a member of the audience had called out: that was what you were supposed to score, not one hundred and fifty. June is right: it isn't about bull's eyes. That's why I feel wretched.

As we throw a few more darts with increasingly dismal results, I make it quite apparent that I have absolutely no desire to play a proper game, let alone 'the best of three legs' as June pretentiously puts it. I am making no effort to add up my scores. She finally gives up.

'You play the piano, don't you, David?' My hope is that June interprets my shrug as showing modesty. 'It's just that Stephen hasn't touched the piano for months and it's gathering dust. I was wondering if you'd like to have it. I don't want any money, but it's in fairly good nick … probably just in need of a tune-up.'

I ignore the insinuation that I am penniless. 'I haven't played since I was sixteen … and don't really have the time to practise.'

'Don't have the time? You seem to spend most of your life watching TV.'

'Don't tell me you weren't watching *Coronation Street* last night.'

'It was on in the background.'

'Well, on the other side there was this amazing darts player.'

'Someone at school did mention it: a cringe-making interview, followed by some sort of a circus act.'

I fold my arms in a limp attempt to be assertive. 'To my mind, anyone that can hit successive bull's eyes without even trying is a cut above a circus act. In fact, I see him as being pretty special.'

'Colleagues in my field would see him more as someone with severe behavioural problems. Apparently Eamonn had to move in and bring the whole fiasco to a halt … So do you want the piano or not?'

Wednesday, 9 November 1977

10 a.m. What, then, was so special? Perhaps nothing was special after all. It seems that James Kelly has not changed the world overnight; in fact, he has made no difference whatsoever. To my profound disappointment, after a wasted hour in Clapham reference library scouring newspaper articles, I could only turn up the odd paragraph alluding to Monday night's bizarre behaviour.

On reflection, there really wasn't much to report. He was hardly likely to be trumpeted as the new saviour of darts on last night's showing. Neither had he come across as the new Uri Geller, whose charisma surely emanates from *believing* himself to be special. James Kelly's seeming eccentricity and awkwardness could, I suppose, be misconstrued as charm – and he is certainly rather beautiful – but Mister Showbiz he is not. And as for what he actually did: his own version of spoon bending – it is of no use to anyone and has zero entertainment value after five minutes. James Kelly is a one trick pony. He had his fifteen minutes of fame and blew it. We can put him into the category of men who swallow razor blades. I will let it go.

3.30 p.m. I have not let it go. On the contrary, I've purchased a book on darts from WH Smith, but have yet to open it. I am intending to spend the rest of this evening in the spare room with my new equipment. But currently I'm stretched out on the sofa, half-watching some 'humorous' play called *Abigail's Party* while leafing through the *Daily Mirror* that I earlier managed to smuggle out of the library. I can still find nothing on James Kelly or darts. But what is it that I want? To meet him, to speak with him – but to say what?

PART 1: BULLS

The dart book lies within arm's reach. If I *am* to meet James Kelly, I need first to prepare. I'm hardly likely to transform myself into a proficient player overnight, but I can at least learn the basics: how to stand and how to hold the wretched things.

There are three main stances. After some clumsy experimentation, I have settled for the third – best foot forward – and then progress to the second stage. This entails gripping the dart between thumb and forefinger while using the middle finger as support. I throw. The dart flies out my hand and momentarily lodges in the wall before dropping to the floor. My throwing action evidently needs some attention. The book suggests that rather than pushing from the shoulder, I should be bringing my lower arm into play and then following through. Now fewer darts are going astray, but I'd be still happier if they would all at least hit the board and stay put.

Although my manual discourages solitary practice, the thought of joining the local darts team, if such a group exists, or even going down to the local pub, fills me with horror. The very idea of displaying total incompetence to strangers is disincentive enough, but the truth is that I am not, and never will be, remotely interested in the game of darts. I might, however, consider, after a little more experience, hiring a private coach to offer me a few practical hints.

I return to *Abigail's Party* just as the mouthy tart's husband is on the verge of a heart attack.

Perhaps I should get the piano.

Thursday, 10 November 1977

The only regular newspaper I read is the local that June pokes through my letterbox each Thursday. As the *South London Press* is a Friday publication, its news is virtually one week old and therefore of even less relevance today than it would normally be. After further detailed investigation of the newspapers in Clapham library, I've now managed to track down three small articles in respectable papers, plus one feature in a particularly prurient one. Under facile headings such as 'Kelly hits the spot', James is pictured aiming a dart while grinning sheepishly at the camera. Each story is pretty much identical: all refer to his erratic behaviour, the common newspaper opting for the glamour angle. Collating these articles, together with information from the TV show, I have gleaned the following facts about James Kelly:

Personal: He is nineteen years old and lives with his mother and younger sister in Outlane, near Huddersfield.

Social: He occasionally drinks and throws darts with friends at his local pub: The Waggon and Horses.

Professional: At eighteen, James became the youngest player ever to win the Yorkshire championship. This year he was the runner-up to Eric Bristow in the *News of the World* championship. He is currently signed to The Belltime Agency, which his Uncle Ken, himself an ex darts champion, runs. James' ambition is to win the Embassy championships in February.

What I've so far learned of The Belltime Agency does not inspire confidence. It consists of just one office in Wakefield, with a reputation in the North of England for handling lesser-known 'artistes'. In 1975, this agency managed a pop group that had one novelty record in the top ten. Five years previous to that, it briefly looked after a ventriloquist that a few people in their late fifties might remember with embarrassment. I would guess that Belltime is a one-man band, with Ken Bell's wife answering the telephone in a phoney voice. Perhaps James Kelly doesn't know any better, but would he actually *choose* to be signed to an agency that books out 'turns' to working men's clubs if this man were not his uncle? It may be that no one else will touch him, especially now, after his less than stable TV appearance. He certainly showed no hunger to become a world champion, nor any hankering after celebrity. I can hardly picture him following Englebert Humperdink at the Batley Variety Club.

I feel totally unprepared to meet him, but there would be no harm in making preliminary enquiries. I could phone The Belltime Agency and introduce myself ... but as what – a fan? 'I'd like to book James for my nephew's Christmas party.' The sensible option still seems to forget the whole thing.

Friday, 11 November 1977

After changing platforms at Wakefield station, I am now on a slow train to Huddersfield. I resisted the temptation to alight at Wakefield in search of The Belltime Agency; that can wait. My current plan is to make my way to Outlane, buy a pint in the Waggon and Horses, find myself an inconspicuous seat in the corner, and observe the scene.

The locals suspend their amateur darts match and move aside for the handsome, blond-haired lad in a cream suit as he glides into position behind the oche to aim his dart. They respectfully follow its graceful arc and descent into the bull's eye before bursting into spontaneous applause. All glasses are raised to their young hero. But his watery blue eyes flash towards the mysterious stranger seated in the corner, the one person remaining impervious to the uproar. Kelly pulls out his dart, sidles over to the stranger and places it in his hand.
'David, I was expecting you. Please throw.'

I shake myself awake as the train finally pulls in to Huddersfield station. I don my grey duffel coat, eat egg, chips and baked beans at the station café and head for the taxi rank. The driver knows the pub, referring to it as 'The Waggon.' After a tedious one-way conversation about Yorkshire weather and London ('I went there once and didn't like it'), I'm relieved to be dropped off in New Hey Road.

Perched on a bar stool with a pint of Sam Smiths, I take in my surroundings. In the far left corner a group of rough looking youths play pinball and Space Invaders. It's only 7.30 and the pool table is still covered up. At a table ahead of me, four weather-beaten locals noisily share anecdotes between card hands. In the right corner, a handsome blonde woman in her mid-forties sits facing an oddly dressed teenage girl with wild ginger hair. They seem to have nothing to say to each other. A muscular, craggy-faced regular in paint-spattered overalls, perhaps in his mid-twenties, sits three stools away from me. Apart from one suggestive remark to Betty, the barmaid, (a bespectacled and even less glamorous version of the tarty woman from *Abigail's Party*), he spends the rest of his time glaring into his personal metal jug. Looking as though he hasn't been approached in days, this gruff individual gives off the impression that he would headbutt the first stranger daring to disturb his privacy.

To the right of the pinball machine, two young men are playing darts. The younger player, a nattily dressed lad with brown hair covering his ears, approaches the bar clutching two empties. I down the dregs of my bitter rather too quickly and move towards him just as Betty is taking the lad's beer glasses. He orders two more of the same and glances at me over his left shoulder.

'How do.' I 'how do' back, echoing his chirpy tone but girding my loins for a second trite exchange. He briefly looks me up and down. 'Not from around here, then.'

'Is it that obvious?' I attempt a casual smile.

'Locals don't usually arrive by taxi.'

'I'm up from London actually.'

'Oh ay?'

Having mistaken his response for a comic impersonation, I emit a false laugh. Luckily, he doesn't seem to have noticed. I cough into my gloved hand. 'Are you expecting James Kelly this evening?'

'Oh, you from the telly, then? Expecting him? No.'

He picks up his two refills.

'No, I'm not from the telly. Do you know where I can find James?'

He indicates the woman and teenage girl sitting in the corner. 'Why don't you ask his mum? Ta, Betty.'

He makes his way back to the dartboard via their table, where he mumbles a few words to the oddly dressed teenager. Her shrill laugh sounds derisory.

I had not envisaged having to decide whether to approach James Kelly's mother, but the teenage girl is already heading towards me. She looks barely seventeen and is draped in an orange overcoat several sizes too big for her. Her green eyes examine my gloves and duffel coat, and then finally squint up at me as though I were a harmless space alien.

'So you're not from the telly. You want to speak to my mum.'

Two terse statements.

'Actually I'm just—'

'Take my seat. Talk to her.'

Two terse instructions.

As we introduce ourselves, my attention is already wandering to a length of white thread dangling from Mrs Kelly's right fist. Three fingers curl round the hidden object to which the thread is attached while her forefinger toys with the thread. Unlike her children, she speaks without any trace of a Yorkshire accent. She is probably younger than she looks, her heavy make-up only enhancing tired and drawn features. Like her son, she has pale-blue, dreamy eyes; like her daughter, her clothes somehow don't match. Without any prompting, and in a far more comforting manner than I find in females generally, she is already talking about James.

'He used to come over for the odd game with Darren, but not any more … well, not during opening hours.'

'Mum, he's not from the telly.'

I glance up to discover her daughter and the trendy darts chap standing guard each side of my chair. Mrs Kelly's edgy response echoes my own irritation. 'Yes, I know that, Jade. He never said he was.'

'Not surprising, looking like that! So what is he, then?' I crane my neck up and to the right, only to receive a second confrontational squint. 'What are you?'

Mrs Kelly now addresses the young man.

'I was just saying to Mister Carpenter that it's a shame James doesn't see his friends in here any more.'

Jade's flapping coat brushes my ear as she edges in towards her mother.

'Mum, they're not James' friends. They never were his friends. Are you James' friend, Darren?'

Darren pulls up a chair. It pleases me to see Jade left standing. Perhaps she's really a fifteen-year-old, trying not to look underage.

'No disrespect to your son, Mrs Kelly, but you know what Jade means.'

'What *does* Jade mean?' I ask.

Mrs Kelly addresses her reply to Darren.

'Well, he can sometimes appear to be a little different.'

'Different? My lovely brother is more like the other side of bonkers.'

She pulls a comic, bug-eyed face that does her freckled features no favours. I force my attention back to Mrs Kelly.

'I realise how odd it must appear, my arriving like this, out of the blue, and enquiring after your son. It really isn't the sort of thing I normally do.'

'So what do you normally do?' asks Darren in a perfectly friendly way. 'Journalist, writer?'

'No, I'm nothing really. I saw the TV show on Monday and was captivated.'

I can't believe I've just used the word *captivated*, which Jade instantaneously mimes back to me. Is Mrs Kelly holding back a grin as she winds the white thread round her forefinger?

'And what did you find *captivating* about my son?'

'Just seeing him throwing darts into the bull's eye like

that, without any effort … it was like watching some kind of miracle.'

'So you're not a darts player, then,' says Darren.

'I'm trying to teach myself, but so far I mostly hit the wall. Mrs Kelly, when you say James can appear to be a little different, do you mean—'

'My brother's different, as in nuts.' Jade has repositioned herself behind Darren with her elbows digging into his shoulders. He acquires an instant ginger wig. 'You two must get together. It would be so captivating for you both.'

I stand up too quickly and feel slightly dizzy.

'I'm sorry. I can't imagine what you must think. I don't know what got into my head to come here. So I'll let you get on with your evening and …'

Mrs Kelly gently motions me back to my seat.

'Mister Carpenter.'

'It's David. I expect you think I'm some kind of crank, but I really believe that your son is doing something special.'

'Then why don't we just *ask* whether or not you should meet my son?'

'Oh, Mum!'

Mrs Kelly unfurls her fingers to reveal a small wooden pendant, which she hands to me.

'Take no notice of Jade. Now hold the pendulum between your thumb and forefinger and let it dangle just over your beer glass.'

Jade leans over and shoves my arm.

'Now drop it in.'

Mrs Kelly lets out a dramatic sigh.

'Jade, do me a favour, just for five minutes? Darren, would you mind?'

Darren playfully punches Jade's shoulder and they move to the adjacent table for a ringside seat of my rising discomfort. My hand has begun to tremble.

'You can rest your elbow on the table but try to keep the pendant still. Now ask the following question: is this a glass of beer?'

'Look, if this is a joke, I really—'

'We need to know your *yes* direction. Now ask!'

'Is this a glass of beer?'

'Excellent, clockwise … wait till it comes to a complete stop. Now you can ask whether you should meet up with my son.'

'Should I meet up with your son?'

The pendant is circling above my glass in a clockwise direction.

'There! A very positive result … you must always listen to your heart, David. Can you meet me here at around the same time next Friday?'

'Yes, I can, Mrs Kelly.'

'Excellent. So I'll take you over *then*. We live almost opposite: at 702, just behind the Stainland sign and to the left of the phone box – white door, black knocker.'

Whether it's the drink or the prospect of meeting James Kelly, I'm suddenly feeling nauseous, and so make my unsteady way to the gents. When I re-emerge, there is no sign of Darren or the Kellys.

Thursday, 17 November 1977

June's piano, now ensconced in my front room, has served as a distraction, rather than any source of enjoyment. I have dug out the old pieces I used to play in my mid-teens, and my current rendition of 'A Walk in the Black Forest' only serves as a reminder that I type rather than play. My lack of creative flair is more suited to running through scales and arpeggios, and by G harmonic minor I have compiled a mental list of all the things I need to pack for tomorrow.

Friday, 18th November 1977

I'm on the same train as last Friday and should arrive in good time to meet James and Mrs Kelly in 'The Waggon' for 7.30. Nothing of much significance has taken place during the last seven days, apart from the arrival of the piano and the purchase of a book entitled *Thus Spoke Zarathustra*. Friedrich Nietzsche was a German philosopher who went, as Jade Kelly might put it, the other side of bonkers. After five pages and two stations, I am already regretting that I hadn't opted for an E. M. Forster to while away this tedious journey. I cannot regard being checkmated at my Monday chess club by a twelve-year-old girl in eighteen moves as newsworthy. Lest the word *club* might conjure up connotations of a social nature, I will list the only three words required for an evening: 'hello', 'check' and 'checkmate', 'hello' being just chess-speak for 'would you like a game?' There is no reason to say 'goodbye', or at least this is the way I prefer it. Unfortunately, one member by the name of William Abercrombie chooses to add words and phrases surplus to requirements, the most objectionable being 'just like that'. This is intended to be his Tommy Cooper impersonation, but might as well be David Frost. He will use this phrase upon checkmating me, and then follow it, not with the traditional handshake, but by a forward thrust of all his fingers and the Tommy Cooper '*zz zz zz*' noise. I've not heard him inflict his moronic behaviour on anyone else, probably because I'm the only person he is capable of beating. However, it is his unique, unorthodox opening gambit, before moving a single chess piece, it is his chilling calling card that is sufficient to put off the most focused of opponents. William's mouth opens wide enough to glimpse his tonsils, he locks his jaw as though rigor mortis has set in and then mimes a voiceless laugh from the grave.

Although I've been throwing darts each evening, I am as yet noticing little improvement and have long given up attempting to hit the bull's eye. Instead, I aim merely to land in the top half of the board. I can usually achieve this with one dart in three, but precisely where each dart might land, Old Moore himself would not dare to predict.

* * *

But now this God has died. And let us not be equal before the mob. You higher men, depart from the market place!

This profound quote prompts me to move from Nietzsche to my food-stained copy of last Friday's *South London Press* in search of bargains at Arding and Hobbs. And indeed they are offering a third off Wilton carpets! Although my heart does not go out to the amateur mimic stabbed to death after performing his Bruce Forsyth impersonation on top of the number 45 bus, I would have gladly offered William Abercrombie as a far more deserving sacrifice for the chop. I've been considering whether to cancel my Tatler cinema club membership for some time now, but next week's offering, *The Sexualist* does whet my appetite, if only to discover exactly what a sexualist is.

Fantasies revolving around possible futures with James, however, remain strictly in the spiritual realm. In a typical scenario, we are seated together at a corner table of the Waggon, needing to say very little, due to the subtle understanding we have of each other's inner worlds. He is wearing the same baggy cream suit and grammar school tie that he wore on TV.

Let it be said, however, that I have not, even for one second, confused fantasy with reality, nor am I in any danger of doing so. If there comes a moment where my presence is being read as intrusive or unwanted, I will immediately withdraw and permanently remove myself from these people's lives. I have never been tolerant towards nuisances and have no intention of turning into such a person.

Without daring to look around me, I make my way to the bar. After a large gulp of Sam Smiths, I turn around and affect a casual glance in the direction of the darts area. It is deserted. A solitary soul is playing pinball. I slowly look right, finally focusing on the table in the far corner. Jade and Darren face each other, their heads almost touching. She is dressed more smartly than last week, but the stripy green top clashes violently with her flailing ginger mop. As they seem oblivious to their surroundings, I summon the confidence to approach and on arrival clear my throat like an ineffectual schoolmaster. Without averting her eyes from Darren, Jade greets me with a cursory 'Mum's home.' Darren has the decency to shake my hand and invite me to join them.

'Evening Mister Carpenter. Fancy a game?'

'I really am hopeless, and all that subtraction defeats me.'

'James would *love* to subtract for you,' oozes Jade. She leans in towards me but Darren playfully pulls her back.

'Actually, Darren, I'm here to meet James.'

Jade now leans right across the table, within an inch of my spectacles. I feel a tuft of her hair tickling my forehead.

'*Actually*, you're to go across to Mum's. It's right opposite, white door, number 702 … big number for you.'

I stay focused on Darren. 'So, is James coming over later?'

'James doesn't go very far without his Uncle Ken.'

'And Ken's in Wakefield,' sings Jade, with a grotesque smile.

I feel a chest pain of disappointment as she eyeballs me,

adding, 'with *James.*' She then signals her boredom by gazing around at nothing in particular.

My subsequent attempt at small talk with Darren has led to my offering him a spare room in London, should he ever be passing through. I'm instantly regretting this, as I watch him scribbling down my address and phone number, but feel immense relief when he doesn't reciprocate with his own details. A modicum of satisfaction is also derived from finally having cut Jade out of the proceedings during our man-to-man exchanges.

'Might be seeing you then,' says Darren, who does strike me as a genuine, if a little over-chirpy, young man. Nevertheless, as I'm leaving the bar, I feel certain that they are both grinning at each other behind my back.

Mrs Kelly has led me through to the kitchen. She clears some knitting from a chair, explaining that it's a new cardigan for Ken, and invites me to join her at a small, cluttered table.

'Cup of tea?'

I spot the pendulum curled up next to a filled ashtray and decide against a jocular suggestion that I consult it.

'Thanks. I've brought a packet of custard creams.'

Although seeming vaguely happy to see me, James' mother is looking decidedly haggard in her baggy house-clothes and without make-up. As she bends towards me with a cup of very milky tea, I notice some silver streaks mingled with her blonde hair. I picture Jade's ginger mop and wonder whether she's adopted. But there is no mistaking the pale-blue dreamy eyes of Mrs Kelly's son.

'Sorry, but you didn't leave a phone number.'

'He's in Wakefield, then.'

'Afraid so – left with Ken this afternoon. What about those two lovebirds!'

'Lovebirds?'

'It started last weekend, after the night you came up. Darren took her to see *Star Wars* on Saturday and they've been gazing into each other's eyes ever since. The poor lad doesn't know what he's taken on.'

'He seems very nice,' I mutter vacantly, as I dunk my custard cream. I just want to go home.

'I know what you mean. You can hardly describe Jade as nice. She'd pretend to throw up if you did. It's just a teenage thing she's going through, although it did start when she was nine.'

She indicates a photo that is sellotaped lopsidedly to the door. Jade's head rests contentedly on her brother's shoulder. James, in the same school tie as he wore on TV, beams at the camera. 'July 1971: our first holiday in Cleethorpes … just the three of us.'

I note the absent father.

'James looks happy.'

'That's because I'd just bribed him with "Give us a big smile and we can all go home." He never did like going away anywhere, even as an infant.'

I stare back into my undrinkable tea.

'Does James use the pendulum?'

'That's funny. No, James is his own pendulum. He expects *us* to ask the questions. So, would you like to see his room?'

I look up in bewilderment. Has she suggested such a thing to compensate for my wasted journey? I feel myself frowning, and prepare to decline this bizarre offer. Instead I hear myself saying, 'Yes, I would like that. May I use the toilet?'

The phone rings. Mrs Kelly picks up the receiver with one hand and directs me out and up with the other.

I'm standing in a ransacked bedroom: unmade bed, magazines and clothes strewn everywhere. An off-white shag pile carpet continues its way up the front wall. On the back wall behind the bed is a large poster of a young black man with deep, sad eyes. Propped up in the corner, behind a hanging wicker chair, is a straight, blowing instrument that might be a clarinet or oboe. I crouch down for a closer look; it's made of brass.

'Wrong bedroom – this is Jade's bombsite. That's her saxophone.'

'Aren't saxophones curly?'

'Don't expect my daughter to choose something conventional! It's a soprano sax and sounds like she's charming snakes, except they'd hide in terror under the bed.'

'So she's a musician, then?'

'*She'd* like to think so. But it's not music as we know it – lots of squeaks and honks. She calls it improvising. James seems to like it – says it gets him off to sleep.'

I show some empathy by mirroring her nonplussed gesture.

'I play the piano … proper tunes though. Is James musical?'

'Is James musical? Ha! You're going to think I live in a madhouse. Well, you asked. He sings, but just long notes that drive me even further up the wall than his sister's screeching saxophone. No wonder I talk to a pendulum. James' bedroom is next door.'

I'm shown into a stark, white room that could be taken for an up-market monastery cell. An old-fashioned, red upholstered rocking chair faces the window. The walls are bare but for a childlike sketch of a tortoise or turtle with markings on its back. The bed is made, and the few articles adorning the room each have their appointed place. On the bedside table lies a book lined with brown wrapping paper. I point up towards the new, unused dartboard. Mrs Kelly sighs.

'Ken replaced the old one a month ago but James hasn't gone near it. God knows what he does up here all day, apart from rock.' She collapses into the ancient rocking chair to demonstrate its annoying squeak. 'Yes, we can hear the creaking from downstairs.'

PART 1: BULLS

The creak, creak, creak has caused my mind to wander until I'm suddenly aware of being closely observed.

'Sorry, did you say something, Mrs Kelly?'

'Yes, I said I'm wondering whether you two can become friends. You might bring a more mature influence to bear.'

I check her expression for any hint of irony, but, like her son, the blue, watery eyes only convey solemnity.

'I thought that perhaps he didn't want to meet me.'

'He was really looking forward to it. But then Ken arranged this trip to his office in Wakefield for a meeting with James' new sponsor. That was Ken on the phone just now and … David!' I'm at the bedside table and have just picked up the book in brown paper. She jumps to her feet. 'No, please don't!' Her raised voice startles me. 'He'll know it's been moved.' I carefully replace the book and move away. She resumes as though nothing has occurred. 'So the new plan is that you can meet them both tomorrow morning. Be at the office by eleven. It's easy to find. I'm not sure that you'll get to see James alone, but at least your journey won't have been entirely wasted. Oh, and James says you can sleep in his room tonight. You're deeply honoured, I must say.'

'But if I'm not supposed to touch anything …'

'James actually *wants* you to sleep in his room.'

We stare at each other in a silence that I find intensely uncomfortable. It's as though Mrs Kelly has delivered an order that I have no right to refuse.

'Is Jade …?'

'She'll spend the night at Darren's. I know! But she's promised me she'll sleep on the couch. In the end, we can only trust in the universe. *You* know what I mean, don't you, David.'

'Oh yes, Mrs Kelly.'

'I'll drive you to the station in the morning. There's a 10.15 to Wakefield. So, I'll bring you up a nice cup of tea at nine.'

OVERTONES

I dream that I wake up in the middle of the night in a cold sweat. I lunge at the forbidden book, rip off its brown paper cover and hastily leaf through the pornographic photos of naked men until I find the one that I'm looking for. Darren's long brown hair is slightly dishevelled; he holds a hand out, beckoning. Suddenly, the door bursts open and James is standing over me. I close my eyes and lay there paralysed as he climbs in beside me.

PART 1: BULLS

Saturday, 19 November 1977

I awake at 8.30 with a throbbing headache and creep down the stairs into the kitchen. Mrs Kelly has second-guessed me with a note on the table.

> *There's a regular bus service from Outlane that passes Huddersfield station. Ken's office is number six, Cheapside, second floor. Then, from outside Wakefield station …*

The journey is straightforward and her instructions clear: left along Westgate, past the Opera House and left again into Cheapside. I walk up a grimy staircase to the second floor. The off-white plastic sign on the door says: The Belltime Agency.

I ring the bell.

'Door's open, son, come on through.'

Behind a large cluttered desk sits Uncle Ken. He looks much the same as I remember, except for black-rimmed National Health glasses that perch halfway down his nose and an old food-stained sports jacket. He is a stout man, but it's not all flab; he can probably handle himself when the occasion arises. An ashtray is crammed with dog-ends and I can smell whiskey and the remains of a bacon sandwich. On the wall behind him is displayed a large framed photo of a younger, fitter Ken, poised to throw a dart. His left arm is draped around the shoulders of a man I assume to be a major darts celebrity of the day.

'So are you a journalist or not?'

'Well, not really, but occasionally I do try my hand at …'

He waves my faltering reply to a halt, asks for my name and scribbles it down. Then, without introducing himself or offering me a seat, launches into his story as though expecting me to take notes. He does not, however, have my full attention as I'm feeling a little disquieted by James' absence. I cannot help but wonder if, yet again, he will fail to show up.

Yes, Ken had indeed been the Yorkshire champion in the mid-1960s and then went on to win the *News of the World* championship in '69. He set up The Belltime Agency, 'on account of my name being Bell,' in 1971, and has apparently managed 'the cream of Yorkshire talent' ever since.

A chubby forefinger guides me through frayed posters and photos displayed around the office walls.

'This shady bunch made their reputations in the sixties. But believe me, they still fetch a decent price round the circuit from here to South Shields. And Jim? Yes, it was yours truly who bought him that dartboard for his thirteenth birthday. And now, seven years on, I represent the future world champion … that's what I call money well spent. So, how can I help?'

I feel cheated, and want to blurt out, 'I'm here to see James, not you.' Instead, I ask how the young James first took to darts.

'It was actually Brenda's idea. She thought it was a way he could apply all that adding and subtracting bollocks to something more practical. We set up the board in his bedroom, and for weeks he just sat on his bed, totting up my score. I remember handing him his first dart. To be honest, I wasn't expecting much and I was right: that dart hit the wire and rebounded. But he didn't flinch or pull a face – just held his focus and threw a second … that's the mark of a potential pro. Of course it was nothing new to see the boy just lock into just one thing and blot out the rest of the world. "It's just you and that dartboard, son," I'd tell him. He liked that. Trouble was he didn't want to play with the other lads. Often he'd not even allow *me* into his room. There were times when I was a bit harsh on the boy, but you could only push him so far before the shutters came down. Off the record, he can still be a bloody nightmare.'

I choose not to respond to Ken's comic expression of helplessness.

'Anyway, the day arrived when I felt he was ready to leave the nest, cross New Hey Road and try his luck at the Waggon. It was a Tuesday, so things would be nice and quiet over there. I remember the precise day because it was his seventeenth birthday: December 11th 1974. I bought him a new suit and he looked the business. Mind you, it took a bit of cajoling to get him out the house. We turned the whole event into this special birthday treat, and he went for it. So there I was with my protégé and ready for some action. We waited for these two older lads to finish their game and I invited the winner to play James. Of course, James wiped the floor with him – the poor sod barely got a look-in.

'And so it went on, gently mind. I gradually widened the field, carted him round some low-key venues until he was playing in the local league. Within eight months, he was playing for Yorkshire … unheard of! And, pretty much, no one could get near him as long as I was supervising things.'

Ken had stopped looking at me some time ago, and is now, clearly, reliving the story purely for his own pleasure. Suddenly he becomes aware of my presence and frowns.

'But he's not comfortable with strangers and he doesn't take to new situations. Excitement's bad for him, see. He always needs me to pave the way, to show him the route. Otherwise things get out of hand, like all that bull's eye shit on the O'Brien show.'

Ken Bell has risen to his feet. His bulky frame has my full attention. 'I weighed up the risk, putting him on that show, but an opportunity like that's hard to turn down. A guest had cancelled last minute and Eamonn owed me a favour. So I took the gamble. It's only once in a blue moon you're going to get anyone to interview a bloody darts player on TV. But I gave him the full build-up and they bought it – big, big mistake … although I hear, Mister Carpenter, that you saw it another way.'

Up to this moment I had barely uttered a sound. Now I am required to explain why I have travelled twice to Huddersfield in the past week, made myself known to James Kelly's mother, sister, and now his manager.

'Well the thing is, Mister Bell, that I found James' ability to throw an effortless stream of bull's-eyes—'

'Yes Mister Carpenter, I'm fascinated to know what you found it.'

'Well, I found it rather wonderful.'

It is evident that my choice of words has been received with even less forgiveness than 'captivated' was last night.

'Now I will tell you just the once, and I speak as James Kelly's uncle, his mentor, his manager and agent, and the best friend he'll ever have … I will tell you that it is not wonderful. The way I see it is that he came across as a fucking freak show. I want to hear no more of this bull's eye bollocks from you or anyone else. Do you understand, Mister Carpenter?'

'I do, Mister Bell.'

'Now, where was I?'

'The TV show.'

'So, I make it crystal clear to Eamonn that the questions need to be set and rehearsed, so that James doesn't lose his way. And then, at the end of the interview, James will throw a few darts and *finish* with the bull. But when O'Brien starts going off script and changes some questions – that's when things start getting a long way from rather wonderful.'

'If you'll pardon me for saying so, Mister Bell, as I saw it, things were looking out of hand before then.'

'Is that right, son? Please tell me how *you* saw it.'

Ken removes his glasses and slips them into his breast

pocket. The creases that appear on his sweaty forehead suggest that I may have gone too far.

'Well, to me, he looked traumatised right from the start. But of course, I don't know him.'

Ken takes a step towards me. 'That's bloody right, you don't know the first thing about Jim. But that's how he is. He would have been just fine if O'Brien had stuck to the routine. But good things come out of bad. Next morning, I get a phone call from this bloke with a funny accent that calls himself CC, probably because no fucker can pronounce his name. Says he's seen the TV show, and heralds James Kelly as the greatest genius since Frank Sinatra. You a fan of old blue eyes, son?'

'Well, I can appreciate—'

'*My Way*: now, that's the song I want at my funeral. Anyway, at first I'm thinking this CC is some cranky fan like you, but then he goes on to offer himself up as a sponsor. He's talking big money, and name-drops this flash company in Hong Kong that his father owns, says he wants to meet me with a proposition. So the next day I turn up at the Palace Hotel in Manchester. And there he is, this wiry looking chink in an Italian suit. He's very laid-back and all smiles, not at all what I'd been expecting … much younger than he'd sounded on the phone, perhaps in his mid-twenties. Anyway, he starts with the carrot: not just money upfront, but also an all-expenses paid trip to Hong Kong for me and the boy. He's already provisionally set up an exhibition match to mark the inauguration of the Hong Kong Darts Federation, which, he assures me, is going to be a high profile event. So he's handing me this whopping great cheque, shaking my hand and grinning from ear to ear as though we're old friends.'

'Was James there at the meeting?'

'Course he fucking wasn't. So I'm trying to slow things down. I need to put him in the picture about boy wonder. I explain that we're not talking about your ordinary teenager.

You can't simply tell James Kelly that we're off to Hong Kong with a total stranger, go and pack your bags. But the chink won't be put off, says we've time to prepare as the Hong Kong gig's not till December 11th. Oh right! It was enough of a palaver just to get Jim to cross New Hey Road and into the Waggon on his seventeenth birthday. "And now lad, for your *twentieth* birthday treat, we're shoving you halfway across the world with some foreigner you don't even know. Anyway, mister positive Ching-Chong-Chinaman has it all worked out. Says he'll introduce himself to James the following Monday – that's the Monday just gone – and spend a week or so getting acquainted. Then on Saturday the 26th – one week today – the plan is for the three of us to fly out, spend two weeks at his place on some island off Hong Kong, do the gig, and return home on December 12th. He impresses me with his knowledge of the British scene by slipping in that this will give Jim a couple of weeks to prepare for "The Winmau" at Lakeside on the 27th. But I'm still not convinced. "So what do I tell James?" I ask the chink. "Tell him nothing," he replies. "Just give me fifty minutes with James next Monday. Trust me."

'Why should I trust him? I'd only just met the cunt … but at least his cheque doesn't bounce. So I arrange with Brian the landlord for us to have the saloon bar to ourselves an hour before opening time and I just tell the boy we're going over for a practice session. CCs already arrived and he's standing by the dartboard. Jim freezes, but CC asks me to leave. He's asking politely but you can tell he means it, like the whole thing's off if I don't. So I leave like a good boy. But I'm not happy. In fact, I'm half-expecting Jim to follow me out. But he doesn't. So now I'm back at Brenda's, pacing up and down in a right strop. She doesn't see the problem, and Jade's just taking the piss, which winds me up even further. After three-quarters of an hour I walk back over and witness a scene of calm serenity. Jim's as good as gold. They're both by the dartboard, smiling at each other. Well, CC's smiling and the lad is sort of gazing back as though he's just been breast-fed. It kind of gave me the willies. Then CC turns to me. He's offering to shake my hand but I have to check with Jim. "Well, son?" But he's just grinning at me as though I'm supposed to be in on a joke. So I shake the chink's hand.'

'Do you know what happened between them while you were gone?'

'Not a clue, but since Monday they've been meeting up for an hour every day. As far as I can see, he's got the lad's total trust.'

'Do they play darts?'

'Fuck knows.' Ken looks at his watch. 'But whatever they get up to, they've got just twenty more minutes to do it.'

'So where are they? I'm here to see James.'

Ken's chin slightly drops. He's peering at me with a slightly derisory squint reminiscent of Jade.

'They'll be back in half an hour. So, as you see, it's all turning out nice as pie. I've made a few pennies, the boy's about to experience his first working holiday, and we'll all be back in time for "The Winmau" just after Christmas. That's your neck of the woods. Frimley Green in Surrey, so you'll get your chance to see our Jim in action there. I'll organise you a ticket. Then we've got the whole of January to prepare for the big one: this new world championship that they're calling 'The Embassy'. Put the sixth of February in your diary, young man, and see darts history being made.'

'Mister Bell, I really want to see James. Mrs Kelly said he'd like to see *me*.'

'Listen, son.' Ken steps towards me. He puts a hand on my shoulder. His breath stinks of bacon. 'Here's the good news. Jim's written you a personal message. Apparently you're not to open it till you're back in London. He won't even tell *me* what it says. Now isn't *that* something!'

I can't answer as I'm holding my breath. He walks over to his desk, rummages through the scattered papers and returns with a small white envelope with the word 'Carpenter' written on it. He stuffs it into my duffel coat pocket.

'Now go home, lad. Jim's got enough on for one day. And I promise to sort you out a comp for the first day of the Embassy. How about that? As a gesture of goodwill ... which may soon run out.'

Ken walks over to the half-opened door. He is signalling me out, but I stand my ground.

'Mister Bell, you cannot imagine ... you have no idea the trouble I've taken. I've travelled up to Huddersfield twice in one week and now I've made the effort to come over to Wakefield. I feel that you're deliberately trying to prevent me from seeing James. I won't be messed around like this.'

I feel my heart race through ten seconds of silence.

'You won't be messed around like this? Who are you?' Ken Bell's voice has taken on a new brittle, metallic quality. What does he mean? Should I repeat my name? 'Who the fuck do you think you are? What right do you have, first harassing Brenda and Jade and now banging on my door, demanding to see someone you saw for five minutes on television? So what are you?'

This is an even more oblique question, to which I have no answer. Is he about to grab hold of my collar? The phone rings. Without taking his eyes off me, he scuttles back to his desk and snatches up the receiver.

'Yes Jim. No! Yes, he is ... no, stay there. Yes, I have. Yes, he's got it. Later. I said *later!*' Ken Bell has slammed down the phone and is heading towards me again. 'So what are you, a freak or a pansy boy? I'm giving you five seconds.'

* * *

Part 1: Bulls

Still shaking from the encounter, I've crossed the road and am standing in a shop doorway. Shivering with the cold, I'm determined to wait until James arrives, even though I know that Ken is observing me from his office window.

Twenty minutes have passed. On the other side of the road two men are slowing to a halt. A young Asian wearing a stylish black overcoat has an arm around James Kelly's shoulder. I shout his name. James turns. He is beautiful. I wave the envelope and he smiles. It is enough for me. As they turn into the doorway opposite, I stuff the envelope back into my duffel coat and run non-stop to Wakefield station.

Sunday, 20 November 1977

As a mark of respect, I waited until this morning before opening James' letter. It reads as follows:

Dear Carpenter,

In three hours from now, you will be sitting with Uncle Ken in the false hope that we will meet. But one day very soon we will study the sacred turtle together. Did you see the picture on my bedroom wall? This will help you with adding up to fifteen.

But for now, here are two examples of subtraction that will take your breath away. In both cases, once 501 has been whittled down to 50, 50 then drops down to zero with a single flourish.

The first example demonstrates how to check out in twelve by throwing eleven darts. This brings the total down from 501 to 50. We then aim the twelfth and final dart at the true target: our beloved bull's eye!

My first three darts total 140, which, when deducted from 501, leaves 361.

My second three also total 140, leaving me with 221.

Now I throw two double 20s and a single 20. This adds up to 100.

Subtract 100 from 221, and we are left with 121 for a possible finish.

I throw triple 20 and am left with 61.

PART 1: BULLS

There are now just two darts to go. Can you guess what I throw next? Yes, Carpenter, I throw an 11. Why? Because I have already calculated that I will be left with 50: the double 25.

BULL'S EYE!

And now for perfection: the perfect nine!

> Dart 1: triple 20 = 60
> Dart 2: triple 20 = 60
> Dart 3: double 20 = 40
> Total: 160
>
> 501-160 = 341
> Dart 4: triple 20 = 60
> Dart 5: triple 20 = 60
> Dart 6: triple 20 = 60
> Total 180
>
> 341-180 = 161
> Dart 7: triple 17 = 51
> 161-51 = 110
> Dart 8: triple 20 = 60
> 110-60 = 50
> Dart 9: BULL'S EYE!

In July, during the *News of the World* championships, a strangely dressed but totally gorgeous girl with masses of black, curly hair visited our dressing room and explained how to extract a special number from a person's name by using this grid.

1	2	3	4	5	6	7	8	9
A	B	C	D	E	F	G	H	I
J	K	L	M	N	O	P	Q	R
S	T	U	V	W	X	Y	Z	

J = 1
A = 1
M = 4
E = 5
S = 1
1+1+4+5+1 = 12. 1+2 = 3

K = 2
E = 5
L = 3
L = 3
Y = 7
2+5+3+3+7 = 20
2+0 = 2
3+2 = 5

This means that the number five is my special number. You will be delighted to learn that it is yours too, even though your name contains four more letters than mine. You must try this for yourself. Just remember that twenty-two is a master number and not to be reduced.

You may phone me on Huddersfield 376007 and ask a question.

Your friend, James Kelly

You may phone me! I would be dancing round my lounge, were I that way inclined. As for the question James wishes me to ask, when the time is right I will invite him to describe his state of mind during those magical moments that precede the release of the dart destined for the bull's eye. But in the meantime, because he is offering his friendship, I intend to reciprocate with a little of my homespun wisdom. I trust that this contribution to our friendship might provide a spiritual environment to counteract the aggression and sarcasm meted out by his uncle and sister respectively. My one concern is his false assumption that I seek help for my innumeracy. But such a trivial misunderstanding is overshadowed by the genuine connection that has now been established between us. In this knowledge, I will no longer be deterred by the likes of Ken and Jade.

Wednesday, 23 November 1977

I have already let two days slip by and need to phone James before he flies out this Saturday. But who might pick up the phone?

Jade is bound to be troublesome, but may also be the easiest to negotiate. I would expect the conversation to be brief and monosyllabic. 'He's not in' might be as much as I get out of her. If this occurs, I will remain calm and patient, otherwise she may well hang up on me.

Mrs Kelly ('Brenda, how *are* you?') will be full of apologies for my abortive mission to Wakefield. She'll by now have heard Ken's version of what took place and will either defend him or apologise further for his inexcusable conduct.

The worst scenario is that Ken answers with: 'You have the fucking effrontery ...' etcetera. His question to me had been 'Who are you?' Now I am wondering who Ken Bell is. What, exactly, is the nature of his relationship to Brenda and her children?

But suppose I hear the words, 'James Kelly speaking.' What reply might suitably mark our very first conversation? Firstly, I will thank him for the letter. Then I'll gently explain that, although I found his description of the perfect nine fascinating, I don't require his guidance with arithmetic. Finally, I'll move on to the main purpose of my call.

'James, I recognise your true gift, whereas the people around you can see no further than the darts player. I'm in the process of writing you a letter to elaborate on this and request that you do not open it until your arrival in Hong Kong. I should point out that I resisted the temptation to open yours until Sunday morning.

Part 1: Bulls

'Having now met your Uncle Ken, I can only conclude that he has no respect for you. In fact, he dismisses your remarkable bull's eye display as 'bollocks'. I see him as a man driven by money and the quest for prestige. He may also be a threat to your future happiness. Do not allow any of these people to distract you from your true self. I feel certain that you understand what I mean by this. For you and I already have ...'

Perhaps I'll phone tomorrow evening.

Thursday, 24 November 1977

7.40 p.m. Had I posted my letter to James yesterday, he would have received it in time. Now I will have to hand it to him personally at the airport on Saturday.

Here, in this first draught, I am appending each paragraph with an appraisal, thus alerting myself to any possible misinterpretation:

> My dear friend,
> Before proceeding, I wish to make myself clear with regard to two issues. Firstly, it is not my intention to pester either you or your family. So, should you consider my presence to be an intrusion, I only need to be told once, and will never approach or disturb you again.

Both honest and commendable.

> Secondly, I can assure you that I am not some kind of religious maniac, imagining you to be the new messiah. Nor am I on a spiritual trip. Even though I was at an impressionable age when the Beatles sat adoringly around the Maharishi, I thought it shallow nonsense, even then. So, although we happen to share the same special number, I have no vision of us as two souls on a path predestined to meet. In fact, I consider numerology to be just another futile attempt to make sense of a senseless universe. I can only describe my own equivalent of religious feeling as a dull ache, brought about by a gradual realisation of this senselessness.

Less honest: I dismiss numerology while secretly delighting in our shared special number. I have resisted the temptation of also dismissing his mother's pendulum divination, as I am as yet unclear on James' opinion of this nonsense.

After observing you on that absurd TV show, it occurred to me that you might feel a similar ache. The vast majority of humanity – those who consider themselves to be well adjusted – are for most of their lives sheltered from this disquieting experience, due to their lifelong efforts to transform meaninglessness into meaning. I have no talent to counterbalance the chronic ache, but you, James, have been richly compensated with your remarkable gift. My heart opened as I watched the darts floating to their appointed destination, for it seemed as though I were witnessing a live demonstration of transcendence. You passed through the prison bars and effortlessly transformed the ordinary into magic, chaos into beauty. For the next twenty-four hours I naively believed that your little TV miracle would awaken people to a new reality. But of course nothing changed.

He may not consider the TV show to be ridiculous.
Might he perceive me as a person without talent? Hopefully, he'll spot some poetic flair in my description of his dart throwing.

I will resume my letter in the morning.

* * *

Earlier this evening I tried to steady my nerves by throwing some darts, but they mostly landed in the wall. Now I feel even more agitated. After a further parade of scenarios, my predominant thought is that in the real world I should not be making this phone call in the first place. One part of me still has no idea why I'm phoning. Am I just making a fool of myself? I can only take courage in the words of Martin Heidegger, who assures me that we are aroused from our inauthenticity by encountering ultimate situations.

I finally lift the receiver and dial the number.

'376007.'

A male voice – so, that rules out Brenda and Jade. I press the phone closer to my ear, straining to identify the tinny music in the background. I hold back, allowing him to continue.

'Hello, who is this?'

Darren, James or Ken. I hesitate a little longer.

'Is someone pissing about?'

My worst scenario: Ken Bell. I need to say something.

'No. Sorry. May I speak with James Kelly please?'

'Who *is* this? Who wants him?'

There's no doubt about it: the same, metallic rasp that had asked whether I was a freak or a pansy boy. I'll announce myself.

'This is David Carpenter speaking. I'm phoning from London. Would it be possible to have a brief word with James?'

'What do *you* think?'

'Is that Mister Bell?'

'So what are you after, lad?'

For some reason, I'm encouraged that he calls me lad.

'You'll remember handing me a letter from James last Saturday in your office. I'm sorry if I—'

'You're sorry?'

'Yes, if I—'

'If you're phoning to apologise, just spit it out without all the fucking trimmings. Well?'

My rehearsed Ken scenario had concluded with my cursing him and slamming down the receiver. But now I am traumatised and feel only shame.

'I'm sorry for my behaviour, Mister Bell.'

'Ha ha. I'm very sorry too!'

The voice has abruptly softened, and risen by half an octave. This is not Ken Bell. I'm speaking with James Kelly, who has just been impersonating Ken with uncanny accuracy.

'I'm very sorry for Uncle Ken. He's such a fool! Hello Carpenter, are you still there?'

'Yes James, I'm here.'

Silence.

'It's funny, isn't it?'

The honest answer would be no, but a lighter tone seems more appropriate.

'Someone in Clapham got stabbed to death last week for doing Bruce Forsyth impressions.'

'Would you like to ask me a question?'

'Is anyone with you in the house?'

'Uncle Ken's over at the Waggon playing darts with Darren, and Mum's in the front room watching *Dad's Army*. She can't come to the phone because it's the last ever episode. Jade's in her room, jamming to 'A Love Supreme'. I love JC, and I know you will. Listen!'

I picture James waving the receiver around in mid-air as I'm subjected to a cacophony of high squeals from Jade's soprano saxophone mixed with a chorus of 'Who Do You Think You Are Kidding Mister Hitler?' During these two minutes, I struggle to recall a little of what I wished to say to him.

James has returned. He is informing me that I've already missed the best section of 'A Love Supreme,' which comprises the chanting of its title. He then demonstrates the chant by singing around fifteen repetitions of a four-note phrase. Apparently, the record is now about to move into its final section, entitled 'Psalm'. This will be Jade's cue to discard her saxophone and commence whooping and wailing, a ritual that will eventually evolve into a war dance. James assures me that although he has never actually witnessed this performance, the combination of sounds that come blasting from the adjacent bedroom always follow the same pattern.

'But sometimes Mum can't stand it, so she'll march to the bottom of the stairs and order the racket to be turned off. That is most disappointing for me, but worse for my sister. She'll storm off into town to meet her stoned friends in the Wimpy Bar. Can you play an instrument, Carpenter?'

'Yes, James, I play the piano.'

'There is an instrument that I will play one day. It sounds like the wind and slowly glides from one note to the next. It's a blowing instrument, but so much sweeter than a saxophone.'

'Is it a recorder?'

'I'm not talking about those squeaky pipes they made us play at Birkby Infants – they just tootle. I heard this wondrous sound on the radio. It was in a programme about the music they sent up into space in the Voyager two months ago. They mostly sent rubbish like Chuck Berry singing 'Johnny B. Goode'. But there was also this swooping instrument. I must have one. Can you find out what it is please?'

'Yes, of course I will. I was actually phoning to thank you for your letter.' There is a brief pause before he launches into a stream of numerical variations on the nine-dart finish. 'James … James, listen. Please stop! Thank you, but I really have no interest in that. I'm writing you a letter that explains my true interests.'

He does stop momentarily, but then his mood instantly switches from exuberance to anxiety. This seems to have no connection with my interruption. He is now expressing his deep concern about the imminent trip to Hong Kong, with particular regard to unpredictable destinations and shadowy strangers. He pauses for breath before lowering his voice.

'I need to know why I'm going.'

'Well, apparently your new sponsor has set you up with an exhibition match to mark the inauguration of the Hong Kong Darts Association.'

'I'm not an imbecile. Please don't ever speak to me as though I were.'

'I'm sorry, I really didn't mean to—'

'CC's a remarkable man. He's already told me the most extraordinary things. CC promises to reveal the true reason for our trip when we meet tomorrow. He says that he understands me. But how can I know who to trust?'

I'm wary of giving another wrong answer. 'You've no good reason to trust *me* till you've read my letter. Can we meet before you leave?'

'CC will tell me what is best. Please phone tomorrow evening at 7.30.'

'Perhaps I could come to the airport on Saturday.'

'Now, don't push your luck, son.'

James has snapped back into his Ken impersonation, which he maintains for the remainder of the call. I feign amusement and remind him to expect my call tomorrow. So ends my first conversation with James Kelly.

Friday, 25 November 1977

Yesterday's conversation turned out to be nothing like I could have possibly imagined, bearing no relation to his halting and ponderous manner on TV. Moreover, I am convinced that had we been face-to-face, he would not have stared at me as he did at Eamonn O'Brien. When I couple today's mentally adjusted picture of James with the young man that smiled and waved to me in Wakefield, I feel that all is well.

I have spent all morning working on my letter. If things go to plan, I'll be handing it to James tomorrow before he departs for Hong Kong, together with a very special birthday present that I purchased this afternoon from an ethnic music shop in Denmark Street, off the Charing Cross Road. When I described the sound to the salesman, suggesting that it might be Japanese, he instantly produced a bamboo flute and blew a long airy note to demonstrate beyond doubt that the instrument I required was a shakuhachi.

The letter, however, is proving to be problematic. My intention is to assure James that although he stands apart from the herd, his burden can be transformed through affirmation. But in the light of my recent experience of him, I may have to lighten the tone. It continues as follows:

> You are not alone. Nijinsky danced, Van Gogh painted, and Kierkegaard converted the emptiness of existence into a living philosophy. You throw darts. The rest of us attempt to ease our burden by either getting busy or depressed – the first to mask the second. However, that ennui of nothingness is never

far away. It is forever luring us back to its stark terrain of isolation, a terrain that can, on occasion, be quite thrilling. Suddenly, objects that were once familiar no longer possess a nametag. For one brief moment, they are perceived purely … as they really are. But to linger in this no-man's-land soon becomes disquieting; to maintain this state of *just seeing* any longer than that brief moment can feel like a madness. Consequently, we reconstruct meaning, thus returning to safer ground. Now, when re-encountering that object, we can once again judge it to be good or bad, wondrous or horrific. The nameless, once again, has a name.

But the majority of mankind mistake the label for the genuine article, adorn the nameless with a word, and then only see the word. This process repeats until the entire universe has been reconstructed into an imagined reality.

It would be prejudiced of me to assume that folk from the North are not acquainted with existential philosophy, but might this language be a tad high-flown for the likes of James? I will bring it down to a more personal level.

Whenever you and I (please permit me to include yourself until you refute it) are in the company of those that live in ignorance, we have no choice but to act out a role in order to fit into their world of so-called normality. Now and again, we misfits stumble upon a signpost that fills us with godlike ecstasy. But sooner or later we are lured back to the land of the 'normal', where the majority of well-adjusted mortals lazily bask in their false assumption that they are secure.

I am questioning the word 'misfit'. But more importantly, I need to simplify these knotty concepts by introducing everyday examples.

Let us observe a 'normal' couple, in their doomed struggle to find common ground. Let's watch as they swap unsettling tales of heaven and hell, in their eagerness to reveal a spiritual side. During copulation, upon catching a glimpse of our wordless terrain, his clumsy attempt to describe the indescribable is reciprocated with an account of *her* peak moment. He swallows back disappointment to discover that her experience occurred, not during their lovemaking, but midway through a Beethoven symphony.

Perhaps a Neil Diamond song might be safer than Beethoven.

Entrance to this fairground of the unknown comes with a hidden return ticket. And indeed it only takes one major incident – a terminal illness or bereavement – to turn light into darkness in an instant. With no point of reference, the hapless victim stumbles into the night. God is now the devil. Labels no longer hide the chasm from view. Words fail to drown the silence or explain away emptiness. Alcohol and television lull him into a temporary and false cheeriness. But such drugs only hide the truth: that the land of meaninglessness is the *only* authentic place in which to dwell. It is my belief, James, that you recognise this land as well as me.

Might he take this to mean that I see his life as meaningless? Time to bring on the star!

According to Friedrich Nietzsche, only a potential Superman can face this void and declare that 'God is Dead!' Only *he* has the courage to grab meaninglessness by the scruff of the neck and transform it to a new and greater meaning through the might of eternal recurrence. Now, let us pray!

TIME IS INFINITE BUT MATTER IS FINITE.
ONCE ALL COMBINATIONS EXHAUST
THEMSELVES, THEY CAN ONLY REPEAT.

So I have written this letter innumerable times to innumerable Jameses and will continue to do so for all eternity.

If you and I can look this fiasco squarely in the eye, raise our glasses, and still proclaim 'Yes!' then we can finally become Gods on earth.

Dear James, I look forward to hearing your response to my ramblings.

Your friend, David

A positive conclusion: we both stand together against a sneering world.

* * *

7.30 p.m. My letter has inspired me. This time I am dialling the Kellys with renewed confidence.

A female voice – wait.

'This is Jade Kelly speaking.'

'Is that you, James?'

'You deaf?'

'I'm sorry. I thought it might be James doing an impression of you.'

'What? Who's that?'

'Are you *sure* you're not James?'

'Jesus Christ! Mum, weirdo on the phone.'

'Jade, I'm sorry. I really thought … this is David Carpenter. May I please speak to your brother?'

'Hello mister TV man … no, you may not. He's incommunicado. That means he's not speaking to anybody, okay? I'll count to ten and hang up unless you have something really interesting to say. Perhaps five will be easier for you. I hear it's your lucky number.'

'But he's expecting me. He asked me to phone this evening. Can you call him over please?'

'No point – locked in his room since he got back. Big trouble – Uncle Ken's gone barmy. More questions please. One …two …'

'Hang on. Why has he gone barmy?'

'Gone barmy. I shall now read you a message from your boyfriend.' She pauses for a reaction. I do not oblige. 'It reads, "CC says that we are to meet at 2 p.m. Heathrow departures. Love and kisses." '

'For God's sake, Jade! Can you please read the thing out properly?'

'Mum – blasphemer on the phone … three.'

'So how *is* your mother?'

'Brain dead, watching *The New Avengers*. You'd need to be brain dead. Next.'

'And how's Darren?'

'Rotting in hell. Four.'

'Wait! I have something interesting to say.'

'Well?'

'I'm a musician like you. I play the piano.'

'Yes, I've heard. You play *proper* tunes.'

'But I play jazz too! I know 'Midnight in Moscow' by Kenny Ball.'

'Five.'

Saturday, 26 November 1977

1.30 p.m. Heathrow I finally managed to finish my letter to James during the interminable tube journey from Green Park to Heathrow. Having enquired about today's flights to Hong Kong, it seems that the next departure is not for another six hours; this I find unsettling. I have commandeered two facing rows of empty seats, and am sitting in the optimum position to observe as many entrances as possible. I am anxious that, unless James is looking out for me, I'll miss him altogether.

I'm on the lookout for three men. James, wearing an old-fashioned cream suit, might be flanked by his two minders: a sweaty beer-bellied Yorkshireman in a grey cardigan and smelly sports jacket, and a casually, but immaculately dressed Asian. Dreamily, I envisage James breaking rank to embrace me.

And now we are seated together in the front section of the plane, while Ken and CC have been relegated to second class. James nods repeatedly, as he mouths each word of my letter.

I knew he would understand.

My eyes open and half focus on the wrapped shakuhachi rolling off my lap. As I crawl to retrieve it, I run into a pair of brown slip-on shoes and pale cream trousers belonging to a man seated opposite. My bleary eyes then settle briefly on a hand that grips a slim book lined with brown paper. I continue upwards, past the grammar school tie, to James' profile. He is looking to his left, where CC stands, smiling gently down at me. Declining his offer of a handshake, I clumsily retrieve the shakuhachi, scramble to my feet, and transfer my gaze to his shining black eyes. Attired in a white, casual jacket, light blue jeans and sandals in bare feet, James' sponsor is certainly younger and more handsome than I remember. CC is a man totally at ease with himself. In stark contrast, James' face, but for a slight frown, is expressionless. He continues to look towards CC after joining him on the seat. He squeezes up far too close to him for my liking. My disquiet is compounded by CC's breezy manner.

'Mister Carpenter, James is delighted that you have managed to see us off.'

His rimless glasses and jet-black hair, swept back without a parting, give him the aura of a successful orchestral conductor. I need to demonstrate that my business is not with him.

'James, where's Uncle Ken?'

These words, the first I have ever spoken to James in person, receive no response. In fact, he seems loath to even look in my direction. I try again.

'We have no need of Uncle Ken, do we, James!' James' mouth slightly parts but no sound comes out. Although his head has now turned slightly towards me, I can still gain no eye contact. CC has begun to speak but I continue to address James.

'James, would you like me to ask you a question?' A barely perceptible nod encourages me to persist. 'Are you wanting to go with this man or not?'

His focus reverts to CC. I feel I've lost him.

'Yes, Mister Carpenter, I can confirm that James wishes to go with me. Please attend to me very carefully.'

This infuriating man is totally contained, his voice calm and alluring. The black smiling eyes draw me back into him.

'Trust me. I am acting solely in James' interests. James and I are of the opinion, as you are, Mister Carpenter, that Kenneth Bell's motives are less than honourable.'

'Why have you instructed James not to speak to me?'

'James, would you like to speak to Mister Carpenter?' James remains totally frozen, his eyes now staring into the floor.

I fractionally raise my voice.

'James, will you at least take my letter?'

His arm reaches out, snatches the envelope and slides it between the covers of his brown-papered book. He stares up at me momentarily, but with that vacancy that had fazed Eamonn O'Brien: neither hostile nor friendly.

CC is now standing. He retrieves a small travel bag and places a firm hand on James' shoulder. 'And now it's time to be on our way.'

I cannot let this moment slip past.

'On your way where? There's no Hong Kong flight for six hours.' CC taps James' shoulder. Like a well-trained animal, he jumps to his feet. I must not allow rising agitation to cloud my thoughts. 'Wait! So when exactly is this exhibition match? When do you arrive back? The Winmau championships start on the 27th.'

CC counteracts my rising tone with an infuriatingly measured response.

'The inauguration is in fifteen days' time: Sunday, December 11th. This gives us more than a fortnight to relax and acclimatise. Everything, including the Winmau, has been tightly scheduled. James will contact you on his return. Now it really is time for us to part company.'

I play my final card.

'December 11th – James, that's your twentieth birthday. Look, I have a birthday present for you. You can probably guess what it is.'

He hastily accepts my gift, but his attention is now focused only on CC. They both stand there silently, as though waiting for me to leave. And so I do.

Saturday, 3 December 1977

A week has passed and I have neither heard anything nor spoken to anyone connected with James. Despite a growing weight of responsibility, I am as yet unsure what action, if any, to take. I fear that CC may have snatched my letter from James, but prefer to believe that he has by now read it many times and may even have posted a reply.

Sunday, 11 December 1977

8 a.m. On this special day, I have risen early. This will allow me ample time to prepare for the international phone call that I intend making within the hour. To clear my head, I list six statements, only some of which I know to be true or false.

1) Today marks James' 20th birthday.
   Answer: true.

2) Today marks the establishment of the Hong Kong Darts Association.
   Answer: true. I have checked with the BDO (British Darts Organisation).

3) Tonight, James will play an exhibition match to mark its inauguration.
   Answer: to be verified within the next hour.

4) James and CC will not be attending the inauguration because:
   a) They never flew to Hong Kong
   b) They are staying at the Palace Hotel in Manchester.
   Answers:
   a) Not known.
   b) False: I phoned to check.

5) James will not be celebrating his 20th birthday because he has been kidnapped by CC. He languishes in a cellar – bound, gagged, and possibly dead.
   Answer: not known.

8.30 a.m. Yesterday's call to the BDO proved fruitful. The gentleman confirmed that the Hong Kong Darts Organisation was about to become established. He also supplied me with their phone number. It's now 4.30 p.m. Hong Kong time, so I'm expecting someone to pick up the phone. I'll speak slowly, but if they respond in Cantonese, I'll hang up.

'Yip?'

This may be a Cantonese word, as their language is monosyllabic.

'Good afternoon, is … this … the … Hong … Kong … Darts … Organisation?'

'There's no need to speak like a retard, mate … unless of course, you *are* one. My … name … Sid Furney. What … your … name?'

'Mister Carpenter – I'm calling from London and trying to contact James Kelly. He's a darts player.'

'Well, you're through to the right department, love. London! How's the weather there? Raining cats and dogs? Very pleasant here in Wan Chai, 90 degrees back in Melbourne.'

'I don't wish to sound rude, but this phone call's costing me a fortune. My friend's name is James Kelly. You should be expecting him. He's due to arrive with his sponsor to play an exhibition match.'

'That'll be nice. We were only planning on throwing a few darts and then retiring to the Old China Hand to get hammered.'

'So you're not expecting him? Is there no inauguration tonight?'

'An augur what? Jack, there's to be an auguration. Get your cassock on! Listen mate, tonight we're having a few tinnies to mark the start of an organised league over here. But I wouldn't jump on the plane if I were you.'

'Well, if he does arrive, can you please wish him a happy birthday from David Carpenter?'

'I could play it to him on the piano if you like. I play a bit of jazz actually, some say rather better than I play darts, cheeky buggers. What was his name again? Kelly? Any relation to Ned?'

I hang up, my suspicions confirmed.

Monday, 12 December 1977

10.30 a.m. Jade answers the phone.

'Well, if it isn't James' beau. I'm afraid he's away with his Chinaman.'

'Jade, just get off the bloody phone and put your mother on.'

'Here are two things my mother will not like. The first thing she'll not like is to hear that her daughter has just been verbally abused with the 'b' word by a London nancy boy. Okay? And the second thing she'll not like is to be dragged away from *The Archers* just after Walter Gabriel has made a confession that holds deep significance for her. So can *I* be of any assistance? Perhaps I can recommend some material to widen your jazz repertoire. How about 'Stranger on the Shore' by Acker Bilk?'

I remain silent. Words are exchanged in the background and the phone is passed to Brenda.

'Hello David.'

'Mrs Kelly, I'll get right to the point. I'm extremely concerned about James. Ken wasn't at Heathrow and James wouldn't speak to me. I'm not even sure that they left the country.'

'Thanks for your concern, David, but he sounded fine yesterday.'

'Where was he?'

'Well, it was a long-distance call. You can tell by that gap before they speak. But he was having a great birthday. It sounded like he was in a really good place.'

'What place?'

'He was on great form but totally hyper. Lord knows what he was on about. Then CC came on to say they'd be back in Yorkshire for Christmas Eve.'

The news that all seems well evokes an irrational feeling of disappointment, rather than relief.

'Did either of them mention the exhibition match?'

'Why would they? They both know I've no interest in darts. And James was on such a high that I wouldn't have noticed even if he *had* told me. At one point he was rattling on about Cluedo.'

'Cluedo?'

'Yes, it's a board game I used to play with the children. Miss Scarlett has to go first.'

'Does she? I expect *Ken* had something to say to the two of them!'

'Oh they refused to speak to him. That didn't go down too well. Talk of the devil … David, can you hold on a tick?'

I overhear Brenda having a brief altercation with a man, who now takes over the conversation. This time it's clearly not James' impersonation of his uncle, but the genuine article. My mind is momentarily consumed by the ghastly vision of Ken poised to throw me down a grimy flight of stairs.

'You're taking the piss. Are you in on all this or not? One word answer.'

'No. The last time I spoke with James was two weeks ago.'

'You phoned him. Why?'

'Because I wanted him to read a letter I'd written – which I can assure you had no connection with whatever is going on. Then he passed a message to Jade saying that I could meet him at Heathrow.'

'Did you see him?'

'Yes, but he refused to even look in my direction. CC tried to assure me that everything was fine but it certainly didn't look fine to me.'

'And that's all you know?'

I refrain from sharing with Ken the little more that I *do* know.

'I expected you to be with them, Mister Bell. Why aren't you in Hong Kong now?'

'I'm not in Hong Kong because Jim turned on me. He delivered an ultimatum: either I stayed behind or everything was off. He wasn't even leaving his room until I agreed. So if you're not in on all this, it's fucking obvious who is.'

'CC.'

'Chinese cunt … Jade, shut it! He arranges and finances the whole thing, sets up this exhibition match and then goes and cuts me out of the trip. Well one thing's for sure, he's got no idea what he's letting himself in for with James Kelly.' Ken lowers his voice to a whisper-like growl. 'But between you and me, I'm arranging a little trip of my own just to let this greasy fucker understand that from now on, it's *him* that's out. He can stuff his sponsorship. I've already pulled James out of the Winmau, so we can get our heads down to focus on the Embassy. From here on in I'll have no one, and that includes you, interfering with our preparation. After February 10th, when my boy's become world champion, you can all be weird together. But until that time, if you as much as send him a postcard, I'll personally squeeze your head through a mangle. Understand? Good. Then I'll hand you back to Mrs Kelly.'

I hear the front door slam. Brenda is back.

'Ken's really showing his age talking about mangles. He's owned a tumble dryer for at least twenty years. I suppose he could stuff you into *that*. So was your conversation helpful, David?'

'I'd be grateful if you didn't share with Ken my suspicion that they didn't go to Hong Kong.'

'Oh, our Ken seems to have his own suspicions. But I'm sure CC's taking good care of James, wherever they are.'

'You really think so?'

'CC's a gentleman. I've been thinking, David. Why don't you come up for a few days over the Christmas? James would love to see you.'

'What about Ken?'

'Don't worry. Tomorrow, Ken's setting off for his villa in Majorca. He'll be gone for three weeks. So any mangling will have to be put on hold.'

Although I've no plans for Christmas, I hardly know these people. I will not be taken in like some orphan. 'Perhaps I'll come up for New Year's Eve.'

'Then it's settled. Come over here for tea … say, about six. Then we'll all see the New Year in together at the Waggon.'

'Okay, thanks. I'll see you then, Mrs Kelly.'

'Call me Brenda. Now, just one more thing. Don't take this the wrong way, David, but you might be a little less aggressive towards Jade. She's rather sensitive.'

Saturday, 31 December 1977

'So how was your Christmas?'

'Well, you know, pretty much the usual: too much food, another Morecambe and Wise Christmas special.'

'And your year in general?'

'Well, I did meet the future world champion darts player. We've become good friends actually.'

Friends?

He smiled at me from the other side of the road in Wakefield.

He wrote me a letter about the perfect nine.

We spoke on the phone.

We met at Heathrow but he wouldn't look at me.

I wrote him a letter, although, thirty-five days later, I'm still waiting for a reply.

Wherever James went that day, he did return home on Christmas Eve. Brenda told me this during a brief phone conversation last Thursday. She'd called to check if I still intended coming to Outlane for New Year's Eve.

'I'll need to reschedule some arrangements. Does James know I'm invited?'

'Yes, but don't expect much. He's hardly come out of his room since he got back … says he's in training and not to be disturbed.'

This hardly comes as a shock. Based on our brief track record, my hopes of any real communication with James are diminishing. What *did* surprise me was Brenda's air of formality, bordering on unfriendliness. With the prospect of a frosty Brenda, a reclusive James and an abusive Jade, New Year's Eve does not bode well. Indeed, I question why I'm still bothering to go, considering the little that's on offer. After *tea*, (will that be a meal or another cup of tepid, milky water?) I can only look forward to a smoke-filled, noisy pub crammed with total strangers. Hardly a conducive setting in which to welcome in 1978.

* * *

Facing Brenda Kelly at her kitchen table is like the waking dream of finding oneself in the wrong house with the wrong family. We have no history and can find nothing to say, not that she's making much effort. Dishevelled and distracted, Brenda looks as though she hasn't slept for a week. For two long minutes, she vacantly shunts her pendulum around the table with the aid of a half-empty pack of Embassy cigarettes. Finally, she looks up, as though remembering that I'm sitting there.

'Shall I get tea?'

Even the prospect of a light-brown cup of boiled pond water has more appeal than further endurance of the current situation. At least tea turns out to be beans on toast and a mug of hot chocolate.

'So how was your Christmas, Mrs Kelly?'

Again she asks to be called Brenda, but her request is stiff and distant. I'm on the verge of asking if there's anything on TV, when she mutters, 'Actually, Christmas was lousy.' The last word sounds at odds with her posh accent, which for the first time strikes me as affected. 'What with James holed up in his room most of the day, Ken sodding off to Majorca … although that's nothing new …' She nods towards a photo on the sideboard of a younger, more accessible Jade. '… plus a sullen teenage daughter, behaving even more obnoxiously since her big bust-up with Darren …'

Her sentence peters out. We are left with a full minute's worth of loud ticking from the kitchen clock.

'So is she out, then?' I ask hopefully. Brenda's silence suggests that she hasn't heard me. I lean forward. 'Did CC return with James on Christmas Eve?'

She starts. 'Oh yes, Jade's coming down for you at 7.30.'

'Down for me?' My spirits sink further: it's now 7.20. I picture a red-cloaked Jade, hurtling down the stairs, ginger hair flying and dagger waving, in the Huddersfield Rep's rendition of *Don't Look Now*.

'Don't laugh, but you've been chosen to witness the premiere of something or other in her bedroom. She says it's to further your jazz education.'

'Brenda!' I finally have her full attention. 'Did CC come back here with James?' She stares blankly at me.

'No idea ... the doorbell rang, and there was James standing alone in the doorway, luggage in hand ... no car or cab outside. You can't get a peep out of him about *anything*, let alone the trip. It's not like he's in one of his states ... no tantrums. He just keeps repeating that he has to perfect his game. But what's going on behind his bedroom door is anyone's guess.'

'Perhaps he's practising his darts.'

'Well, that's the thing. He doesn't let me in any more ... keeps his door locked. But I *have* sneaked in and ...' She seems about to smile but then changes her mind. '... and there's no dartboard.'

'No dartboard?'

'It's not on the wall any more. And yet Ken says he's playing better than ever.'

Ken? Can things get worse?

'Ken's back? You know what he said he'd do to me!'

Brenda shunts the pendulum across the table.

'And *I'm* saying he won't lay a finger on you. If you don't believe me, ask for yourself.'

Purely out of politeness, I gather up the pendulum and clear a space in front of me. Resting my right elbow on the table, I grip the thread between my thumb and forefinger and allow the pendant to dangle in mid-air. It immediately begins to swing from side to side.

'That's not clockwise!'

Brenda shrugs.

'Well, at least it's not anticlockwise. It's telling you that you're in with an even chance.'

I ignore Brenda's tired smile and let go of the thread.

'I thought Ken was supposed to be away till the New Year.'

'He decided to return early – got back Boxing Day afternoon. And since then he's been taking James over the Waggon for long practice sessions before opening time. Well, it gets James out the house, even if it *is* only to cross the road. And I've never known Ken happier. Of course, I haven't told him about ... the round patch on the bedroom wall.'

'Has Ken asked about CC?'

'No, and he throws a fit if his name's mentioned. Come to think of it, I've not heard from CC since they both phoned from abroad on James' birthday.'

'Has James mentioned him?'

'No. James acts as though the whole trip never happened.'

'And I don't suppose James wants to talk to me.'

'Oh, he's expecting you after Jade's ... whatever it is she's about to do for you. In fact, he's asked for a chair to be placed outside his room.'

'What for?'

'Lord knows! And Jade's promised James that when she's finished with you, she'll come downstairs and leave you two alone in peace.'

An horrendous cacophony of tuneless modern jazz has erupted above our heads. I jump nervously to my feet. Brenda pulls a cigarette from her Embassy pack. 'I'm afraid that means that Jade is ready for you.'

A notice is pinned to Jade's door. With an orange crayon she has scrawled:

```
ASCENSION

LET US RISE TO HEAVEN TOGETHER

J C
```

I tentatively push open her door, but the overpowering roar of a saxophone from her hi-fi drives me back out on to the landing. Brenda stands at the foot of the stairs, eying me while drawing on her fag. Tentatively, I enter the room, leaving the door slightly ajar behind me and continuing to grip the brass handle. Then I turn. The sole source of light glows red from a bedside lamp. There is no sign of Jade. Her soprano saxophone lies on the bed.

Suddenly, the wardrobe door flies open and an array of flapping, multicoloured garments make for the opposite wall. Large plastic bangles spin on flailing arms, as each hand twirls purple silk scarves. Her face is covered with black netting that hangs from turban-like headwear, and from the top of the turban protrudes a long ostrich feather. She freezes for a few seconds and then hurls herself at me. She has grabbed my hands and pulls my arms up above my head. I am pinned to the door and feel the cold brass handle digging into the small of my back. The involuntary sound of nervous laughter emitting from my mouth is barely discernable from the cacophony.

The saxophone solo has screeched to its climax. Now the other drugged-crazed musicians join in, thus recreating the tuneless din that I'd first heard in the kitchen. The trumpet (surely not the sort that Kenny Ball plays) makes its entrance like a terrified chicken. Throughout this solo, Jade bounces on her bed, hop-scotching around her instrument. As the ensemble re-enters around the trumpet's dying squawks, I realise that my hands are still above my head and that my teeth are tightly clenched in a rictus grin. As a second, deeper sounding saxophone enters the fray, Jade is repeatedly yelling one word at me, as she trampolines off the bed and flaps her scarves across my face.

'Pharaoh, Pharaoh!'

She's back on the bed, this time on all fours, the ostrich feather pointing towards my stomach, as she cries out 'Dewey, Dewey!' This continues throughout a new trumpet solo that buzzes like an angry wasp. The ensemble dives back in, and the din gradually subsides until only the ticking needle click remains.

'Close your eyes. Close your eyes *now*!'

She has clasped my hands and is pulling my arms down.

'Jade, you must not do ...'

'Eyes closed now!'

'I'd rather you not do anything of ... a sexual nature.'

'Do not move or look. I will have to write that down.'

The record has been turned over, and my eyes remain tightly shut throughout three more anarchic saxophone solos. Like a captive who has given up any notions of escape, I gradually adjust to, and even attune to, this alien sound world. My eyelids relax to a lush light-headedness.

Something has been placed on my head, and a light fabric now hangs down to tickle my face. But I pay it no attention, as I allow my body to sway in time to an urgently repeated saxophone phrase that summons the piano in for its solo.

'Open your eyes, David.'

Through the cobwebbed netting that hangs from my turban, I observe Jade sitting peacefully on her bed in the lotus position. Her half-closed eyelids lightly flicker: red-lit ginger hair sprouts in every direction. Softly, she chants a new mantra.

'McCoy,' she whispers. 'McCoy.'

The piano has made way for a double bass that seems to gurgle up from beneath the ocean. Jade's hands delve into the intertwined scarves. She slides out her soprano saxophone, puts it to her lips and holds a low, sustained note. Magically, the low note gives birth to a second, high note. Two notes seem to be sounding at once. Then the high note breaks free and takes on a life of its own. As it skips to and fro, transforming into subtler shapes, I catch myself smiling my own smile as I become aware of my body. Her solo unfolds, evolves to its climax and finally merges with the record. Now, just silence but for the repetitive needle click.

She has removed the saxophone from her lips and settles it back among the nest of scarves. She is gazing at me as though there is a question in the air. What I really want to say is that her solo was beautiful, but instead, I produce two limp claps. I can no longer hold her gaze and turn towards the door. Her voice is soft. 'I'll tell James you're ready.'

'No, Jade, tell him I'm *not* ready. I need some air. I'm going out for a walk.'

I'm halfway down the stairs, when Jade overtakes me.

'Mum, nancy boy's going for a walk. He's not seeing James after all.'

Brenda hovers, bleary-eyed, in the lounge doorway.

'Is something wrong, David? James is waiting for you.'

'I just need to clear my head. Can you please tell him that I'll be back soon?'

'Back from where? It's very dark and cold out there. At least put on an overcoat. Here, I'll lend you James'... best not to tell him.'

I turn right, into a biting wind. After having waited almost two months and travelled nearly two hundred miles to meet someone, that very person is now waiting for *me* as I walk in the opposite direction. Why? It is not that the prospect of meeting him has waned in significance, rather that my recent experience has befuddled my brain. I am presently at a total loss as to what it is I want from James Kelly. I'll walk until my mind clears.

After a few more houses, I have reached open fields on either side of me, passed a deserted bus shelter and now stop at a sign pointing towards Marsden Gate. Light from the lamppost illuminates a track that cuts through the field to my right and peters out amid a few scattered farmhouses. A string of dangling Christmas lanterns links a partly built house with two adjacent caravans.

I am perched on a dry-stone wall, huddled in James' blanket-like overcoat. I feel elated, yet somehow displaced, as though I have no notion as to how I arrived here. As the saxophone improvisation continues to echo in my head, I hazily reassess my feelings towards Jade Kelly. The warmth I feel is not sexual or romantic but filled with gratitude for her selfless gift.

All the while, I've been staring unconsciously at a parked motorcycle and sidecar covered with stickers and miniature flags. For some moments, I have also been vaguely aware of loudening footsteps on the track behind me, but my tranquil mood protects me from any fear. Even though the man has drawn close and is now scrutinising me, I continue to remain perfectly calm, despite his massive frame and strange appearance. This bear of a man is wrapped in a brightly coloured patchwork quilt covered in political badges. On his head perches a fake white turban from which long tufts of blond hair protrude. By his side, propped up on the wall, is a double bass; an appropriate instrument for a giant. I muse philosophically that I might also have been wearing a turban, had Brenda not tactfully removed it as I was leaving the house. He offers his hand.

'Luke.'

'David.'

Luke's accent is similar to Ken's, but with a higher pitch and a singsong quality that belies his size.

'So, David, you enjoy the sensual sound of a saxophone, pardon my alliteration.'

'I've never taken much interest before tonight, and I don't believe in meaningful coincidences but ...' The notes that I had momentarily imagined in my head have in actuality been drifting from one of the caravans at the end of the track. This musician, however, is far less assured than Jade, and his instrument emits a more masculine tone. We both listen to the player stumbling through a series of attempted scales and intermittent phrases. 'Summertime' is started and abandoned. '... but this is the second time in the last thirty minutes that I've both heard a saxophone being played *and* seen a turban!'

'Ah, now that'll be Jade. Isn't she something else! But I'm surprised Jamie lent you his coat. So how come you know these wonderful people?'

I improvise sign language to denote that 'it's a long story', while fighting the uncharacteristic urge to stroke Luke's headwear. This is Jade's doing. As I reach up towards the silky fabric, the giant obliges by lowering his head for my inspection.

'I gave it to the boy two years ago. There was a *two for the price of one* sale in Brighouse. Jamie instantly declared it to be "an utterly wondrous object", like he does, then wore it just the once.'

The aspiring saxophonist has now launched into a lame approximation of 'Blue Suede Shoes'. I gaze back towards the two dimly lit caravans, fifty yards down the track, tranquillised by the giant's singsong voice.

'Barrie and his missus used to live on the top floor of Barkisland Hall, looking after Joe Kagan's mansion. As Lord Joe hardly ever lived there, he said they could both stay for free if they kept an eye on the place, caretakers like. Then Barrie's missus went and did something she shouldn't have. So Barrie moved out to the caravan and I mostly kip in the one next door. Barrie's a builder by trade and spends most of his time converting the farmhouse out there. He pays me to help out. Well, at least he *says* he'll pay me when things have straightened out. We've just been having a jam. Barrie reckons that his new relationship with the baritone sax is a safer bet than marriage. Do you like Mingus?'

'Is that a Yorkshire speciality, like haggis?'

'It certainly is. You must promise me that you'll ask Jade for some.'

I nod gratefully and return his gentle smile. That I have taken in little of what this intriguing stranger has said is of no importance; it is enough to relish this unusually tranquil mood that recalls memories of idle chatter in the dormitory after lights-out.

Luke is loading his double bass into the sidecar of his motorbike.

'I'd give you a lift but don't have a spare crash helmet … not that I require one myself, being a Sikh, like.' He perches on the edge of the sidecar. 'It's funny, if you'd have asked me what religion I was four years ago, I would have told you that I wasn't anything … unless you'd class anarchy as being a religion.'

I shrug my shoulders, genuinely enthralled and happy for him to chatter on.

'I wouldn't have even been able to *spell* Sikh back then, but four years ago they brought in this daft law making crash helmets compulsory. And me being an anarchist, I stuck to my principles. Can anarchists have principles? Perhaps they *refuse* to have principles. So I bombed around Huddersfield helmetless, often with Jamie on the back. He thought it was hilarious. I was forever getting nicked. Then I got my brainwave, and nine months later I'd converted. It's a very open religion you know. They'll take anyone. So whenever I got stopped by the pigs, I would preach Guru Nanek's message of love and understanding to them. Some policemen can be most unsympathetic. In fact, one or two thought I was just taking the piss. Well, perhaps I was. Then it dawned on me that a lot of Sikhism was stuff I already believed, like trying to balance a virtuous life with a sense of social justice ... all that malarkey. I started really getting into it. Only ten minutes ago, I was telling Barrie, "Look mate, you don't even have to be celibate," because he's always been a bit of a lady's man. But I don't get the feeling he's about to sign up.'

'So did they start letting you ride around town in your turban?'

'No. So I waged a full-scale battle: campaigns, graffiti, the lot ... even led a protest march through town. And you know what? I won! Last year they went and changed the law. They should make me the eleventh Guru! The tenth died in 1708 so they're bound to be ready for a replacement by now, eh?'

I grin back at the odd fellow as I turn up the collar of James' overcoat.

'I'm not needing a lift anyway, thanks. I only came out for a breather. Best to get James' coat back without him noticing. Perhaps I can buy you a drink at the Waggon later, if that's permitted in Sikhism.'

'Well it is and it isn't. I've been banned from the Waggon since *last* New Year's Eve. But that's another story.'

* * *

I'm seated outside James' closed bedroom door, listening to the creak, creak, creak of his rocking chair and feeling as though I'm taking confession, except that James has nothing to confess. After the exhilaration of Jade's performance and my recent encounter with Luke, this is decidedly an anticlimax. For the past fifteen minutes James has been talking incessantly about the upcoming Embassy championships and I'm actually feeling bored. From the other side of the door, he has been studiously informing me that there is first to be a play-off between four British players, including himself, to qualify for the final sixteen. Now, he's in the process of laboriously naming each of the eighteen players involved. Admittedly, I'm mildly surprised to learn that he is actually required to qualify, but he offers no explanation. Instead, I'm being plied with each player's age, country of origin and seeding. I take no interest in any of this and am unconvinced that James does either. At one point I feign enthusiasm, if only to prove that I'm still sitting there.

'I'd assumed that it would be mostly British players.'

'This really is a world championship: two Americans, two Swedes, two Australians, a Canadian, two Welsh, two Scots, and one Irishman.'

'James, are you *really* interested in any of this?'

'Oh yes, Carpenter, I truly am. I *have* to be. It's the only way. And you have to be also.'

My patience is running out.

'Will you please stop calling me Carpenter! My name is *David*. Carpenter's my *surname*, for God's sake.' Silence. 'And who says I have to be interested? Uncle Ken?'

'So, there are four rounds. The first is the best of nine legs … David.'

'What.'

'If you really claim to be my friend, I expect you to be there to support me in Nottingham on February the sixth. That's a Monday, and it's the first round. By then, I will have got through the qualifying round without any problem.'

'And what else must I do to qualify for your friendship?'

'You must stay away from me between now and then. For the next forty days, I need to prepare without any disturbance or interruption.'

'How are you preparing, James?'

'When I'm not practising at the Waggon with Uncle Ken, I prepare here, in my room.'

'How can you concentrate with all that racket coming from Jade's bedroom?'

'Jade is a part of my preparation.'

'And why have you taken the dartboard down? Is that part of your preparation too?'

'Yes, it is.'

'There was no exhibition match in Hong Kong, was there! They weren't even expecting you. I wonder if you've even *been* to Hong Kong.'

'I *have* been! And while I was there, I learned a Mongolian song about a horse. Shall I sing it to you?'

'No thanks. I've heard enough weird music for one day. Why didn't you answer my letter?'

'Because I didn't know how long it would take to reach you over Christmas.' He slips a thin envelope under the door. 'By February the eleventh I'll be world champion. The prize money is £3,000.'

'Less Uncle Ken's ten per cent.'

'Twenty per cent ... Are you going to tell him?'

'Tell him about what – the missing dartboard? Tell him that you never arrived for this supposed exhibition match? I *did* speak with Ken after you'd left. He said he was planning a little trip of his own. It sounded like he intends going after CC.'

'Are you going to read my letter?'

'I'm opening it now.'

'I do want to be honest with you, David.'

I have read the twenty words, and crumple the sheet into James' overcoat pocket. I'm rattling the handle of the locked door.

'Is this a joke? Did you read even one word of the letter I spent days writing to you? Or perhaps you just couldn't grasp it. Perhaps it went right over your simple head.'

'I did read it! You must stop shaking my door.'

'I thought you were special. You're not special, are you! I got it wrong. Ken was right after all: you *are* a freak show. I owe him an apology. Well, I won't keep you from your preparation. You'd better get back to throwing invisible darts at your imaginary friend on the wall. It's probably the only friend you've got.'

'Please don't go. Are you still there? Do you have any more questions for me?'

As I turn towards the top landing, I see Brenda and Jade listening at the foot of the stairs. They are also witness to the rising anguish in James' voice.

'David, you *have* to take an interest. You *have* to be with me in Nottingham!'

Now on the bottom landing, I pass silently between mother and daughter. Jade attempts to hand me something, but on discovering that both my fists are tightly clenched, she stuffs it into James' overcoat pocket.

'Ken said to give it to you: your complimentary pass to the Embassy. And like the man says, you *have* to be there. Now I'd better go up and see what you've done to my big brother.' As she arrives on the top landing, the door swings open to let her in.

Brenda is seeing me to the front door.

'Has James said something to upset you? You're sweating. Perhaps you need a little sit down before we go over.'

'A drink's what I need. I'll see you both there.'

'Jade's not coming. She's trying to avoid Darren. But I'll follow you over in a bit. I don't want to arrive too soon. It's usually my job to lead Ken back to the house around three in the morning.'

'Ken's over there now?'

'Yes, and he's floating on a cloud. It would take a lot more than you to spoil things. He just wants James to be left alone until after this wretched match. Oh, just one more thing before you go. Jade handed me this note ... something you said to her. It's not that I don't trust you, but as her mother, you can understand my concerns. Perhaps you'll explain it to me later.'

* * *

Seven weeks ago, I was sat perched on this same barstool, hoping to catch sight of James Kelly. Two stools along, a solitary regular stared sullenly into his personal metal jug, while two youths played darts. Darren, the younger of the two, handed his empties to Betty the barmaid. We chatted. That following weekend, Jade would become his girlfriend.

This evening, Darren, in scruffy T-shirt and jeans, is throwing darts alone. He appears distracted and bored. Seven weeks ago, Jade sat facing her mother at the corner table, but this evening, the morose, craggy-faced regular, still glowering into his beer, occupies that table. Although the paint-splattered overalls have been replaced with a smart suit and open-necked shirt, his unspoken message is still to keep well clear. Betty attempts some small talk as she empties his ashtray, but he barely looks up.

I had expected the bar to be packed and noisy, but there are no more than twenty locals quietly chatting. The exception to this depressingly low-key atmosphere is an overweight man on his feet and in full flow, boisterously entertaining a seated group. Although he has his back to me, the smoker's rasp is instantly recognisable. This is Kenneth Bell, agent and manager to the future world darts champion.

The songs from the jukebox are taking on an uncanny, pre-ordered pattern. Hearing Elvis's 'My Way' confirms why I shed no tear when he died this August. Next up is Marc Bolan, warbling his way through 'I Love to Boogie'. This was his final hit, over a year ago, unless you count hitting the tree and expiring this September. And why are we now being blasted with 'White Christmas' on New Year's Eve? Could it be because Bing was gonged in October? But there is no disc of death for November, unless of course Rod Stewart's relatives are keeping the news under wraps.

After a second pint of Sam Smith's, the accelerating repartee in my head now craves an audience. I take the bold step of joining Darren at the dartboard. He nods, listlessly throws a dart and mumbles, 'If one more fucker puts on "Mull of Kintyre", they'll get one of these between the eyes.'

Without turning his head, he hands me the three darts. I throw, and miraculously they all land in the 20. Darren gives me a side-on glower and retrieves the darts.

'Been practising, then?'

'That's the first time I've scored more than 25, apart from one lucky bull's eye. Perhaps alcohol really *does* steady the hand. So did you notice? We had Elvis, who died in August, then Marc Bolan—'

'Then Bing Crosby … just trying to keep myself amused.'

'Charlie Chaplin popped off on Christmas day. We could have had "Smile".' I make a feeble stab at singing: '*Smile, though Jade's heart is breaking*,' and follow through with a comedy northern accent. 'So it's all off with your sweet lass, then?'

'He shrugs, and throws 85.

'Did you see her? She say anything?'

'This evening I saw Jade Kelly in a whole new light. I had no idea she was going to be *that* good – on the saxophone I mean.'

'So you got the full JC experience, then?'

'No, it wasn't at all religious, just that way-out, modern stuff. I think I could get into it.'

'No, not Jesus Christ … John sodding Coltrane. Yeah, way-out, man! I bet you were one of those hippies, weren't you. So how old are you, Mister Carpenter?'

This curt version of Darren bears little resemblance to the chirpy, trendily dressed lad that had politely shaken my hand only seven weeks ago. But I persist. Perhaps he could do with some male company.

'I'm thirty, and, believe, me, I despised hippies. *Make war, not love*: that's what Friedrich Nietzsche would have said, had he been at Woodstock.' Darren hurls three darts in quick succession. 'Look, Darren, I didn't mean to intrude. I'll leave you to it. Happy New Year.'

He rips the darts out of the board and wheels round.

'Well that's exactly *it*, isn't it! Hardly the most ecstatic New Year's Eve I've ever had. This time next year I'll be like Barrie over there.' Darren points to the craggy-faced misery on the corner table. 'You're looking at a man that's *really* had his share of women trouble. Jade talked him into buying a second-hand saxophone to take his mind off things. Now he can't put the bloody thing down … says it gives him solace. Just as well he lives alone. It sounds like a dying bull.'

'That's so odd. I heard him practising just a while ago. I was chatting to some tramp that'd just left Barrie's caravan. They'd been improvising together.'

'Let Luke hear you calling him a tramp and he'll brain you. God, no … Ken's putting it on again.'

It's not 'The Mull of Kintyre', but a familiar medley of two old rock songs: 'Daddy Cool' and 'The Girl Can't Help It'. As Ken elicits a cheer from his seated audience, I picture James staring wildly into the TV camera. Darren points accusingly in Ken's direction.

'Ken reckons he's finally heading for the big time, now that darts is about to become fashionable. And of course our man owns fifteen per cent of the main attraction.'

I correct Darren with an air of confidentiality.

'Twenty per cent. So you've seen James playing recently?'

Darren stares at the board and shakes his head.

'He's untouchable. Throwing like they're radar controlled. But it's more than that. Since his little holiday, he's a changed man. Not like he's turned into your regular bloke ... that's never going to happen. But there's something different about him. He's calmer, less unpredictable, almost talks normal to you. And that bull's eye stuff's all gone, except when he needs one. James is now just playing to win – and he's *really* set on winning the Embassy.'

'Perhaps that's CC's influence.'

'No, what attracted James was CC's *indifference* to winning. CC was always dead keen, but never for the game. He didn't give a damn about tournaments and leagues. Mind you, he's one hell of a player himself, but just throws for fun. They were always laughing together. And CC took a real interest right from the start, I mean in James as a *person*. We all know how wonder-boy loves people to ask him questions. Well, CC did that without any prompting. James had never got that kind of attention from anyone before. Brenda's never had any ambition for him, and Ken – well Ken's Ken. CC was the opposite of Ken and really brought out the best in James.'

I picture James looking anxiously up at CC in the airport.

'Well, I think James was frightened of CC.'

'You're wrong. It's Ken he's scared of. CC could actually calm James down. But it always did seem an odd set-up: CC offering to sponsor James only as long as he could have some *personal involvement*. Ken found that one hilarious.'

'Why?'

'Oh, come on – James and personal involvement just don't go together.'

'Oh, I thought you meant ...'

'What, that CC was after getting into James' pants? Well, that would be nothing new. Anyway, when it became clear how well the two of them were hitting it off, Ken came on board and let CC do his thing. I liked the guy: very laid-back, friendly –

loaded, but never chucking it in your face. Anyway, he's totally out of the picture now. Buggered off back to Japan.'

'You mean Hong Kong.'

'James said Tokyo. And then there's the difference *you* made.'

'Me?'

'Oh yes, he was forever on about his friend Carpenter. He told me he was really looking forward to seeing you.'

His friend Carpenter! I am already regretting my earlier aggression but continue to feel furious towards him.

'James no longer interests me. In fact, I feel disappointed in him. He's let me down.'

'He's *what*? How could he have let *you* down? He hardly knows you.'

I, of course, have no answer. But if I really *have* severed my connection with James, then whatever am I still doing here among these people that are a part of his life and not mine? Without James Kelly, his tribe: Darren, Jade, Brenda, Ken, and Luke no longer hold any significance for me.

Darren nods towards the bar.

'Alright, stand by your beds. Ken's just spotted you. His beer gut's headed this way.' I'm looking around for the nearest exit. Darren's chirpiness has returned. 'Hold tight mate, we might squeeze a round out of him. Hi, Ken. I believe you two have met.'

'Well, if it isn't James Kelly's number one groupie still poking his nose in. So what'll it be, lads? Betty, three pints of Sam Smiths!'

'Mister Bell, I promise you I didn't come here to disturb James. I also owe you an apology for my outburst in your office. It was—'

'Get a load of this, Darren: "My outburst!" That's poncey London talk. But if Brenda tells me that you've been talking bull's eyes with Jim, outburst will take on a whole new meaning. Betty!'

PART 1: BULLS

'James has made it clear that he needs to be left alone. I totally respect his wishes.'

'Oh, we like a bit of respect, don't we, Darren!'

'We do, Ken.'

'And did he make anything else clear to you, Mister Carpenter?'

Darren is now also eyeing me as I sweat under James' thick overcoat. But Ken leaves the question hanging; he screws up his face into a cross between sneer and smile, and lurches off towards the bar.

Darren snorts.

'Totally pissed, but he wouldn't harm a fly. He's all mouth.'

'So Brenda keeps telling me.'

We watch him stumbling back towards us, precariously balancing the three pints.

'Well, did he, son?'

'Did he what, Mister Bell?'

'Did the boy tell you anything I should know about?'

'No, Mister Bell, he didn't.'

He hands us our pints and clamps a clammy hand to my shoulder. His cigarette smoke makes my eyes water.

'Alright, let's get one thing straight: whatever goes on in Jimmy's subnormal mind, and whatever he's been up to with we-know-who, no longer concerns me.' He reaches his arm around my head and takes a deep drag before continuing. 'And that's because, A: we've seen the last of mister slitty-eyes, B: the boy's playing like a dream, and C … What do you think C is, son? What is James Kelly about to become?'

'The Embassy world champion, Mister Bell.'

Ken shouts over to a drunk, leaning against the jukebox. 'Alex, man, let's hear it one more time. Yes!'

The song instantly triggers my recollection of the TV interview stumbling to a halt. Eamonn O'Brien can barely wait to introduce the guest group: 'They've a top ten hit with

'Daddy Cool' and they're called ... yes, you've guessed it: Darts!'

'And here she is: the lovely lady herself!'

Ken waves to Brenda as she emerges from the lounge bar looking rather glamorous. Darren and I observe Ken envelope her with hugs and slobbering kisses while spilling half his pint.

'So what's the story with those two?' I ask Darren.

'He's been on and off with Brenda for years. Lord knows how she puts up with him. But there's no way he's going to lose contact with Jade.'

'With Jade?'

'She winds him up something rotten but they're very close.'

'How do you mean?'

Darren looks back towards Ken and laughs at his antics.

'It's good to see Ken back on form. But he's being a bit premature with all this champion of the world stuff. OK, James has turned things around, but it's still not going to be the walkover Ken's making it out to be. For a start, he's not actually there yet. He still needs to qualify for the final sixteen. There's only room for two more British players, so there has to be a play-off between four of them. Alan Glazier's in that group, so nothing's for certain.'

'Why does James need to qualify?'

'Because he hasn't played enough matches this year to be seeded. And the fact that Ken suddenly pulled him out of the Winmau this month has gone down badly with the BDO. It also left the door open for Bristow to walk that one. Eric's got a tendency to scare the shit out of James just by winking at him. And then there's John Lowe – lovely bloke – except that James beat him earlier this year. So gentleman John'll be looking for him. And when *Lowe's* on his game, which is ninety per cent of the time, he can wipe you out in minutes.'

'I thought you said James is untouchable.'

'That's only when all the conditions are right and there's nothing to upset or panic him. This is going to be a big event with TV cameras, and we all know what happened the last time James had a camera stuck in his face. But Ken's right: as long as he stays focused, he's in with a big chance.'

The evening gradually takes on a warmer glow, with drink, chat and more darts. Sadly, the drink does not continue to improve my playing skills. At least Darren is showing patience and seems grateful for the company.

My attention is suddenly drawn to an open window at the far end of the bar, through which a white turban has appeared.

'Come on Mister Belltime! Just pass out a Newcastle Brown so poor old Luke can see in the New Year. And the lad wants … you sure about that? Says he wants a double Advocaat. With a what? He says with a cherry in it. Sorry Jamie, but your manager doesn't approve.'

I'm surprised to discover that the bar is now packed, and the clock above the fireplace is reading ten to midnight. Ken has pulled away from Brenda and is heading unsteadily towards Luke's taunts. Meanwhile, Brenda, a little unsteady on her feet, is about to join us. Strands of hair hang down her face, and her lipstick is smudged.

Brenda's standing a little too close to me and I'm feeling slightly aroused. Darren asks her if James is really outside with Luke, but she playfully pushes his shoulder and continues to focus on me. I enjoy the smell of Brandy on her breath, as her thumb and forefinger gently press my upper arm.

'Now David, I have something for your ears only, so Darren, if you wouldn't mind.'

'Well, I'll leave you to see in the New Year together. I'll settle for the Punch and Judy show instead. We're coming up to the bit were Punch attempts to remove Judy's turban.'

I glance towards the far window.

'So, is James out there without an overcoat?'

'David – the note.'

'Note? You mean James' letter. Did he tell you?'

'No, the note Jade gave me. Have you still not read it? I didn't want Darren to know, what with things as they are between them.'

I remove three items from the right-hand pocket and transfer James' letter and the Embassy pass to the left pocket. I then straighten out the crumpled sheet of notepaper and, for no apparent reason, pass it to Brenda without reading it.

'So would you prefer me to read it aloud *for* you?'

I nod, and grin sheepishly, like a naughty schoolboy. Although earlier events have become muddled in my head, I'm now recalling that very moment when I uttered the words that I know to be scribbled on the notepaper. My eyes had been closed when Jade said: 'Don't move or look. I will have to write that down.'

'And so I'm standing there,' I explain to Brenda, 'in your daughter's bedroom, invited by her, and with her mother's permission ...'

'For a musical performance.'

'... For this totally weird *happening*, like hippies used to have. It was very good, mind you, incredible actually. You have two amazingly gifted children.'

'David, why have you got your eyes closed?'

'Because this is what it was like, this is what she wanted. Jade *told* me to shut my eyes. Then she's flapping these scarves in my face. And all the while there's this wild music winding up to a frenzy.'

'She's forever playing that noise. It's called 'Ascension'. Go on.'

'Then she's pulling my arms up above my head.'

I feel liquid dripping on to my hair.

'You really don't need to demonstrate. Here, let me hold your drink for you.'

'This is not a normal situation, as you can imagine. It really isn't. And it's then that I say to her …'

'I'd rather you not do anything of a sexual nature.'

I open my eyes and lower my arms. Brenda is looking up from Jade's note and either smiling or frowning, perhaps both at the same time. She hands back the note and the remains of my beer.

'So, do you find my daughter attractive?'

'Well, she's seventeen and I'm thirty … of course not! But I was so disoriented … tated. Then later, when she was sitting cross-legged on the bed, playing so passionately, yes, I thought she looked very beautiful. But by that time we were … well, somewhere else – we'd transcended. I mean, it was one of those moments when a door opens and you get a brief glimpse of how wonderful the world can be without people like William Abercrombie.'

'Who?'

'Oh, you really wouldn't want to know William.'

For the first time, I'm looking directly at Brenda but am still unable to interpret her smile, as she peruses her daughter's note.

'What a quaint phrase: "… anything of a sexual nature". It reminds me of the *News of the World*. "And then he did something of a sexual nature". Some of those stories used to really turn me on but nowadays they tone down the juicy bits. David, I really don't believe that Jade was about to do …'

'Please don't say it again. But why ever did she write it down?'

'Well, I can see why she would have found it noteworthy.'

'But why then hand it to you?'

'To wind you up – haven't you noticed? It's her second hobby after playing the saxophone.'

'So why are you embarrassing me with it now?'

'Oh, you've become all sober suddenly. What a pity! Perhaps

I'm checking, as Jade's mother, that nothing *did* happen.'

'Well I can assure you that so far in my life, nothing of that nature has ever happened.'

'You're a virgin, David?'

'Would you like a megaphone? I'm trying to tell you that I found the experience spiritual rather than sexual, and also a little overwhelming. I needed to clear my head, so I took a walk. And that's when I met Luke.'

We both look towards the open window. The show is over.

'Oh, Luke will have gone off with James to see the New Year in. That's what they usually do.'

'What, back to your place?'

'No, to Marsden Gate with the lovely Barrie ... now *there's* a fit lad.'

'He doesn't look very healthy to me.'

'Fit, not healthy. So what happened with you and James? He sounded upset.'

'Oh no, no, no.'

'Well, thanks for the explanation – I'll just have to imagine how much damage you've inflicted on my other baby. But at least we've cleared up the bedroom incident. "Thirty-year-old virgin left alone with provocative teenager". All things considered, you behaved like a gentleman.'

'It's not just *Jade's* hobby, then.'

'Alright, I'm teasing you. But you're more attractive than you think. You've got a nice face.'

'I used to stare into a mirror until all I could see was two eyes, a nose and a mouth. Just separate bits stuck on to the front of my head.'

'You've got brown eyes like Darren's.'

'It says hazel on my passport, otherwise I wouldn't really know.' I look away into the crowd. Ken is attempting to attract Brenda's attention while trying to stand upright and fails on both counts. 'Ken wants you.'

'Sorry David, he's calling me over for the countdown. Have a happy New Year, virgin from the South.'

She kisses me lightly on the mouth and rejoins Ken.

The whole place is on its feet, craning to view the television that perches high on a shelf in the corner. The TV presenter is working up his audience for the final moments of 1977. O'Brien had valiantly struggled with James. Now, relaxed and in his element, he is delivering a sentimental spiel over the massed pipers of somewhere or other, as they blast out 'The Mull of Kintyre'. Darren walks out in disgust.

I hover alone by the door, observing the scene from within my bubble. I could almost be back home, stretched out on the sofa, watching all this on TV, staring at the closing moments of my very own *Coronation Street*. And as the final minute is counted down, I imagine Jade cross-legged on her bed, blissfully chanting: 'A love supreme.' Meanwhile, in Marsden Gate, I picture Luke endeavouring to envelope James with a bear hug as Barrie delivers a shaky rendition of 'Auld Lang Syne' on his baritone saxophone.

I catch myself mouthing the words 'should auld acquaintance be forgot' as the Waggon slowly reverts back into its subgroups. Brenda is struggling to pull Ken up from out of his chair, but his mind is on other things.

'Alex, man, put it back on. Give us another blast. Betty, where's Betty?'

Betty is bolting the front door for a lock-in.

As I turn to take one final glance back at the bar, I cannot think of a single reason why I would ever wish to see any of these people again. I'll not miss them and they've already forgotten me.

* * *

I have stepped out into the street. The continuing murmur of their chatter confirms that my presence has left no impression whatsoever. But this is as should be. For whatever it was that I had been hoping to achieve over the past seven weeks, has now reached its conclusion.

I look across the road, and up to the drawn curtains of James' vacated bedroom, in the certain knowledge that there is no more that I wish to know.

I have propped myself up in the side alley. This must be the very spot where Luke and James stood earlier. But the window provides insufficient light for my purposes. I move on.

I have crossed the road. My back slides down the Stainland sign until I'm sat, knees up, on the cold pavement, outside number 702.

I have fished out the envelope that James had slid under his bedroom door. I hold the crumpled sheet six inches from my glasses.

For a third time, I am reading aloud his unintelligible reply to my letter.

> *Carpenter, I am sorry that you are lonely. But how can I answer your question until you ask it?*
>   *James Kelly*

PART 2
DARTS

13 January 1978 – 6 February 1978

At the tender age of twenty, it would seem that Eric Bristow is unstoppable; well, he certainly thinks so. But this young man's bravado can be justified by his two recent wins in December. No fewer than 111 players from around the globe battled it out for the £2,000 prize at the Winmau World Masters. In the finals, Yorkshire's Paul Reynolds almost managed to level it at two apiece, but in that all-important fourth leg, he just missed a double top finish, allowing 'The Crafty Cockney' past to clinch the trophy. In the same month, despite the World Cup eventually passing to Wales, Bristow, and England captain John Lowe still managed to win the pairs. The one small blot on Eric's copybook occurred during the Cameron's Master Invitation, when Welsh wizard Alan Evans knocked him out in the quarter-finals.

The New Year has got off to an explosive start. On Sunday night at the Empire, Leicester Square, the joint was jumping, not to the sounds of disco, but to the enthralling spectacle of Bristow and Lowe locking horns for the British Open. The fact that Lowe was the reigning champion didn't deter Eric from going in for the kill at 2–2 and pocketing another £1,000.

Over the New Year I came to realise that my behaviour towards James had been unjustified and have since decided to carry out James' wishes: I am taking an interest in darts.

James Kelly's TV appearance had jolted me from a long slumber. That single event on a Monday evening in November led me to embark on a quest. Despite Ken Bell's insistence that James' 'bull's eye shit' was just the result of Eamonn O'Brien's unscheduled questions, I remained convinced that, to the contrary, bull's eyes lay at the heart of things. And despite my discovery that James Kelly was the holder of prestigious trophies and had built up a considerable track record, I still refused to believe that he had one grain of interest in the game of darts. Indeed, my initial contacts with him confirmed this belief.

Then, on New Year's Eve, for reasons still unknown, something changed. From behind his bedroom door, he was suddenly insisting that his one ambition, his true aim in life was to become the Embassy world champion. Having enthused about the prize money and suchlike, he then demanded that I was not to disturb him until his moment of victory. My disappointment and ensuing bitterness led me to accuse him of dishonesty and having let me down. I ridiculed James, virtually calling him a simpleton. But still he entreated me to demonstrate my friendship by trusting him and taking an interest. Now, thirteen days later, my head has cleared and, putting his nonsensical note to one side, I do feel ready to trust him.

Saturday, 14 January 1978

The 123 bus, having crawled through Woodford and Walthamstow, is now on its final leg towards Tottenham. This slow pace is due to Saturday markets and the resulting queues of shoppers at every bus stop.

By the time I'm ready to disembark, just two blocks from the Mayfair Hotel, I have devoured every word of the January edition of *Darts World Magazine*. Since New Year I've read up on everything I can lay my hands on. Information on the subject is hard to come by, so this magazine is a real find.

Within the hour, I will be watching my first live darts match. Moreover, I'll be in the presence of two players that have made it to the Embassy: Alan Glazier, and the world number one, Eric Bristow. Both are members of the London team. This afternoon they are playing at home to Essex in the inter-counties championship.

The receptionist points me towards a cavernous function room. I pay my 80p entrance, take a programme, and am immediately deafened by sixty conversations struggling to be heard above the new Donna Summer record. The stage is still being set up, its centrepiece being the new Lynmar darts cabinet, which houses an unused Winmau board. This solid pine cabinet has a lighting system that eliminates shadows from darts already thrown, and costs £160. I know this fact, having earlier perused the ad in *Darts World* while the bus waited at Blackhorse road. I also recognise an electronic scoreboard that Highway Electronics have just put out for £140. I'll sit as close as possible to this machine so that I can follow the scoring.

I'm sharing a table with three men, all wearing identical blue and white sports shirts. The man to my left is hunched over the table, filling out a form. The emblem on the back of his shirt informs me that I'm in the company of the Essex team. He suddenly lurches up, and a gaunt, bespectacled, acne-ridden face emits a grunt that I take to be his greeting. I offer my congratulations on their 8–4 win over Hampshire last month. He seems impressed by my knowledge and indicates the man seated opposite.

'Meet the man that gave Cliff Lazarenko a right scare. Took the first leg off him in eighteen darts, didn't you, Ron.'

Ron is a red-faced man, already dripping sweat into his lager. He glances up from his form.

'Then the bugger comes back to win 2–1.'

He shakes off another bead of sweat and returns to his form filling. I struggle to place Lazarenko into the scheme of things. Yes, he is one of the four following players in the Embassy play-off:

Cliff Lazarenko (Hampshire)
Bill Lennard (Lancashire)
Alan Glazier (London)
James Kelly (Yorkshire)

I follow up with a second morsel of my freshly acquired knowledge.

'Funny you should mention Cliff, because he's in the Embassy play-off. They're letting two more English players through to the last sixteen.'

I receive a dubious look from acne face.

'And?' says Ron.

'Well, there's also Bill Lennard, who plays for Lancashire. But the third one, strangely enough, is here today: Alan Glazier.'

'Well who's just dropped down from the skies, the prophet Mohammed? We fucking *know* he's here today. Jesus Christ!'

Ron slugs down the remains of his lager. A much older man

in suit and tie, sitting to Ron's right, has taken a sudden interest. He points a finger at me.

'Look mate, I don't know what this is leading to, but Ron, here, is about to play Alan. So please make your point or be on your merry way.'

'It's just that the fourth player in this play-off happens to be a close friend of mine: James Kelly.'

The finger slowly descends, as the smart gentleman lowers his voice.

'Friend of yours, is he?'

'Yes, James plays for Yorkshire. We spent New Year's Eve together.'

'I know who he plays for. *You* know who he plays for, don't you, Len.'

Len's acne edges towards me. 'Got a few problems, your close friend then?'

I grin like a corpse. 'Are you referring to the television interview?'

'Well, he certainly did the game no favours. I turned over to *Coronation Street* to stop me puking up. We played Yorkshire in October. I'd say that – your friend – tends to play something John Lennon describes as mind games, rather than darts as we know it.'

Ron lets out a chortle. 'Still whipped you 2–0!'

Rather than rising to the bait, Len excuses himself in order to 'get his arm in'.

'Here's the thing,' says Ron in a hoarse whisper. 'In around an hour, my mate Len's going to be shooting it out with Eric. Now, whatever Bristow has to say for himself *away* from the oche – and he's got quite a lot to say – is none of my business. But I can assure you my son, that when he's up there playing Len, he'll be doing one thing only and that's playing darts. Get it?'

'I get it.'

'I'm glad you get it, because that is not what Kelly does'.

'I think that's because James doesn't like playing darts very much.'

The older man nearly spits back a mouthful of lager. 'Well, that'll be it then. Problem solved. That must be why he doesn't even fucking show up half the time: he doesn't like playing darts. So where was he for the *Masters*? Playing netball?'

'Actually, James was playing an exhibition match in Hong Kong. He couldn't get back in time.'

The two men seem to be enjoying this. Ron chimes in.

'Couldn't get back in time – for the Masters? Bet that pleased Ken!'

Balancing a fresh pint, Ron sets off for the practice boards, shaking his head and muttering, 'Couldn't get back in time.'

This leaves me with the older man. He slides across to Ron's vacated seat.

'So what are you doing here?' No answer springs to mind. 'You a fan or what?'

'Actually I'm writing a piece.'

'A piece of fucking what?'

'It's an article about James Kelly, for *Darts World*.'

But, for Eric Bristow, the upcoming Embassy world championships will have an even greater significance than even the Winmau Masters. The Embassy is being taken very seriously indeed, and not just by the players. Not only is this a new world championship, but it will also receive an unprecedented five-day coverage on BBC2, with a total of three hours of broadcasting. Highlights will be shown each evening from Monday, 6th to Friday, 10th February. Darts is about to come into its own and Bristow, already seeded number one, will wish to consolidate his position. With his 'made for TV' personality, I'm sure he won't fight shy of becoming a household name. But will he win? Well, the

*game I am about to witness will hopefully demonstrate
that, at club level, it's anyone's game.*

'So you *are* a journalist then!'

'Not really, no.'

'But you *are* a friend of Kelly's.'

'I am.'

'Then you'll be knowing his manager, Ken Bell. So tell me, is
the fat slimebag still screwing your friend's mum?'

'Ladies and gentlemen, welcome to the Mayfair Hotel,
Tottenham, and to what promises to be a classic encounter
between London and Essex. May I first introduce you to the
team managers?'

My new acquaintance leans over the table towards me,
grins in my face and joins the MC on stage. The Essex team
is introduced one by one, to varying degrees of applause, plus
the odd thrown-in knowing comment. A young lad with black-
rimmed glasses and fair hair is greeted with 'Come on, milky
bar!' The London boys arrive to the bigger reception, being the
home side. Alan Glazier gets a particularly warm welcome and
Bristow offers a playful V-sign in response to a joker calling out,
'Who?' The MC, after urging us to participate in the interval
raffle, hands over to the match referee, and its 'game on'.

*And I can now bring us bang up to date here at
the Mayfair Hotel, where the London boys are already
a tidy 7–2 up against Essex. I have just witnessed
Ron Etherington going down 0–2 to Alan Glazier,
who showed top form by firing a sixteen and a fifteen
darter.*

*And now it's the turn of Len Coles to take on
the Crafty Cockney. Earlier this afternoon, Len, still
smarting from the drubbing he recently received from*

Yorkshire's golden boy, James Kelly, tells me that he has nothing but respect for Bristow. 'The moment Eric's at the oche, he leaves all that swagger behind. He's just there to play darts.'

But who's playing darts now, as Coles goes out in sixteen throws to take the first leg, then immediately follows up with 180 to kick off the second. A lesser player would be fazed, but Bristow throws a cool 140, followed by 125 and 127. Then, with a double 14, he's checked out in thirteen darts and it's one a piece. The third leg's a spellbinder! Despite Eric throwing two tons, Coles is simply unstoppable, clinching the decider in sixteen arrows.

But does this cause uproar? Well, of course not. It's just another game in an inter-counties match, like so many others being played all around the country. Yes, Bristow lost on the day, but his team won 9–3, and I'm sure that Eric would value a team victory above personal defeat. But it does go to show that if an average Essex club player (no offence, Len!) can trounce the world number one, then the Embassy surely has to be up for grabs. And it must be remembered that the game of darts is now worldwide, with top players arriving from Canada, the USA and Europe. So to predict the outcome of such a contest would be foolhardy, and I, being a newcomer to the game, and a fan rather than a player, should be the last person to have any opinion taken seriously. But I know where I'm placing my money!

Earlier, I referred to the twenty-year-old Yorkshire lad that has caused such a stir in the darts world in these past two years. Apart from being runner-up to Eric in the News of the World, 1977 was a tough year for James Kelly. A combination of illness and unpredictable behaviour caused some doubt as to whether he would ever fulfil that early promise he had shown as a teenager. Moreover, he had to pull out of the Winmau in December due to prior commitments. But having had the rare privilege of observing James at close quarters in recent weeks, I can reveal that any doubts can be laid to rest: the Kelly boy has never been so focused. In fact, he confided to me that nothing will stand in his way until he is world champion – and James is not one to spout empty rhetoric. In the words of his manager, Kenneth Bell, 'James is playing like a dream!' My prediction, for what it's worth, is that, come February 10th, we are in for a major upset. Watch this space!

Thursday, 19 January 1978

6, Cheapside
Wakefield, Yorks.

Mr Carpenter,

I'll come straight to the point and answer your question. I have no objection whatsoever to you submitting your so-called article to *Darts World*. This is not because I would like to see it published. To be frank, son, you stand more chance of getting it printed in the fucking *Beano*. But I'm sure old Cotter could do with a bit of a giggle down there in darkest Croydon. So you have my blessing.

However, if it has so much as crossed your mind to send this literary gem to James, you'll no longer be requiring your Embassy pass unless you bring your guide dog, as by then I'll have had your eyes poked out with rusty darts.

Incidentally, you may be intrigued to hear that since James' return to the UK, I have received an anonymous death threat from someone with a Chinese accent. If by any chance you are still in communication with Jim's ex-sponsor, please inform him that I am trembling in my boots.

In earnest,
Kenneth Bell

Monday, 23 January 1978

Darts World,
2, Park Lane
Croydon, Essex

Dear Mr Carpenter,

I am in receipt of your proposed article for *Darts World Magazine*. Sadly, we are at present unable to make use of your report of the London v. Essex match as it has already been covered by one of our regulars. In any case, I have to point out that these pieces always take the form of reviews (as opposed to articles) and are displayed separately under *BDO Inter-Counties Championships*.

I have to say that your speculations on the upcoming Embassy championships, although entertaining in their own way, come across as rather biased. Furthermore, if you can excuse my bluntness, your lack of knowledge and insight into the world of darts is evident throughout your article, although, in fairness, you do admit to being a newcomer to this sport.

Might I suggest that you capitalise on this by reflecting on your first impressions of our world: the atmosphere, showmanship etc. You might perhaps observe your local team, Lambeth, playing a couple of home matches and then consider whether you see them as a microcosm of the local community or whether they strike you as something rather separate from the general fabric of society (I must say that I find us a pretty odd lot!). I am not suggesting a thesis, but something light and brief, say 500 words maximum.

As you rightly point out, the televised world championships will expose thousands of first-time viewers to darts, so the type of article that I am suggesting would be timely.

Regards,

John Cotter (editor)

Friday, 27 January 1978

'Excuse me, but how far back were you standing?'
'Sorry mate, could you say that again?'

As I sit here in the function room of Fern Lodge Social Club, awaiting the start of a super league match between Lambeth and Walthamstow, gazing into the foam of my Guinness, I conjure up a French battlefield in the fifteenth century. Two bored British soldiers are firing broken arrows at an upturned wine barrel to see who can land nearest to the cork. Feeling a trifle chilly, it being mid-winter, they haul a slice of tree trunk into their tent and fashion something a little smaller and more dart-like to throw at it. The tree rings suggest a scoring system, with the inner circle scoring the highest. As play proceeds, they manage to slowly drain the one remaining wine barrel, and soon discover the optimum amount of imbibed wine required to steady the throwing arm.

And now, as the British Empire relentlessly establishes itself, a new breed of soldier can be observed in the drinking clubs across the globe, steadying his arm with a selection of new and exotic brews.

Meanwhile, in America, coal miners from Pennsylvania and barge workers along the Erie Canal are honing their skills and showing New Yorkers how it's done.

But naturally, it's the British who lead the way in taverns across the country, raising the game to a new level. Once again, booze-carriers come to the fore, as a brewery by the name of Hockey and Sons lays three beer crates, each measuring three feet, end to end, thus setting the throwing distance. When the crate size is reduced to two feet, one extra crate needs to be added on, thus cutting the required distance between player and board to eight feet. The toe-line becomes known as the 'hockey', eventually shortened to 'oche'.

This throwing distance of eight feet, although still the standard length overseas, has recently become, as all you Darts World *readers know, a bone of contention on these shores, as our distance of a mere seven foot six is about to increase by three and a half inches for international events. I'm sure you all enjoyed Les Treble's provoking article that ridiculed the seven foot six throw as making the game too easy. I wonder what he makes of those stubborn men of Nottingham who still insist on throwing from six foot. Let's hope that when the Embassy circus rolls into their city in February, they'll not move the oche!*

'I said how far back, exactly, were you just standing?'

Turn left outside my flat, continue to Clapham North tube and cross the road. Take the first side road opposite, and after two hundred yards you will arrive at Fern Lodge Social Club.

As there's no one on the door, I walk straight through into the clubroom and scan the walls for a dartboard.

'You lost, guv?'

'I've come to watch the darts.'

'It's in the function room, door round to your right.'

I enter an inner room that contains a smaller bar, two pool tables and a cramped corner stage. A short, squat man in his mid-thirties takes aim, while his opponent chats to the chalker, who scrawls both players' names on the blackboard: Max and

Jim. In the far corner, a small queue of chattering players faces the practice board. There are no team shirts to differentiate Lambeth from Walthamstow. A gaggle of players, wives and girlfriends cluster near the makeshift stage, seemingly oblivious of the game in progress. Two tables have been pushed together to face proceedings, but the one official seated there reads a magazine. In fact, apart from the chalker, I seem to be the only person paying any attention to the game in progress. Everybody else is contentedly smoking, drinking, or exchanging repartee over the Abba and *Queen* soundtrack. There is no outward sign of organisation, and yet a procedure is clearly taking place, as new players and chalkers come and go.

Both my block of flats and Fern Lodge Social Club seem to share a sense of community from which I am excluded. Fortunately, a community is not something that I wish to become a part of. Apart from June and her son, Stephen, I know the names of my neighbours only through reading the envelopes on the communal doormat. I nevertheless assume that a community thrives above my ceiling. Similarly, the community that I have just discovered within five hundred yards of my flat and am currently observing from my corner seat in the function room, seems totally unaware of my existence. For me, invisibility brings forth a melancholic contentment: a feeling that I can only describe as, no, not loneliness, James, but separateness. This self-awareness sits well with my third pint of Guinness.

Now a pool match has begun. Each individual in this separate group seems in some way connected to the two players. They all buzz around one another, only occasionally giving the pool table a cursory glance. The darts group is unaware of the pool contingent and neither group seems perturbed by the other's chatter.

There was one slight technical hitch at the start of the century: a decision needed to be made as to whether

PART 2: DARTS

darts was just a game of chance rather than skill. If, in fact, darts was a game of chance, this would render it an illegal activity, and so a court case ensued. When none of the court officials was able to replicate the pub owner's triple 20, it was declared 'game on' legally for pubs and clubs across the country.

In 1927, The News of the World newspaper launched its own championship, which is still going strong; in fact, my good friend James Kelly was last year's runner-up. It was not until 1954 that the National Association standardised playing rules ... or at least so they thought!

The one player that still holds my attention is the short, squat man who is once again poised behind the oche for his second match: Max versus Tony. So this is Max. He wears a fifties' style black leather jacket, and sports a totally incongruous Hitler moustache. His brilliantined jet-black hair is piled high. Black winkle-pickers poke out of drainpipe trousers and each knuckle bears a tattooed letter. Max is taking the game very seriously, as opposed to his opponent who is more wrapped up in maintaining a running joke with his girlfriend. Mister Brilliantine's array of mannerisms – blowing on the dart before each throw and muttering after any slight mishap – would mark him out as a 'character', if anyone were noticing. His playing style irritates me. Although he's hitting respectable scores, there is nothing at ease about the man. Every muscle is taut, his arm action jerky, and the energy he puts into each throw could launch a javelin. While observing him, I simultaneously visualise floating bull's eyes. James Kelly's defocused, dreamy flow that somehow merges with the target is far removed from what I'm witnessing now. Why am I even watching this? Have I inadvertently turned a wrong corner and strayed from what drew me to James' world in the first place? This is not my world;

it is not James' world. James cannot truly want this.

They shake hands, Max nods congratulations to his victor and leaves the stage, muttering and shaking his head. He is passing me on his way to the bar.

'You what?'

'I just wondered how far back you were standing.'

'I'm still not with you, my old son. Knocked back one too many Guinnesses, have we?

'Good for you.'

'Good for me?'

'Guinness is good for you. But don't you think that all players should play from the same distance?'

As Max scratches his nose, I read the word *hate* on the knuckles of his left hand.

'If you're saying what I think you're saying ...'

He holds his breath for five seconds and then stomps off towards a group standing near the pool table.

I had only required the man's opinion as to whether the distance should be standardised, but the raised voices and subsequent aggressive gesticulations in my direction cause me to gather my belongings and stagger towards the exit.

Monday, 30 January 1978

Dear James,

Do you believe that nothing ever happens by chance? Well, I don't. I prefer to believe that, rather than fate or destiny working behind the scenes, there is only coincidence playing tricks amid the chaos. However, sometimes coincidences can be fun, so here are two for you.

You are about to embark on a journey to Nottingham with a mission to emerge as the finest marksman in the land. On your arrival in Nottingham, may I suggest that you first make your way to the castle to take some inspiration from the statue that guards its walls. Here is your predecessor, Robin Hood, acknowledged to be the finest archer of all time. Perhaps, in a few months from now, the authorities will be replacing Robin with a statue of James Kelly!

And so to coincidence number two. Hire a taxi from outside your house and head up New Hey Road for the M25. Exit at junction 25 and take the A644 towards Mirfield. Your destination is Kirklees Priory: Robin Hood's last refuge …

Robin is unwell, and allows the prioress to bleed him with her blood-iron. But this woman, knowing full well that Hood is a criminal, wanted dead or alive, proceeds to over-bleed him. He sounds three weak bugle blasts to attract the attention of Little John, who is residing nearby. But alas, John arrives too late, for an accomplice of the prioress has already mortally wounded Robin. With his remaining strength, he fires an arrow from the opened window and instructs John to bury him wherever it falls.

Alas, the story does not hold up, for the site that nowadays marks his gravestone lies more than seven hundred yards from where he supposedly fired that arrow. In truth, even a man of Luke's proportions could have only managed a third of that distance with a longbow. Back in his heyday, Robin had also been reputed to have the strength to split a tree branch from three hundred and thirty yards, surely another fiction. But the fellow was probably fictitious in the first place. Whether he existed or not, could it be fate that you, James, the young pretender, reside less than four miles from his grave? No, it's just another coincidence.

I enclose a booklet entitled *The Adventures of Robin Hood,* which I hope you enjoy, if only for its illustrations. On the subject of illustrations, I admit that of all my failings, the most spectacular is my inability to draw even a stick man. Your turtle drawing at least *looks* like a reptile, whereas my woefully inadequate cartoon depictions of the main characters from Sherwood Forest (enclosed within the booklet) may need some explanation ...

You, naturally, are the hero – Robin – and that's supposed to be a longbow you're pointing towards the Sheriff of Nottingham. In my amateur cartoon production, the evil sheriff is being played by – please don't show him – Uncle Ken. On your right arm is the fair (ginger?) Jade Marian, and the object held to her mouth is meant to be a bugle. I had tried drawing a soprano sax but it was beyond recognition. The scene to your left depicts the sheriff being manhandled by that giant of a man: Little John. There is only one contender for this part: Luke.

Part 2: Darts

I find it difficult to bring up how badly I behaved towards you on New Year's Eve and truly regret certain things that were said. I can only live in hope that there will be some forgiveness on your part when you learn that I have since been acting on your request: I am now taking a genuine interest in darts. To show commitment, I can even recite the names of the other fifteen qualifiers for the Embassy championships. Furthermore, I've actually watched two of them playing in a live match!

I was delighted to hear how easily you won your play-off against Bill Lennard, just as you predicted. I will, of course, be there to support you next Monday. I originally considered booking into Ye Old Bell Hotel near Retford, due to its proximity with Sherwood Forest. Instead, I've settled for some cheaper digs near the centre of Nottingham. I'll give you the phone number, just in case you wish to contact me. The accommodation is called Lindum House and is just a twenty-minute walk from the club. I'm due to arrive late Sunday afternoon.

Your friend (and supporter!),

David

Sunday, 5 February 1978

After having been informed that Burns Street is on the other side of town, the taxi driver finally drops me off at my digs. Lindum House advertises itself as a carefully restored Victorian Gothic building, built in 1864. My bedroom couldn't feel less Gothic, its centrepiece being a portable TV with a dodgy indoor aerial. I peruse my evening alternatives to *Blake's Seven* and *Bless This House* in a copy of Friday's *Nottingham Evening Post* that has been left on the sideboard. Tonight, the Theatre Royal reopens its doors after a year of renovation with Ken Dodd's Laughter show. Unsurprisingly, this has been sold out for several weeks. I settle for a film at the ABC entitled *Cinderella X*, described as 'an adult fairy tale with Buttons undone!' It will have to suffice.

Monday, 6 February 1978

8 a.m. I am in need of a larger towel than Lindum House supplies and have already troubled the grouchy landlord with a request for written directions to tonight's venue. Fortunately, the *Nottingham Evening Post* advertises a store, situated in Tanners Walk, actually called Supertowels. Their timely ad, reads: *Emergency sale Monday, 9.30 sharp. All overstocks must be cleared on auditor's instructions.* I can also rest assured that the verbal exchange with Supertowels' shop assistant will be more erotically charged than anything that occurred during the mind-numbing *Cinderella X*.

1.30 p.m. Supertowels proved to be as good as their word, but lugging the bulky package from Tanners Walk to Nottingham Castle was a bad idea. And now, as I stand before Robin Hood's statue, I'm tempted to drape my new, overstocked, pink-and-white-striped bath towel around his neck and make a run for it. This would hardly detract from the figure's dignity, looking as it does more like an oversized garden gnome than a revered hero.

3.30 p.m. The landlord thumps twice on my bedroom door.

'Phone call – you can take it in the hall.'

Without any preliminary greeting or introduction, the caller is rattling on in a singsong Yorkshire accent.

'Ye Old Bell Hotel was *your* bright idea. It's very rustic and all that, but Retford's thirty bloody miles from Nottingham. *And* we're both left holding the babies, so to speak. Brenda had no intention of coming in the first place and Ken's booked himself into the poshest hotel in town. Just as well – he'd throw a fit if he knew that CC was here. We really need to make a move soon, so don't let their story go on for too long. The dynamic duo's written the whole thing down ... reams of it. See you later.'

'What story? Who is this?'

'Thanks, Luke. Hello, pansy boy. This is your boyfriend's sister. In exchange for your cartoon masterpiece, we've written you our very own tale of Sherwood Forest. I'll start, James will continue and I'll finish. Are you sitting comfortably?'

'Jade, I've no idea what you're on about. Shouldn't James be practising?'

'Then I'll begin. A mysterious archer, recently arrived from Asia, sends a message to the Sheriff of Nottingham, requesting an urgent meeting. His assurance that this meeting will lead to the capture of Robin Hood is sufficient bait to entice the sheriff to keep the appointment. The stranger, claiming to be a champion marksman, proves his prowess with a display that leaves the sheriff open-mouthed. He then tells his story.

'He has travelled from Thailand to settle an old score with Robin Hood, who, five years ago, had killed his brother in a duel. The stranger's plan is to lure Robin to an appointed clearing in the forest for an archery contest to decide who is the greater marksman. But the sheriff and his men will be prepared: they'll surround the clearing and capture Robin before he has time to fire a single arrow. In return, this stranger from Thailand requires that the sheriff pays him a handsome fee, but not until the ambush has been successfully carried out. The wary sheriff needs further proof that Robin will accept this challenge. So one of the sheriff's henchmen accompanies the stranger deep into Sherwood Forest to meet with Little John. John gives his approval, a secret location is set, and the henchman reports back to the sheriff that all is above board. Over to James.'

'Jade ... hold it up ... no, higher ... so I can read it properly. Three days later, Robin arrives at the secret location and is finally standing face-to-face with the dark-skinned foreigner. Robin shows no fear, but smiles at him and even shakes his hand. Naturally, the sheriff and his men are observing proceedings from behind the trees, content that all is going to plan. They patiently await the appointed signal: the instant when the Thai archer reaches into his sheath for the first arrow. Now both of us will finish the story together. Luke, you'll have to hold up the last page.'

In perfect synchronisation, brother and sister recite the conclusion.

'Right on cue, the sheriff and his men burst out from the undergrowth to surround Robin. But the Thai stranger spins round to aim his longbow at the sheriff's right-hand man, who falls like a stone, an arrow between his eyes. Robin now swings into action, pinioning a second henchman. And now Alan a Dale and Friar Tuck have joined the fray: Tuck snatches the sheriff's purse containing the foreigner's fee and merrily throws it to Alan. The fuming sheriff tries to intervene but they play piggy-in-the-middle with him. The purse is lobbed to Robin, who finally tosses it to the mysterious archer. The evil sheriff tries to lunge at him but Little John bursts on to the scene and bars his way. The foiled sheriff can only look on in disbelief as Robin and the foreign archer once again smile and shake hands. It turns out that they were old friends all along and their devious plan has worked. The end. See you later.'

* * *

Turn right out of Lindum House and right again along Waverley Street.

7 p.m. I have saved the walk from Lindum House to Talbot Street until this precise moment. This is so that I can arrive at The Heart of the Midlands nightclub just as they are opening the doors for 7.30. My excitement edges towards nervous anticipation at the thought of finally watching James Kelly playing for the world championships. All this excess energy put me off lunch and I'm now feeling slightly light-headed.

Cross the road and walk along the edge of the Arboretum. This won't save time but is more pleasant than continuing along the main road.

I peer into the aviary and explain to a parrot why I'm so anxious, why James' success is of such importance to me. The parrot cocks his head but is saying nothing. I squawk and move on.

Waverley Street leads into Goldsmith Street. Continue past the church on your right and a university building to your left until you reach a row of cafés and curry houses. You're almost there.

But I don't want to be almost there. It's far too early, and I'm strutting like a hysterical penguin. I'll stop for a snack.

Talbot Street is the next main turning on the right. You'll find the club fifty yards down.

I am now observing the club from the opposite side of the road. My stomach is churning, possibly due to excitement, but more likely as the result of the hot chocolate and Mars bar I stuffed down in the café. If this really is the heart of the Midlands, it's in dire need of a transplant. Can this shabby old building really be staging a world championship? Yes, it seems so, for the poster is advertising P. J. Proby from 1–4 February and the Embassy World Darts Championships from the 6th to the 10th. I had also anticipated a long queue, but punters are casually wandering through the doors in small groups. I fish out my envelope and cross Talbot Road.

'So what's this, then?'

'It's my pass.'

'It won't get you in here, sir. Who gave it to you?'

'Kenneth Bell: James Kelly's manager.'

'Shall I send someone in to get him?'

'God, no.'

'Then that'll be £1.25 including programme.'

I had expected the place to be heaving, but there are, as yet, only about a hundred in the main hall and perhaps another thirty up in the balcony. I carry my pint to a lone side table from where I can observe the proceedings while maintaining a low profile. According to the listings, James is third on. This is the order of play:

Leighton Rees v Barrie Atkinson
Eric Bristow v Conrad Daniels
Nicky Virachkul v James Kelly

The first match isn't due to start for another thirty minutes. The sole action on stage is a BBC producer barking last minute instructions to his crew. A few players wander in and out through a door presumably leading down to the dressing rooms. I can't imagine there being rooms for all sixteen players, but some seem perfectly content to mingle with their friends and supporters in the auditorium. Leighton Rees, an older player of considerable bulk, makes his unsteady way down the stairs from the balcony and towards the dressing room without spilling a drop of his lager. I spot Eric Bristow casually chatting with a handsome young Thai player that I assume to be Nicky Virachkul. Both men appear totally relaxed and out to enjoy the occasion.

Brother and sister plus giant chaperone move as one mass

towards a table at the front, as though guided in by radio control. All three then glide into their respective chairs, seemingly to a prearranged seating plan. Kenneth Bell, clearly not a member of this tight clique, shuffles along a few steps behind, appearing a little off balance. He pulls up a chair to join them, but then instantly leaps to his feet as though he's just sat on a sharp object. Ken lights a new cigarette from a glowing butt, starts to make his way towards the stage, but changes his mind and rejoins the trio. He is agitated; there is sweat on his brow. Jade and James glance at each other as Luke rises to his feet. Ken retreats and skulks back towards the rear stairs that lead up to the balcony. The big man resettles and links arms with James, whose left arm is already being cradled by his sister. Jade wears a silk headscarf, perhaps the one she flapped in my face on New Year's Eve. James sports a white dress shirt and red braces. Luke's blond hair hangs down in a pigtail over a loose-fitting, flowery caftan.

Not wishing to intrude, I continue to observe James from my vantage point, waiting for clues as to his state of mind. Suddenly, he turns around, gazes at me, and smiles. It is the same open grin he shot at me as I'd stood in that shop doorway in Wakefield. This has happened too quickly for me to respond, as he has now already turned back towards Jade. She leans into him and they share something that is surely about me. But I feel that their words are kindly. I am also reassured that James, at this moment, seems relaxed and at ease. And so I, too, relax and take a first sip of beer.

The music has been turned off. Tony Green, the MC, is welcoming the audience and the BBC viewers to The Heart of the Midlands nightclub, 'where we are about to commence round one of the very first Embassy professional championships.' He thanks Embassy cigarettes, Olly and Lorna Croft and all the officials, then introduces the two players that are about to do battle: Barry Atkinson, the Australian number one, making his debut in the UK, versus the number three seed, Welsh wizard: Leighton Rees. Game on.

It soon becomes evident that Atkinson is not being allowed time to settle into his game, and the rotund Rees eases his way to a 6–0 victory. He raises an empty lager jug to his appreciative Welsh fans, steps down from the stage and makes straight for James' entourage. They chat amiably for some minutes. Then, to my surprise, he strolls over to me, and perches, rather precariously, on my table.

'David Carpenter?' Rather than offering my congratulations, I nod foolishly and rescue my drink. 'I've had a word with our James and he's suggested that I'd make a good Tuck.'

'Oh, Did he?'

'So I'm putting myself forward, all sixteen stone of me, if it's all the same to you. Good! Well that's settled. Have a good evening now, boyo.'

The American champion, Conrad Daniels, has already been introduced, and the atmosphere intensifies as Eric Bristow is now summoned to join him. Considering that Bristow is number one seed and reigning world master, this first round match would, on paper, seem a formality.

Things are not going well for the Londoner – perhaps he's a little too relaxed – and within fifteen minutes Eric is trailing by two legs. But it's not long before he pulls it back to two legs apiece. The atmosphere in the hall is electric. I, however, am feeling disconnected from the growing excitement that surrounds me. In fact I'm hardly watching the match at all and can summon up no anticipation for the outcome. My mind is totally occupied with one recurring thought: that within minutes of these two players' exit, Nicky Virachkul and James Kelly will be taking the stage … this is unless James freezes and remains stuck to his seat. Why is he still sitting out-front? Surely by now he should have gone downstairs to either the practice area or a dressing room. And if he does make it on to the stage, how will he react this time to the TV cameras? Will he throw bull's eyes until Olly Croft has to lead him away?

Bristow has lost his match 6–3 and is out of the tournament. There's lukewarm applause for the American, as Eric sidles off to be interviewed. Most punters seem too wrapped up in their personal post-mortems to notice that the Thai player is already on stage. His striking good looks and gleaming smile get a reaction from a small group of young female fans.

'And now ladies and gentleman, the Yorkshire champion, and runner-up to Eric in last year's News of the World championship: James Kelly.'

For a few moments, James glances to his right and left, while Luke and Jade still clutch his arms – and then he's up there with Virachkul. They exchange smiles, shake hands like old friends, then both look out to the audience and receive some generous applause. I suspect that some are amused that the boys look less like typical darts players than members of a pop group. Nicky Virachkul is much the slimmer and shorter, his black T-shirt and jet-black hair reminiscent of a young Elvis; James is a podgier, larger framed, blond Bowie. As they throw a few practice darts, I'm relieved to see James' composure, as he calmly works his way around the board, looking for triples.

James throws first: it's a bull's eye. This gets a knowing reaction. He turns round, looks up towards the balcony and nods. In these initial moments I feel that it's all over; I'm fighting the overwhelming urge to leave and head back to London. James has turned back to face the board. He focuses, and throws triple 20. His third dart, triple 17, evokes a few grunts and whispers from the connoisseurs.

'One hundred and sixty-one.'

When Virachkul's first dart also finds the bull's eye, the two players beam at each other, as though sharing a private joke. Nicky follows this with a triple 20. But the third dart lands just left, only making the triple 5.

'One hundred and twenty-five.'

James throws three darts: all triple 20s. It's now clear to everyone that he's going for the perfect nine. The TV producer waves his arms in panic. A perfect nine has never been televised, and now, of all times, there is some kind of technical fault. Tony Green has called for order, as Virachkul casually throws three 20s. He makes way for James, who needs just two triple 20s and a double 20 to pull this off.

The first dart finds its mark. People are moving forward. Luke is on his feet, but Jade tugs him back down. James is moving in slow, yet fluid motion, as his second dart arcs up and glides home into the triple 20 … one to go.

Players are emerging from their dressing rooms and the crowd is again being asked to settle. Only the TV producer walks away in despair. I catch sight of Ken Bell pacing and clutching his head. His eyes are probably tight shut as the final dart sinks into the double 20.

Neither player seems aware of the pandemonium; they could be playing a friendly match on a remote beach. Amid the general hubbub, I only become aware of Jade's proximity when I feel her warm breath in my ear.

'What do you think of Nicky? Shush, don't say anything.' She presses a sheet of folded drawing paper into my hand. 'James wants you to have this: the unofficial programme. Now, let the magic commence!'

Jade kisses me lightly on the cheek and slips back through the punters, who are now on their feet, giving James a standing ovation.

What do I think of Nicky? Is Nicky Virachkul her new boyfriend? I unfold the sheet and instantly recognise it to be the solitary decoration that had adorned James' white walled bedroom: the drawing he later referred to as the sacred turtle.

The second leg commences with Nicky throwing a triple 20 and two double 20s. This leaves 361. James steps forward to throw the three darts that will signal the end of the match and his career.

Double 1
Double 2
Triple 3
'Fifteen.'

I enter a world of total calm, without questioning this surreal turn of events. I merely wonder why, after following a pattern of doubles, he should then choose to throw a triple. Virachkul, paying no attention to his opponent's bizarre score, throws 83. This brings his remaining total down to 278.

James' next three darts divide the crowd into two opposing camps.

Double 3
Double 4
1
'Fifteen.'

Some jeer, others smile. What is seen by the jeerers to be another disgraceful episode of the James Kelly freak show, the smilers interpret as an outrageously theatrical display of exhibition darts that has no regard for match play.

Virachkul calmly continues his own game with 140. He now only requires 138; James still requires 471! He throws.

Double 1
Triple 2
7
'Fifteen.'

Virachkul's double 12 secures the second leg. But all eyes are now on James, who is slowly dream-walking to the front of the stage. He briefly looks up to the balcony, then slightly bows his head. Nicky takes a seat, sips his water and waits patiently until James has completed his ritual and is ready to resume. Neither player responds to the growing boos and catcalls, as James kicks off the third leg.

PART 2: DARTS

Double 2
Double 3
5
'Fifteen.'

As James Kelly continues to throw combinations that total 15, more people are losing interest and wandering off to the bar for refills in preparation for the next match. It seems that by the fifth leg, only Jade, Luke and I are continuing to give the remaining legs our full attention. My sole distraction is Ken. I watch him pacing aimlessly, running down like a clockwork drunk, and finally slumping into a solitary seat at the back of the hall.

As the match proceeds to its inevitable conclusion, I feel increasingly at ease, mesmerised by the elegant spectacle of James Kelly. He is flowing at his own pace and to his own rhythm, neither traumatised nor distressed, neither playing to win nor lose, totally unperturbed by the world around him. The man is at peace with himself. Whether or not Nicky Virachkul comprehends James' actions, he drifts in and out without interfering or reacting.

James lands the penultimate dart of the match: a bull's eye. This is surely the final dart he ever intends to throw. His opponent checks out with double 18 and the match is over. Nicky Virachkul has won 6–1 and is through to the next round; James Kelly is out of the tournament and will never again, I suspect, stand in front of a dartboard.

The final sequence of events, from the moment of James vacating the stage, to his exit from the club, takes approximately ten minutes and is carried out like a carefully rehearsed army manoeuvre. Apart from the two loose cannons – Uncle Ken and me – all other parties seem to have practised their roles, knowing where to position themselves and when to move.

James marches briskly down the steps to rejoin Jade and

Luke at their table. Luke and James link arms and then stand. Jade remains seated. Leighton Rees is already posted by an emergency exit, ten yards from the stairs that lead down from the balcony. As Luke and James head towards this exit, a Chinese man in rimless spectacles and a black Italian suit is swiftly descending the balcony stairs. Ken, who has been observing developments through a drunken haze, now catches sight of CC. As he shambles over to intercept him, Rees steps forward to block his way. Luke pushes the emergency doors, allowing CC to exit onto the street.

I reach James, just as he's about to head through the doorway and towards a waiting car. The passenger door is being held open by CC, who nods back towards me. James half turns and flashes a smile, but his eyes remain elsewhere. He is handing me a package: the book lined with brown wrapping paper. Now, in a bungled attempt at a hug, my chin momentarily nestles between his left shoulder and neck. He wriggles free and steps out. Luke slams the emergency doors behind him. Rees releases his hold on Ken. But Ken remains frozen, looking utterly lost and bewildered. I open the book and read the inscription on its first page.

> *Dear Carpenter,*
> *Thank you for your trust.*
> *I am now returning to Matsudo.*
> *James Kelly*

PART 3
ARROWS

28 April 1978 – 11 December 1978

Friday, 28 April 1978

Darts laid to rest.

In the quarter-finals of the Embassy world championships, Nicky Virachkul beat Conrad Daniels (the American who had knocked out Bristow in the first round), and Leighton Rees beat fellow Welshman Alan Evans. Leighton and Nicky met in the semis and the Welshman scraped through 8–7 to play John Lowe in the final, which he won 11–7. And so Leighton Rees is now the Embassy world champion and £3,000 better off. During his earlier match with Evans, he managed to compensate the BBC for missing James' nine-darter with the first-ever televised ten-dart finish. He will not, however, be collecting the Concord trophy for the achievement, as this will be presented to James Kelly for his perfect nine, should anyone ever find him.

I gleaned the above information from the March edition of *Darts World*. Within one minute of James' bizarre exit from the tournament, I could find no reason to follow the proceedings, and so too took my leave from the club. I used the same emergency doors, which Luke kindly reopened for me, in the knowledge that I had no chance of following James ... not that I wanted to. I stepped out on to a dark and desolate Talbot Street, just as a red Toyota was turning right into Goldsmith Street.

There also appeared in the March edition of *Darts World*, an article about Leighton Rees. It contained the following piece of trivia: apparently, on 18 December 1976, Rees finished a game in 141 darts by only aiming for the bull's eye, and managing to convert 34 double bulls and 52 single bulls. Whether James knew about this – they seemed to know each other at Nottingham – I may never know. *Darts World* decided against publishing my article, instead reducing it to a brief reader's letter. I have since cancelled my subscription.

I have also given away my darts and board to June's son, Stephen. This seems a fair enough swap for the dilapidated piano they palmed off on me. During the handover I couldn't help but run my finger over the solitary hole in my dartboard's bull's eye: visible proof that my third dart had found its target.

David Carpenter, giant of jazz.

Perhaps not, but I have at least learned the three chords required to play a basic twelve-bar blues. I can also play 'I Got Rhythm' off by heart. I recently purchased a jazz magazine entitled *Crescendo*, and have just sent off for the navy-blue musician's tie they have on offer at £2.40.

Chess laid to rest.

William Abercrombie began hanging around a singularly unattractive female member of the club called Sharon – the fact that her arms are covered in large moles is the tip of the iceberg – and it was his subsequent insufferable behaviour that led me to resign. I realise that this might be perceived as an over-reaction and can only say in my defence that the sight of them gazing into each other's eyes between moves proved intolerable.

James and David

How odd our names look together. When we parted company on New Year's Eve, I was incensed by his request to terminate all contact before the Embassy, while at the same time requiring my trust. On reflection, my aggression that evening gave James good reason to mistrust me and consequently pretend that he really did have ambitions to win the championships.

On our final parting, I felt both sadness and elation: sadness that I would almost certainly never see James Kelly again, but elation that somehow I had played an unwitting part in the successful plan to outwit Kenneth Bell.

I feel convinced that James was entirely responsible for his own actions at Nottingham. Yes, perhaps the man he was acknowledging up in the balcony, CC, wielded, and continues to wield a certain influence over him. But I cannot believe him to be James' puppet master. I do, however, suspect him of being James' lover.

Matsudo

Matsudo is a Japanese city, northeast of Tokyo. The train journey takes around thirty minutes. On 26 November, James and CC did not fly to Hong Kong. They, in fact, flew to Tokyo, and in February they returned there. I know nothing more about Matsudo and have no idea why they went, or what they are doing there now.

The sacred turtle

Around four thousand years ago, a character by the name of Hsia Yu was standing by the banks of the River Lo in Central China, when he observed a giant turtle emerging from the water. He was drawn to some unusual markings on its shell, and on closer inspection noticed groups of small dots, each group enclosed within its own square. There were nine small squares in all. Hsia Yu, convinced that there was some logical pattern to these groupings, converted the dots into numbers and constructed the following grid:

4	9	2
3	5	7
8	1	6

Amazingly, each line adds up to fifteen, horizontally, vertically and diagonally. James' sketch of the sacred turtle once hung on his bedroom wall. Jade then passed it on to me at the club, and it is now laid out in front of me. Known as the Lo Shu Square, it is the system that James used to throw as many combinations of fifteen as it took to lose the Embassy championships, initially choosing available trebles and doubles. I am guessing that CC requested him to do this. I have no idea why.

The book lined with brown wrapping paper.

I first spotted this book on James' bedside table and vividly recall Brenda reprimanding me as I reached to pick it up. That night, I dreamed it contained pornographic photos. The next sighting had been at Heathrow airport, tightly clutched in James' hand. He finally handed it to me just before leaving the club in Nottingham, and it now also lies in front of me beside his sketch of the sacred turtle. The book is entitled *Zen in the Art of Archery* and was written in 1953 by a German professor by the name of Eugen Herrigel, who recounts his experiences while learning Japanese archery under the tutelage of a Zen master in Tokyo.

Archers fire at targets, aiming for the centre. Is this not synonymous with the bull's eye? In a letter, James once defined his 'beloved bull's eye' as 'the true target'. There has to be a connection.

Zen

The word means little to me. I do recall once skimming through the first couple of chapters of *Zen, a Way of Life* (one of those yellow-sleeved manuals in the *Teach Yourself* series), only because I was attracted by the author's odd name: Christmas Humphreys. I now intend revisiting this book with more reverence.

Charlie Chaplin

Four grave robbers recently dug Charlie Chaplin up and made off with his coffin. That's about as funny as *he* was. I must update Darren, should I ever see him again.

PART 3: ARROWS

Saturday, 29 April 1978

I'm finding this book by Christmas Humphreys, with all its talk of emptiness, detachment and non-self, most appealing. In all modesty, I would say that I see some of these qualities within me.

Zen in the Art of Archery, however, is leading me towards a new understanding of James. If only he had shown me the book earlier! The author travels to Japan to learn Zen archery from a master by the name of Kenzo Awa. As early as chapter one, there is talk of the marksman aiming at himself. Were these not the words that James used in the TV interview? When asked whether he would be affected by the new throwing distance between oche and dartboard, he replied: 'It makes no difference. I aim at myself.'

Later, in chapter five, it recommends that one attains a state resembling drowsiness on the verge of sleep: a precise description of James as he is preparing to release a dart. I now see why this book meant so much to him and feel honoured that he should pass it on to me ... not that I have any practical use for it. I certainly have no intention of taking up archery. But should he ever choose to make contact, I'll at least feel able to discuss the subject with a modicum of knowledge.

My overall conclusion is that James is now furthering his Zen archery studies in Matsudo under the tutelage of CC. I would also guess that James and I are at the end of our journey. My original instinct was right: James was, after all, doing something special. He is now where he should be, and somehow I helped him along the way. That is as much as I could ask of myself. The end.

Sunday, 30 April 1978

'Hello David, it's Brenda Kelly. Happy New Year!'

'Four months late, but thanks anyway. I hadn't expected—'

'What … to ever hear from us again? I'm not surprised. What must you have thought of us all? I was rather out of my head at the time.'

'You mean with all that pendulum nonsense.'

'No, that's not what I mean, David. But I wouldn't expect you to believe in a sixth sense.'

'Is that the same as a third eye? I've just been reading about how to fire an arrow and hit the target with your eyes closed … well, two of them closed. It's in this book that your son gave me before he left.'

'Oh, that book! Well at least it won't be glued to his side any more. He's probably picked up a new transitional object by now. I do like that phrase! It's the stage after sucking your thumb; Jade's is her saxophone. I've also been doing some reading. It's for this course I've just started, called Basic Counselling Skills. Apparently, Ken's not just paranoid, he's also schizoid.'

'Well that would explain it … but it's not all in his head, you know. He had every reason to feel cheated. You must have heard what happened in Nottingham.'

'God, not that again! I've heard Ken's version a hundred times and still don't know what he's on about.'

'It's simple enough. He was tricked, Mrs Kelly – lied to.'

'CC's not a liar. In fact, he put me in the picture right from the start. He was always straight with me.'

'But not with Ken.'

'It's James that comes first, not Ken. I was only acting in my son's spiritual interests. I trusted CC and so did James. The agreement was clear: if James enjoyed that first trial trip, they'd return in February for a longer period.'

'That's not what you said when I came up on New Year's Eve. You told me that James wouldn't talk about that first trip.'

'Actually, James talked about it incessantly the morning before you arrived … made a right old drama about it being a guarded secret. He likes that sort of thing.'

I swallow my lurking resentment.

'And have you heard from James since?'

'Regularly. And CC was in touch yesterday … said he needed to speak with you urgently. That's why I'm phoning. I'm to tell you that he'll be ringing you tomorrow evening. I gave him your number … hope that's alright.'

'No, it's not. What does he want?'

'He said it was about Ken.'

'About Ken? I have nothing to do with Ken.'

'Well, Ken thinks you're involved in all this. It's better if CC explains.'

'You haven't given Ken my phone number?'

'No, but he has your address. You wrote to him about some article you were writing. I always guessed you were a journalist.'

'I am not a journalist. Please tell Ken that I have no connection with any of this and no wish to have anything more to do with him.'

'Well, it's a bit late for that. He's worked himself up into a right old pickle. Get this: he's convinced himself that he's being followed, that someone wants to kill him and that I'm having an affair. I've suggested primal therapy. Oh, Jade wants a word.'

For once, the prospect of speaking with Jade comes as welcome relief.

'Hello, nancy boy. Have you mastered "Stranger on the Shore" yet?'

'Actually, I've started reading Crescendo magazine. I'm also studying a book on how to play jazz.'

'Give up. You can't learn jazz from a book. Or find people to play with.'

'I don't know any people. But I've learned the chords to a twelve-bar, and the blues scale to play over it. I've also memorised 'I Got Rhythm'.'

'No, I didn't suppose you'd actually know any people. You could try playing along to records. Okay, suggestion number one: learn 'Village Blues'. It's a three-chord, twelve-bar in C, third track of Coltrane Jazz. Are you keeping up? Suggestion number two: ditch the tune to 'I Got Rhythm' but keep the chord changes to the first sixteen bars. Now you can jam along to 'Big Nick'… that's track six of Coltrane. McCoy, Jimmy and Elvin are the rhythm section.'

I'm struck by her knowledge and reminded of her warm heart.

'Thanks, Jade. Do you have any more recommendations?'

'Yes, track eleven of Coltrane for Lovers might appeal to you.'

'What's it called?'

'Nancy. So are you prepared?'

'Prepared for what, Jade?'

'For Uncle Ken. He's coming to get you!'

PART 3: ARROWS

Monday, 1 May 1978

Contrary to Jade's hopes, I have not been cowering under the bed for the past twenty-four hours for fear that Kenneth Bell is about to burst in through the door with a machete. I have, however, been anxiously awaiting CC's call.

'Mister Carpenter?'

The sound of CC's well-spoken, laid-back voice reminds me of waking up in Heathrow airport.

'Yes, it's David.'

'Excellent! James is standing right here beside me. I'll put him on the line in a moment. He is so looking forward to speaking with you. Please first allow me a few words. I can imagine how you must feel towards me, but it's been impossible until now to explain all that has been taking place. But rest assured that all our efforts have been worthwhile. Even in this short space of time, James has progressed faster than anyone could have imagined. He's surpassed all expectations. It has never been known for a novice to reach second dan within four months. James is already shooting like a master. Oh, hang on … and he never even had to do his first dan … hello …. Carpenter?'

I remain silent for a few more seconds to readjust to the fact that I've been victim to one of James' childish impersonations.

'You let yourself down with that last sentence, James. CC speaks far better English than that.'

'Oh, he just put me off by yelling, "Cut it out". That's not proper English either. Are you enjoying the Zen archery book? Chun Chow insisted that I got rid of it … but it was supposed to be a present too. That's CC's real name … well, his Christian name, except that he isn't Christian. His surname is Lee … Mister Lee.'

'James, just tell me if you're okay.'

'I wasn't okay when we met at the airport. I couldn't speak because you weren't to know our secret. And I wasn't happy to go anywhere, even though Chun Chow had tempted me with exotic photos and beautiful descriptions. But Jade, Mum and the big man were all telling me that I should go. And so I did. But now that I'm here for a second time, everything is okay, thank you. Japanese people look at me in a better way than people do at home, so I'm not missing any of them … especially Uncle Ken. He's a pig, don't you think? My room in Matsudo is perfect: white and empty, except for my red rocker. The big man had it shipped over. I'm also learning the seven stages of shooting and lots of Japanese phrases. My favourite is moka-moka su-su.'

The frantic pace of James' ramble is reminiscent of New Year's Eve. But this time he is happy and I am magnanimous.

'I'm glad to hear that things are going so well for you. Have you really reached second dan?'

'Ha ha, no dans at all I'm afraid – they won't even let me shoot arrows yet. I have to practise with this rubber contraption called a gomuyumi until I perfect my action and learn the form. I need to tell you why Kyudo is superior to darts but Chun Chow is waiting to talk, so I'll send you my list of reasons. Were you impressed with my performance against Nicky V at the Embassy? I thought it was breathtaking, but CC says that this is wrong thinking. He's shaking his head at me right now. He wants the phone. I'll write. Bye, Carpenter.'

'Mister Carpenter, I'm so sorry about that. He really must stop this foolishness. I find nothing amusing about these impersonations. How are things with you?'

I'm angered that CC has taken over the conversation and have no intention of engaging in friendly chatter. I adopt a formal tone.

'Mister Lee, I would be grateful for some straight answers.

Why did you instruct James to lose the Embassy by throwing combinations of the Lo Shu Square? If it hadn't been for the book that James gave me, I'd still be totally in the dark.'

'I agree that you are owed an explanation, but I was in no position to provide one until now. I am in the process of writing you a letter that will enlighten you with regard to a host of things, including the sacred turtle. As for Herrigel's book, I'm relieved to see the back of it.'

'I assumed that you'd given it to James in the first place.'

'Most certainly not – Herrigel's concept of Zen archery is his own romantic myth. It has no fundamental connection with Kyudo. There are certain parallels, but the notion of it not mattering whether or not one hits the target is ludicrous. However, this call is for a very different reason. I'm aware that Kenneth Bell has been to my father's offices in Hong Kong with the sole intention of bringing the maximum amount of disgrace upon my family. Now that he has returned home, there's little I can do from this end.'

'Well, that makes two of us.'

'I also fear that his intentions may well bring misfortune down upon himself.'

'Well, that sounds an excellent result, so long as it prevents him bringing misfortune down upon me.'

'Your reluctance to help is perfectly understandable, even though it is not you that he wishes to harm.'

'Perhaps, in your country, threatening to poke people's eyes out with rusty darts isn't classifiable as wishing a person harm.'

'James and I are merely asking that you and Mister Crane weigh up the facts. You will then be in a better position to reach your own decision.'

'James didn't ask me anything. And who's Mister Crane?'

'Mister Crane will be paying you a visit in the coming few days. He'll brief you with an update of Kenneth's current state of mind. This should enable you to assess the degree of danger that Kenneth is putting himself in.'

'Mister Lee, I really don't have the faintest interest in Kenneth's state of mind. My only interest was in James. Now that things have worked out well for him, I've no intention of seeing any of these people ever again.'

'I implore you to reserve your judgement. My letter will provide you with the information you require. Only then can you ascertain whether there is still a possibility of steering Mister Bell from his delusional path of self-destruction.'

'Can't you understand? Brenda tells me that he's unstable. Ken actually believes that I was involved in this business. He's even told Jade that he's coming to get me!'

'All I ask is that you read my letter, agree to meet Mister Crane, and then make your own decision. I promise to respect whatever line of action you take.'

'Well Mister Lee, I've already decided. I want no involvement with any of this nonsense, or with this Mister Crane, whoever he might be.'

'Oh, you've met him on at least two occasions. He looks forward to seeing you.'

Wednesday, 17 May 1978

This morning I received CC's letter and am intrigued, not so much by its contents as by its interminable length. Notwithstanding the improbability that this tome from a total stranger might contain anything of the remotest significance, I will nevertheless keep an open mind. But how am I expected not to prejudge a letter that begins in the year 1949?

Matsudo

Dear Mister Carpenter,

On 1 October 1949, the lives of two men changed forever. On a rostrum in Tiananmen square, as Mao Zedong was proclaiming the new Chinese People's Republic, my father, Lee Ying Yuen, was crossing the Chinese border into Hong Kong. Mao was nearly fifty-six; my father was twenty-two. Mao would not have approved of my family's business interests and so Hong Kong seemed the obvious choice of resettlement, being less than fifteen miles from his home in Shenzhen.

With his father's blessing and a small bundle of money, Ying Yuen was determined to transform himself into an international businessman within five years. And sure enough, by 1952, having taken advantage of the cheap labour force, he had established a flourishing factory in the New Territories. By 1955 he had taught himself English, moved into export and had saved sufficient money for a three-week trip to the country he had dreamed about since childhood.

Considering the devastation that Japan had wreaked on his homeland, my father's admiration for the Japanese, together with his longing to travel there, bordered on the perverse. He would brush aside any talk of the countless deaths and atrocities, by pinning all blame on the Japanese military, which, he maintained, had ridden roughshod over both politicians and populace. Those two dreadful and entirely unnecessary bombs were his conclusive evidence that these people were victim to unfortunate circumstance rather than violent aggressors. Alongside this moral stance, his money-eye was trained on the Japanese economy, which had already been kick-started by the war in Korea.

Whyever is he telling me all this? So far this is no more than a dull lesson in modern Chinese history. I have little interest in history and none in China, although I quite enjoy sweet and sour pork. In fact, last year, to celebrate my thirtieth birthday, an old school friend (who hasn't been in touch since) took me to the Lido restaurant in Gerrard Street. I mostly enjoyed the ethnic experience but drew the line at chopsticks. Why design cutlery that makes eating near impossible? No wonder the Chinese are so thin. Our one disappointment was jasmine 'tea', in actuality nothing more than perfumed water, which they had the nerve to charge for. We later popped into the Stockpot for a proper cup. OK, back to the mid-1950s:

And so, on 15 February 1955, Ying Yuen perused his map and drew a triangle: Tokyo, Kanazawa and Kyoto. The first city offered material excitement, the second, culture and the third, spirituality. I was born in Kanazawa precisely one year later. My father never made it to the third city.

Ying Yuen arrived in Tokyo in late March amid celebrations. Two conservative parties had merged into a new *Liberal Democratic Party* that was promising higher living standards. The week whirled past with a surfeit of sightseeing that left him totally drained.

As the train headed north, his guidebook assured him that Kanazawa would provide gentle strolls by the river, Kaga cooking and the perusal of fine lacquerware. It made no mention of my mother.

With no plan in mind, Ying Yuen set off southwest from Kanazawa station and soon found himself in Ohmicho market. The dazzling displays of unrecognisable seafood and vegetables buoyed his spirits. He tried out a few mispronounced Japanese phrases on the stallholders, who mostly responded with nods and smiles of encouragement. After a further five hundred yards, he came across the People's Culture Centre. Its frontage displayed a placard in English that read: 'SOCIETY TO INTRODUCE KANAZAWA TO THE WORLD – FIRST FLOOR'.

Ying Yuen copied this into his notepad, proceeded to the first floor and showed the words to the receptionist. After a dainty bow, she launched into a string of questions in Japanese. Then, relieving him of the notebook, she backed away into an office. Five minutes later she reappeared, now accompanied by an anxious male colleague.

'I am manager. One moment please.'

He returned my father's notebook and hurried down the stairs. A further ten minutes passed before he returned, a little dishevelled, gasping, 'We find someone,' before retreating back to his office.

Meanwhile, the receptionist had returned to her seat and was busying herself with a pile of letters. My father's growing impatience had now almost outweighed the fear of giving offence. But just as he was about to take his leave, my future mother arrived on the top step and they instantly fell in love. Or to quote Yukari's words eighteen years later, 'In that moment, we saw each other.' I suspect that it was the only moment in which they ever really did see each other.

'I am so sorry. I will take you from now till one o'clock. Then, from two o'clock, I will be taken over by Miss Masaki. Follow me please.'

The reciprocal arrangement required no exchange of money. She would provide a morning tour of the city in return for a conversation in English. Then, after an hour lunch break, Miss Masaki would lead the afternoon tour in return for *her* English practice. Of course, Ying Yuen never did meet Miss Masaki.

Within the month he had returned to Kanazawa to propose, and to the utter horror and disbelief of Yukari's family, they married on 18 July. I was conceived that evening on Phoenix Hill in Kenrokuen Park.

Three pages in and CC is conceived. Unbelievable! Not only does he assume that I'd be interested in how his parents met, but that I'd be fascinated to know the precise location where they copulated. Come to think of it, I did see a Japanese film at the Tatler last year ... something about the realm of the senses. Not much of a story, but it was chock full of Japanese rumpy-pumpy. Perhaps CC senior should have met Miss Masaki after lunch. I expect they're all at it.

And so I was born and raised on the north point of my father's triangle, imbibing my mother's respect for the old values and traditions, alongside my father's constant craving for progress and all things material. There was a fierce argument as to whether my name should be Japanese or Chinese, but my father's pride won out. Thereafter, Ying Yuen and Yukari were to resolutely face in opposite directions: she forever looking back, and he forward. It was hardly surprising that after that first moment, they would never again really see each other.

Yukari had been raised in a nearby fishing village, and I would often secretly watch her gazing into the Asano River as it drifted her back to the place of her childhood. Her parents were Buddhist, but my mother's instinctual relationship to natural objects and creatures was closer to Shinto.

Their problems were immediate, immense and insurmountable. There was nothing remarkable in itself to see Chinamen in Japan. In fact, Yokohama already had its own Chinatown, besides which, my father was regarded as a respectable and conservative businessman. Even the language and cultural barrier might have been overcome, had Ying Yuen and Yukari found anything in common, apart from their initial lovesickness. He interpreted her spirituality as self-indulgence, referring to it as a pastime; she interpreted his forward thinking as the epidemic of greed that was sweeping through the cities. And I, of course, was forever caught between the spiritual and the material, the old and new, in the impossible attempt to please them both. There was also the dual attraction of being holy and wealthy.

Here in Japan, the absent husband and father has always been commonplace: working long hours for the company, followed by socialising with male colleagues into the night. But my father took this behaviour one step further by spending months away on business trips, mostly in Hong Kong. The short periods that

I remember him being home with the family were never easy. He was what you English might describe as a Victorian father, insisting on silence at table and an 8 p.m. curfew. But he wished to be seen as a man with progressive ideas: I was regularly taken aside for paternal lectures that were filled with warnings against all forms of old-fashionedness, and then shepherded towards his notion of common sense. I, of course, both feared and worshipped him, believing him to be the perfect male adult. This opinion was to change dramatically.

I could certainly do with some drama. But my speculation is that dramatic change in Japan moves at a more leisurely pace and with less drama than in Great Britain. My evidence is as follows:

1) I recently yawned through the first ten minutes of a TV documentary about Japanese theatre. It's called Noh and rhymes with slow.

2) CC's next paragraph commences with the phrase: 'as I turned eighteen', suggesting at least another seven year of memoirs!

As I turned eighteen and began my studies at Kanazawa University, father would take me on occasional trips to Hong Kong to experience a taste of my future life in his business. I became familiar with a few members of his staff, and, in particular, a rather coarse Filipino woman who was always fawning over him and administering to his every need. I continually fended off her persistent efforts to befriend me until the day she admonished me for showing insufficient respect, considering that she and my father shared a flat. I was later to learn that they had a child. I felt totally incapable of confronting my father with this revelation; neither could I bear to break such news to my mother. Instead, I informed him that I wished to transfer my business studies course to another university.

During my year at Kanazawa University, I had been drawn to the martial arts, and Kyudo in particular. Training became a priority, and I would be up at dawn with other enthusiasts. But I felt frustrated that our Kyudo instructor chose not to differentiate between Kyudo and any another sports activity. When I expressed to him my hunger for a spiritual connection, he was not only sympathetic, but pointed me towards a master by the name of Hideharu Onuma, who ran a Kyudo school in Matsudo. Such a move would serve two purposes: firstly, I would no longer have to bear witness to the lie my father was living. Secondly, I would have the opportunity to immerse myself more fully in Kyudo.

Despite father's disapproval and mother's tears, I transferred my business administration course to Senshu University. This would afford me the opportunity of at least meeting the master and demonstrating my willingness. Although father mocked my attachment to the spiritual, he could not help but acknowledge my commitment. Soon I was spending more time at Kyudo school than at university. Although I made regular trips home, I never made reference to his secret life.

And let's hope that I'll also be spared any more references to his father's secret life. I should at least be thankful that he's skipped over his mother's pregnancy. I could speculate on how, after overhearing his parents' squabbles from the womb, CC might have been adversely affected during his teenage years. Or

I could take a well-earned break from this self-indulgent epic and trawl through the remaining decades over a cup of tea and pack of custard creams at the café on the common. I'll opt for the latter.

A wise choice!

Once my studies were completed, I became a partner in his business and consequently began spending longer periods in Hong Kong. The flat that he had shared with the vulgar Filipino woman had become unoccupied, as she and the child, for reasons unknown, had returned to Manila. Their affair had apparently been common knowledge among my father's employees, who never fought shy of discussing scandals between themselves. The flat is on Cheung Chau: one of the larger outlying islands off the mainland. I have grown to love this island, and continue to use the flat as a retreat from city life.

Since working for my father, I have been regularly commuting to Matsudo to continue my training whenever possible, and have recently attained my third dan. There was, of course, no dojo in Hong Kong. So, as a very poor substitute, I would often play darts in the Old China Hand in Wan Chai. It was there that I came across Sid Furney, who I believe you spoke with on James' birthday. He is an entertaining, although sometimes provocative gentleman, whose real talent lies, not with darts, but as a jazz pianist. Sid is often to be found at the piano in the lounge bar.

Towards the end of last year, my father sent me to England to establish contact with major food importers in Chinatowns across the country. It was on Monday, 7 November, as I sat watching TV in my hotel room in the Manchester Palace Hotel, that I first caught sight of James Kelly throwing bull's eyes.

It is here, Mister Carpenter, that our paths first crossed, as we simultaneously bore witness to something extraordinary. My immediate reaction was to phone Master Onuma, but my euphoria was met with a cool response that left me most disheartened. 'Even if the boy does have remarkable abilities, the notion of bringing an Englishman to Japan to train for something he has almost certainly never heard of, in a language he doesn't speak, is foolhardy.'

But I would not be deterred. The following morning, I phoned Kenneth Bell with my offer to sponsor his client. I admit that my bait of a non-existent exhibition match was deceitful. But I could think of no other way to engineer a meeting between James and sensei. When Mister Bell and I met in the foyer of the Palace Hotel, I immediately felt repulsed by his manner. But once I had waved a cheque at him, his brashness turned into false charm. So it was agreed: James and I would meet the following Monday in the Waggon and Horses.

Love is an over-used word. I love my mother; I do not love my father. As James stood facing me when I entered the bar, I cannot deny that I felt an immediate surge of love for him. What he felt towards me, I have since come to recognise as a desire for attachment. But it was not in any sense parasitic. His desire was expressed with warmth, humour and enthusiasm: three qualities that he continues to exude in abundance, and which I find impossible to resist. It seems that James is either attached or unattached – and I do not mean detached. He often appears to be perfectly content in either state; it is other people that feel the discomfort. His closeness to you and me is accompanied by deep fondness, whereas his attachment to Mister Bell has a darker connotation. I nevertheless suspect that when he deems an attachment to have ended, he is capable of severing the tie, with no regard as to whether the relationship was endowed with goodness or badness. Nor is there concern for the people left behind.

Why he should have felt such instant warmth towards me I cannot say. However, in *your* case he had come to feel something of the kind even before you two had spoken. Mrs Kelly had asked what you found remarkable about her son. Your reply – that when he threw a dart, it was as though he was performing some kind of miracle – caused James to smile. This was not because he found your pronouncement foolish; he simply felt an instant fondness for you.

My second deceit was to misinform Mister Bell that he would be accompanying James and me on the forthcoming trip. This, of course, was out of the question, but I would need to devise a strategy. I also had just twelve days in which to gain James' trust, intrigue him with Kyudo, and persuade him to fly with me to Japan in secret, rather than to the non-existent exhibition match in Hong Kong. Only naivety and blind enthusiasm could have driven me to believe that I would succeed in convincing this total stranger to consider such a crazy venture. Although I did succeed, I am now beginning to regret having not heeded sensei's wise warning.

And so you should! Blind enthusiasm? Blind stupidity, more like. Do warnings come any clearer? This sensei fellow spelt out that your whole idea was idiotic. This café only has Bourbons; next time I must remember to bring my own pack of custard creams.

During our fifty minutes alone in the bar, James and I threw some darts and chatted about our lives. I described Matsudo city, showing him photos of Master Onuma and the dojo. He spoke excitedly about his sister and her music, but then flipped into extreme anxiety as he relived the TV experience. I was intrigued by these abrupt emotional changes and his total immersion in whatever he happened to be describing or responding to. It was as though he could wholly inhabit one world, then seamlessly relocate to the next, leaving no trace of the first. It is this genius for being in only one place at any one time that makes him a world class darts player, and would surely provide him with a natural aptitude for Kyudo. This total immersion could, I suppose, count as one of James' peculiarities, if indeed one chooses to regard James as peculiar; I do not. I would classify his irritating penchant for impersonation more as immaturity, and surmise that his compulsion to hold long sustained notes is linked to his close connection with Jade and the music that she improvises. Life with James has the added challenge of endeavouring to separate his unconsciously eccentric behaviour from the mischievous and sometimes devious play-acting. I would even venture that James sometimes deems it in his best interests to appear a little odd!

Was my behaviour questionable? I admit that during and subsequent to this meeting I can be justly accused of planting romantic images of Japan and archery in James' mind. But I have since learned to my cost that, not only is James perfectly capable of looking after himself, but he also refuses to be led by anyone.

For CC to accuse James of play-acting is not only hypocritical, it also shows a total lack of understanding. James' behaviour is James; there is no pretence. As for James refusing to be led, it is my perception that he has been misled.

From the very start, I gave Mrs Kelly my word that nothing would proceed without James' full consent or her prior knowledge. I outlined my hopes and even furnished her with a brief background to Kyudo. Her response was positive: welcoming any pursuit that might open doors creatively for her son. In addition, she hoped that the spiritual element of Kyudo might also fill a much-needed void. She agreed that James' passion for bull's eyes and his tendency to repeat one action until it is perfected were two more reasons why he might adapt well to the path. In short, she embraced the whole project wholeheartedly, but counselled me with regard to her son's behaviour, emphasising that to indulge his every fear merely escalated internal drama, whereas a lighter touch usually caused the fear to evaporate. I was flattered by her pronouncement that my friendship with James would surely be of great benefit.

One unfortunate side effect of Mrs Kelly's support was her well-intentioned but misjudged gesture of purchasing and presenting James with that misguided work by Eugen Herrigel: *Zen and the Art of Archery*. The book was to become an obsession with James and rarely left his sight. I was most relieved when he finally agreed to pass it on to you.

It is not Herrigel that is misguided. During our recent phone call, Mister Lee demonstrated his ignorance by insisting that to hit a target is of real consequence. Surely the desire for a favourable result, combined with its resulting pleasurable sensation of success can only be egotistical. Perhaps I should forward CC a copy of Teach Yourself Zen to put him straight on this matter.

There were occasions when Mrs Kelly's subterfuge became a little overzealous, for example, expecting you to believe that her son had spoken of *Cluedo* rather than Kyudo. However, her later surprise, to discover there to be no dartboard in James' room, was genuine. Although she is not averse to a little mysticism herself, she cannot grasp that, in Kyudo, the *physical* target eventually becomes redundant.

Despite James' fear of the upcoming trip, he took to the idea of deceiving Mister Bell with gusto, clapping his hands with glee on being told that we would soon be flying off to a secret location. It was as though we were embarking on a mischievous game of espionage. He seemed positively relieved to hear that his Uncle Ken could not be invited, and welcomed any escape route from the man's clutches. He even suggested a simple strategy: 'I'll just throw a fit and refuse to go unless Ken stays home.' His plan not only worked, it demonstrated how he is perfectly capable of working himself up into a state of agitation out of thin air when it suits him. In short, he can be something of an actor. Unfortunately, his actions also marked the beginnings of Mister Bell's antagonism towards me.

I wish you had not come to Heathrow. Your well-intentioned presence only led to more deceit. To be blunt, we feared that you might disclose our plans to Kenneth. Whether or not you can appreciate our mistrust, I can certainly appreciate yours: you had just cause to be suspicious upon seeing James in such distress. His unhappy state was due not only to his escalating fear of boarding the plane but also his decision to remain silent rather than having to lie to you. This tipped him into an unreachable turmoil. His sole consolation was the shakuhachi that you had given him and it was only with some coercion that he could be persuaded to leave it outside the dojo.

Mrs Kelly was right: once the plane was airborne, James proclaimed flying to be the only way to travel, proving himself to be far more fearless than myself. He also took well to the simply laid-out bedroom in Matsudo that I had prepared to reflect his own room in Outlane. So, all things considered, the obstacles that I had envisaged simply did not materialise.

Our first meeting with Hideharu Onuma was inauspicious. My role was not merely as an interpreter. I was also expected to mediate between the reluctant master and his new, exuberant, and rather wilful novice. Sensei exhibited a coolness that bordered on hostility, suspecting James' skills to be superficial and ego led. James was not helping matters, by treating the whole subject of Kyudo with little deference or humility. I was starting to regret the whole enterprise when sensei suddenly announced that he would set James a task: he was to return to England and then deliberately lose the world championship with a disciplined display of non-ego and grace. Only on accomplishing this task would he then be accepted at the Matsudo school for a trial period. James needed no time to consider. He accepted his task with high excitement. For James, this was a game of the highest order.

It had been during our very first meeting in the Waggon and Horses, as I listened to James enthusing about numerical combinations, that I drew him the Lo Shu Square. He was so entranced by this grid of nine squares with its totals of fifteen that he began drawing countless sketches of the sacred turtle, one of which he pinned to his bedroom wall. I believe this is now in your possession. We subsequently chose the square as a discipline to incorporate into our darts practice. I could also see how this system might be utilised to both satisfy Master Onuma and thrill James.

Following our meeting with sensei, James was invited to observe a tournament in which I was competing. He was enthralled by everything he saw: the traditional clothing (he said I looked like a kung fu film star!), the tall, slender wooden bows, the great distance from which one had to shoot, and the smallness of the actual target. But it was the slow, set ritual that finally won him over. I felt most heartened. Perhaps my initial instincts had been right all along.

Three weeks later, we flew to Hong Kong for six days of recuperation. Our time was mostly spent in and around my flat on Cheung Chau Island. James immediately took to Cheung Chau like a second home. His constant and rather infantile joke was the similarity of my name: Chun Chow, to the island Cheung Chau, and I was duly proclaimed king of the island. I was further heartened to observe James befriending a youth that cleaned the flats and who enjoyed joining in with this tiresome joke. He was from a poor family that lived in a cramped apartment in the New Territories. I cannot recall the young man's name, but believe his father was Mongolian, and that he could speak the language. He and James taught each other songs, and they would sometimes take a stroll round the harbour. I hope they stay in touch.

Occasionally James and I caught a ferry to the mainland to join Sid Furney for some darts at the Old China Hand in Wan Chai. By the way, Mister Furney did remember to pass on your birthday greetings. James loved Sid's eccentric piano style. Indeed, on our second visit, he insisted bringing along his shakuhachi and, without invitation, began improvising with Sid. Although, to my ears, the results were lamentable, they both enjoyed the experience hugely, laughing uproariously at each other. I was obviously missing the joke.

Two days before our return to England, I received an anxious phone call from a junior partner in my father's Hong Kong offices, enquiring why I hadn't put in an appearance. I made my excuses, explaining that I was on vacation and had in any case sent a full report of the UK trip to my father, who was back home in Kanazawa. He persisted that it would be in my best interests to meet him immediately, as a serious problem had arisen. The problem, I was soon to discover, came in the person of Kenneth Bell.

Although I do not in any way hold you responsible, your phone call to Mrs Kelly sparked a fire that I am still endeavouring to extinguish. Brenda told me how Kenneth had leaned over her throughout that call, struggling to decipher her responses to your concerns. He was feeling betrayed by the three of us: James had insisted that Kenneth be left behind, I was usurping his position, and you were masterminding the whole enterprise. The prospect of anyone attempting to steal his protégé, just as he was poised to manage a world champion, was unbearable.

Under the pretext of a pre-Christmas break in his Majorca villa, he flew to Hong Kong and visited my father's offices under an assumed name, claiming to be an importer of Chinese goods. He managed to convince the sales manager that he and I had recently met in Manchester to negotiate an alliance between his company and ours. By the end of this visit, he had ingratiated himself with certain members of staff, who were happy, for a price, to wag their tongues about any matters connected with my family. By the conclusion of his second visit, he knew every detail of my father's affair and the address of my parents in Kanazawa. During his third visit, he planted the rumour that I was having a homosexual affair with his nephew.

It is common knowledge in the workplace that my father had this affair and that it had ended some time ago. It is also highly likely that he'd had affairs before and continues to do so. No one in Hong Kong really cares. But such knowledge would mortify my mother.

Mister Bell's second accusation is double-edged. In Hong Kong, to be homosexual is a criminal offence. Furthermore, if my father receives such information, he will disown and disinherit me without a second thought. Such are his morals. It now appears that someone, perhaps in a misplaced attempt to protect me, has put out a death threat. If this anonymous individual happens to have Triad connections, then Mister Bell needs to take the threat very seriously. It is imperative that he curtails any further action for his own safety, let alone his own peace of mind.

Finally, after reams of useless information, Mister Lee has revealed his true motive: he wishes to save his own skin. But, true to form, he professes his actions to be selfless. It is no less than his duty to protect his parents and save Ken from himself. Ha! Such are his morals!

On Christmas Eve James returned home alone. It was agreed between us that he would, to all intents and purposes, focus on the Embassy to the exclusion of everything and anyone else. He agreed to train in the manner that Mister Bell required, and make no further mention of my name.

Two days later, Mister Bell arrived back in Yorkshire and was pleased to learn that I had not made an appearance. He was further heartened by the apparent change that had come over James.

Although I had spent the New Year in Japan, I did actually return briefly to Huddersfield in late January, with the specific task of enlisting two new recruits for the next stage of our covert operation. As you are aware, James is very close to his sister and would have certainly kept her fully informed from the start. As for Luke, one should not underestimate his role in the scheme of things. He can always be counted upon. And so my next task was to prepare Jade and Luke for February 6th.

In Nottingham, Luke and I enjoyed contributing to the tale of Robin Hood that James and Jade were determined to narrate to you over the phone. In truth, it was Jade's idea. She was unable to resist furnishing you with a little plot that would pre-empt what was to unfold before your eyes later that evening. I trust that you took their playfulness in good spirit.

On the evening of the 6th, I did explain to Nicky Virachkul, your mysterious archer from Thailand, that James would be playing to a system, but that it would not encroach on his opponent's game. Nicky, who is a calm, easy-going man, took it all in his stride and proceeded to play his own game without being thrown by the spectators' reaction. And without the support of Leighton 'Friar Tuck' Rees, I believe James would have lost his nerve. Leighton has always been kind to James. Despite not being party to what was taking place, he stood by us till the end. It goes without saying that

Jade and Luke played their parts of Maid Marian and Little John to a fault. The sheriff was outwitted.

The purpose of this letter has been to provide you with a clear understanding of events to which you have hitherto been an uncomprehending witness. My hope is that you now utilise this knowledge to assure Mister Bell that my intentions have always been honourable and that James is happy in his new endeavours. My additional hope is that by combining your unique grasp of the situation with Mister Crane's closeness to Mister Bell, you can both bring this pathetic man to his senses.

It may turn out that there is no real external threat to Mister Bell's life. If this is the case, it still does not alter the fact that he is forging his own path of destruction. It seems prudent to cover all options.

In conclusion, one can only hope to make some reparation for the damage done.

Warmest regards,

Lee Chun Chow

I would have welcomed 'in conclusion' two pages ago. Well, my conclusion, Mister Lee, is that I do not consider your intentions to have been honourable. Therefore, even if Ken and I were the best of chums, I would be in no position to assure him of anything of the sort. And why would I wish to assist you in making reparation for the damage that you have caused, considering that it's Kenneth Bell that wishes to do me damage? And as to your shameful part in ridiculing me with the Robin Hood tale, no, I do not take your 'playfulness' in good spirit.

Tepid regards,

Mister Carpenter

Thursday, 25 May 1978

The Lee family

Having now digested the letter, it is still beyond me why this man assumed that I'd be in the slightest bit interested in the history of China or the Lee dynasty. So what is his purpose? If it's to allay my doubts about him, then he's failed. He portrays himself as well meaning, yet admits to deceitful behaviour. He purports to have good intentions, yet makes no allusion to buggering James Kelly. If such practices are against the law in Hong Kong, who am I to argue? And after so many years of Lee senior's infidelity, surely his wife would have some inkling by now. If not, perhaps it's about time she *did* know. Let things take their natural course I say: cause and effect. Or as Christmas Humphreys would put it – the law of karma. Why upset the balance of the universe?

Ken Bell

Well, perhaps he *deserves* to be murdered by a Triad. He's surely built up enough bad karma to be bumped off for several reincarnations to come. Why should I lift a finger to help him, just to assuage CC's guilt? Not that anything I'd say would make any difference, other than to push Ken further over the edge.

'Well, Ken, Mister Lee's motive for making off with your pension plan was entirely honourable. He truly felt that James would be far happier playing bows and arrows in Japan. We knew you would understand.'

I don't think so.

Zen in the Art of Archery

I can see why James so loved this book, with its talk of

suchness and the non-self. I'm gladdened to learn of James' lack of humility or seriousness amid these po-faced Japanese archers. I imagine they go about exuding misplaced religious fervour as though they have discovered the one true path.

Mister Humphreys refers to Zen archery as only one of a *host* of paths, including judo and flower arranging. I have discovered that Toby (his nickname) leads a Zen class on Monday evenings at the Buddhist Society in Victoria. I intend paying him a visit after a little more meditation practice. I have already begun sitting in Zazen for short periods of time with the aim of peppering my day with peak experiences. This will surely raise my level of consciousness to a new spiritual height.

Brenda Kelly

Brenda had actively encouraged the friendship between James and myself, suggesting that a mature influence might benefit him. Now I learn how she enticed CC with similar words. Those of us who do not consider the pendulum to be a reliable arbiter can only conclude that Mrs Kelly is somewhat indiscriminate in her choices for her son's companions. And considering that she knew nothing about either of us, why did she arbitrarily close ranks with CC while shutting *me* out? Brenda knew precisely where things were heading. Yet she either didn't trust me sufficiently to be included, or, worse, was simply not taking me seriously. Either way, I feel slighted. Her intended acquisition of counselling skills will require a certain degree of honesty and straight dealing. For play-acting she should best apply to the Huddersfield Players.

David Carpenter

Yes, here I am, a heading in my own right, worthy as anyone else to be up there. I will not be belittled. I am no figure of fun, and yet have on occasion been treated as such. I can excuse

Jade's initial treatment of me as the wiles of an adolescent girl, whereas Uncle Ken would be hard pushed to show kindness towards a starving Ethiopian. But I am most hurt by the Robin Hood tale that was dangled in front of me as a cruel prank. Shame on you, James; this is the one blot on your copybook. I acted in blind faith, offering myself unceasingly as a faithful foot soldier, so that you might achieve whatever you were striving for. Moreover, I took on my role with a degree of seriousness that has not been reciprocated. For them to have teased me with a trailer of coming events that I could not possibly have foreseen was nothing less than insulting. But for you to have joined in is not what I would have expected.

David and James

In spite of these criticisms, I see our connection as being far from over. Perhaps my role has shifted from friend to anchor, for surely James Kelly is adrift in a foreign land among strangers who seem intent on imposing their own set of incomprehensible rules on him. Although James has an inner strength, I don't perceive him as thick-skinned or worldly. Admittedly, there were sound reasons to have transferred his creative energies from darts to a more fulfilling pursuit. Nevertheless, he's been shepherded to a place not of his choosing. And we could all take some responsibility for leading James into his current state of uprootedness. As things stand, it's my belief that he has no one but myself to support him from a neutral corner.

Big Nick

I have finally grasped how the tune of 'Big Nick' fits the chords of 'I Got Rhythm'. However, once JC has embarked on his manic solo, I can see absolutely no connection between what he's playing and Mister Gershwin's composition. At least I'm managing to plod along to 'Village Blues', only because it moves at a slow pace and is in the key of C.

I now subscribe to Crescendo magazine and may well send Jade a copy of an article about the new Vandoren soprano mouthpieces. My musician's tie arrived on Monday.

Charlie Chaplin

On the selfsame day that Chun Chow wrote his letter, the little fellow's coffin was discovered. It had been buried ten miles from the original grave.

Mister Crane

I know of no one by this name.

Tuesday, 30 May 1978

9.30 a.m. I have just received a phone call from Kings Cross station. Mister Crane turns out to be Jade's ex-boyfriend Darren, who will be paying me a visit within the hour. I've met Darren Crane on three previous occasions, all of them in the Waggon and Horses. During our first meeting he introduced me to Brenda and Jade Kelly. On the second occasion, I foolishly offered my flat as a stopover, should he ever be down in London. By our third encounter, on New Year's Eve, he had split up with Jade. He has a job interview this afternoon and hopes to be returning to Huddersfield the same evening. So, thankfully, he doesn't intend to use my flat as a guesthouse and I won't be lumbered with his company for too long. It's not that I find him particularly objectionable, rather that I'm not at present feeling at my most sociable. I will now attempt to make the lounge presentable.

11.20 a.m. 'Sorry about that – I was lost the minute I stepped onto the fucking platform. Where's the lav?'

Having directed him along the passage, past my usual assault course of cardboard boxes filled with half-read books, I collect two cans of Fosters from the kitchen.

Darren's small rucksack offers further evidence that he is not intending to stay overnight. He looks dapper in a dark grey suit, although the brown hair covering his ears still gives him the look of a member of The Merseybeats.

'Take a seat. Fancy a drink, Darren?'

He sprawls back into the armchair as I clear a space for myself on the sofa.

'Perhaps just the one … I've never been for an interview in my life. This is Ken's bright idea – another one of his, so-called, connections. He says the bloke owes him a favour, you know, usual Ken. I say usual, but you wouldn't recognise him these days, poor sod. He's even lost weight, although that's not a bad thing. Anyway, if I get the job, I'll be moving down here in June.'

I am reluctant to discuss either Ken, or the prospect of Darren looking for London digs.

'Did you read that Charlie Chaplin's body was stolen?'

'Stolen from where?'

'From his grave … then they rediscovered it a few miles away. You remember we talked about him and other dead people on New Year's Eve.'

Mister Crane is now on his feet, his attention taken up surveying my cluttered room.

'Did we? I don't really get American humour.'

'He was from South London, not that far from here, actually. So are you still playing darts?'

'When James did a bunk, Ken thought I might step into his shoes. But I wasn't up to it. I play the odd match for Yorkshire, but only make the B-team. Just as well really … Ken's no longer up to it either. So what's it like round here? Clapham's right posh, isn't it?'

'It's pricey nearer the common. This is more the Stockwell end.'

'So where's your local darts team?'

Darren is now peering out of the window opposite, as though searching for it.

'Lambeth play just down the road from here. They're not much good though, apart from one chap covered in tattoos. I wrote an article for Darts World about them.'

'Must have missed it. So you *are* a journalist, then! Looks like you live here alone by the state of it. Bring back the birds, do you? Serenade them on the piano? Or are you a bachelor gay?' Darren gives me a wink, opens the piano lid and bashes out 'Chopsticks'. He is already outstaying his welcome. 'So give us a tune, David.'

How much longer can I maintain this sham of camaraderie?

'I'm not quite ready for a public performance. But I'm learning to play the blues. I was chatting to Jade last month and she gave me a few tips. Have you seen her?'

'No, but I hear she's growing nuttier by the day … soon be overtaking her brother. We're out of touch. Best thing really, you know … to finish something completely, move on, as Brenda would say.'

I politely ask Darren to abort his painful variation of 'Chopsticks'. He slumps back into the armchair, clearly bored. I struggle to restart the conversation.

'Mrs Kelly was telling me about her counselling course. She's discovered that Ken's schizoid.'

'He's been called most things. God, Brenda's really into it … asks how I'm feeling and all that bollocks. Can't imagine how Ken puts up with her. "Where do you feel your anger?" She actually asked him that last Friday in the Waggon – with me standing there! He just stared at me like some lost mongrel – told me later he's thinking of moving out.'

I put my feet up, as though I'm used to having mates round for a beer.

'I wasn't aware he'd moved in.'

'Well he's always had one foot in the door. But the poor guy's had enough on his plate without Brenda urging him to love himself. And he's got plenty of reason to feel pissed off, the way he's been messed about.'

Was that an accusatory glance? What has Ken told him?

'So you heard what happened at the Embassy? It was really quite a spectacle.'

Darren lights a cigarette and throws the dead match towards the bin. It misses.

'Spectacle? All I know is this: James Kelly took a dive.

That's unforgivable … and to make Ken look such a twat. I'm not surprised the old boy's been up to no good.'

'He was up to no good before the Embassy: going to Hong Kong and making trouble for Chun Chow. That's what all this is about. And I wouldn't be caring now if Ken hadn't got it into his head that I'm partly responsible.'

'And aren't you?'

I swivel round towards him and plant my feet on the floor.

'No. Not in any way – I hadn't a clue what was going on till CC wrote to me. You don't know half of it. And he thinks I can help? Well I can't. I don't even know Ken Bell. And if I did, I certainly wouldn't want to help him. God, I like the man even less than James does. And even if I did like him, why would I help anyone that, according to Jade, is coming to get me?'

My manic reply is far more than I had intended to say. I lean back into the sofa a little drained and emotional. Darren grins.

'I wouldn't take too much notice of Jade. Listen, perhaps I don't know half of it, but here's the half I do know. Finally, after years of managing third-rate talent, Ken believes he's got a world champion on his books. Then up pops a sponsor with a bulging wallet. Ken takes the bait. This flashy Asian poof introduces James to a thing or two, and now our wonder-boy also takes the bait. He's whisked off to Japan. Yes, I told you on New Year's Eve that it was Tokyo and not Hong Kong, but you wouldn't have it. So now Ken's gutted and wants revenge. But Ken, being Ken, goes too far. Then, for whatever reason, James is encouraged to do some weird stuff in Nottingham (not that he ever needed much encouragement) and flies off again with his new best mate. Meanwhile, Ken starts receiving sinister death threats that push him further over the edge. And as if things couldn't get worse, Brenda's asking him to love himself. So what's the other half?'

'Me, I'm the other half! There's this mentally unhinged man

who, even before he became unhinged, threatened to put my head through a mangle. Now he's convinced himself of my significance in the plotting of his downfall. And I'm supposed to help him? I think not.'

'Believe me, Ken's in no fit state to put his own socks through a mangle. The one time I worried that Ken might have done something stupid was just before Christmas. When James arrived back home without CC, I did wonder if Ken had managed to bump the Chinaman off.'

'I think he's Japanese.'

'Same thing. Anyway, last week, CC phoned to suggest that you and I meet up. He reckoned that because you now know the full story, you're the right person to reason with him.'

'Reason with Ken?'

'Well, assure him that it's all been in James' best interests, etcetera.'

'Telling Ken the full story would just make it worse. Look, you're the one that knows him. He'll listen to you. Just tell him to take back any accusations he's been making, and to give up interfering in Chun Chow's life. Assure him that James is perfectly happy and is now leading a more fulfilled life.'

'Oh right: "Calm down, Ken. James is now leading a more fulfilled life." That should get me a punch on the nose – bad as Brenda telling him to love himself. You know what I think? James and Ken were doing just fine until people started interfering, having James believe that he was destined for better things.'

'You're implying that I'm one of those interfering people. Well, perhaps I did believe that James deserved something better.'

Darren stands up. Am I in for a Ken Bell repeat performance?

'Better than what, for fuck sake? Please tell me, what's better than the prospect of becoming a world champion? James has just thrown away two professional careers: his and Ken's.'

'I really don't care about Ken.'

'But the man's getting death threats!'

Darren is starting to get agitated. I stretch back out on the sofa in a bid to lower the tension.

'Then he should go to the police.'

'They're hardly going to listen to a pisshead on the verge of a nervous breakdown. So, you'll not be speaking to Ken?'

'No, I will not.'

Darren is in the hall collecting up his belongings. 'Then I will. I'd take care if I were you!'

Sunday, 25 June 1978

Almost four weeks have passed since Darren Crane's visit. Mercifully, I've heard nothing more from him or Chun Chow. It goes without saying that I've made no contact with Ken Bell, and have no intention of doing so. I did, however, receive the following letter from James.

8 June 1978, Matsudo

Dear Carpenter,

Darts was fast but Kyudo is slow and therefore superior. Kyudo is so slow that you have to pass through eight stages just to shoot one arrow. You must try it immediately. Now, imagine that you are wearing a black, three-fingered leather glove on your right hand, and holding a very tall, wooden bow. Here are your instructions.

Stage 1: Ashibumi: stance

Face sideways and plant your feet at a 60-degree angle.

Stage 2: Dozukuri: balance

Place the centre of gravity on your hips and rest the bottom tip of the bow on your left kneecap.

Stage 3: Yugamae: readying the bow

Take hold of the arrow with your right hand. Now grip the bow with your left hand and look up towards the target.

Stage 4: Uchiokoshi: raising the bow

Raise the bow above your head, keeping the arrow horizontal.

Stage 5: Hikiwake: drawing the bow
Draw the bow apart, equally to the left and right.

Stage 6: Kai: the full draw
Clear your mind and direct the arrow towards the target.

Stage 7: Hanare: release
Let go!

Stage 8: Zanshin: reflection
Retain your position and reflect on the energy that remains.

Did you try it? You are fortunate that no one is watching. I'm unable to reach even the second stage without getting something wrong. I'm not even allowed to hold a real bow yet! The master has little time for me and is always critical when he does. He is also severe with CC, who's preparing to take his fourth dan. I do not like the master.

Playing darts was dirty but Kyudo is clean. Back in Yorkshire I was surrounded by filled ashtrays and darters playing in the T-shirt they'd slept in. But here, the dojo must be spotless before one arrow is fired. Clothes are freshly laundered, and the bow is treated with great respect. The dojo is like my bedroom.

Darts was tactical but Kyudo is direct. There used to be strategies and computations; now there is simplicity. Here is me, there is the target. The objective, Carpenter, is to be both here and there. You must always remember this!

Darts was loud but Kyudo is soft. The hubbub of darts was confined to a small space filled with clinking glasses and harsh voices. The quietness of Kyudo emerges from slow, silent movements in a large space.

All these improvements suit me very well.

Because this bedroom is almost identical to my room at Outlane, I rarely think of home. But when I do, the Yorkshire home I imagine is not with Mum, but at Marsden Gate. For this is where I will eventually live with Jade and the big man. That is if Barrie and Luke ever finish building it. But before then, when I leave Japan, my dream is to move to Cheung Chau. That is my paradise island.

Although Barrie employs the big man to work on his new house, Jade tells me that they spend most of their time either jamming or quarrelling. This is because big man Luke has not yet been paid for his work. But he's far more proficient on double bass than Barrie will ever be on baritone sax. Jade would have mocked their version of 'Auld Lang Syne' on New Year's Eve, but it was *her* idea in the first place for Barrie to buy such an unwieldy instrument.

I am learning to play the bamboo flute that you gave to me at the airport. What a happy coincidence that you should give me a Japanese instrument to take to Japan. Did you know that it's called a shakuhachi? Jade has sent me a John Coltrane LP called *Giant Steps*. She says I have to learn a tune called 'Naima' on my shakuhachi and recommends that I play it whenever I am having dark thoughts. She has also sent me a tape recording of her latest music: long, winding notes that turn into rainbows. I often sing along to her soprano saxophone, as it guides me through the eight stages of shooting, but our sounds are unpopular with students in the adjacent rooms. After my practice and before bedtime I try holding single notes on the shakuhachi until my breath runs out. Although the sound is still very shaky, I can hear each low note splitting off into much higher notes that seem to whistle and hum. The first time I heard these celestial sounds, they were drifting from Jade's room as she played her soprano. I will write and ask her about it. I did tell CC, but he has no interest in such things.

I do miss making music with other people. When CC and I were on Hong Kong Island last December, I used to jam with a jazz piano player called Sid Furney, who also thought he could play darts. At that time, I could only play three notes, but our music still sounded wondrous. I've told Jade all about Sid and she wants to meet him one day.

I was sad that Mum spent all her time with Uncle Ken on New Year's Eve. He doesn't deserve to be with anyone. But she often visits Barrie when Ken's not around. She calls him the lovely Barrie.

I have an unhappy memory from that night:

The big man and I stand shivering in the side alley of the Waggon. I am watching you through the window, fearful that you will never wish to speak to me again.

It is excellent that we can be friends once more.

Darren tells me that you are the worst darts player in the universe – far, far worse than Sid. So it is time for you to change direction and take up Kyudo. CC has given me the address of the one Kyudo group in the whole of London. You must go there to study the eight stages of shooting.

We are arriving back at Heathrow in the early hours of December 1st. Then, just ten days later, my mother will be organising a small party to celebrate my 21st birthday. She has promised to only invite people that I wish to see. I am hoping that there will just be the six of us: me, you, Mum, Jade, CC and the big man. I know that you will have many questions to ask me.

James

———————

I must admit to having performed a mimed approximation of the eight stages of shooting behind drawn bedroom curtains and in front of my wardrobe mirror. Although I initially felt utterly foolish, by stage eight my imagination had taken flight: I had convinced myself that I was 'retaining my position' just as nobly as any Japanese warrior.

Next Wednesday, I plan to attend a public lecture that Christmas Humphreys is delivering at the Buddhist centre in Victoria. It is entitled 'Doing Buddhism'. In preparation, I've already subscribed to The Middle Way. The May edition contains a transcription of an interview with Mister Humphreys that was recently broadcast on Radio 4. He certainly comes across as extremely clear minded for a seventy-seven-year-old. Here is the gist of what he has to say.

1) We are all one, merely parts of the divine principle.

2) The idea of a separate self is illusory.

3) We are the result of all that we have done and must therefore take full responsibility. This is the law of karma.

I do hope that this divine principle is not synonymous with God. I will discuss this with him on Wednesday, should the opportunity arise.

Wednesday, 28 June 1978

I have walked from Victoria station and find number fifty-eight on the posh side of Eccleston Square. Having arrived twenty minutes early, I enter the ground-floor library and begin inspecting each section as though I knew my Theravada from my Mahayana.

An old crone, almost bent double with arthritis, has silently arrived at my right elbow.

'May I help?'

'Oh, do you work here?'

'I'm a volunteer.'

'Can you direct me to the Zen section? I'll be attending Christmas Humphreys' class from next Monday.'

'You're here for Toby's talk? I'm afraid you will be unable to join his class until you've spent a while in Basil's beginner group.'

'How long is a while?' I utter the words as though I'm inventing a koan.

'Months, years … until you are *ready*.'

'Could it not be seconds? Is there a discount if I experience instant enlightenment?'

The crone is not up to my banter.

'Basil's group is held upstairs and there you stay until you're summoned downstairs to join Toby's advanced class.'

'I was given to understand that Buddhists regard such concepts as *beginner* and *advanced* to be in the illusory world of duality.'

'Well, tonight's talk is upstairs and will begin in fifteen minutes. You are at present downstairs. If you consider up and down to be illusory concepts of duality, I'm afraid you're going to miss the talk.'

Although the front row is still empty, I take the middle seat of the second row. The room slowly fills, and by the time that tonight's speaker is being introduced, only the chair in front of me remains vacant. This affords me a perfect view of the imposing figure that has now arrived centre stage and looms over me. Christmas Humphreys is tall and thin, with snow-white hair and a handsome skull for a head. Large ears support black-rimmed spectacles. He is immaculately attired in a dark pinstripe suit, and the austere frown marks that lead diagonally from mouth to chin add to the overall theatrical effect of a retired Shakespearian actor about to deliver his after-dinner speech. Will his tones be mellow?

'THE UNBORN, UNORIGINATED, UNFORMED ...'

No, his voice is thunderous. He is the headmaster and I must not fidget.

'WHAT DO YOU *DO* ALL DAY WHICH IS CHANGING YOU?'

Just as I have managed to disentangle this odd sentence and am on the verge of formulating an answer, a willowy young woman in a fluffy, hand-embroidered afghan coat makes her way to the front row and noisily settles herself into the seat in front of me as though she were arranging a nest. I am now staring into a thick, tightly curled crop of jet-black hair. Fastened to this joke afro wig is a collection of wooden clothes pegs. My vision is now totally blocked.

'WHAT IS YOUR RELATION TO ALL OTHER FORMS OF LIFE, ALL EQUALLY YOUR BROTHERS?'

My attempt to digest yet another strangely constructed sentence is further impeded by the increasingly disruptive rustling sounds in front of me. After having rummaged through her small pink rucksack, she half turns to fish out a notepad. I manage to catch a brief glimpse of her profile, or more specifically, the metal ring through her nose. If I were a pupil I would report her; if Toby were a headmaster he would expel her.

Part 3: Arrows

'LOOK TO YOUR RELATIONS WITH ALL THAT LIVES. IS IT INDIFFERENCE, OR AT LEAST ANIMOSITY TO ALL THAT GET IN YOUR WAY?'

I can now barely comprehend one word, as my mind is elsewhere. Surely, anyone that puts clothes pegs in their hair and wears a nose ring cannot be a genuine Buddhist. Perhaps she's a leftover punk.

'MEANWHILE, WE SHALL LEARN TO WORK ALL DAY ON THE TASK OF RAISING CONSCIOUSNESS TO THE LEVEL OF ITS HOME. WALK ON!'

My inner rendition of 'You'll Never Walk Alone' accompanies enthusiastic applause, as Mister Humphreys bows to his audience and invites questions. The weird girl has now raised her hand and I shut my eyes, expecting the worst. She has a Welsh accent.

'Mister Humphries, are you a theosophist?'

The chairman of the Buddhist Society, the man that single-handedly brought Buddhism to the west, tilts his head downward with no perceptible change of expression. He lowers his voice.

'The theosophical movement certainly had its influence. And yes, there is a great deal of Buddhist thought contained in H. P. Blavatsky's *The Secret Doctrine*, particularly in her description of the law of karma. But no, I am a Buddhist.'

'Are you a Christian?'

'I believe I have answered your question. Anyone else?'

Toby has made a stately exit and is now replaced by the arthritic old woman from the library, who is inviting us to the basement kitchen for tea and biscuits. As people file out, I remain seated, so as to observe the Welsh punk gathering herself up. As she passes down the aisle, wide black eyes adorned with Dusty Springfield mascara briefly flash in my direction, then instantly refocus towards the door. She is wearing silver lipstick.

We have reassembled in the basement kitchen. As I scan the room for any sign of Christmas Humphreys, I'm simultaneously aware of the annoying woman staring at my shaking hand, as it precariously dunks a custard cream. I have no idea why she's choosing to observe me, but suspect that no one else in this room would deign to speak to her after such an ignorant outburst. I will surprise her with a direct stare. She lowers her head and I return to a floating biscuit.

PART 3: ARROWS

Thursday, 29 June 1978

Had last night's dream been only of Jade, I might have woken slightly more refreshed. Why did it have to feature both of them, like some double-headed gorgon with wild red hair and flapping silk scarves, merged with clothes-pegged black curls and nose jewellery? How crass that her dream-name should have been Davina, that they should have simultaneously materialised as mischievously grinning sisters, luring me towards them and seductively inviting me to link my hands with theirs. Had I been naked, even Sigmund Freud would have thrown up.

I approach Davina with the coded greeting: 'hello again.' This is intended, not as an acknowledgement of recognition, but as a hint that in a previous incarnation we had been man and wife. Jade provokes, Davina bows.

Although I have little time for dream interpreters, I will concede that dreams might possibly serve a useful purpose. However, that usefulness diminishes rapidly as their half-remembered traces continue to linger the following morning, causing one to feel utterly miserable and unsettled for days to come. The phrase: *hello again*, bears no meaningful significance whatever, other than having been used in last night's talk during an anecdote to illustrate reincarnation. *Hello again* happened to be the words that came to Toby when first laying eyes on his future wife.

The trouble is, of course, that I am now desperate to see 'Davina' again, and am pinning all my hopes on her being at the Zen class next Monday.

Monday, 3 July 1978

She is. Earlier, I caught a glimpse of her disappearing into the upstairs room. Now I am seated on my mat, cross-legged and in agony, as part of a large circle of similarly pain-racked participants. Davina sits facing me. Her glazed look suggests drugs rather than nirvana. A book entitled *The Zen Teachings of Huang Po* is being passed around the group as each student in turn reads one paragraph aloud. Basil Sladen pads around in a well-worn suit and a slightly skewed red-and-cream-striped tie. Basil is the antithesis of Christmas Humphreys. Rather than the Shakespearean actor, he is more a benign version of Batman's adversary: the Penguin. In last Wednesday's talk, Toby had made much of treating life as fun, but, perversely, delivered his lines with an air of gravitas; Basil exudes warmth and humour without a trace of self-consciousness. Zen has nothing to say, Basil has little, but Toby has enough to furnish a second library. Toby's theatrically timed pauses invariably led to the sledgehammer punch line, whereas Basil is interspersing silence with the occasional, pithily profound gem. Because he makes no attempt to put on a show, his natural eccentricity is enigmatic.

I am handed the book, and opt for a soft, clear tone that might suggest that I already have some grasp of the material.

> *Rid yourself of all your previous ideas about studying Mind or perceiving it. When you are rid of them, you will no longer lose yourselves amid sophistries.*

I aim the final sentence towards Davina, who is now staring back.

PART 3: ARROWS

Regard the process exactly as you would regard the shovelling of dung.

She smirks and looks away. In fact, she fleetingly eyes the drab man in a sports jacket and brown corduroys who sits diagonally opposite her. Basil strikes the gong for a ten-minute meditation before tea break. The drab man's eyelids begin to flutter, as though falling into a blissful trance.

'Have a nice sleep,' quips Basil.

In the kitchen, this wretched fellow in sports jacket and cords immediately buttonholes me. He is balding and has dandruff. He announces himself as Alan, in a northern, but not Yorkshire accent.

'Welcome, my friend! What brings you to our little coven?' He intones the question as though he's Buddha's closest disciple. I fall into his trap with an idiotic reply alluding to the raising of my consciousness. 'Oh very good, they'll move you downstairs in no time. That's Toby talk: lift! lift! That's one of his favourite war cries. I'd forget about all that if I were you, unless you crave the drama and fireworks. All you'll get upstairs in our beginner's class is pure and simple sitting … very boring. We just observe our breath. There's nothing more to it than that. If you're looking to raise your consciousness, then Toby's your man. Not that you *will* raise it, as there's nothing to raise. You'll just *feel* uplifted. Won't last, mind you … nothing does. Everything changes. Now, the boss doesn't actually recommend meditation … very controversial, but that's Toby. His latest thing is NTBT – *the next thing to be done*. We're encouraged to constantly seek new ways to improve our karma in preparation for the next incarnation. Well, there's none of that here in Basil's class as there is *no thing* to improve. So we're forever at the beginning with no prospect of advancement. Running on the spot, or rather, sitting on it – hardly appealing for a newcomer like yourself! The majority of us, when we finally receive the call of promotion downstairs to the advanced class, prefer to remain beginners with Basil. Hey Jax, can you make an extra cup of tea for our new friend?'

I have taken in little of Alan's pompous monologue, due to the constant distraction of 'Davina's' afro hair-do hovering at the edge of my peripheral vision. But now I am within three feet of the metal nose ring. She hands me a teacup, places her own cup down on a nearby shelf and hugs Alan.

'David, Jax – Jax, David … it's his first time.'

'He was here last Wednesday. Weren't you here last Wednesday?'

Welsh, but more like rapid gunfire than singsong from the valleys.

As Alan moves off towards the sink, intoning that Zen is doing the washing up, David and Jax, Jax and David lunge for their teacups and sip in silence, eyes down. Then, as she takes a tiny step forward, her Jimmy Hendrix hairdo, now held in place by a new coloured assortment of plastic pegs, wobbles slightly. I address her hair.

'What's a theosophist?'

'No idea … that's why I asked god.' More concentrated tea drinking. 'Basil should be ringing the bell soon.'

'What for?'

'Zazen. We'll be sitting for forty minutes.'

'That long! So don't you like Christmas Humphreys, then?'

'I don't know him. But Alan says he's really a theosophist.'

'And a Christian? Perhaps he's all three.'

Jax shrugs. I make no physical response, for fear of spilling my tea, but press on in desperation. 'I've just finished reading a book Mister Humphries wrote called *Zen, a Way of Life* because a friend of mine gave me this other book called *Zen in the Art of Archery,* which is what my friend's doing now. He used to be a darts player, my friend, James Kelly … that's his name. But now he's given it all up to practise Kyudo. That's a form of Japanese archery, but very spiritual. There's a Kyudo group in West London and I'm going along in the next couple of weeks.'

'Say that again.'

'What, all of it?'

'The name of your friend.'

'James – James Kelly.'

'The darts player?'

'Well, as I said, he *was* a darts player but now—'

'Holy fuck!'

Basil is ringing a hand bell. As the group begin to make their way back upstairs, Jax has joined Alan at the sink and is whispering to him. They're both staring at me.

Zazen not only involves sitting cross-legged for forty minutes facing a wall. The objective is to observe the breath while passively acknowledging any thoughts that pop up, then to let them go. Were I to divide the past thirty years of my life into forty-minute segments, and then rank each segment as to its suitability for Zazen, this current forty-minute segment would score zero. Putting aside the excruciating pain in my knees, the remainder of my being comprises entirely of thoughts, not just strung together but one on top of the other. Moreover, they are not being observed passively. The one respite is *Zen walking*, during which we all stride very slowly and purposefully in a large circle around the room, casting our eyes down at forty-five degrees. Jax follows behind Alan, and they both seem to be deeply immersed into whatever we are supposed to be immersed in. Then it's back on the mat for the final fifteen minutes of mental torment.

I've finally located my shoes halfway down the corridor. As I bend down to tie the laces, my head brushes an afghan coat hanging from the rail. As it is being removed, I hear Jax asking the one question too ludicrous to have appeared in last Wednesday's dream.

'David, do you fancy a drink?'

Jax has already downed a vodka and lime, and is currently firing a string of questions at me, all of which relate to my connection with James Kelly. I am further unsettled by the news that Alan will be joining us imminently.

'So you really know him? You two are actually friends?'

'Yes, but only since last November.'

'And he's given up darts to do what?'

'Kyudo: it's a form of Japanese archery but very—'

'And you're going to this place to do it in a couple of weeks?'

'Well I don't know if I'll actually get to do it. But yes, I am.'

'I'll come with you if that's alright. Is that alright?'

'Well, yes but—'

'And will James Kelly be there? My God!'

'He's in Japan till December.'

'Shit. Well, I'll come anyway. Look, here's my number. I'm usually home from college around 5.30. Okay?'

'So, Jax, how come you know of James Kelly?'

The one question that yapped on incessantly through Zazen is left unanswered, as Alan bounds over to commandeer the conversation.

'There's nothing in the Dhammapada to say you can't get plastered – is there, my love? I assume you're on the usual.'

His hand rests on her shoulder. I'm surprised that she doesn't shudder.

'Well actually, Alan, it states that he who stupefies himself with drink, destroys his roots. Double vodka and lime please … what's your poison, David?'

'Not for me, Jax … I try to follow the Dhammapada whenever possible.'

Alan fends off my look of disapproval.

'I've heard tell that Chögyam Trungpa himself is not averse to knocking back the old sake or three. So, my friend, I hear you're a mate of James Kelly.'

'Yes, I am. Look, I'm sorry to appear unsociable, but I'm going to have to leave you stupefying yourselves. Perhaps next Monday night.'

Perhaps not.

Tuesday, 11 July 1978

I have been informed by the London Kyudo Society that their next introductory workshop will take place on Sunday 30th. This is still nineteen days away. I phoned, but Jax was not in, so I left a message that I would meet her outside Acton Town tube at 2.30 on that date. Unfortunately, the message was taken by her drugged and/or drunk female flatmate (at least it wasn't Alan) who ended up calling me Phil. I cannot bring myself to phone again and feel little motivation to return to the Zen class, so I will take my chances.

I'm in the process of replying to James' letter, which I will complete once I've attended the Kyudo workshop. The act of writing to James somehow reassures me that I *am* in fact his friend and that I am not meeting Jax on a false pretext.

Part 3: Arrows

Sunday, 30 July 1978

Jax turns up only fifteen minutes late, wearing a sky-blue tracksuit and red headband. No sign of clothes pegs, black mascara or silver lipstick; just the nose ring. Her reply to my greeting is a hummed pattern of seven staccato notes: five on the same pitch, the sixth moving up a tone, and the seventh returning to its initial pitch. Then, thankfully, she bypasses any awkward peck on the cheek by clapping her hands to signal the commencement of our expedition.

We have walked five hundred yards along Gunnersbury Road, and the sound of a wasp trapped in a jam jar still shows no sign of abating. I gesture to our left.

'The Passmore Edwards Cottage Hospital,' I announce, as though we'd just stumbled upon the Taj Mahal.

'Hm mm mm mm mm mm mm.'

I edge us towards the commemoration stone.

'Laid by Lady Rothschild on 9 June 1897. Now that's almost exactly one hundred years ago … not that coincidences bear any significance. Okay, what *is* that tune?'

'The Ramones – "Teenage Lobotomy" – latest album – *Rocket to Russia.*'

'Very catchy!'

'Hm mm mm mm mm mm mm. I need caffeine.'

We are in a greasy spoon on the Uxbridge Road. Jax is sprinkling hash into her roll-up. I anxiously look at my watch.

'Best not to arrive late … look, can you do that outside? Thanks.'

She's now strumming her fingers on the plastic table.

'I've got something for you. I want you to send it to James

Kelly. Will you do that? You *have* actually met him, haven't you?'

Have I actually met him? Well, I spoke to him at Heathrow airport although he wouldn't reply. Then I met him on New Year's Eve on the other side of his closed bedroom door. Have I met him?

'I've already told you: we're friends.'

And so we are.

'So how do you know him, then?'

'Through a friend of a friend – Your Alan's probably heard of Darren Crane: he's another darter who plays for Yorkshire. Darren used to go out with James' sister and was over at my pad last week for a couple of beers. So what do you want me to send him?'

'It's a sketch I made of him last July. He's going to adore it.'

A short distance along Twyford Crescent stands the Church of England High School. Small groups, mostly Japanese, are chatting to one another as they head towards the sports hall. Most of them are carrying tall slender bows encased in cloth covers. We arrive in a crowded corridor, midway through an informal announcement: a children's party in the gym is running late but should finish within ten minutes. My idealised vision of the spotless dojo that James had described makes way for the reality of a school gym populated by partying kids. But Jax has now gained my full attention as she finally chooses to embark on her story.

She is a third year student completing an arts degree at Goldsmiths College and shares a bedsit in New Cross. She joined the Buddhist Society last May and opted for the Zen class as it seemed the furthest one could possibly get from God.

Recognising Alan as a fellow outsider, Jax was drawn to the very exuberance that drove others away. She allowed him to latch on to her, tolerating his constant desire to impress. During a tea break, Alan's dry analysis of the eightfold path suddenly switched to asking her out for a date. Although clearly not her type, Jax surprised herself by accepting his offer.

'Well, the word *date* wasn't actually mentioned. The phrase, as I remember it, was "a surprise outing". When we arrived at the Alexandra Palace, I hoped it might be a band, or at least a live TV show. Then I saw this banner saying *News of the World* – and if that wasn't bad enough, *Darts Championships*. I nearly burst out crying. How a man could imagine that any human being, let alone a young woman, would wish to spend an evening watching fat blokes playing darts was mind-boggling. Believe me, trainspotting in fog would have been a better option. But dear Alan is heavily into his darts. He'd recently attended the area finals in Sheffield, where some player from his hometown had just got through. So naturally he assumed that I, too, would be riveted. Would you have been?'

Her widening eyes remind me of heroines in silent films.

'Me? What, riveted to darts? God, no!'

'So I'd been sitting there for an eternity, pretending to be enthralled by Alan's mind-numbing commentary and knocking back vodka and limes to fend off deep depression. Then suddenly I found myself gawping at the stage like some love-struck groupie. It wasn't just the fact that James Kelly was totally gorgeous that knocked me out; it was how, in an instant, he totally transformed from this lumbering, awkward lad struggling inside a body too big for him, into … a ballet dancer. No, that's not it. It was something about his poise: utterly still, and yet somehow moving at the same time … You haven't a clue what I'm on about.'

'But that's just how *I* saw him: poetry in motion.' I hum six descending notes. 'It's a song by Johnny Tilllotson … before your time.'

'Do you want to hear the rest of the story or not?'

I nod sheepishly.

'I just *had* to sketch him. So later I slipped backstage, and was led to a separate room away from the other players. He was sitting across from this smelly fat bloke who immediately tried to get rid of me.'

'Ken Bell: James' manager. I hate the man.' My virtually inaudible interjection is ignored.

'But James didn't seem in the least put out that I was standing there. He was in a dreamy world of his own. I came over totally star-struck and could only think to ask him whether he'd like to know his expression number. You see, I do numerology, and people usually take an interest if it's about their destiny. Well, James did more than take an interest. He became all animated, walked straight up to me and insisted that I show him how it all worked. So I drew him the grid, and while he was studying it, I made this sketch. But I never managed to give it to him, as the smelly fat bloke finally kicked me out before I'd finished. Then I forgot all about it until I saw him being interviewed on telly. What a star! He left that Irish git, O'Brien, standing. It was like watching performance art. I remember getting smashed that night and dreaming up ways to meet him again. But by the next day it all seemed a bit schoolgirlish. Then when you mentioned him a third time, I just couldn't ignore destiny.'

We are now inside the sports hall and have been ushered to a line of long wooden benches that line the wall on the far side. A slightly built and gently spoken man called Lawrence has handed out pamphlets and is now taking us through the schedule.

'After a brief history of Kyudo, I will explain the eight stages of shooting. There will then follow a demonstration.'

Twenty minutes later he has only reached stage three.

'Yugamae is the preparatory stage. This will lead us to the actual movements for shooting.'

Jax leans across and whispers in my left ear.

'Jesus, their whole buggering army would have been decimated before stage two.'

It's 4.15, and the news that stage five, hikiwake (the moment when the bow is finally drawn apart), can be carried out in three different ways, brings forth a muted rendition of *Teenage Lobotomy*.

'Hm mm mm mm mm mm mm.'

Three Japanese girls glance back and giggle into their hands. Jax gives them a jolly smile and wave. They abruptly assume their former positions.

Lawrence remains focused.

'Stage six, kai: the full draw... Although this could be regarded as a completion of hikiwake, it might also be considered as a condition of endlessly drawing the bow apart.'

'Endlessly, endlessly,' intones Jax.

Lawrence glances up at her and bestows a fatherly smile. Jax is on her feet.

'I'm off for a smoke if that's alright with everyone. I'm sure I'll be back in plenty time for stage seven.'

She isn't, thank God.

The demonstration has begun. Lawrence has changed into traditional costume and reappeared with two Japanese women. The slow graceful moves lull me into a pleasant, soporific haze. Both women have taken their turn, and all arrows have landed within the tiny target that is set up about twenty-five yards away. It is now Lawrence's turn. He takes three formal steps forward and stands the bow upright. He kneels, half-bows and then, while holding the upper part of the bow with his right hand, uses his left to remove the kimono sleeve from his left shoulder.

Now, back on his feet, Lawrence stands with legs apart and toes pointing outwards. As his head gracefully turns towards the target, his torso remains facing the onlookers. Although most of his bare chest is now exposed, he lacks any self-consciousness or awareness of an audience.

The silence is broken by a sound that can be heard emanating from building sites and is commonly known as the wolf whistle. The Welsh she-wolf leans against a set of wall bars, smoking a joint. Lawrence nocks the arrow, rests the lower tip of the bow on his left kneecap and releases: bull's eye!

It's question time. As Jax raises her hand, my fear of a repeat performance is about to be realised.

'So Lawrence, have you come across this bloke in Japan? What's his name, David? The one that's teaching James how to do all this bollocks.'

'Master Onuma,' I mumble.

With a treacherous nod, I pass the ball to Lawrence, who remains courteous.

'There are so many masters in Japan. I'm only acquainted with my own teacher.'

'So how can we find out if this one's any good? And another thing, Lawrence: if someone's really good at darts, I mean really shit-hot, do you reckon he could get even better than *you* at Kyudo?'

'I know little about darts, but there's no reason why not. On the other hand, being a first-class darts player, or even a competent archer, will guarantee nothing in Kyudo.'

'I've another question – do you mind?' She is rummaging through her pink rucksack and pulls out a copy of *Zen and the Art of Archery*. 'I've been doing a spot of research. It's this bit on page eighty-one, where Eugen challenges the old guy to hit the target in the dark. And then he bloody goes and does it. What do you think of that, then? If we all get you to close your eyes and have a go, what do you reckon on your chances?'

He smiles and speaks evenly without a hint of impatience or irritation, 'No chance at all, I'm afraid.'

'And one last thing.' I am now, for the first time since early childhood, tugging at a woman's sleeve. 'There's some nasty bloke that my friend here really hates. With a few lessons, could my friend bump this geezer off with one of your arrows?'

Sunday, 3 September 1978

Dear James,

It has taken me some weeks to write this letter as I've been working hard to finish the enclosed sketch. Are you marvelling at my meteoric progression from cartoon stickmen to professional artist? Well, if you are, I can assure you that my artistic leanings are still on par with my darting skills. So who *really* drew this sketch? And how did I come into possession of this fine piece of artwork?

Your first letter to me, last November, related an incident that took place during the *News of the World* championships. You described a strangely dressed girl entering your dressing room. She sketched you, then proceeded to calculate your special numerological number. Well, that girl's name is Jax (I suppose it's short for Jacqueline) and here's the sketch she drew that day. She took quite a shine to you, considering your TV appearance to be performance art, whatever that may be. So, do darts players have groupies? I won't even hazard a guess at her appearance eighteen months ago, when you saw her. But her current look consists of a nose ring, silver lipstick and clothes pegs in her hair. What a sight! She insists she's not a punk, but a living art form reflecting the despair around her. I expect her mother feels the despair alright! So how did I, of all people, come across such a specimen?

Having recently reread *Teach Yourself Zen*, I took myself off to the Buddhist Society to attend a lecture by its author. Upon learning that Christmas Humphreys did not consider meditation to be an essential ingredient of Buddhist practice, I decided against joining his advanced class and opted instead for a more practical session that included Zazen: a far purer approach than that favoured by the theatrical Mister Humphreys. It is here that Jax and I were thrown together. As her acquaintance happened to be a darts enthusiast, I brought your name into the conversation. From that moment, she seemed to find me of great interest, insisting that I take her to the Kyudo workshop.

Now, I expect it's obvious to you that I do not normally 'click' with girls. What I really mean is that they don't like me much. Take your sister as an example. So actually being asked out by someone, for whatever reason, is an event that is bound to cause me sleepless nights and anxious dreams.

It was on the day of the workshop that Jax handed me the sketch, asking that I forward it to you. Since then, I've spoken with her twice on the phone. On the second occasion, she made me promise to bring her along when we meet up for your 21st birthday on December 11th. Jax has made it quite clear that if this does not happen, she will have nothing more to do with me. You would think that I would be glad of such an offer. But for some unaccountable reason I have become rather fond of her, in spite of our having little in common. Can you understand? Would you mind?

I'll not be replying to Chun Chow's letter. I have nothing more to add than what was said during our phone conversation. I trust that he will not be offended. However, you could inform him that my meeting with Darren Crane has not changed my mind: I want no involvement whatever with Kenneth Bell and his paranoia. That he is a potential danger to himself and others is not my concern, but Jax's suggestion that I bump him off with a Kyudo arrow is taking things rather too far.

I consider it a good omen that you have not warmed to the so-called master. Furthermore, I would urge you to keep your independence and maintain a respectable distance from such people. These zealots consider themselves brimming over with spiritual wisdom, just because they've learned a set of silly rituals.

If you should ever feel cast adrift and in need of solace or advice, remember that I am always here to support you in any way I can. I very much look forward to seeing you in December.

Your friend,

Carpenter

PART 3: ARROWS

Wednesday 6 December 1978

The *South London Press* is not a riveting read. Every Thursday, for the past two years, June has poked her food-stained copy through my letterbox as a neighbourly gesture. I have never requested her to do this. Nor have I thanked her or reciprocated with a similar gesture. But still it arrives and still I leaf through, in the certain knowledge that nothing from front page to back will catch my eye, other than what's showing at the Tatler in Stockwell. (*Saucy Nymphos* was such a disappointment that I may well cancel my membership.) The possibility that it may contain something of any interest is further reduced by the fact that the news items are always six days out of date, it being a Friday publication. But this morning, having returned home with my pint of milk from the Co-op, I'm mystified to find the bedraggled specimen dangling from my letterbox one day early.

I settle down with a mug of tea and two custard creams, the newspaper lain across my lap. Despite my irritation that they've made the paper even less readable by decreasing its overall size and typeface, I still embark on my usual mindless ritual of flicking through the dross. But now I'm catching sight of headlines and phrases with a totally unfamiliar ring:

'Mirfield couple's miracle baby'.

'Devastation as vandals wreck Rawthorpe Secondary School'.

'Rail prices hit £10.80 for economy return to London'.

I return to the front page and discover that I have been perusing yesterday's edition of the *Huddersfield Examiner*.

The single question that takes precedence over who might have posted the newspaper through my letterbox is: why?

What exactly does this mystery paperboy wish me to read? I spend half an hour scanning every article and advert, but find nothing. I work from the back, starting with the sports news and fail to even find darts results. I thumb through each TV and radio listing (perhaps there's a *Best of the Eamonn O'Brien Show*) or a documentary about darts. I read each letter to the editor, searching for the names Kelly, Crane or Bell, scrutinise household goods for sale, job ads and mid-season sales. There is nothing in this newspaper that has any connection with any person or event that has touched my life in the past year. I stuff it into the paper bin, curse mankind and turn my mind to other things.

Christmas Humphreys suggests that by welcoming all thoughts as passing illusions, they will soon dissipate of their own accord, but by 2 a.m. they have long outstayed their welcome. I get up for a pee, snatch the paper from the bin and make one final attempt, this time scanning through the weather forecast, a concert review, even a recipe for Lancashire hotpot, before scattering it across the room.

PART 3: ARROWS

Thursday, 7 December 1978

The phone rings.

'David Carpenter speaking.'

'It's Darren Crane. How you doing?'

'Fine. You?'

'Bearing up under the circumstances. I don't suppose you'll be going, then.'

'Going where?'

'Oh, didn't Brenda phone? She was supposed to phone you Sunday. That's why I shoved the *Examiner* through your box. I was down for another job interview. I rang your bell, but you were out. You *did* get it?'

'Yes, I got it and I can recite the whole paper to you backwards. In fact I could answer a quiz on it. Go on, test me. Ask me anything.'

'Well, if you must. Try this one: who snuffed it last Friday? Three letters.'

'What?'

'Ken … Ken Bell. Ken's dead – run over by a lorry. He'd just stepped out of the Waggon, totally pissed of course, and was crossing New Hey Road when—'

'Can you slow down a bit?'

'They were probably Ken's last words to the lorry driver. Get it?'

'Just tell me the story, Darren,'

'So, I'm throwing a few darts with Barrie. Ken storms in. He goes for Barrie, socks him in the nose. Then in walks CC and—'

'No, I'm not getting any of this. What was CC doing in there? Was James with him?'

'They'd both arrived back from Japan earlier that day. No, James was home. Apparently he'd locked himself in his bedroom. Look, that was my last coin. Brenda says you were supposed to be coming up for James' birthday but under the circumstances ... Speak soon.'

The newspaper is strewn around the lounge. I hastily reassemble it and turn to the one section I'd omitted: the obituaries.

> BELL, *Kenneth passed away suddenly on Friday, 1 December, aged 46 years. A much loved husband and dear dad. Will be very sadly missed by his wider family, friends and clients. Funeral service will be held at Outlane Methodist Church, Huddersfield on Monday, 11 December at 1.30 p.m., followed by interment at Pole Moor cemetery.*

And so, in the end, it was neither the Hong Kong mafia nor my bow and arrow that took out Uncle Ken. The task fell to a luckless lorry driver. The poor fellow was given no choice but to squash the owner of The Belltime Agency into New Hey Road, just moments after he'd stumbled from the Waggon, too drunk to look right, left, then right again. This certainly makes for a far more plausible and fitting end to the life of Kenneth Bell than a revenge killing. My one regret is that the date of the funeral clashes with James' birthday. I'll phone Brenda this evening.

***

'Brenda, it's David. I've only just heard. I'm so sorry.'

'David? Oh, is that David from London? I meant to phone, but it completely slipped my mind, what with so much going on this end. James wants to know if you're still coming up? We've had to call off the birthday party of course, much to his relief.'

'Oh.'

'And I didn't think you'd want to travel all the way up here just to attend Ken's funeral. You were hardly bosom buddies … although I suppose you and James could catch up with each other after the burial.'

'Well, it's hardly an occasion for catching up. It must have been a terrible day for you.'

'It would have been a pretty lousy day for Ken, even if he *hadn't* died.'

'Wasn't James arriving back from Japan that same Friday?'

'Yes, but not till midday, so we were hoping for a bit of a lie-in. When the phone rang in the middle of the night – well around six in the morning actually – Muggins was expected to go down and answer it. Ken just cursed and pulled the pillow over his head. The operator asked if I'd accept a reverse-charge call from a Mister Lee. CC said he was phoning from Heathrow and had to speak with Mister Bell urgently. He was sounding very rattled.'

'That's not like CC.'

'Exactly. So something was wrong. I rushed back up to the bedroom and finally herded a disgruntled Ken downstairs and on to the phone. God knows what CC was saying to him but Ken was blowing his top.'

'Can you remember what Ken said?'

'Oh, stuff like "I'm on to you" and "You must take me for a bloody fool". Then he slammed down the receiver and stomped off into the living room. I tried asking him if there was a problem, but all I could get was, "Oh yes, Brenda, there's a problem. At least there's going to be one hell of an 'f' problem when the 'c' arrives." '

'I suppose he *would* have been angry if CC was intending to show his face on your doorstep.'

'So was Ken really expecting James to find his *own* way from

Heathrow to Huddersfield? Fat chance! Anyway, I left him to stew, went back to bed and slept through till eleven. When I got downstairs, Ken was snoring in the armchair: the result of washing down his breakfast with a few Newcastle Browns. I set about tidying up while Jade flitted in and out, making a nuisance of herself. I'd heard them both talking earlier from upstairs, but she refused to tell me what they'd been talking about. So we both went about our own business.'

'When did James and CC arrive at yours?'

'Just after twelve … I was coming out of the kitchen when the doorbell rang. Ken barged past me and opened the door to James. They were talking on the step for about thirty seconds before Ken headed off down the front path.'

'Could you hear what they were saying?'

'No, and James still has no intention of telling me.'

'Where was CC?'

'Outside, by the car … I hurried out to greet James, but I really wanted to keep an eye on Ken. CC was bent over, unpacking the boot. I was about to warn him, but Ken walked straight past, crossed the road and disappeared into the Waggon. That was the last time I saw him alive.'

'Did you think to follow him?'

'Why should I have done? I felt relieved that he hadn't attacked CC. And if he wanted to drink himself into a stupor, at least he was out of *my* hair for a while. CC and I shook hands. James collected up his stuff from the car and went indoors. He was very subdued.'

'And where was Jade?'

'She may have been helping, but I can't remember. I invited CC in, but he said … and I can recall his exact words because they were so odd sounding … "I have to make reparation with Kenneth." I warned him that he hadn't picked the best time for a conciliation, but a big part of me just yearned for them all to go away.'

'So CC followed Ken into the pub?'

'Yes, and by that time James had locked himself inside his bedroom. Then Jade dramatically announced that she was off to find Luke. Good riddance to the lot of you, I thought.'

'And what did *you* do?'

'I opened a bottle of plonk and collapsed into the armchair. I must have drifted off to the wafting sound of James' Japanese flute. The next thing I remember was a shout from upstairs, then screeching brakes and a thud that turned out to be a car crashing into the back of a truck. As I watched them load Ken's body onto the ambulance, all I could think was that at least he died healthy.'

I choose to keep the ensuing fifteen seconds of respectful silence, rather than fill it with untactful reminders of his bulging stomach, sixty fags a day and probable alcoholism. I then speak in the hushed tone appropriate to such an occasion.

'It's just a shame that his last days were so miserable. Poor Ken … You know what? If it's all the same to you, I feel I should come up and pay my respects. Do you think it will be okay to bring a friend?'

Friday, 8 December 1978

'May I speak to Jax please?'

'Who shall I say is calling?'

'David Carpenter, from the Zen class ... James Kelly's friend.'

'Jax, for you – it's Phil.'

'Jax, it's me, David ... no, not Phil. How does David sound like Phil? Anyway, slight change of plan. There's bad news and good. Which do you want to hear first?'

'Bad.'

'James' twenty-first birthday party is off.'

'Shit! And the good news?'

'I'm taking you to a funeral.'

PART 3: ARROWS

Monday, 11 December 1978

11.15 a.m. Huddersfield. We are sitting in the Wimpy in King Street. Having survived twenty minutes of Jax's intermittent humming and chip flipping, I celebrate by ordering a Brown Derby. On Saturday I had my hair trimmed, and this morning, before setting off, I changed into my dark grey suit and musician's tie. Jax, however, has not dressed for the occasion. She flicks a final cold chip off the plate. Then, after adding one last flourish to her sketch of me, she packs the sketchpad and pencils into her pink rucksack and chirpily announces that she's off to buy a hat for the funeral. I don't ask whether she'll be shopping for something that will be in keeping with the brown trench coat and purple Ramones T-shirt, but she has at least made a small gesture of respect for the dead with black lipstick and a shiny black plastic skirt.

11.45 a.m. I've long finished the donut and am spooning up puddles of melted vanilla ice cream and chocolate sauce when Jax reappears. She is wearing a flat-brimmed black hat, complete with a veil that hangs down past her chin. I call it a veil, but it's more like a remnant of net curtain that's been stapled to the front rim of the hat by a drunk with impaired vision. I am dressed for a funeral, Jax for a beekeeping course.

'You look like Morticia Addams in mourning.'

'From the little I remember of the fat slob, there's not much to mourn about. I can't imagine anyone bothering to turn up. How did you say he died?'

'I told you. He was run over by a lorry.'

'Terrific. Let's party.'

With so much time in hand, we decide to walk to Outlane. This proves to be a bad decision. Jax has decided not to remove or even raise her veil, in order to 'get some practice in'. She attracts attention, not only by her appearance but also by walking into walls and lampposts.

'I'm *so* looking forward to getting another eyeful of James Kelly. Did I tell you that I do numerology? James' expression number is 5? I'll do yours. So that's fourteen letters. I'll need to work it out.'

'I'll save you the trouble. Mine's also five. James told me in a letter ... not that I go in for any of that nonsense. I'm surprised you'd want to know anything about me anyway.'

'Why would I offer to work out your number if I'm not interested in you, Phil? Joke! So tell me something about yourself that will surprise me.'

'Well, actually I've been learning to play some blues piano.'

'Hm mm mm mm mm mm mm.'

12.50 p.m. We arrive at the Waggon with forty minutes to spare. I had expected to see a hearse, or at least a few cars parked outside 702 opposite. But the only vehicle is Luke's motorbike. I refrain from informing Jax that the Kelly family live right across the road from the pub.

The bar is deserted but for 'the lovely Barrie', as Brenda had described him on New Year's Eve. Barrie is still propping up the bar and supping from his personal jug, as though he hadn't moved in almost a year. He's dressed for a funeral, but actually looks quite perky for once.

Jax wastes no time.

'I'm Jax.'

'Barrie Collins.'

The nasty gash on the bridge of his nose, together with his chiselled features and broad shoulders give him the look of an attractive middleweight TV wrestler, the type that mums cheer. Jax takes a step closer.

'And this is David. He's a close friend of James Kelly.'

'Oh, right,' is the extent of his acknowledgement of my existence.

I make an effort.

'I hear you were with Ken just before—'

This time I'm totally ignored.

'So Jax, which side of the family are *you* from?'

'I'm from the other side, aren't I, David!'

'She certainly is, Barrie.'

As he peers into the veil, his broad grin reveals a missing tooth. Betty finally appears and I order three drinks in a final bid to establish myself.

'I heard you playing 'Summertime' on your sax last New Year's Eve.'

Barrie gives me a sideways glance.

'How come?'

'You'd been jamming with your friend Luke and I bumped into him outside your house.'

'Luke and I have fallen out – reckons I owe him money, the lazy bastard.'

'I'd been round at the Kelly's, having a chat with James.'

'More like upsetting the lad, the way Bren tells it. So lass, you're from Welsh Wales, then?'

'Blackwood … and David was raised on a plantation in Alabama. He's a blues man, direct descendant of Blind Lemon Jefferson. You'd never guess to look at him. Are you a local, Barrie?'

'Born and bred – I was living up in Barkisland Hall, sort of caretaking for Joe Kagan till the wife ran off with some posh git. So then I moved to Marsden Gate to renovate the farmhouse. It's just up the road from here, past the church on the right. But I'm mostly living in a caravan till the house is finished.

Mine's the blue one next to Luke's hovel. He was supposed to be helping me but he's fucked off again: the story of his life. So how well did you know Ken Bell, pet?'

The maiden demurely lifts her veil. 'Ken? Oh, intimately, didn't I, David!'

Without deigning to reply, I grab my half a bitter and retreat to the corner seat, leaving them to their pathetic flirting. After five minutes, I observe Barrie scribbling something onto Jax's sketchpad. He gives me a cursory nod and takes his leave. Jax joins me.

'A fireplace fell on his nose, or something like that. Says he's off to collect Bren. Who's Bren?'

'James' mother – that's odd. I would have expected Brenda to be with the funeral party. It's already a quarter past one. Right, the church is five minutes up the road. Let's go.'

'And who's Luke?'

'He's the local eccentric. I expect he invents things that don't work.'

'David, have you ever dropped acid?' I think back to test tubes in the chemistry class. 'You know, LSD. Have you ever taken it?'

'Good God, no – why? Have you?'

'Oh yes.'

'When?'

'About twenty minutes ago.'

We are now standing outside the church. Luke's motorbike screeches to a halt. After allowing Darren ten seconds to clamber out of the sidecar, he bellows, 'Last call for Luke's funeral rides,' before roaring off up New Hey Road. Mourners are filing past Jax as though she were the Outlane spectre. But Darren cannot resist.

'So who do we have here? There's no booze allowed inside, my love, even though it *is* Ken's send-off.'

'Darren, this is Jax. Where's Luke off to now? Or is he banned from here too?'

'Off looking for James ... he was supposed to be with the main party.'

As the double vodka and lime disappears behind the veil, a voice whispers, 'What party?'

Darren peers into the netting, as though observing tropical fish. 'Anybody home?'

'Bubbles can be so loud. Come under here with me, Darren. Have a listen.' Darren lifts the veil to reveal two anxiously darting mascaraed eyes.

'You alright in there, love?'

'No. Where's the corpse?'

'Ken's due here any minute, what's left of him. We'd better get in, David. It's nearly half past.

'Do we sit anywhere?'

'No, we're in the back row. Chun Chow's saving us some seats. They don't have pews here, just those uncomfortable hard-backed chairs. Bloody Methodists! I didn't get that job, by the way.'

Jax, now in beatific reverie, perches cross-legged in the aisle seat to my left. Darren is to my right. CC, seated three vacant seats from Darren, stares solemnly towards the pulpit. I whisper to Darren, 'It's somehow incongruous to see him here.'

'Not as incongruous as seeing you ... So what are *you* doing here? Day out with the girlfriend?'

Jax has returned to her version of consciousness. She swivels round to ogle the red stage curtains that hang directly behind us. She's now stroking them sensuously with both hands.

'Wow, are they going to bring the coffin on stage?'

Darren stretches across and lifts the veil.

'They still put on Christmas shows here. They're rehearsing *Scrooge* now.'

'What, right now? Oh listen, Darren. This must be the overture. Who's the stiff on the organ? Is it Scrooge?'

'That's my father.'

I intercept the conversation.

'That's some bang on the nose Barrie's got.'

'Ken landed him one before Barrie knew what was happening. He could have torn Ken apart, but that's when CC walked in. Look, here come the leading players.'

I scan the select group that follows the coffin but only recognise Jade. She steadies a distraught woman in her mid-fifties, whose dyed-pink hair and face-lift only accentuate a shrivelled frame, ravaged by illness. I then spot Brenda. She is seated with Barrie in the second row. They are arm in arm. But there's still no sign of James. I now feel certain that he will not be attending the service.

'*We meet in the presence of God, who holds the key to life and death. We meet to remember the life of Kenneth who has died, to give thanks, to forgive.*'

There's a shuffling to my right, as CC pulls out a handkerchief to dab his eyes.

'*... And this life-affirming song, written by Charlie Chaplin and requested by Kenneth's devoted wife, epitomises to Doris how, particularly in recent months, her dear husband could still smile in the face of adversity. But now it is the hearts of his loved ones that are aching.*'

Darren nudges me as the Chaplin record crackles through its final chorus.

'CC's not finding anything to smile about. He seems even more cut up than Ken's missus.'

'*The strike is over, the battle done.*
Now is the victor's triumph won.'

Suddenly, Jax is on her feet. I pull her back down. She's mumbling in my ear. 'David, it's the raffle ... a Victor Triumph. Somebody's won a car. Did I give you the number that broken-nose Barrie wrote down? No, I've got it. Just look what he's written!'

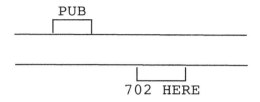

'Yes, I can see. Please Jax, people are looking.'

'This is simple: seven equals G, then O, then two ... here. GO TO HERE. I have to go!'

And she's gone! My prayers are answered.

I joyfully sing along to 'The Lord is my Shepherd', offering heartfelt thanks for Jax's early departure, and feel further uplifted as Jade slowly mounts the three steps to take her place before us. Clutching her soprano saxophone, she is looking uncharacteristically spruce, like the head girl of a boarding school. Her clothes actually fit her and the colours blend. She must have received help from external sources. Her voice resonates with confidence.

'I'm going to play "Naima" by John Coltrane. You can imagine how much Dad detested modern jazz, but I haven't chosen this tune just to spite him. I did enough of that when he was around. But he also understands me enough to know that I'm not about to launch into "My Way", even for his funeral. I'm also not going to pretend that he was always there for me. But I *will* say that when he *was* ... well, he could be twice as cantankerous as his daughter and I loved him very much. So this is for you, Dad, like it or not.'

I feel inappropriately moved by this revelation that Jade not only had Ken for a father, but that she is professing to have loved such an obnoxious man.

A high, sustained note heralds three shorter ones. Then, after a brief improvisation, we are led back to the original, sombre theme, now laced with delicate embellishments. (Get me! Perhaps I should try my hand at a review for *Crescendo* magazine.) Jade allows a moment for the final note to reverberate, gazes dreamily around her and rejoins Ken's widow on the front row.

Kenneth Bell is in the ground and Pole Moor cemetery is all but deserted. As I observe groups of departing mourners, I feel no more a part of this fraternity than when I sat, alone and invisible, in Fern Lodge Social Club. I nod to Ken's widow, as she passes by with the support of two elderly gentlemen. Brenda and her daughter pause momentarily, but none of us know what to say. We shake hands and they move on. Barrie trails behind them, cracking graveyard jokes with Darren. Luke had arrived too late for the burial service and is now rushing off again, clutching a bunch of battered flowers. I even give *him* a nod, but he has no idea who I am. The one lone figure in the far corner, seated on a gravestone and staring down over the valley, would, in a dream, be James. But of course, it isn't James.

Chun Chow briefly turns to mouth my name and then continues to stare out into the distance.

'I have caused all this suffering. Why did I reject Master Onuma's warnings and plough on regardless with such a misguided scheme? Mister Bell had every good reason to feel badly towards me, even to wish me harm.'

Quite so! Why should I make things easier?

'Did Ken ever actually harm you or your family, Mister Lee?'

'In the event, no. When I wrote to request your help, I had genuine concerns that he was still actively seeking revenge for my deceit. Later, I learned from Mrs Kelly that he was becoming incapable of getting himself onto a bus, let alone a plane. When did you last see him?'

'New Year's Eve – and he couldn't have been happier. You were the last person on his mind.'

'It's true. Once James had begun to play his role, Mister Bell had no further reason to punish me. These were his final weeks of contentment, and for good reason: I had been banished and James seemed set for victory. But I was poised to snatch away his dream, leaving him with nothing but a crippled wife and failing business. That night in Nottingham, as James threw fifteens, I watched Kenneth from the balcony. He was wandering in circles like a wounded dog. Then he spotted me, just as we were about to leave. Barely able to hold himself up, the ensuing confrontation was pitiful. Kenneth's mouth opened, but no words came out. We found it amusing: shame on us.'

If Mister Lee is vying for my sympathy, then I need to put him straight.

'But you went ahead anyway, regardless of the damage you'd cause. You hurt Ken just as he'd hurt James.'

'You are right not to separate us. Kenneth and I are failed Svengalis. James chose neither darts nor Kyudo. *We* did. And why? Because we believed that he was capable of attaining a higher level than either of us could dream of. In the end, I was no better than Kenneth. Only our methods differed. The irony is that Mister Bell proved to be right. It was he, not I, who really understood how to manage James. Initially, my liberal attitude bore fruit. But in the long term, it has proved disastrous. And now James has turned against me, just as he turned against Kenneth.'

'But for different reasons.'

'No, for the same reason: our fatal error was to assume that he would treat darts or Kyudo with any seriousness. Both Kenneth and I are from the furrowed-brow school of hard work and commitment, whereas James' gift is his featherlight touch. He has no need to be serious.'

Momentarily, CC's face relaxes. His dark eyes smile at me.

During this shared image of the infuriating man-child that has caused us so much disruption, I can see why a certain sort of man might find CC attractive. But his gaze soon returns towards the valley and self-flagellation resumes.

'The day that we abandoned Kenneth in Nottingham marked the start of his decline. Less than a week later, upon receipt of a further death threat, his obsession for revenge increased tenfold. But now his rancour was infused with a complete lack of reason and fuelled by alcohol. It was evident that he was in more danger of destroying himself than others. I vowed that on our return I would face him, admit to my wrongdoings and make reparation. This was my intention as I entered the pub, just minutes before his death. Initially my appearance was a timely diversion from the ugly scene that had developed between him and a neighbour.'

'Barrie Collins.'

'I tried reasoning with Kenneth but was drowned out by his abusive tirade. He was adamant that we were all out to destroy him.'

'He did have a point. Everyone but me seemed intent on bringing him down: you, Jade, Luke, Brenda ...'

'You have omitted the one offender that Kenneth held ultimately responsible for all that had taken place. In fact, his final sentence, as he stood at the door, contained a vile description of what he was about to inflict on James in the next ten minutes. But he didn't live long enough to cause further harm.'

'Well, *my* conscience remains clear. Why ever should *I* have come to Ken's aid? I hardly knew the man. But not one of his friends or family bothered to support him.'

'I agree. No one seemed to care that Kenneth was falling apart, least of all James. He has always treated the whole episode as a game and still shows no sign of grief or remorse. But everything's a game to James, even Kyudo.'

For the first time, there is bitterness in his voice. I feel a brief tinge of sympathy.

'I can see that James has hurt you.'

'It was not his intention.'

'And has it ever been your intention to cause James harm?'

'Never! And make no mistake, Mister Carpenter, James is far more capable of looking after himself than most people assume. I have grown to realise that he cares for no one but himself. It is doubtful that sensei will put up with James' disrespectful behaviour for much longer.'

My next question tumbles out before CC has quite completed his sentence.

'Have you been having sex with James?' I clench with embarrassment. Chun Chow wearily levers himself up from the tombstone. He smiles but remains silent, so I add: 'Not that it's any of my business.'

'David, I wonder if it's more your business than mine.'

'What do you mean? It's *you* that's the homosexual.'

He touches my shoulder. I flinch.

'Yes, it's me that's the homosexual. Have I ever slept with James?'

'Had sex with him.'

'I have not.'

'But would you like to have sex with him?'

'There was a time when I would have liked to. What do you think of that? Would *you* like to, David? He does seem to care for you.'

I am looking back, around the deserted graveyard, filled with irrational panic.

'What do you mean? Are you making fun of me? I've got a girlfriend, thanks. She's around somewhere, which is more than can be said of James. Care for me? I begin to wonder if he'd have even acknowledged me, had he bothered to turn up.'

CC's hand, once again on my shoulder, now feels comforting.

'I can assure you, David, that when he thinks of you, which is probably not often, it is with great fondness. The truth is that you are only on the periphery of his world. James requires a safe distance from which to exhibit certain emotions. His distance from you is sufficient for him to demonstrate this feeling of care, friendship, love. Call it what you will.'

'I call it *friendship*.'

CC removes his hand and takes a step back.

'But be warned, David! Attempt to venture closer or impinge on his way of being and you will see a very different side to James, a much uglier side. There are only two people truly close to James: Jade and Luke. That will never change. Those three are locked together like a coven. You and I remain on the outer circle.'

It is high time to dampen all this overblown drama, surely induced by gravestones and misty Yorkshire valleys.

'As a fellow member of the outer circle, can you share information as to why our fair-weather friend has failed to show up?'

CC sighs.

'Two hours ago, James decided that he had something more important to do than attend Kenneth's funeral. But that's how he functions. I've long since given up trying to anticipate his unpredictable behaviour.'

'And where might he be now?'

'He's probably with Luke. Let's see if his motorbike is parked outside Marsden Gate.'

We pass silently through the gates of Pole Moor cemetery and turn right, back towards the church. Marsden Gate shows no sign of life. I indicate the house beyond the two caravans.

'That's the farmhouse that Barrie Collins owns ... the surly bloke that Ken laid into. My girlfriend and I bumped into him in the Waggon earlier. Did you actually get to meet him?'

The cheerier scenery has lightened CC's mood.

'He was being held back by Darren at the time. So no, we were never formally introduced. But it appears that I am about to be offered a second opportunity.'

Darren and Barrie are perched on the steps of the main entrance to Outlane Methodist Church. Ties loosened, puffing on cigarettes and touching shoulders, they appear totally at ease with each other. Barrie's masculine and craggy features, accentuated by the gash on his nose, are in stark contrast to the younger and prettier Darren with his flowing brown locks.

Darren springs to his feet and shakes CC's hand. Barrie remains seated and sullen. He mumbles under his breath.

'Off to revisit the scene of the crime, are we?'

'I have no intention of making light of the tragedy. I'm Lee Chun Chow.'

'Yes, I know who you are. I was referring to GBH actually.' Barrie indicates his wound. 'It's lucky for Ken you came in when you did or I would have brained him.'

Darren, adopting the role of sidekick, grins at Barrie.

'Yes, I guess it was Ken's lucky day. But it's the lorry driver that *I* feel sorry for.'

'They won't prosecute. Ken was boozed up. The guy in the car behind the truck didn't come off too well either.' Barrie points up at me. 'And you want to keep an eye on that lass of yours. She's running amok, lad … acting like I'd just revealed the meaning of life to her. She spouted off a load of twaddle, then … get this … informed us that she was off *to be with her James*.'

He points away to the right and stubs out his cigarette on the wall. I'm disinclined to grace Barrie with a reply after his earlier snub. Neither have I any desire to expend any more time or energy on Jax. I turn to Darren.

'I'm not that desperate to find her. Did you speak to Jade at the cemetery?'

'No, I wasn't too fussed either – managed to avoid it. She went off with her stepmum back to Wakefield. Shouldn't think she had much to say to me anyway.'

Darren then addresses CC with respectful formality.

'So, Mister Lee, where was James? I'd expected to see him at the service.'

'That had also been my hope. He decided to spend time back at the house. I think you can guess why, Mister Crane.'

Darren avoids CC's quizzical gaze.

'So, did I tell you, David? I didn't get that job. But I'm thinking of moving down anyway. I'm going to become a Londoner.'

'Yeah, sure,' grunts Barrie, as he gets to his feet. 'So are we all off to the Saxon then, or what? The wake's due to start around now. See you later perhaps.'

We cross over at the Waggon, to discover Jax, sans hat and veil, perched on the wall outside number 702. She has settled into a trance-like state of contented reflection. Perhaps her disoriented mind is replaying a ghostly playback of Ken's road accident. But Jax's angelic smile assures us that all is right in the world, and a gently flowing hand gesture bestows her blessing on us both. This all strikes me as even more alarming than her behaviour in church.

'Where's James?' I ask for the second time today.

'Gone, gone, gone! They've all gone. James and baby Jesus were carried off in the Viking's chariot. I've made a sketch. Shall I show you, David?'

She looks up at CC with a sudden expression of awe.

'Oh, are you the master? Should I bow?'

'No, please don't get up. My name is Lee Chun Chow. James calls me CC.'

'I'm Jacqueline Stewart. David calls me Jax, don't you, sweetheart!'

I face her from a respectable distance.

PART 3: ARROWS

'Jax, did they say they where they were going? Was it to the Saxon?'

'Ha ha. Yes, the Viking has set off to vanquish the Saxons. But I don't need to join them, because now I carry everything inside me. Oh yes! I have James Kelly inside of me. Our bodies and souls are one. I've finally had tantric sex with a ninja. James Kelly *is* a ninja isn't he, CC! We made love on his squeaky old rocking chair next to the boy-child. Then he showed it to me. *You* know what he showed me, don't you CC? And then he demonstrated how he did it.'

'How he did what, Jacqueline?'

'How he killed his Uncle Ken.'

CC is passive, showing no emotion.

'And what, exactly, did he show you?'

'You know, oh master: his wooden pipe – he kept repeating its name. James found it funny that I couldn't pronounce it. I made him stop laughing at me and got him to write the word down under my sketch. Can you speak Japanese, Master CC? Look, here's the word. How do you say it?'

CC glances at the sketchpad and then stares angrily at the ground.

'It's pronounced foo – kee – yah. But this really is a lot of nonsense.'

I examine the word on the sketchpad and turn to CC.

'What is this? What's a fukiya?'

But Chun Chow is already walking away.

9 YEARS LATER

PART 4
OVERTONES

15 October 1987 – 12 December 1987

The inquest

Both the driver of the car and a pedestrian confirmed that the lorry driver had not been speeding. The post-mortem showed a high level of alcohol but no other substances were found. The Crown Prosecution decided not to press any charges against the lorry driver.

Fukiya

I discovered two meanings for the word 'Fukiya':

1) Take a train from Okayama station and in fifty minutes you will have arrived at Bitchu Takahashi. From there it is only a forty-minute bus ride to the small town of Fukiya, where you can visit the old mineshaft and factory museum.

2) The fukiya is a bamboo pipe that serves two purposes. A ninja might utilise it as a snorkel while underwater in order to remain undetected by the enemy. He might also blow into it to fire poisoned darts. The fukiya is a blowpipe.

James Kelly the murderer

Of course James Kelly is not a murderer. He did not kill Uncle Ken with a poisoned dart. There is no mystery. Ken Bell died under the wheels of a lorry. It would hardly surprise me, however, if James, just for his own amusement, had confided in Jax that he was responsible for killing Ken with a poisoned dart.

Jacqueline Stewart

I left Jacqueline Stewart sitting on the wall outside number 702. For all I know or care, her skeleton is still propped up there nine years later, her skull beaming the same beatific grin at horrified drunks as they emerge from the Waggon and Horses. I haven't heard from her from that day to this and have no wish to ever set eyes on her again.

The Zen class

Only because the preceding four years had been so uneventful, Monday, 18 April, 1983 stood out as a day containing the grand total of two pertinent events, the second triggered by the first. So-called world events, for the most part, leave me cold. It is therefore noteworthy that the bombing of the United States embassy in Beirut should have particularly moved me. I don't mean that the sixty-three deaths moved me emotionally (although it must have been terrible for the families etc.). This event gave me what I can only describe as a nudge. It moved me to wakefulness. For the first time in five years I meditated. During that meditation I recalled that the Zen class used to take place on Monday evenings. A rush of spiritual inspiration, mingled with anxiety that Jacqueline Stewart might still be there, made for a most unsettling few hours before setting off for Eccleston Square.

The arthritic woman was still hovering in the library, waiting to pounce with one of her profundities. But this time I spoke briskly and to the point, thus preventing her interrupting with some crass pseudo Zen utterance.

'Good evening. I used to attend Basil's beginner's group and now consider myself ready to join Christmas Humphreys' advanced class. I assume that it still takes place here in the library at 6.30.'

'Ah.'

'Do you have a problem with that?

'Yes, I do.'

'In that case, I'll have a word with Toby when he arrives. That is unless you have any say in the matter.'

'I'm afraid that Mister Humphreys passed away last Wednesday. There will, however be the usual beginner's meeting upstairs. I suggest that you first introduce yourself to Alan Dipper. He's in the kitchen.'

'Where's Basil?'

'Mister Sladen passed away last December.'

I decided not to stay, and have not meditated since.

The Kellys

Jacqueline Stewart's one credible and coherent utterance: that *her James* had been whisked off in Luke's sidecar, drained me of any remaining motivation to track James down. The thought of hanging around the Saxon Inn, surrounded by more strangers, in the vain hope that James might show up for Ken's wake, was enough to call off my futile pursuit. I headed straight back to London.

I heard nothing more from James and made no attempt to contact him. The one occasion that I did hear anything more from, or about, the Kellys, was five years ago, on 11 December 1982. Halfway through a particularly uproarious episode of *The Young Ones*, I received a phone call from, of all people, Brenda Kelly. She had just been on the phone to James in Matsudo to wish him a happy twenty-fifth birthday. Because he'd mentioned me, she decided to give me a ring. I didn't ask what James had said about me. In fact my contribution to this dull and faltering conversion was minimal. I certainly had little interest in her news that she was now in a fulfilling relationship with Barrie Collins. Nor did I really care that Jade had moved to Wakefield, that James was thinking of moving to Hong Kong and that Luke was still moving all over the place. After she had run out of moving people, there seemed nothing more to say, and our awkward exchange was terminated. I returned to the final section of the comedy show with increased vigour, even laughing aloud when Neil fell through the ceiling – anything to wipe all memory of the telephone conversation from my head. It had taken me four years to banish the Kellys from my every waking moment, and they clearly were not welcome back.

Super, smashing, great.

Fourteen years ago, in the summer of 1973, I had spent a dull week in Clacton-on-Sea to celebrate my twenty-sixth birthday. Desperate for stimulation, I booked myself a ticket for *The Comedians* at the Ocean Theatre on Clacton pier, even though I wasn't a fan of the TV show. Apart from when Russ Abbot, the drummer of the Black Abbots, took centre stage with a passable impression of Tommy Cooper, the first half was a pretty dreary affair. The second half, however, opened far more promisingly with Jim Bowen. I recall his act, not so much for his dry, understated delivery, but for an unforeseen event that made headlines in the *Daily Mirror* the following morning. Bowen was forced to abandon his performance due to an official in white overalls jumping on to the stage and yelling out two announcements, unfortunately in the wrong order.

'Ladies and gentlemen, I'm sorry to interrupt the show, but the pier's on fire. Please don't panic.'

It wasn't exactly the pier that was on fire, but the Steel Stella big dipper. I've never ascertained whether the screams emanating from the cars journeying above the theatre roof during Bowen's act were due to the thrill of the ride or the perception that they were about to go up in flames. The theatre was evacuated, no one was injured and I finally found some stimulation at Clacton.

Eight years later, Jim Bowen began presenting a quiz show called *Bullseye*. His inane catchphrase – 'super, smashing, great' – did not in any way encapsulate the subtleties of his live act. The show required its contestants to throw darts at an artificial board and answer questions from the category in which their dart landed. There were also guest appearances by celebrity darts players, who would throw for charity. This show, which has now been running for six years, at least demonstrates the accuracy of Kenneth Bell's prediction back in 1978: that the game was about to go big time.

All that jazz

Until last month, the piano lid had been lifted at ever decreasing intervals. Jade was right on two counts: jazz cannot be learned out of a book; playing along to records is no substitute for the real thing. And although I continue to subscribe to *Crescendo*, merely reading articles and reviews has hardly improved my musicianship.

To rectify matters, I have finally enrolled in a jazz piano evening class at Goldsmiths College. I would have preferred not to walk the corridors formerly trodden by Jacqueline Stewart, but could find no other course this side of London. The tutor was rather dismissive of my rendition of 'Big Nick', unless his comment, 'You play like Elton John,' was meant as a compliment. But subsequent to my identifying his Huddersfield accent, we have, at least, found some common ground. I have so far attended three sessions and can easily be identified as the unshaven man hunched at the back in a duffel coat taking copious notes. I have yet to humiliate myself in front of my talented classmates. If this reluctance to reveal my total lack of improvisatory skills continues, I may well have to resign myself to jazz academia and settle for talking jazz rather than playing it. In fact, I am already becoming au fait with the strange language that the jazzers use. Here are five examples:

Head – the theme

Bridge – the middle section of the head, usually consisting of eight bars

Changes – the chord progression

Fours – four bars of improvisation, usually alternating with the drummer

Comp – to accompany a soloist.

I did once post an article to *Crescendo*, vividly describing my initiation into the world of John Coltrane. I managed to convey the passion and intensity of the music, while shielding my potential readers from the anarchic intimacy of Jade Kelly's bedroom. The editor replied, suggesting that I try my hand at reviewing 'a live gig'. It's never going to happen.

Thursday, 15 October 1987

It's around 7.45 and I've just switched over to *Bullseye*. I'm stretched out on the sofa and my left arm dangles over a can of Fosters. Kevin's dart has landed in the film category and Susan has answered correctly. It's time for Jim Bowen to bring on tonight's guest celebrity darts player, who will throw for charity.

'This young man achieved great success in the mid-seventies. He retired from the game at the top of his profession and now lives in far-off shores. But he's made the trip from Hong Kong to be on tonight's show. Ladies and gentlemen, please welcome … James Kelly.'

Rather than that surge of excitement I'd experienced almost ten years ago, I now feel stark bewilderment, as this new James Kelly appears before me. Yes, his step is still ungainly and his movement lumbering. But this time there is no betrayal of fear, no hint of hesitation. He is actually *charming* this presenter with a firm handshake and broad smile. Trendily dressed in a black T-shirt and faded blue jeans, he looks healthier and more muscular than ten years ago. Backcombed hair replaces the old-fashioned parting, and a natural tan adds to his assured demeanour. Jim Bowen casts us a knowing wink, as a few young females signal their approval. James is invited to throw three sets of darts. He obliges with an effortless 180 on each set and accepts the £500 cheque for Oxfam. Jim's special guest gives a cheery wave to the audience and is gone.

I have slammed the ball of my hand into the off-button and am pacing the room in a rising fury that takes me by surprise. Of course I'm shocked by this sudden manifestation of James Kelly. I'm even feeling a little sick. But it's more the incongruous image of James as part of the human race that has thrown me into turmoil. It is as though Jim Bowen has transmitted his show into my living room for the sole purpose of ridiculing me.

'Well, look what we have here! I give you, not the James Kelly of your imagination, but the genuine article: as normal as the ordinary folk that he's waving to. Whatever were you thinking of, son?'

I experience the worst night of my life, tossing and turning in a world that is unravelling and crashing down around me. Now James is banging on my door, insisting that he is the real James. He demands that I let him in. There is one final almighty crash.

Friday, 16 October 1987

The interpretation of dreams: what do they *really* mean? They mean virtually nothing, as per usual. Still in pyjamas, I glare out of the front room window, projecting my fury onto the Clapham Road. I then slowly adjust to the rearranged landscape that can be held indirectly responsible for my dream-filled night. It seems that, just for once, the universe and I have been in synchronicity, for it has chosen to wreak havoc on my behalf. The traffic is at a total standstill, the lamppost opposite has bent over to support a fallen horse chestnut tree. Every movable object has found a new place of rest. I switch on the radio, slump into the sofa, and time each reporter from across Southern England: not one is capable of lasting sixty seconds without repeating the words destruction or devastation. Apparently, I've slept through the worst British storm since 1703.

I am briskly marching southward, towards the common, dodging the maze of debris and upended dustbins, in search of my nearest tree action. Sure enough, massive branches block the Southside road to the common. Iron railings lay alongside roof tiles and the contents of people's front gardens. Shall I be South London's very own Friedrich Nietzsche? Shall I straddle this massive log that blocks the traffic, to preach my sermon to the lost, wandering fools of Clapham?

'Can you not see how you've brought this upon yourselves? It is not God's wrath, rather the voice of blind nature. The God of chaos, with one careless flick of his hand, has demonstrated how easily you can all be crushed to no purpose. This is a timely reminder, dear commoners, that you have no purpose! But who

is now before you? Could he be the Superman, proclaiming "yes", in the face of this motiveless enemy?'

But the sighting of a newly opened café in Venn Street eclipses any urge to clamber onto a snapped tree trunk. Instead, I opt for a fry-up.

I have pushed today's *South London Press* to one side, and am perusing the breakfast menu (twelve combinations of the same items) when I hear a vaguely familiar female voice.

'You're Dave, aren't you?'

I continue to stare into the menu, despite the bare, plump, female arm covered in large moles, dangling within my peripheral vision. The sole reason that this obscene object continues to vie for my attention is that I have prior knowledge of the arm's existence. I force myself to look up.

'The name's David actually, but you won't know me. I don't know anyone this far south. Bacon, egg, baked beans and two fried slices please.'

Her thick neck swivels back towards the kitchen.

'Willy, it's Dave from the club.'

The offending female arm has been replaced by a hovering male shadow. I find myself peering into a wide-open mouth that attempts to gape even wider. The horror! After a ten-year reprieve, I am once again pinioned by a silent, deathly grin that could only emanate from one person: William Abercrombie from the chess club. He swiftly follows up with a Bruce Forsyth catchphrase.

'Nice to see you, to see you nice!'

'So you've given up the Tommy Cooper impressions, then.'

'Respect for the departed ... but what do you reckon on my Brucie then?'

'Your Brucie is totally indistinguishable from your Tommy Cooper.'

'He's on the box on Sundays now, in *Play Your Cards Right*.

"It's gonna be a good night if you play your cards right." That's his latest one.'

'Yes, very good! Did I order a tea? Not too milky.'

'Do you still go to the chess club? The other half put a stop to us going – said we had better things to do.'

'I can't imagine. So how's life with another half?'

'Couldn't run the business without her. Sharon's got a real flair for it, she has. We're about to invest in those BP shares. Sharon's got a nose for such things.'

'She thinks it's a good time for it, does she?'

Abercrombie's jaw begins its long journey downwards but stops midway. His head nods towards the front door.

'So what do you think to all this, then? I bet my TV aerial's perched on top of the bandstand in the middle of the common by now.'

'What do I think? I'd say it's a wake-up call.'

'It certainly woke *us* up. We live above the café. Well, you can imagine!' I stare back into the menu, hoping he'll dematerialise. 'Hey Dave, you know how Tommy Cooper died, don't you?'

I shake my head.

'Just like that! Do you get it?'

'This may surprise you, William – or do you prefer Willy these days?' Abercrombie shrugs. 'You may find this hard to believe, Willy, but I know of someone who was actually murdered for doing a Bruce Forsyth impression.'

'That bad, was it?'

'Fortunately, we'll never know. But the gentleman was knifed on top of a number 45 bus. The article was in this very newspaper almost ten years ago, November '77 to be precise. I was reading it on a train to Huddersfield, visiting a friend of mine. He's a darts player, who, you may be interested to hear, was the special guest on *Bullseye* last night.'

'Super – smashing – great!'

'That'll be the one. Now this friend of mine – James Kelly's his name – really *can* do impressions, not of celebrities though. No, James does, or at least used to do impressions of his friends and family.'

'Why did he do that, then?'

'Because it amused him … but you know what?' I stand up. 'Now *you* do impressions, Willy, so you should be able to offer me your expert opinion. Do you think that, on request, you could come up with an impression of yourself?'

'Why would I want to do that?'

'Never mind why. But how would you go about it?'

I sit back down, as the mole-infested arm delivers my fry-up.

'Sharon, David here wants me to do an impression of myself.'

'Why would you want to do that?'

'That was my very question.'

'I'm not asking you to do one. I'm just asking how you'd go about it.'

'Well I suppose I'd exaggerate my characteristics, like they do on *Spitting Image*. It still seems a weird thing to do.'

'But just supposing you *were* a bit weird, a bit out of the ordinary, like my friend James Kelly.'

William turns to his other half as she delivers my tea.

'David's friend was on *Bullseye* last night.'

Without any trace of Bowen's northern accent, Sharon mumbles 'smashing, great' and shambles off to the next table, as though I'd offended her.

'It's *super*, smashing, great. At least get it right, petal! Now, where were we? So if I were a bit weird like your friend …'

'Just conjure up someone you know who's a little unusual.'

'Do I have to know them personally? I don't know that many people.'

'It can be anyone. Now imagine that person is also a talented impressionist. Have you got someone yet?' Abercrombie's eyes are tight shut, his mouth wide open. He nods. 'Now, Willy, imagine that they are on TV and in front of a live audience.'

Abercrombie's face takes on the look of a grinning death mask.

'I'm there. What now?'

'Now, this strange person, who is a brilliant impersonator, wishes the audience to believe that he's not in the *least* bit strange. So he does an impression of what he would be like if he were completely normal. Can he do it?'

Abercrombie's eyes pop open. The smile fades. 'Well, no he can't. It would be difficult, what with the peeling skin and knives for fingernails.'

'You've lost me.'

'Freddy Krueger – I took Sharon to see the new one – *Dream Warriors* it's called. And just as she was going to sleep, I leaned over and whispered right into her ear ...' His knees bend and he delivers the hoarse impression into my right ear '... If you think you'll get out alive, you must be dreaming!' He shouts back to the counter. 'Do you remember me doing that, Sharon? If you think you'll get out alive, you must be dreaming!'

He takes Sharon's hostile stare to mean that she does.

Saturday, 17 October 1987

'Is that you, Brenda?'

'Brenda who?'

'Sorry! Is Mrs Kelly there?'

'Oh, that Brenda – she moved to Marsden Gate two years ago – shacked up with Barrie Collins. This is Mrs Worth. You must be one of Barrie's friends. He does my decorating every other year. Did the lounge last year in magnolia. So I won't be needing him now till next year. Shall I give you their number?'

'Yes please. I'm actually a friend of James.'

'James! Now, there's a right odd bod. Always was. He went off and joined some bunch of weirdos in Japan. But I did see him around here a little while back. He was on telly the other night, you know – that Jim Bowen quiz show.'

'Bullseye.'

'It's not really my cup of tea, that sort of thing. I prefer the documentaries, but Brenda told me he was going to be on, so I thought I'd better give it a go. Her lad hasn't changed much over the years.'

'You've known him a while, then.'

'Oh yes. He was in the same class at juniors with our Janet, not that he ever approached her. Well, he did once and she never forgot it. He was an odd one then and by all accounts he's got even worse. Totally off his trolley! Ah, here's Barrie's number. It's 376027. So have you seen James recently?'

'Apart from on Bullseye, that's the first time I've seen James in ten years. I thought he'd really changed. He seemed much calmer.'

'Probably drugged up to the eyeballs. Believe me, those people never change. They just get better at acting the part.'

'You mean pretending to be normal.'

'Funny how they turn out – I had his sister down as a right smart lass until ... But that's another story best left. Anyway, give them all my best regards.'

Sunday, 18 October 1987

'Hello, 376027.'

Male, low growl with a Huddersfield accent.

'Hello, this is David Carpenter from London. Am I speaking to Barrie Collins?'

'Not if you're trying to sell me some new fancy contraption I don't need.'

'We met a few years back. I'm an old friend of James. I saw him on *Bullseye* last Friday and wondered if he was still around.'

'That was recorded three weeks ago. He's back in Hong Kong, or Honkers, as he likes to call it. He wants *us* to move out there. Fat chance! So how do I know you, then?'

'Well, the last time we met was on the day of Ken Bell's funeral. My girlfriend and I popped into the Waggon on our way.'

'Well, I can't say I remember you, but the loopy girl with the black veil would be hard to forget. Did you marry her?'

'I never saw her again.'

'Well, you're best out of that one, son. Hang on a tick, she's running out the door. I'll give her a shout. Brenda! Someone called David, David Carpenter – says he's an old friend of James. For Christ's sake Bren, I can't talk to two people at once. Sorry, you still there? Says she'll write, and do you want to leave a message?'

'I just wanted to ask her what she thought of James' TV appearance: whether she thought he was putting on an act.'

'You mean why didn't we get a repeat of the Eamonn O'Brien farce?'

'James did seem a lot more at ease this time round.'

'He was okay because this time we all bowled up at the studios and grabbed the front row: me and Bren, Darren, Luke – not that *we've* got anything to say to each other these days. James just kept looking our way and talked to *us*. That's all it took ... made him calmer than Perry Coma. Does that answer your question?'

'Not really.'

Sunday, 25 October 1987

Dear David,

Sorry we didn't get a chance to chat when you phoned, but I was running late for my Samaritan shift. I never did finish that counselling course, but the Sams keep my hand in. Most of our callers are pretty run-of-the-mill compared to my family. I don't include Barrie of course. He's a brick, or is it a rock? As for Ken, James and Jade, lord knows how I'd have got through without 'mother's little helpers?' But those days are long gone and so are my family. One by one, they all left me, David. But it's Ken I miss the most; only Jade would understand that. He could be such a warm-hearted man when he wasn't drunk or shouting his mouth off. Even James loved him once, but that was long before you met us all and James started turning against him. I do wish James wouldn't turn against people. Once poor Ken's dreams were shattered, he became good for nothing and an easy target. But at least he went down fighting. His wife Doris only lingered on for another three years. Not that I knew her. We'd never even met. But she knew who *I* was of course. I didn't attend her funeral. It just didn't seem right. Besides, I didn't want to bump into Jade as she and I had fallen out badly. We haven't spoken in years. She still lives in Doris's house in Wakefield when her band isn't touring. Well, it was Ken's house really. He was there when he wasn't with me. At least, I assume he was. People say that Ken was cruel to James, but I won't have that. He certainly never hit him. I would have sent Ken packing if he had.

After the funeral, when I asked Chun Chow how things were going with James, he sounded disheartened: 'I'm afraid that his rather cavalier attitude has resulted in slow progress.' You know how CC talks! Well, I did warn him. We all know how easily James can shift between being difficult and impossible if things aren't going his way. A year later, CC seemed on the verge of delivering him back home. But somehow they managed to struggle along for another eighteen months before the final move.

CC's other concern was the growing number of cranks that were writing to James and even trying to track him down in Japan. This situation had come about through ... wait for it ... a James Kelly fan club! This was being run from London by a *very* worrying individual! But before we get to her, I just have to tell you about one particular 'fan' who changed the course of James' life.

In the spring of 1981, James finally got round to phoning me, the unstoppable James of old, enthusing about a Mongolian singer called Delger. This chap had been writing to James from London and was in the process of moving to Hong Kong. Apparently, Delger had got it into his head that James should learn a particular style of Mongolian throat singing – I think it's called something like 'Gloomy'. So he began posting James cassettes and written instructions, assuming that they would be of great interest. Well, it turned out that Delger was right: James declared it to be 'wondrous'. And as James never does anything by halves, he was soon insisting to CC that in order to further his studies in this Gloomy singing, he *had to* move to Hong Kong immediately. As usual, I discussed this latest turn of events with CC, who, I must say, sounded pretty relieved by these developments. It turns out that CC was already making provisional arrangements for James to move into the flat he owned on Cheung Chau Island. Because they'd stayed there on previous occasions, the bedroom was already laid out to James' specifications. CC even suggested buying a second flat opposite the one he owned, so that Delger could live nearby, if need be.

That summer, CC flew with James to Hong Kong, settled him in the flat and promised to ship over his gran's rocking chair. On CC's return to Japan, he phoned to report that he'd left James looking happier than in a long while. CC's one regret was that he wasn't able to meet Delger, who wasn't due to arrive till the following week.

In the seven years that James has been living in Hong Kong, we've only spoken at Christmas and on his birthdays, but he's always sounded cheerful. He did once hand the phone to Delger, but all I got from him was a Mongolian song that sounded more like a didgeridoo. I hear that Luke and Jade have been over there a few times but I'm never informed of anything. That's because Luke's never around (no change there) and my daughter won't speak to me. Did you know that Jade and the big man work together these days?

During our phone chat last Christmas, James suddenly declared his latest idea: Barrie and I *must* – he really does overuse that word – we *must* leave Marsden Gate and move to Hong Kong. He had it all worked out: we would live on Cheung Chau, in the flat opposite … with Delger, I suppose! And Barrie (who can't stand hot weather or Chinese food) would work for CC's company. I know it's all fantasy but I must admit to having leafed through a few travel brochures.

You must have been surprised to see James on telly the other night after what had happened the first time. Whoever could have talked him into a repeat performance? Well, now that you've heard about Delger, it's time to introduce infiltrator number two.

Although James has never mentioned the name Jacqueline Stewart, both CC and Luke have repeatedly warned me not to have anything to do with her, should she ever attempt to make contact. Do they think I'm that gullible? I'm quite aware that James has built up what you might call a cult following over the years. *I've* certainly had my share of inquirers – you, of course, being among them. So I'm the last person needing advice on how to handle difficult people. (You were never difficult, David.) Yes, I did receive a very polite letter and, no, I did not reply. It seems that this young woman, who refers to herself as Jax, sees herself as James' manager. She enclosed a very home-made looking issue of a fan magazine she'd been publishing. It's called *Divine Marksman* and is full of photos, sketches, press cuttings and even interviews. She must have even taken the trouble to visit James in Japan, because there's a sketch of them both, with James in his full Kyudo regalia. There's also a more recent photo of James in Hong Kong. A foreign gentleman is posing behind him with his hand on James' shoulder, but he doesn't look particularly Mongolian. Miss Stewart's letter informed me that she'd provisionally set up James' guest spot on *Bullseye* and, with my permission, intended chaperoning James from Hong Kong to London for the appearance. I had to laugh. As if James needed my permission to do anything! The only person he takes any notice of is Luke.

So, finally to your question: was James putting on a

persona for the TV cameras? I can agree with Barrie up to a point. Jade and Luke had already spent time with James in the dressing room. (Apparently, Jax had also been in there, but Luke, for some reason, kicked her out.) Then, the sight of us all grinning up at him from the front row must have boosted his confidence. But *that*, David, as we both know, is not the whole story, for as you rightly observed, it was still a performance. To my mind, the true answer to James' behaviour lies in this book I'm enclosing.

Now, the last time I gave someone a book, it led to all sorts of trouble. When I gave James *Zen in the Art of Archery* during that crazy time, CC was not amused. He made it very clear that I was poking my nose into a subject I knew nothing about. Well, this time round it's something I *do* know about. We studied *The Divided Self* by R. D. Laing on my counselling course. Anyway, tell me what you think.

It's hard to believe that in less than two months it will be James' thirtieth birthday. What's more, I'll be seeing him twice in one year! So when did you two last meet up? I guess it must have been December 11th, 1978. Now *there's* a date to remember: Ken's funeral *and* James' twenty-first. Some birthday! Anyway David, here is James' address: I'm sure he'd love to hear from you.

> 31a, Lung Tsai Tsuen,
> Cheung Chau, New Territories,
> Hong Kong.
> Best wishes,
> Brenda Kelly

Friday, 30 October 1987

Dear James,

I recently reread a copy of my very first letter to you. What must you have thought of me? Your correspondent can only be described as an insular and rather arrogant man who mistakenly believed himself to be elevated to a lofty and inaccessible spiritual plane. Have I changed? Buddhists say that everything changes; cynics say that nothing changes. So my answer is both yes and no. The very fact that I can claim to be less arrogant proves my ego to be very much intact, but I would hope that I have at least become less insular.

I refer to myself only to illustrate a point. It is certainly not something I enjoy. In fact, the instant I embark on this unhealthy indulgence, I feel the discomfort of bestowing such inappropriate importance on my archenemies: **self** and **personality**. I have emphasised these two words in order to suggest that personality is a false cloak of confidence under which we venture out into the outside world, thus edging further away from our true self (non-ego) and towards a false and inauthentic self (ego). Thus we contract for our own protection rather than expand towards fulfilment. (You may wish to read R. D. Laing for a fuller explanation.)

Such a man was David Carpenter, aged thirty. He weighed up the pros and cons of contraction and expansion, then charted his options.

Contraction/ expansion	Contraction perks	Expansion perks	Contraction fears	Expansion fears
Silence/ sound	People will leave me alone	Heartfelt speech to express feeling	People will ignore me	People will attack me
Inactivity/ activity	Nothing need change	Health and fitness	Illness	Physical injury
Solitude/ company	Increased spirituality	Relationship and intimacy	Withering	Suffocation by love

Though I yearned to expand, the common escape route from a cocoon was denied me. For how could I don the false cloak of personality without the requisite acting skills for such an undertaking? And if such skills go hand in hand with strong personalities, then I have never been in the running, as I possess virtually *no* personality. But may I suggest, James, that you have always worn *your* colourful personality cloak with nonchalant ease.

Putting acting aside for one moment, would you not at least admit to being something of a performer? Is this not a requirement for both darts and Kyudo? No matter how much one focuses, there has to be some awareness of one's audience, perhaps even some pleasure to be derived from being the centre of the spectacle. Your appearance on *Bullseye* may have demonstrated another of your skills in this area. I recall on one occasion just how easily you managed to convince me that you were Uncle Ken. Another incident of this nature was your uproarious Chun Chow impression, although it failed to amuse the man being impersonated. My guess is that when you are feeling mischievous, you perform these accurate impersonations solely for your own pleasure. However, when you are feeling fearful, your skill is put to use as a coping mechanism. It is on these occasions that the impersonation is no longer of others, but of yourself. When you turn into James Kelly the *personality*, your false self comes to the rescue of your real self. I am curious to know whether this concept holds any meaning for you.

The last letter I received from you was during the summer of 1978. You had just moved permanently to Matsudo and were bursting with the joys of Kyudo. Did you ever manage to master 'Naima' on the shakuhachi? What a pity that you missed your sister's beautiful rendition at Uncle Ken's service. I'm sorry to hear that Jade and your mother are not on speaking terms. What became of Jade? I can hardly imagine her as a mature woman.

I counselled you to keep a respectable distance from any deluded souls within the Kyudo fraternity believing themselves to be spiritually superior and am delighted to learn that you have since moved on. Pray tell what you have moved on *to*! Your mother informs me that a gentleman from Mongolia has been involved. How intriguing.

I replied to your first letter of that year, enclosing a sketch drawn by the selfsame person who is now, I am informed, the editor (perhaps too grand a word?) of a fanzine entitled *Divine Marksman*. And you, James, are that marksman. But what else is Jax up to? Beware!

During my brief but intense liaison with Jacqueline Stewart, I found her to be self-seeking and unpredictable. I learned to my cost that such an unsavoury combination is not the ideal recipe for a fulfilling personal relationship. However, in a business partnership it could prove fatal. In hindsight, I feel that she used me in order to reach you. I have little doubt that she will now use *you* to gratify her own selfish needs. Due to my unwitting part in bringing together this unhealthy liaison, I now feel some obligation to offer you the above assessment, in the hope that you will tread very carefully.

When Chun Chow requested my help to save Uncle Ken, you may recall my reluctance. I continue to feel that my non-intervention was justified, even though he was dead before the year was out. I had very much hoped to see you on the day of his funeral, or at least to wish you a happy birthday. But you were nowhere to be seen. This is not in any way a criticism, but I had at least expected to see you in church.

Please do not feel obliged to reply to this letter. I suspect that I am just a faded memory in your eventful life. But if you do find time to write me a brief note, it would be good to hear from you.

With fond regards,
David Carpenter

Wednesday, 11 November 1987

I have just received this letter from James. True to form, it can only be described as a reply in the sense that it postdates my letter to him.

Dear Carpenter,

In thirty days' time I will be thirty years old and you will be here in Hong Kong with us all to celebrate my birthday. You must attend my party on Friday, 11 December.

You're going to love Honkers so much that you will immediately want to live here with me on Cheung Chau. I have already told Mum and Barrie that they are to move out of Marsden Gate to live in the flat opposite. They will be our neighbours!

So who will be here with me? Everyone is coming: Jade, who has agreed to make it up with Mum, and CC, who has agreed to make it up with me. Then there's the big man, who will *never* make it up with Barrie, and even Darren, who has agreed to make it up with Jade.

Ten years ago, I enthused to my sister about Sid Furney's wondrous piano playing. Well, Sid's coming too! He will be guesting in Jade's band for her gigs over here. There may also be one or two surprise guests. But I cannot promise that Delger will make an appearance.

I KNOW YOU WILL COME because of the four questions that you wish to ask me.

I KNOW YOU WILL COME so that we can finally

sit facing each other in the same room, just as we have always wanted.

I KNOW YOU WILL COME because CC has already made your arrangements.

Now I want to tell you about overtones.

Although Heinrich Hertz did not invent the hertz, it is named after him. One hertz equals a single unit of vibration that lasts for one second.

Sound is vibration. There can be no sound until we vibrate something in the air. Vibrate an object fast enough and it will produce a fixed pitch. Vibrate an object at 65.406 hertz and you will hear a very low C, two octaves below middle C. This is impossibly low for me to sing, but Delger can produce the note with ease.

But there is no such thing as just one note. Yes, Carpenter, it's true! You may *think* you are hearing just the one, but there is a whole rainbow of them, all softly ringing out above the note that you are hearing. This lowest note is known as the fundamental, or first harmonic, and the rainbow of higher notes blend together perfectly because of their precise relationship to the fundamental. Each note that rings within this rainbow hanging above the fundamental is called an overtone, and each overtone has its allotted place.

But how can this happen? When we pluck a string, it vibrates along the whole of its length and produces the fundamental pitch. But it also vibrates in halves, thirds and quarters, etc., etc., to produce notes that get higher and higher.

Taking that low C as our fundamental, let's continue up to the 6th overtone.

Not only is it possible to sound an overtone at the same time as its fundamental; the overtone can also be coaxed to stand apart from its parent, as though it possesses a life of its own! I used to listen to Jade producing overtones on her soprano. But Delger can actually sing them, just by shaping his tongue and mouth in a certain way.

Now that Delger has taught me to sing overtones, you must also start learning the technique as soon as possible. Then, by the time of your visit, you will be sufficiently competent to join in with us at the performance! It is essential that you choose to study Mongolian khoomii singing rather than Tibetan overtone chanting, which is not singing at all. You must also gain some understanding of tagnain before attempting shahaltai, in order to acquire the basic technique for producing harmonics.

Although I love to hear Delger sing up to the fifth overtone, this first series of notes still remains within the bounds of basic harmony. But the sixth overtone is something else: it is a flat seventh blues note. It is heaven. It is the bull's eye!

CC will soon contact you with information as to where you can learn to voice your own overtones.

With love,

James

PS. Jade needs to know whether you still remember how to play 'Big Nick'.

PART 4: OVERTONES

NOTE	OVERTONE	HZ	RATIO	DESCRIPTION
C1		65.406	1/1	Fundamental
C2	1st	130.81	2/1	Octave
G1	2nd	196	3/1	Perfect 5th
C3	3rd	261.63	4/1	Octave
E1	4th	329.63	5/4	Major 3rd
G2	5th	392	6/5	Perfect 5th
Bb	6th	466.16	7/4	Flat 7th

Friday, 13 November 1987

Who does he think he is? How dare he still presume to tell me what I must do and where I must go? You *will* be in Hong Kong, indeed! We haven't spoken for nearly ten years, and with a click of his fingers, he expects me to fly across the world for a meeting that, no doubt, he will not attend. And even if he does, he'll have no interest in anything I have to say. That is clear from his 'reply' to my letter.

James is learning to sing two notes at once. So naturally, I am expected to follow suit. At least darts and Kyudo had a target. Jade did warn me from the start that her brother was bonkers. And whyever should Jade care if I can still remember how to play 'Big Nick'? Admittedly, I have recently learned to recognise the difference between a flat nine and a sharp eleven, but in practical terms I doubt that I could now even bluff my way through 'Midnight in Moscow'.

Chun Chow phoned me this morning. His manner was cold and unfriendly, not that we had ever developed any close bond. But he might have at least enquired how I have fared over the years. Perhaps he's saving the pleasantries. I am to meet him for tea, tomorrow afternoon in Fortnum and Mason. I hope he's paying.

Unusually for me, I have spent the last two evenings out, purely as a means of distraction from recent events. Yesterday, I attended the Alan Glazier darts night at The Dorset Arms in Clapham road. This is the second time I've witnessed Alan Glazier in action, although had things turned out differently, it would have been the third. The first occasion was on 14 January 1978 at the Mayfair Hotel, where he beat Ron Etherington 2–0. The second would have been twenty-three days later, in the first round of the Embassy. But by the time that he had lost 6–4 to Alan Evans, I was halfway back to London. Last night he easily put paid to all but one challenger.

This evening I took myself off to the Lewisham theatre for 'a wrestling bonanza, featuring the sensational wrestling midgets'. The one sensational moment of the evening was provided, not by a midget, but by Steve Logan, as he elbowed his arch-enemy Indestructible Skull Murphy between the eyes, knocking him senseless. As all Buddhists know, no one, not even Skull Murphy, is indestructible. Today's supposedly unlucky date, Friday, 13th, should not be held responsible for this ignominious defeat. Rather, the law of karma would indicate that Skull had it coming.

Saturday, 14 November 1987

Victoria line from Stockwell to Green Park, turn left along Piccadilly, cross over to the Ritz, and Fortnum and Mason is on the corner of Duke Street St James', opposite the Royal Academy.

Chun Chow has aged. He is thin and pale, possibly ill. We sit at a table for two, by the rear bay window, consuming toasted muffins and house breakfast tea. My inquiry after his health produces a philosophical shrug. His voice is uncharacteristically flat.

'You're to go to Stukeley Community Centre on Sunday week – that's the 22nd. The workshop commences at 10.30. Wear comfortable clothing. Here are the details and receipt. I have paid in advance.'

'I'm to go, am I?'

'Yes, you are, bearing in mind that this is all nonsense, the usual James Kelly nonsense. The nearest tube is Holborn. Stukeley Street runs parallel to High Holborn.'

'So why should I go if it's all nonsense?'

'For the same reason that you chose to watch darts matches and attend Kyudo workshops.'

Rather than feeling insulted, I experience a brief moment of kinship.

'Is Hong Kong James' permanent home now?'

'I presume that he still abides in my old flat on Cheung Chau and that Delger lives in the ground-floor flat opposite. His latest demand is that Brenda and Barrie move to the island. I'm expected to find Barrie a job. There is only so much one can do.' The curt tone masks sadness and resignation.

'You've already been very generous.'

'I gave Mrs Kelly my word that I'd do everything in my power to ensure that her son was looked after. When my father died in 1981, I took over his Hong Kong company. However, I chose to run it from a distance, as there was no further need to be there. Nor did I wish to see James again. I have not returned since.'

'You haven't stayed in contact with James?'

'I gifted him both the flats in the summer of 1981 and that's the last I heard from him. It was Jacqueline Stewart that asked me to contact you. She sees herself as James' manager these days. But what there is to manage is unclear.'

'Have you seen her since the day of the funeral?'

'She came over to Japan once and I was not impressed. She was suggesting ways to raise James' profile … as though I'd be interested in such foolishness.'

CC is clearly wilting. I slightly raise my voice.

'Was James interested?'

'He most certainly was. James was always enamoured with the idea of fame … ironic, as he also hated people staring at him. And naturally, he enjoys the attention of such an attractive young woman. But I see her only as an opportunist.'

'Exactly! Well, I've warned James. And Brenda tells me that Luke's of a similar persuasion.'

'Luke is fiercely protective of James' interests. He and Miss Stewart have crossed swords more than once. I have always had the utmost respect for Luke, but he is not someone I'd choose as an adversary. "The big man" is the one person that James heeds, and I hear that Luke has already begun to bring his influence to bear.'

'What about Delger? He must have some influence on James.'

His voice becomes brittle.

'I don't know the man. I never met him.'

CC clearly wishes to change the subject so I switch tack.

'Did you see James on TV last month?'

'I did not.'

CC is now visibly flagging. He stares vacantly out of the window as I maintain the conversation out of politeness.

'Are you still practising Kyudo?'

'Yes, I have always believed in commitment.' He looks round at me, at first tiredly, and then with the first trace of a smile. 'I was making an indirect reference to James' lack of commitment, not yours. I have no idea whether you have any particular commitment to anything. I know absolutely nothing about you.'

'What would you like to know, Mister Lee?'

With a barely perceptible shake of his head, he reaches into the inside pocket of his jacket.

'You fly out of Heathrow on Wednesday, 9th at 12.30 p.m. with Cathay Pacific and arrive on Thursday 10th at around 3 p.m., Hong Kong time. This envelope contains an open return ticket plus your hotel reservation at the Mandarin Oriental for the first three nights. I've been informed that you're welcome to stay with James, should you wish to extend your visit. I assume you'll be going. Or do you have other commitments? '

I ignore the hint of sarcasm.

'Why are you paying out all this money for me?'

'I believe you can answer that question for yourself. I'm not doing it for you. I'm doing it, as ever, for James. I am paying out more money because James has asked me, albeit indirectly, to do so. You and I have always shared the same weakness for acting on James' every whim.'

Our eyes acknowledge this strong and irrational connection.

'James tells me that you'll be there for his birthday.'

His back straightens.

'He knows full well that I have no intention of being there.'

'You seem angry with him.'

CC leans back into his chair.

'Over the years, my anger has faded into disappointment, even disillusionment. James Kelly is not the person I had taken him to be. But that is my failing, not his.'

'Is it your failing that James gave up Kyudo?'

'No, Mister Carpenter, I had long given up on him by then. It was fortuitous, and in retrospect, inevitable that he would eventually latch on to something or somebody new. I'll get the bill.'

'There's something you're not telling me. James did something, didn't he?'

'Yes, James *did* something, but he can speak for himself. Go to Hong Kong, David. It will be worth your while. I have it on the best authority that, finally, James *will* speak for himself. And Jade wishes to know whether you still remember how to play ...' He extracts a slip of paper from his shirt pocket. 'A tune called "Big Nick".'

Sunday, 22 November 1987

Despite the continuing tube disruptions caused by Wednesday's fire at Kings Cross, I arrived at the Stukeley Community Centre on time and have joined the circle of participants. A thin, wiry man seated to my right introduces himself to me as Dominic. He is our workshop leader. Directly opposite, a short, squat, shaven-headed man sits on his chair but with both legs tucked up in the lotus position. With eyes half-closed, his lips move silently under a Hitler moustache. He has caught my attention, not due to his pretentious pose, but because I am convinced that I know him. This seems most unlikely. I know few enough people even with full heads of hair, and would certainly steer clear of anybody that made such an exhibition of themself. I mentally file through the men that I encountered at the Buddhist Society: Toby and Basil are dead, and this is certainly not Jacqueline Stewart's pretentious boyfriend.

This distraction has caused me to miss Dominic's introduction, but I now catch him breaking the ghastly news that we are to introduce ourselves to the person to our left. In my case, this happens to be a large and singularly unattractive middle-aged lady in a black leotard. I introduce myself to her right ear, so subverting her blatant attempt to blot out my existence by burying herself in a handout.

'Hello, my name is David. I'm a Zen Buddhist.'

Her name is Margaret and she declares herself to be an amateur opera singer. This, I can imagine. Because she has declined to inquire into the life of a Zen Buddhist, and I have reciprocated by choosing not to investigate which particular aria she is currently crucifying at her local operatic society, our conversation peters out just as others are becoming more animated. She returns to her handout, and I straighten my spine and close my eyes until further notice.

Dominic gently brings the room to order.

'Please say your name and state briefly what brought you here today.'

He turns to me and suggests that we 'go round clockwise, like the Buddhists do.'

I aim a knowing half-nod at Margaret, before offering my details to the moustache of the shaven-headed man opposite.

'My name is David and I have arrived here via darts and Kyudo.'

My eyes flutter to a close, thus signifying that I would prefer not to be questioned on these matters. After a respectful fifteen-second silence, Margaret expresses her concerns that Mongolian throat singing might injure her singer's throat. It is soon the turn of the man still precariously perched on his chair in lotus position.

'Hello, the name's Max. Yeah, I chant. I do lots of chanting. So I'm hoping that this will help my chanting.'

I turn towards our leader and raise my hand.

'Dominic, with great respect to our friend, am I correct in thinking that it's actually the *Tibetan* Buddhists that chant and the Mongolians that sing tunes?'

Dominic moves the open palm of his left hand to within a few inches of my face.

'Perhaps we'll have time to discuss those differences after lunch. I'm sure that our work today will help you with your chanting, Max.'

Max nods in appreciation and then glances quizzically in my direction.

Each person has now spoken. The room is full of self-styled shamans and healers. This is apart from Carmen: a tiny, gorgeous Asian girl with a schoolgirl fringe, who claims to be a drummer. Dominic has explained the harmonic series and also enlightened us with the irrelevant and improbable information that the planets Pluto and Neptune would collide but for the fact that their harmonic ratio is three to two.

The ancient Tibetan greeting of sticking out one's tongue has gone down very well, with loud hoots of laughter from Margaret, obviously delighting in such unseemly behaviour. Dominic is now taking us through the day's agenda.

'Today will be split into two sections: this morning you will learn tagnain khoomii, and after lunch I'll be demonstrating shahaltai. Tagnain, also known as palatal, is a technique for producing overtones, and shahaltai is the Mongolian guttural sound that is added to these overtones.'

I scribble down the instructions for tagnain as we try out the sounds.

1) Shape your tongue like a spoon.
2) Place the tongue tip on the hard palette.
3) Form the shape: 'oo', like a puckered kiss, but sing 'ee'.
4) Gradually change from 'oo' to 'ee', moving slowly through the following vowels:
oo ... awe ... aah ... aye ... ee.

Amid our cacophony of vowels, Dominic has become the centre of our attention. This is because an extraordinary high whistling sound, rather like a spinning top, seems to be spiralling above his head. He calls a halt to the exercise and recommends patience, assuring us that our individual overtones will emerge naturally as part of the practice, and should not be forced.

'As there are fourteen of us, I suggest we split into pairs. So find yourself a partner, and take turns listening to each other sounding the vowels.'

I make my way towards the shaven-headed man with the Hitler moustache, but he has already commandeered

Carmen. Everybody has moved away from Margaret and I am stranded.

Margaret and I sit facing each other. She is explaining why this upper tongue position is most unnatural for a trained classical singer.

'I have always been taught to keep one's tongue at the base of the mouth to prevent throat constriction.'

Margaret lets rip a couple of high-pitched warbles to demonstrate her classical technique.

'I think you'll find, Margaret, that Mongolian throat singing actually requires a constriction of the throat.'

'Well I'm not prepared to take that risk. We have a concert on Tuesday. Why don't you have a go, and I'll listen.'

'Okay. Here goes: oo … awe … aah … aye … ee.'

'Extraordinary! Let me have another listen. Yes, there it is. Can't you hear? You're actually doing it! You obviously have a natural gift for shouty.'

I disguise the pleasurable feeling of my newly acquired skill with a correction of her pronunciation.

'We'll be learning shahaltai after lunch;. This is tagnain. So I'm doing it, am I?'

'I'd say you've mastered it. Dominic, could we borrow you for a moment? We have an early success.'

Dominic apologises to the couple he is working with, and arrives for my encore.

'Yes David, you have the beginnings of tagnain, but try to relax your jaw. Now, maintain the pursed lip position. Can you hear the overtones?'

'Not really. I can just feel my head vibrating and I'm starting to feel sick.'

'Well, why don't you have a rest and listen to Margaret for a while.'

Margaret clutches her throat.

'I'm a little concerned for my voice actually. We have a

concert on Tuesday. I'd rather hear more from our Zen Buddhist friend. It's rather relaxing actually. I might even fall asleep.'

Everyone but me brought a packed lunch. Having abandoned a fruitless search for a café in an area geared up for weekday office workers, I have, perhaps unwisely, ended up in a pub. I order a pint.

I've finished my Stilton ploughman's, and just as I'm setting about my second pint of *London Pride* to the soothing accompaniment of my very own tagnain khoomii, I spot the shaven-headed man with a Hitler moustache heading towards my table. He sets down his pint, and as we shake hands I read the word *love* tattooed on his knuckles.

'It's Max, isn't it? I'm David. Sorry if I was staring earlier, but I'm sure we've met.'

'You mentioned darts. That'll be the connection. I used to play for Lambeth in the Super League, but that's going back a few years. Perhaps we bumped into each other on the circuit, although I'd be surprised if you recognise me from back then. I was a bit of a teddy boy ... totally messed up, out of control, like ... on the hard stuff. It got so bad I had to take drastic action. I ditched all my bad habits and totally turned things around. I don't usually drink any more but some of those people at the workshop are jangling my nerves.'

'Now I remember where we met! I can even remember the word tattooed on your other hand.'

Max scratches his nose: H ... A ... T ... E.

'That's the only bit of me I never changed. I got the idea from Robert Mitchum in *The Night of the Hunter*. So where exactly did we meet?'

I slug down half of the pint to quell my rising panic. 'I've not seen it, but Meatloaf had the same tattoo in *The Rocky Horror Picture Show*. We met in Clapham actually ... in Fern

Lodge Social Club. Well, we didn't exactly meet, not in the sense of sitting down and having a chat, like we're doing now. I was writing an article for *Darts World* at the time. I'd been drinking then, just like I am now. And the funny thing is that I hardly ever drink when I'm out … not that I'm out much. Well Max, I'd say it's time to rejoin the troops. "Back on your head", as the joke goes. That's the punch line. Do you know the rest of it? I don't usually remember jokes, but this one's rather amusing. This bloke goes to hell. Remind me to tell you in the tea break.'

'I know the joke.'

Max gives his nose a second scratch.

'Welcome back to our little circle! We'll soon be working on our feet, so let's hope you haven't eaten too much, or are on the verge of an afternoon snooze. Well, it looks like we're all assembled, apart from Margaret. So, now it's time to discover our shahaltai voice: the hallmark of Mongolian throat singing. In order to produce this guttural sound without damaging your vocal cords, ensure that both your chest and throat are open. For those of you already familiar with the practice of supporting the voice in Western singing, I must emphasise that it is of even greater importance here. With shahaltai, we are placing the sound far back in the mouth and then constricting it. Let's begin with a normal 'ee' and then move the sound back. You should immediately notice the tongue moving upwards.'

Although I'm making the sound, I have no understanding of *why* I'm making it. This is due to two major distractions that have averted my attention from Dominic's introduction. In reverse order of importance, the dark brown eyes of the pretty Asian girl have been flashing in my direction since we arrived back. I swear that she even smiled at me once. Whether she is the cause of my increased heart rate is unclear, due to distraction number two: Max is now sitting bolt upright with both feet planted firmly into the floor. He also appears to be muttering as he stares unblinkingly at me. I can only surmise that Carmen has taken an interest in the situation and is observing me for this reason alone.

'So, this time, choose a partner you haven't worked with, perhaps someone you haven't yet spoken to. Then sing through the five vowel sounds we practised earlier. As we're down to thirteen, I'll partner the odd one out, so to speak.'

Before I've had time to rise from my chair, Max has arrived in front of me, just ahead of Carmen. I stand tall, in a simultaneous effort to impress Carmen and to maximise my six inches height advantage over Max. I then address him in an assertive tone that I hardly recognise.

'Dominic has just suggested that we should work with a new partner.'

'And I'd suggest we've some unfinished business.'

In an efficient physical manoeuvre belying her tiny frame, Carmen steps in, grabs my hand and pulls me into a corner. She then sets up two chairs and eases me into one of them. With eyes clenched shut I launch into the exercise.

'Oo … awe … aah. Margaret said she could hear something. What do you think? Oo … awe … aah.'

'It's okay David, Max has been partnered by Dominic.'

I open my eyes.

'So why have you and Max been staring at me since we returned? Do you two know each other?'

'It's not unusual to bump into the same people at these events. It's a small world. But no, I don't know Max.'

'Well it's certainly not *my* world. I never go to these events. In fact, I don't really know why I'm here today.'

'Oh, I think you do.'

'What's that supposed to mean? Were you and Max discussing me when you two paired up this morning?'

'No, but he *was* acting a little oddly.'

'Oddly? I'd say he's nearer psychotic. The last time we met, he had Brian Ferry hair and winkle-picker shoes. I said something he took the wrong way and he's obviously been harbouring it for ten years. I think he wants to murder me.'

Carmen smiles as though she's my carer.

'I've heard how dramatic you can be, David.'

'Oh please don't do this. Don't act as though you know me. I don't know you. In truth, I don't know more than about six people.'

'You're raising your voice a little. No, we haven't met. My name's Carmen. I'm pleased to meet you.'

Her hand is warm. This is our second physical contact.

'Yes, I remember your name from the introductions. You also said that you're a drummer. Aren't you a bit short for a drummer? Are your arms long enough?'

Carmen's brown eyes twinkle.

'I play in a jazz band called Crescent.'

'When you say jazz, are you referring to traditional, bebop, post-bebop or cool?'

'We just play music by John Coltrane.'

'I see. So that would cover more than one genre.'

'I suppose it would. You seem very knowledgeable, David.'

'Oh, it's just a hobby really. I read *Crescendo* and attend jazz piano evening classes. The one thing that holds me back is that I can't actually play. Are you professional?'
'Yes, I'm returning to Hong Kong next week for a short tour.'

'That's a coincidence: I'm off to Hong Kong myself in a couple of weeks.'

'It's no coincidence, David.'

Carmen closes her eyes and sounds the vowels as though she's been transported to the foothills of Mongolia.

'Well done everybody. Give yourselves a clap! Let's take a well-deserved tea break and reassemble at four. In the final hour, we'll take a brief look at dandilakh. This is a technique that utilises the locked 'L' in front of each vowel to achieve tongue flexibility. As Max has had to leave early, we're now back to even numbers, so you'll all be able to pair up again. I suggest that you finish the day in the same pairs.'

Carmen and I drink tea and chat in the kitchen. For once, my hand isn't shaking. She is certainly a more calming influence than Jax was.

'So, do you know Lee Chun Chow? He set this workshop up for me.'

'No, David ... I set it up for you.'

'But he asked you to.'

'No, Jade Kelly asked me to. Do you remember Jade?'

I picture flailing silk scarves and an ostrich feather.

'Jade is hard to forget. But I thought it was her brother that had wanted me to come here.'

'I've never met James, but I'm so looking forward to meeting him.'

A jealous impulse causes me to steer the conversation back to Jade. 'How come you know James' sister?'

'We met in 1979, on the jazz course at Leeds College. I'm a year older than Jade, so she must have been eighteen when I first heard her play. I'd never heard anything like it. She was into stuff none of us was listening to. But, of course, by *that* time, you'd had a private performance in her bedroom. It really made me laugh when she told me about it.'

I feel betrayed.

'Well it didn't make *me* laugh. It's still a very special memory, actually.'

'Jade didn't do it to make fun of you. She actually thinks of it as her first-ever gig. You must have been an inspiring audience.'

'Yes, I did find it inspiring. There was certainly nothing comical about it.'

'I'm sorry. It only made me laugh because she was so serious when describing it.' She lets out a brief, rather masculine chuckle and I smile back at the row of tiny white teeth. 'It's just the image of you covered in scarves. Anyway, we stayed in touch after college and I joined her band Crescent in June '85. Then, last year, James' dad came on board.'

'James' dad?'

'Oh, he's an amazing player. Anyway, the plan is to link up with Sid Furney in Hong Kong. He's an Australian piano player I met when I was last over there.'

'James mentioned Sid Furney in his last letter.'

'Yes, they're old friends. James wrote to Jade about Sid years ago. Apparently, he and Sid used to jam together at the Old China Hand. Piano and shakuhachi: what a wild combination! We're hoping to talk them into a reunion on the 11th.'

'James' birthday.'

'As it turns out, Crescent are playing a residency at the Fringe Club that week, so it will make a great party venue. Then we've one final gig at city hall on Saturday. We're just support, but it's a prestigious gig. Oh, and Jade has asked me to ask you if you still remember how to play ...'

'Yes, I know the question. You're the third person to ask, and the answer is: no, I don't know how to play "Big Nick".'

'Well, I'll see you at the Fringe Club, David.'

I'm the last to leave. Max is waiting for me outside.

'I am not a cheat. No one ever accused me of cheating till you came along.'

I take a step back.

'I wasn't accusing you. I was merely enquiring whether matches were still being played at a distance of seven foot six inches. A new rule was about to come into place and ...'

'I'd just lost ... been thoroughly pounded by Tony ... *Tony*, of all people! Then you had the fucking nerve ... I still had another match to play that night. We lost because of you. We lost, *and* we were relegated because of *me*. No, we were relegated because of *you*. Okay, choose. Which hand? Love or hate?'

'Love please.'

Love and hate

Perhaps I should have chosen hate, for there was no love in Max's love-hand as it sunk into my solar plexus. Although I now know the true meaning of being winded, I am at least thankful that he stopped there, rather than follow through with his hate-hand. This would have surely given me my first experience of a broken nose. Being winded is a shocking, rather than upsetting experience. The perpetrator, however, was clearly upset by his deed. I recall him apologising and possibly even crying. But I was too doubled up in pain to be certain.

The love life of David Carpenter

Almost ten years ago, an outrageous, ginger-haired, green-eyed teenager performed a strange and wonderful ritual for me in her bedroom. Later that day, her mother told me that I had a nice face and then kissed me on the mouth. The kiss lasted around two seconds.

Six months later, a Welsh punk with Jimi Hendrix hair and a nose ring invited me for a drink, asked me to take her to Yorkshire and left me at a church.

And now, after nine and a half years of abstinence, I have fallen for a five feet nothing Asian drummer with a schoolgirl fringe who, by no coincidence, is an old friend of the aforementioned ginger-haired female. I have not been so immature as to interpret Carmen's parting words to me: 'Well, I'll see you at the Fringe Club, then,' as code for 'David, I've fallen in love with you.' I have, however, added our brief moment to my growing list of incentives for travelling to Hong Kong.

PART 4: OVERTONES

Monday, 23 November 1987

Dear James,

Well, it seems that in sixteen days' time I will be flying to Hong Kong, courtesy of Lee Chun Chow. Bearing in mind that I've never travelled further than Huddersfield, it does seem a rather long trek in the hope of meeting up with someone who, if they run true to form, will either fail to show up, or make a swift exit through a side door. But lessons have been learned. As I no longer hold any expectation, I intend treating this trip as pure indulgence, irrespective of whether you finally decide to make an appearance.

By my standards, the last few days have been eventful, culminating in my being punched by an ex darts player for something he thought I'd said ten years ago. We crossed paths at yesterday's overtones workshop, where I also met Jade's friend, Carmen. She informed me that it was actually *Jade's* idea, not yours, that I should attend the workshop. This is one of many issues with which I intend to confront you, if, during my visit, you deign to be available for confrontation.

Carmen also tells me that Crescent is performing at your party. I am most intrigued by their line-up: Jade, Carmen, Sid Furney and … your father!

Your ex (?) sponsor has booked me into the Mandarin Oriental, which sounds like a Chinese brothel. It's most unlikely that CC will be making an appearance. He made it clear to me that he has no wish to see you. In fact, his attitude was very frosty towards you, and not particularly friendly to me either.

I'll be arriving early afternoon on Thursday, 10th, so perhaps you can phone me at the hotel, or at least leave a message with the address of the Fringe Club. If I hear nothing from you on my arrival and am not feeling too jetlagged, I may even venture out to Cheung Chau on the Friday morning to personally wish you a happy thirtieth. I am certainly looking forward to meeting Delger, who, I'm sure, will offer an informed and unbiased opinion on my initial efforts at tagnain khoomii. At the workshop, an amateur opera singer assured me that I was producing my very own overtones. I remain to be convinced.

Hoping to see you soon,
David

PS. Your reply to my last letter made no reference to my severe misgivings with regard to Jacqueline Stewart. A further warning bell was sounded by CC during our recent meeting. He regards Miss Stewart as an opportunist. I trust that this rising tide of unease will provoke an appropriate response.

Wednesday, 9 December 1987

Turned right outside the flat, crossed the road, took the Victoria line from Stockwell to Green Park, changed to the Piccadilly line for Heathrow, boarded the 747, hung around for two hours at Bahrain airport while Arab men gawped at Western women, adjusted my watch from 11 p.m. Wednesday to 2 a.m. Thursday, and belted in for the eight remaining hours. Thank heaven CC booked me into *Marco Polo*, and not economy class.

Thursday, 10 December 1987

4.45 p.m. Hong Kong time The plane managed to land safely at Kai Tak Airport without become entangled in washing lines. Finally, after journeying through teeming Kowloon and crossing a flyover that offered intimate views into people's front windows, the A1 airbus has arrived outside the Mandarin Oriental. The forty-minute bus journey has filled me with anxiety. There are clearly too many people here, and frankly, I wasn't expecting to see so few white faces. In ten years' time our lease on this colony is due to expire, and on first impression it is quite beyond me why we would have wanted it in the first place.

6.15 p.m. The Mandarin Oriental is most certainly not a Chinese brothel, and I now regret having not changed into a suit and tie. My spacious en-suite accommodation includes a balcony that overlooks the harbour, thus affording a view infinitely preferable to one that might have featured ten thousand Chinese people darting in and out of winding alleyways.

8.30 p.m After fifteen minutes of air-conditioned bliss, I succumbed to jetlag by nodding off for two hours and now fear that my ill-timed siesta will lead to a sleepless night. There's been no message or phone call.

10.20 p.m. Around an hour ago, I was wandering the streets of Wan Chai, when a neon sign, with its promise of gyrating Filipina go-go dancers, lured me through the doors of the Popeye Bar. This unsavoury establishment is in Lockhart Road, just a few doors up from the Old China Hand, where I am now counting out the remains of my money. This is the English-style pub that Sid Furney and other members of the newly formed

Hong Kong Darts Organisation had been planning to visit after their mythical inauguration celebration.

After my third bottle of Tsing Tao, I ask the Australian barman whether Sid still plays piano or darts in the lounge bar. He replies that Sid still frequents the pub but, alas, the piano and dartboard are long gone.

I am now in a Sichuan-style restaurant called the Sze Chuen Lau, also in Lockhart Road. The pomfret in chilli sauce was rather overlaced with chilli for my conservative palate. Only now, as I crunch into my toffee-apple desert, and down a pint of ice-cold water, do I read the warning in my guidebook with regard to the spiciness of Sichuan food. I'm feeling extremely queasy, and hope not to suffer any ill effects from my first authentic Chinese culinary experience. I hail a cab.

Friday, 11 December 1987

'I'm sorry to disturb you sir, but this letter has just been delivered at reception. The lady has requested that you read it as soon as possible.'

'What lady? Was she Chinese?'

'No, sir.'

'What's the time?'

'It's 9.30. Breakfast is still being served on the first floor until 10.30. Or perhaps you would prefer room service.'

'Do you serve English food, like toast? I'm not feeling very well.'

In fact I'm feeling extremely unwell. I awoke at 5 o'clock in a sweat, with bellyache and a hangover. The envelope contains a small sketch of James playing his shakuhachi. A pair of quavers dance above his head, and under the sketch is a scribbled note.

> *Trail of the divine marksman.*
> *First stop: Peak tram ticket office.*
> *Be there 11.30.*

The note is unsigned. But I have no doubt as to its author, or of her renewed intentions to aggravate me. In his letter, James had alluded to surprise guests. The prospect of meeting Jacqueline Stewart, in whatever her latest bizarre guise might be, is a surprise I can do without.

Two slices of thickly buttered toast barely compensate for the milkiest cup of tea since Brenda Kelly's undrinkable effort on the night I slept in her son's bed. As the Peak tram is only a five-minute cab ride away, I opt for a walking route that the receptionist has kindly mapped out for me. I follow the walkways through the Prince's building, behind the cathedral and down on to Garden Road.

11.15 a.m.   I am approaching the entrance to the ticket office. To the left of a fountain, a hawker is selling Cokes and Vitasoy from a cold barrel. Next to him stands a young European boy. He's about nine years of age and dressed in khaki shorts and a grubby *I love Macau* T-shirt. The child is rather chubby, with light-brown curly hair that dangles down over his ears. I notice him only because he's been eying me while intermittently perusing a sheet of paper. Finally, he settles himself onto the low wall that encloses the fountain. He studiously fashions the sheet of paper into a paper plane, and launches it in my direction. It glides for a few seconds, before nose-diving at my feet. I scoop it up, walk over and hand it back to him.

'Are you lost?'

He shakes his head.

'My mum and nan are at the top. Can you buy me a Coke? I've got the money.'

I pull a Coke from the ice-barrel, pay the hawker and hand it to the boy. He steps back a few paces, closes one eye, and relaunches the paper plane in my direction. This time it grazes past my right ear.

'Don't you think that's rather childish behaviour for a boy of your age?'

'Yes, I do, actually.'

'Well, it's really irritating, so please stop.'

'Do you like Honkers? We've been here for three days.'

'No. So far, Honkers is not to my taste. Can you recommend Macau?'

The boy retrieves his paper plane to carry out minor repairs.

'They eat dogs. Perhaps you'd like it better here if you didn't wear so many clothes.'

'I'm not feeling very well. And I didn't expect it to be so warm here in December. No, please don't do that again.'

'I'll do it just once more. Can you buy my ticket for me? I've got the money.'

'You're not going to throw that thing at people inside the tram, are you? They might think I'm your father.'

'Of course I won't. And I really don't think anyone would think that.'

Mercifully, the boy has become silent, and remains well behaved for the duration of the brief tram ride, even allowing our fellow passengers to dismount before us. As we emerge, he points towards some tables outside the Peak Café directly opposite.

'There they are: Mum and Nan. Come on!' He rushes over to the younger woman, as her older companion stands up to greet me.

'David, we've kept a seat for you. Come and join us.' Under the white sunhat and bifocals, Brenda Kelly's bronzed face, enhanced by a radiant and seemingly genuine smile, has lost its bags and sags of a decade ago. With or without the aid of cosmetic surgery, she has successfully replaced the drained look of old with a second glow of youth. She stretches. 'Isn't it fabulous? I could live here forever. And perhaps we will, although Barrie's arm's going to need a bit more twisting. Are you OK, David?'

'No, not really.'

I sit, and turn towards a young woman with closely cropped ginger hair, slightly puffy cheeks, and sunglasses two sizes too big for her. Jade engages me in a comical handshake.

'Jesus, David, did you pack your duffel coat as well?'

'Jade, I would never have recognised you! I'm not feeling terribly well, actually.'

'So you won't be joining us later for deer penis and double-boiled owl. Have you two been introduced? David Carpenter, my son, big Nick – well he was little Nick when you last saw me. How old would Nicky have been at the funeral, Mum?'

'Around fifteen weeks,' replies Brenda, rather coolly.

I peek round at Nicky.

'I don't remember seeing any babies at Ken's funeral.'

Jade grabs her son's hand and pulls him towards her.

'That's because little Nick was being baby-sat by his Uncle James. Big brother was looking for any old excuse to dodge the funeral.'

Brenda glances up but avoids eye contact with her daughter.

'That is just not true. James wanted some time alone with his new nephew. It's *you* that didn't want to go.'

'Well, Dad had given me such a lousy time about getting pregnant. But he was making a drama about everything by then. And you weren't exactly supportive, were you mummykins? And hardly the perfect role model.'

'It was a difficult time, David.'

'Mummy had an affair, cracked up and needed a shrink.'

'It was rather more than an affair, and he was *not* a shrink. It was a requirement of the counselling course.'

'Well, what a lucky coincidence! And then came our final bust-up when I sided with Dad on his final day on this mortal coil. But we're fine again now, aren't we, mother of mine?'

Jade grins, Brenda doesn't.

'Not *fine*, exactly.'

I try to lighten the atmosphere.

'Ken once threatened to put my head through a mangle.'

'That's my dad! So, that January, I moved out to Doris's. You remember your Auntie Doris in Wakefield, Nicolas Picolas?'

'Sort of,' mumbles NP, struggling to escape.

'Of *course* you remember! She was your other mummy till

you were three, while I was in Leeds … Grandad's wife.' Nick shrugs and breaks free. Jade turns back to me. 'Auntie Doris died in '82. I stayed on in her house when I wasn't gigging.'

'Carmen told me about the jazz course. It sounds like your band's done pretty well.'

'As well as you *can* do, playing stuff that doesn't sell and no one can dance to. Our final gig's at city hall tomorrow, then it's back home. So did you enjoy Dominic's overtones workshop? I bet you fell for our drummer. Everyone does.' Jade follows up her old taunting smile with a semi-sung 'Carmen *likes* you.'

I swiftly move on.

'I'd assumed that the workshop was James' idea. Carmen told me it came from you.'

'James and I discussed it together. We thought it would do you good.'

'Thanks. Well, I suppose getting punched in the stomach toughens you up.' I stoically acknowledge Brenda's sympathetic murmur and counter Jade's snigger. 'So Jade, tell me about your big brother. Is he still together with Delger? Wasn't it Delger that instigated this whole overtones craze?'

For once, Jade is momentarily lost for words.

'Ah, Delger! Let's save Delger for tomorrow morning. That's when you're going over to Cheung Chau. You're to be at James' by 10.45. The ferry takes an hour. I don't suppose you're *with* anyone, David?'

'I might be.'

I turn towards Brenda and enquire after Barrie. She shrugs.

'So-so. He decided to stay in and practise for tonight's concert. As I told you in my letter, Barrie's not that keen on hot weather or Chinese food so he's going to need some coaxing to move here. But here's the *good* news. CC's just made him a very generous job offer. Apparently he still has good connections out here.'

'And what would *you* do over here, Brenda?'

'I've just completed a feng shui course, so I could take on a few clients.'

The sound of Jade's derisory laugh hasn't changed in ten years.

'Well, that should be pretty novel for the Chinese!'

Brenda purses her lips to signify a termination to the exchange and I fill the pause.

'And how about you, Jade? Are you married?'

'You mean who's Nicky's father? Well David, what naughty boy came up to my bedroom around nine months before he was born?'

'You know very well that I didn't touch you that night.'

'Well Mum, lord knows what might have happened if I hadn't made him keep his hands on his head.'

Brenda cannot resist. She tips her bifocals and casts me a quizzical glance. 'David?'

'Oh, you're both trying to embarrass me again. You have no idea, Brenda, just how much your daughter used to scare the life out of me.'

Jade leans forward, pulls a scary face and then relaxes back into her chair.

'Well you should at least take partial responsibility for my pregnancy, David. If you hadn't rolled up at the Waggon that night, Darren and I might never have got together that weekend.'

'And split up the *following* weekend,' snaps Brenda.

'Oh, we lasted a couple of weeks longer than that. And Darren's ended up being a good dad to Nicky, hasn't he, Mum?'

'Ended up is right. It took him nearly six years to have anything to do with either of you.'

'But now the two of them get along famously. You love your daddy, don't you, Nicky?'

'I keep telling you, Mum: call me Nicolas. My name is Nicolas Crane.'

Jade squints up at him and gently pokes his stomach.

'It's just a phase. He doesn't want to be a Kelly any more, do you, Nicky Wicky?'

Nicky dive-bombs the paper plane into his mother's glass of 7 Up. Jade fishes it out, launches it at my forehead and gives herself a round of applause.

'So, Master Nicolas Crane, did you manage a direct hit too?' He shakes his head and breaks into a Jade-like grin.

Brenda hands me a tissue. 'It wasn't Nicolas's idea, David. My grandson's far more mature than my daughter. Jade thought it would be a symbolic act. Is that the right phrase, darling?'

I wipe my face and turn to Nicky.

'Is your dad over here with you?'

'Nope. Can you guess how I knew it was you I was meant to throw my paper dart at?'

'Tell me, Nicolas Crane.'

'Because the plane's got a drawing of you on it. The lady with the black curly hair gave it to me. You're much fatter now, but it's still you.'

I straighten out the soggy sheet and am transported back to a Wimpy Bar in Huddersfield. It is the day of the funeral. I'm sitting rather stiffly, in my dark grey suit and navy-blue musician's tie.

'She's *here*, isn't she?'

Jade half-yawns.

'She *was* here. I must have upset her.'

Brenda glances up at me while rummaging through her handbag.

'Jade was incredibly rude to her. David, just tell me why they're all ganging up on this poor girl.'

'Yes, David, tell mummy what this poor girl's like. David should know. He's actually had *relations* with Jax in the past.'

Brenda has fished out her pack of Embassy.

'Oh, I'm so glad to hear that you finally lost your virginity, David.'

'Well, actually—'

'You're the one man with a bit of sense around here. I can call you a man now. Why is everyone being so hostile towards this young woman? At least she's encouraging James to become a bit more involved again.'

'Well, as I see it …'

Jade clutches her head in exasperation.

'Has anyone asked my brother if he *wants* to become more involved? Mum, how can you possibly like someone that's just using James? Even *he's* stopped speaking to her.'

'I only said I liked her Welsh accent. Whatever she's supposed to have done, there was no call for such foul language. You've got a mouth like your father's.'

Jade grasps my wrist.

'Help me out here, David. *You've* been on the wrong side of my dad. If he were here, how do you think *he'd* deal with the bitch?'

For once, I have no problem with Jade's turn of phrase.

'Mangle time! And I'd help Ken turn the handle.'

'There you are, Mum! Our knight in shining armour has arrived, cunningly disguised as a nancy boy. Joke!'

I pull back my arm. Brenda lets out a dramatic sigh and lights a cigarette.

'David, surely you'll agree with me that using bad language in front of a nine-year old is unacceptable.'

Nicky sidles up to me and shakes his head.

'Bad words!'

Knowing his mother, I'm unsure how to decipher the boy's boggle-eyed expression. Jade leans over and musses his hair.

'Come on, son, I only asked her to leave town.'

Nicky presses himself against my shoulder.

'Mum told the lady to fuck off back to the land of her fathers.' Jade playfully cuffs his cheek but he is not deterred. 'And this morning, Uncle James said something *much worse!*'

Brenda waggles her Embassy pack at him.

'Well, I'm sure we don't wish to hear *that* again, thank you very much. So, David, is this Jax really as evil as everyone's making out?'

'Well, not evil exactly, but she's a troublemaker. In fact, I've already written to James, urging him to be wary. I'd intended getting over to Cheung Chau this afternoon to reinforce my opinion, but I'm not feeling up to it.'

Jade shakes her head. 'He would have ignored you. Luke's the only person that gets through to James. That's why I left the two of them together for the day. As we speak, the big man is hopefully hammering the final nails in the bitch's coffin.'

Brenda is on her feet.

'Oh, really! I'll hear no more of this infantile language. Does anyone want a drink? No? Good!'

She struts into the café. Jade leans back and stretches out her legs.

'Then they'll be catching the 5.30 ferry. The gig starts around 9. My multitalented brother will be one of our guest musicians tonight. And you'll be another!'

'I—'

'James has chosen a Monk tune called 'Hackensack'. It sounds totally mad on the shakuhachi. And Barrie's almost mastered the head of 'Summertime'.

'I should hope so. He started on it ten years ago. But I've decided not—'

'Oh no you don't! We play 'Big Nick' in B flat, like on the record. Is that okay for you?'

'B flat is about as okay as F sharp. Perhaps I should be getting back to the hotel for a snooze. Hopefully I'll perk up by this evening.'

'See you around 8.30, then. The Fringe Club's number two, Lower Albert Road. Nicky, say goodbye to Uncle David. Give him a big sloppy kiss.'

PART 4: OVERTONES

Nicky arrives back beside me and whispers in my ear.

'The Welsh bitch has written you a message. It's on the back of the drawing.'

> *Trail of the divine marksman*
> *Now continue along Lugard Road for one mile.*
> *Join me on middle bench to view Kelly's Island.*

* * *

After what can only be described as a gruelling route march, no view on earth, however spectacular, could possibly compensate for my throbbing head and sweat-soaked clothes. Despite the temptation to stretch out on the bench that overlooks the outlying islands, I would rather jump off the edge than join its occupant, who, not for the first time, obscures my view with her dense mass of black curls. Jacqueline Stewart is clearly indiscriminate as to whether she denies me a view of Christmas Humphreys or the South China Sea. Only the thin gold ankle chain round her right ankle offers a clue to her outlandish dress code of old. She gazes round from her sketchbook, looking bleary-eyed but annoyingly beautiful in her light blue halter-neck sundress.

'There's James' island ... the small one nearest to us. He's going to love this drawing. It's the only way to show him Cheung Chau from this perspective. He's far too lazy to walk up. James can be a bit of a slob sometimes. It's good to see you, David.'

'Why's that, then?'

'Oh, come on! You're not still sulking after all these years? Please be nice. I need *someone* to be nice. Come and sit next to me.'

'I'd rather stand, thanks.'

'I really need to speak to you. God, it looks like you're on your way out. Have you got any last words? And you've put on weight, or is it the cardigan? So how do I look then?'

'Awful.'

'Don't say you've gone off me, David! Once upon a time you fancied me like fuck. Did you ever get to hear the Ramones?'

'No.'

'Richy left in August, but he was never going to replace Marky. Hm mm mm mm mm mm mm – it's still a brilliant song! Whenever I hear 'Teenage Lobotomy', I think of you … but in a *good* way, David.'

'I'm moved.'

'So what are you up to these days? Not that I ever knew what you were up to in those days.'

'Perhaps that's because you never asked me. Well, I'm still doing now what I was doing then. And are you still a drug addict? I expect it's easier to get your supplies in this part of the world.'

'You're kidding. This is the last place you want to be caught with anything. But if you're on about *that* day, it was just one tab of acid … half a tab actually. So shall I tell you what I'm up to these days?'

I'm in no mood for innocent smiles and seductive eyes.

'Brenda tells me that you've made it to the top: James Kelly's self-appointed fan club secretary.'

'*And* editor of his fanzine.'

'That must keep you very busy.'

'Well, you can scoff, but *Divine Marksman* has built up quite a cult following *and* generated some business.'

'Cult following usually amounts to a small collection of freaks.'

'Well, *you* look about ready to sign up. It's a *joke*, David. But did you actually pack that *scarf*?'

'I'm not well. What do you mean: *generated some business*?'

'I now work for James. I'm just what he needs.'

'That's certainly not the opinion of those around him.'

'So they'd they prefer him to stare at the walls all day? Well, at least Uncle Ken would have been proud of me. I've already accepted three exhibition matches.'

'And has *James* accepted them?'

'He will. Then there's a potential sponsor in Manila with money to burn. I also set up Crescent's mini tour of the Far East, but that was just as a family favour. Actually, my day gig for the last three years was in the A&R department at Chrysalis records. Can you believe that? But now I've branched out with my own management company. So far, it's just me, but early days. Are you okay?'

'No. Are there any toilets nearby?'

'This path loops back to the Peak Café. Let's walk together and talk about old times.'

I slump down on the bench but maintain a respectable distance between us.

'Do we really have old times to talk about?'

'Of course we do. I often think about that day we spent together?'

'Would that be the day you embarrassed me at the Kyudo workshop?'

'I was thinking of our trip to Huddersfield, you know: Ken's funeral. That's a day I won't forget.'

'I'm amazed you can remember anything about it.'

'I remember telling you that I knew how James had killed Ken.'

'Then you'll be relieved to hear that CC and I decided against reporting the murder to the authorities. You might also remember telling us that you'd just had tantric sex with a ninja. But spare me your reminiscences of the intimate details right now. I'm not feeling up to it.'

'Oh that bit was true enough. But I realised the next day

that James had just been making fun of me, that he never would have *really* done anything so terrible. Do you think James would ever do anything terrible?'

'I've no idea. Look, do you mind if I set off ahead? I don't think I'm going to last out.'

Jax edges closer along the bench and grabs my arm.

'Please, it's really important to me that we talk about this. Do you remember that word he wrote down on my sketchpad?'

'Yes, I remember. The word was 'fukiya': Japanese for blowpipe. Apparently, your ninja lover had just confessed to having killed his uncle with a poisoned dart. Your startling revelation flew in the face of the inquest's findings. According to your theory, Ken hadn't, in fact, died from fatal injuries after being steamrollered by a ten-ton truck. Had the coroner analysed the two gallons of Sam Smiths in Ken's blood, he would have no doubt uncovered the secret ninja concoction that actually did the dirty work. What an amazingly cunning murder!'

'Don't poke fun at me, David. Yes, I later realised what an idiot I'd been, but you believe anything when you're tripping. It's so cruel to mess with people's heads like that. Why would James do that? Was he just making fun of me too?'

'I expect so. James *has* been known to play little games for his own entertainment.'

'This wasn't a little game. He started to wave that stupid wooden pipe in my direction, bragging about how he'd killed Ken by blowing a poisoned dart at him. That was already freaking me out. But he couldn't leave it there. He had to stick one of his darts in the pipe and aim the fucking thing at my head. Yes David, I know how stupid it all sounds, but I really did believe it.'

'But I didn't believe it, CC didn't believe it and nobody believes it now. So why are you bringing up this pathetic story again after all these years?'

'Because James and I never mentioned it again … and it's only now that I can see what a horrible trick he played on me that day. Perhaps he's capable of more horrible tricks, now that we're not getting on so well. Why don't you ask him tomorrow?'

'What are you talking about? Ask him what, tomorrow?'

'Just ask him if he'd do anything to hurt me. Then tell me what he says. I'd ask him myself, but he won't speak to me. That's his sister's doing. She hates me, and so does Luke.'

'Jade and Luke don't hate you. They just want you to stop interfering.'

'How *dare* they! Name me one other person that's been looking out for James in the past five years. His sponsor dumped him on Cheung Chau, his sister only really cares about her stupid saxophone and his mother's only here because there might be a job in it for Barrie. As for Luke … he's never been capable of spending more than a day with anyone. I'm the one person that's been trying to help and they all despise me for it.'

I soften at the sight of her rising distress.

'Jax, do you *honestly* believe that James wants your help?'

'He did, till they all turned him against me. David, tell me what I've done. Am I really so dislikeable?'

Jax's sad, childlike expression dissipates my half-formulated hurtful response. No, there is nothing to dislike. I should say something positive.

'Brenda likes your Welsh accent.'

Jax jumps up, takes two paces towards the cliff edge and spins round to face me. Her huge black eyes are filled with tears.

'Fuck off, David! I thought I might at least count on *you* as a friend.'

I hoist myself up from the bench and walk towards her. The combination of grabbing her hand and looking down towards the ocean brings on a sudden bout of nausea.

'If you really want my advice …'

She pulls away, leaving me with just the sea view.

'Stuff your advice up your fat arse. I'm visiting Carmen tomorrow morning on Cheung Chau. She's about the only one I can trust. Oh, I'm sorry, David. I didn't mean to be unkind, but you do look a fucking mess. So go on, give me your advice. What do you think?'

'Two things: the first is that you should go home.'

'Unhelpful, but thank you … and the second?'

'I think I'm going to throw up.'

'Are you being metaphorical? No, you're not, are you.' Jax scoops up her belongings from the bench in preparation for a hasty retreat. 'Well, I'll let you get on with it. I'm no good with ill people. But you will do that for me, won't you! You'll ask him? No, don't try to answer. Just nod and then tell me tomorrow. Thanks David. I'll call you. It's been great catching up.'

I've no idea how long it took to hobble from the remains of last night's pomfret in chilli sauce back to the vacated table outside the Peak Café. In my delirious exhaustion, I likened myself to the lone survivor of a failed expedition, whose sole consolation was the absence of a welcome party attending his ignominious return. For I am in no doubt that the mere glimpse of Jax, or any member of the Kelly family, would have been enough to send me scuttling back from whence I had come.

Having finally hauled myself off the café seat, I could barely face the prospect of even the short walk to the Peak tram, let alone summon sufficient energy for the final leg back to the hotel. I managed to ward off throwing up in the tram or the cab, thus saving the final remains of my stomach for the hotel foyer. Once back in my room, I must have totally stripped off, before collapsing onto the bed.

***

PART 4: OVERTONES

Four hours later, I awake with a start, drenched in sweat.

By the time I've showered, changed, forced down half a club sandwich at the bar, hailed a cab and been dropped off at least a quarter of a mile from the destination I had requested, I'm feeling even weaker than I did five hours ago.

By 8.45 I'm standing under a banner that advertises the Fringe Club. As I stare upward, a car suddenly careers off the road, cuts within six inches of my toes, and actually enters the building. I follow behind and wait. The driver, a young Chinaman in designer casuals, parks, jumps out, and saunters towards me.

'I'm so sorry. Are you okay?'

'I wasn't expecting a car to drive into the club.'

'No, you wouldn't. I don't believe we've met. I'm Benny Chia. I run the place. A Volvo wouldn't be my natural choice, but this one's built like a tank. There's the odd occasion when I leave here a little worse for wear.'

'David Carpenter – I'm a friend of the Kellys. They're having a party here tonight.'

'There's no special event this evening to my knowledge, apart from it being the last night of Crescent's residency. You should just catch the end of their first set. You do seem a little overdressed.'

'Actually this is my musician's tie. I'm writing a short review for *Crescendo*, and may be jamming with Jade Kelly's band in the second half. Today's her brother's thirtieth birthday. You know, this building doesn't really look like a club.'

'We only took it over four years ago. The building used to be a dairy cold storage warehouse, although it was only the gweilos that ever wanted milk. But I expect you could do with something a little stronger after your near-death experience. Please follow me.'

Carmen Lo's diminutive frame behind the drum kit belies the thunderous yet intricate drum solo that echoes round the filled club. Now, the giant on double bass begins to underpin her interlocking rhythmic patterns with his own insistently repeating pedal note. This Little John of modern jazz engulfs his bass as though it were a toy. Indeed, he looks capable of whirling it around above his head, or even hoisting it over his shoulders like a sack of potatoes. But a gentle giant he is not. Indeed, one could easily picture the big man putting his instrument to work as a stone-age weapon with which to fend off invaders from the audience. Or, should matters get out of hand (perhaps a group of punters might find the music too way-out for their taste), he may choose to bludgeon them to death.

Jade Kelly (tenor and soprano sax) looks very much the bandleader in her maroon French beret and black top. She smiles benevolently at the duo from the side of the small stage as her head nods gently to the backbeat. She takes a slow, casual walk to centre stage while restating the head, and then purposefully brings the sax down to indicate the final chord.

Jade has taken up the mike.

'Coltrane recorded just two albums in 1964. You've just been listening to "The Drum Thing", from the first album, *Crescent*. Please show your appreciation for the amazing Carmen Lo, working considerably harder than Luke Kelly, who never even made it to a second note.'

'Only know the one, ma'am.'

'I'm afraid the big man's going to have to dig out an extra two for the opening riff of "Acknowledgement". This is the first track of what many consider to be JC's finest hour, and his second album of that year, *A Love Supreme* … that's if anyone can find Sid, our piano player. Ah, I've just spotted another fine pianist in the audience. Sorry to disturb you from your memoirs, Mister Carpenter, but would you care to help out? It's OK, David. Don't panic. Here comes the main man. David Carpenter, by the way, is one of our special guests to be featured in the second half.'

I ignore the smattering of applause and continue to scribble gibberish, rather than meet the public gaze.

'And one final announcement for those who've just wandered off the street: It's only fair to inform you that the Kelly family are having our own little shindig tonight. We're celebrating my big brother's thirtieth birthday, not that anyone knows where he is. Okay Carmen, dinner is served.'

The gong signals three quartal piano chords that support the saxophone's free-form call to prayer. The three-note bass riff pulls the band into tempo. Jade's solo builds to maximum intensity, until it is finally lulled by the band's soft chant: A love supreme! A love supreme!

'And now our piano player will take us into the break with a collection of Monk compositions. These tunes are featured on the one album that JC and Thelonious recorded together in '57. Then, it's the turn of our guests. So what's up first, Sid?'

'That'll be "Nutty".'

'Well, I'll dedicate this one to my nutty brother, James. Take it away, Sidney.'

I have abandoned my review, retreated to a less conspicuous table, and am currently resorting to my version of survival mode: elbows dug into the table, thumbs under the chin to support my throbbing head, and the remaining eight fingers providing acupressure to my forehead. Thelonious Monk's angular, percussive melodies have been less than soothing, and Sid's announcement that there will be a fifteen-minute interval comes none too soon.

To be suddenly flanked by two attractive young women would, under normal circumstances, lie somewhere between fraught and petrifying. However, in my present, vulnerable state, Jade and Carmen are like two angelic nurses materialising at my bedside.

Jade ruffles my hair.

'What's that round your neck, David?'

'Actually it's my musician's—'

'Never mind. You *are* still coming up for "Big Nick" after the break, aren't you!'

'I very much doubt if I'll live that long.'

'But if you do, we'll each take a two-chorus solo. Take yours between mine and Luke's.'

'A solo? No problem. I'll give you my rendition of "A Walk in the Black Forest".'

'Now, don't be silly. I told you before: it's just the "A" section of "Rhythm Changes".'

'What?'

'The first eight bars of "I Got Rhythm" – just solo around the B flat pentatonic scale and you can't go wrong. Oh, hang on.'

Luke is waving at her from the stage.

'Right, James has arrived. Must go. Carmen, sort this sad man out.'

'Hello David, you're looking rough. Were you writing your will?'

I squint at her through half-closed eyes.

'Why do I have to go up there and humiliate myself? Can you promise to drown me out, so no one notices?'

'Just play how you feel and it will be fine. Jade tells me

you're coming over to Cheung Chau tomorrow morning to spend some time with James.'

'So I've been informed.'

'Well, I'm staying in the flat right opposite James' place. I'd like to invite you over for lunch when he's finished with you. Will you come?'

'No.'

'Oh! Why not?'

'Because Jax will be there with you.'

'Jax is arriving mid-morning. She'll be long gone before you arrive. Be over for one. I'll cook you some authentic Sichuan food, just the way my grandmother taught me.'

'Then I'm definitely not coming. I was poisoned last night in a Sichuan restaurant.'

'Okay, I'll do you a nice plain omelette and salad. James Kelly! Can you believe that I've been his neighbour for a week now and still haven't even caught sight of him yet? I've only ever seen a photo.'

'I know the feeling.'

'And here he is! Wow, now I see what Jax means. Are Luke and Jade holding him up?'

'No, I've seen this entrance before. It's more like an entourage, like when Mike Tyson comes into the ring.'

'He's rather better looking than Mike Tyson. In fact he's totally gorgeous. My God! Oh, Sid's calling me up on stage. So you'll definitely come and visit me tomorrow? Wonderful!'

Sid's flourishing arpeggio cues 'Happy Birthday', as James, Luke and Jade settle themselves down at a front table with Brenda and Barrie. But just as Carmen is resting her sticks back on the snare, there is a minor incident. Out of nowhere, Jax has popped up in front of James. She seems to be having words with him but it is difficult to know whether James is responding. Now Luke is on his feet and standing between them, towering over Jax. Carmen jumps off the stage, grabs Jax's arm and tries ushering her away. But Jax has shaken her off and is strutting over to my table.

'Jesus, they're all so fucked up. You *are* still going over there tomorrow?' I stare straight ahead. 'Then you'd better do what we said, right? Ask him! I'll phone your hotel tomorrow night, okay?'

'I'd rather you didn't.'

I return to survival position to the sounds of Jax storming out of the club.

Sid Furney is thin and lanky, with sunken cheeks and a mane of patchy black hair. His strident Australian accent has commanded our attention.

'Okay ladies and gentlemen, it's guest time. We're going to break with tradition by kicking off with the top of the bill and then work downwards. Is that alright with you, young Barrie?' Brenda nudges him for a response.

'I could do with a spot more practice.'

'Brenda tells me it's a lost cause. Now then, let's get down to business. Before I bring on the star of the show, here's a little story to set the scene.

'Around ten years ago, a smart young businessman by the name of Lee Chun Chow used to rock up at the Old China Hand for a game of darts. We'd swap tales: him telling me about the life of a Japanese archer and me telling him … well, you don't want to hear about that. Anyway, one evening he waltzes in with this totally weird blond bloke with an even weirder accent … not that I hear a peep out of him at first. He won't even look at me. To break the ice, I ask the lad if he fancies a game of darts. Yes, alright, don't rub it in! It's taken me years of therapy to rebuild my self-esteem. Anyway, fifteen minutes later, to save face, and get the demolition job out of my system, I sit down at the piano and start banging out … well a Monk tune actually, called "Hackensack". Jesus, what an about-turn! Suddenly you can't bloody shut him up. He's all over me, declaring that I'm a musical genius and demanding that I play through my entire repertoire.

'Two nights later they're both back in, but this time the Kelly boy's brought his bloody Japanese flute with him. And now he's literally dragging me to the piano. "Come on, Sid, we must play 'Hackensack!' " *Must*, mind you, like I've got no choice! There's a famous interview with Monk, where this really dumb interviewer asks him if he thinks there are enough notes on the piano. I can't remember his answer, but however many notes there are on a shakuhachi, James, unlike his daddy, really did only know the one. But, believe me, he blew the shit out of that note. Even if he had known all of them, I'd still lay odds that a master shakuhachi player would pronounce the theme of "Hackensack" to be totally unplayable through that wooden tube. But from whatever angle you look at it, our version of the Monk classic that night had to be its worst ever rendition. From that day on, whenever the world was getting me down, the mere thought of it has brought me out in chuckles and seen me through. Anyway, ladies and gentlemen, we are gathered here this evening to witness a recreation of that musical epiphany from all those years ago. But I suggest we first offer a silent prayer that the boy has improved. As I make my way to the piano, please welcome the birthday boy ... James Kelly!'

James, attired in a lightweight baggy cream suit and black T-shirt, has taken the stand. His upper torso is twisted awkwardly towards the piano and the shakuhachi points down at Sid, who gently eyes him with an almost imperceptible smile, as though reminding him of their little secret. After an eight-bar piano intro, Sid signals James in for the second eight, and they play the jagged theme in perfect unison. The drums and bass slam in together for the second chorus, Jade reinforces James' line during the middle section and Sid solos through two choruses. James turns to the front, scrunches up his eyes, angles the shakuhachi towards the microphone, and embarks on a wild flurry of notes that either have no connection to the chords, or are following his own logical system of improvisation in a parallel jazz universe. The quartet grin delightedly at one another, but James' face maintains an expression of intense concentration as he motors through two choruses, embarks on a third, but then peters out as he awakens to his surroundings. He casts an anxious glance back at Luke, who takes up the baton with a fierce bass solo. Jade finally steps in with the theme to take the piece out, and ushers James to the side of the stage.

I unashamedly admit to shedding tears when listening to 'Lady in Red'. But am I *truly* moved by Chris De Burgh's glorious tearjerker? I am not. For me, authentic emotion is rare. I have experienced it no more than twice in a decade. So, before this evening, when was the last time that I was truly moved? It was while witnessing James Kelly's first ordinary miracle, as he threw bull's eyes on the Eamonn O'Brien show. And now, having just witnessed his second ordinary miracle: a senseless/miraculous jumble of notes, and moments after his audience yet again fails to grasp what has taken place, I am reminded why I love James Kelly.

Jade is back at the mike, all smiles.

'Our next guest has the unenviable task to follow that! Fortunately, he's been working on this timeless song from *Porgy and Bess* for longer than anyone can remember. Rumour has it that it's the only tune he knows. But luckily for him, it fits into our scheme of things. Coltrane actually featured this ballad on his 1960 album, *My Favourite Things*. So please give your appreciation to Barrie Collins on baritone, and marvel at his inimitable interpretation of the Gershwin classic.'

Barrie's rendition of 'Summertime' is a shaky, but thankfully, brief affair, his solo mainly consisting of the first four notes of the blues scale. Towards the final chorus, a stranger has appeared from behind the drum kit, and is now wandering aimlessly around the stage, shaking a tambourine. Nobody seems to be taking much notice of him and he is certainly doing no harm. I'm not too sure what Mongolians looks like – I may even be getting them confused with Eskimos – but I'm fairly certain that this man is not Chinese. I can only assume him to be Delger.

Jade summons up a smattering of applause and elicits a drum roll from Carmen.

'And now, ladies and gentlemen, all the way from South London, to assist us with our arrangement of "Big Nick", I give you … David Carpenter.'

Sid has sat me down at the piano and I'm clutching at his shirt cuff.

'Sid. Help! Tell me what to do.'

'Just lock into the bass, son.'

'No, that's not help.'

'Okay, play wrong notes like they're the right ones and they'll think you're a genius.'

Now Jade is hovering over me. She responds to the blind panic in my eyes by actually guiding my fingers over the five pentatonic notes required for a rudimentary solo.

'How many more times? It's the verse of "I Got Rhythm" – just eight bars repeated, for God's sake!'

As Jade turns away to count the band in, I feel I'm about to black out. But when she suddenly swivels back round, aims her soprano between my eyes, and fires the 'Big Nick' theme into my forehead, I am suddenly very wide awake.

As I poke randomly at the B flat pentatonic scale, my lamentable solo is not solely due to incompetence, for I am being distracted. The Mongolian tambourine man, jigging furiously to the backbeat while grinning in my direction, is little more than a minor irritation. But James, cross-legged on the floor, at the far side of the stage, is really unnerving me. It's impossible to tell whether he's blowing into his shakuhachi or sucking it, for I can hear no sound. Babies suck, and it is his defocused gaze, as the instrument loosely dangles from his mouth, which conjures up a suckling infant.

I am jolted back to reality by the sound of two hands applauding my solo, but Brenda's enthusiasm is swiftly dampened by a sideways glance from Barrie. Luke's solo leads into swapped fours with Carmen, my four-bar contribution amounting to the ultimate understatement: total silence. Jade finally plays us out with the quirky, circus-like theme.

Three of us are preparing to make an exit. I already have one foot on dry land. James and Delger (am I imagining that they are hand in hand?) are about to step off stage from the opposite side. But Jade swiftly takes centre stage. She adopts crucified traffic cop position, thereby indicating that no one is about to leave.

'Okay, big man. You go left and I'll go right. Let's round 'em up!'

Luke heads over towards the duo, as Jade turns to head *me* off. Her arm scoops around my waist and she murmurs in my ear.

'So, nancy boy, your big moment has finally arrived.'

'I don't want any more big moments.'

'Oh yes you do. This is that big moment to snuggle up to your boyfriend. Make the most of it. It's the closest you'll ever get.'

Jade pecks my cheek and drags me unceremoniously towards James and Delger, who are simultaneously being herded by Luke towards centre stage. His 'sorry boys, but you're going to have to hand over your weapons' routine gets a few titters as he relieves them of the tambourine and shakuhachi. The two captives gamely play their parts with a touch of pantomimic protest. Jade then makes her announcement.

PART 4: OVERTONES

'To mark the finale of this section of the evening, three of our guest artists will now add their vocal contribution to a tune entitled "Africa", taken from the 1961 album, *Africa/Brass*. But tonight, ladies and gentlemen, we are replacing Coltrane's brass section with our very own overtones choir.' Jade beckons me but my legs are not responding. 'Come on over boys, there's nothing to it. The whole piece is in E. You simply hit and hold that note whenever I give the signal. Don't be shy. Out you come. That's it: birthday boy in the middle and you two each side. Now, bunch up. It has to be said that two of these guys are no strangers to overtone singing. But the third wouldn't know an overtone if one smacked him in the eye. Spot the impostor! Give them an E, Sid. So here's what to listen for: if you shape your mouth and tongue a certain way – that's it, big brother.'

I'm pressed up against James' right shoulder and thigh, my head six inches from his head. I half turn, but can only catch his profile, as he puckers his lips and sucks in his cheeks to demonstrate the changing vowel sounds. Jade gives her brother a thumbs-up and continues.

'Now ladies and gentlemen, can you believe that it's possible to sing two notes at once? Yes, that Yorkshireman in the front row.'

'Someone should have told Don Everly. He could have sung his own harmony.'

'An excellent point, Barrie! So here's how it works. The low note, that's the one we can *all* hear, sets off higher notes vibrating. We're talking overtones. For any musos out there with dog ears, listen out for high octaves, perfect fifths and major thirds ... then finally, if the wind's in the right direction, minor 7ths.'

Jade has positioned the mike stand in front of us and whispers something to James. He instantly grabs hold of my right shoulder and Delger's left. Thighs are squashed even tighter together and heads are now almost touching. James' clenched fingers are now digging like claws into me, and the resulting pain instantly extinguishes my former embarrassment.

Now Luke is passing by. He inspects each of us in turn like a drill sergeant.

'Atten … *shun*! David? James? Delboy?'

James tightens his grip. I make a valiant attempt to transform my grimace into a casual smile and can only imagine that all three of us are nodding compliantly and standing a little straighter.

Luke's bass riff is bouncing between two notes an octave apart, and I assume that the higher E is the note that we are imminently required to sing. Carmen enters with a pulse, rather than a time signature, Sid begins to roll an ambiguous chord and Jade cues us in. As I tentatively sound the tagnain khoomii that Dominic taught us, so James' grip lessens. I am visualising Margaret, the amateur opera singer, showering me with praise and encouragement for my vocal efforts. My emerging confidence seems to have inspired James and Delger, who are now also ooing, aahing and eeing, thus creating a backdrop and cushion for Jade's soulful solo. We are eventually signalled out towards its climax and only reintroduced for similar vocal backing duties to support the first section of the piano solo, then rested again as Sid takes off.

Now only the piano and bass are left playing, as they pump out one single note in a fast repeated rhythmic pattern, like Morse code. I suddenly catch sight of Carmen and Jade. They have abandoned their instruments, and are now standing closely together and observing us from the front of the stage, far right. This time there is no need for a signal; the repeated bass and piano pattern is our obvious cue. For the first time, I can clearly discern the combined effect of our vocal trio, although it is impossible to single out my own voice. James' hand still hooks around my shoulder, but no longer holds any tension. As the drums and bass slowly fade to silence, I listen passively to our merged voices as though I have no part in the music making. Sid and Luke have now also stepped forward and taken up symmetrical positions to their counterparts. Although their focus is also directing towards us, I feel no self-consciousness or sense of performance, as the ethereal whistling sound, suspended above our heads, whirs in its own dance of slowly transforming colours. Our original, fundamental note has long since evaporated, and the evolution of each succeeding overtone now feels somehow less and less associated with sound and more intrinsic to the very act of breathing out. Now, each effortless outbreath is indistinguishable from the inbreath, and lasts an eternity.

We all three stop simultaneously and there is silence. No one is clapping.

Saturday, 12 December 1987

... And there is silence.

It is the premiere of a Broadway musical and the understudy has made a hesitant start. The audience chat among themselves, fidget, or even mock the poor wretch with a few titters to demonstrate their disappointment that the star has failed to show up. Then, miraculously, she establishes a foothold and slowly builds from strength to strength. The audience have quietened and become attentive.

She has reached the final chorus, hits the money-note with a heart-rending vibrato and finally brings her torch song to a triumphant close. Snapping out of her ecstatic trance, she gazes out at the audience who, for ten seconds, remain silent. Then suddenly, just as though the stage manager had snapped on all the houselights, the crowd burst into rapturous applause. They are on their feet. A star is born.

This is not what happened last night. There was certainly no rapturous applause, and quite possibly no applause at all. I do remember that Brenda's table had become occupied by a group of noisy men far too engrossed in their own banter to have noticed anything on stage requiring a response. So neither would there have been that preceding ten-seconds worth of silence, but only the usual buzz one might expect from punters who had long since dispensed with the onstage entertainment and were now entertaining themselves.

None of this mattered to me, as I stood on stage, dreamily watching James being escorted through a side door by his father and sister. I say that I was standing, but in actuality Carmen was holding me up and asking whether I felt capable of moving. She led me to a battered old leather couch at the back area of the bar and whispered a reminder of tomorrow's meeting. Without replying, I stretched out, closed my eyes and smiled. The smile was, no doubt, caused by the pleasurable sensation of a warm hand entering my trouser pocket.

Luke Kelly

I vaguely recall trying to help Luke load his bass into the boot of Benny Chia's Volvo, but this must have been a couple of hours later, as Benny had already locked up the club and was offering me a lift back to the Mandarin Oriental hotel.

In the back seat of the Volvo, Luke and I were engaged in a rambling conversation about turbans and motorbikes. At one point he was cursing 'that bloody rocking chair' that had belonged to his mother. Then he was jokingly fending off my incessant questions about his early life. Yes, he had married Brenda when she became pregnant, and they lived together for a short while. Not surprisingly, he did not find married life to his taste and so moved out when James was around eighteen months old.

'It wasn't so much being married, more having to live inside four walls. We still haven't got round to getting a divorce. I don't suppose we ever will. Jamie prefers it that way.'

I asked him at what point he had become a tramp, but can only recall Benny's raucous laugh from the front seat. Then I threw up.

Delboy

Delboy is the nickname of a TV comedy character by the name of Del Trotter. It is also the nickname that Luke has bestowed upon Delger. I had no opportunity to introduce myself to Delger after the performance, as he was the first to leave the stage and was subsequently nowhere to be seen. I will no doubt bump into him, if I can follow the scribbled instructions on the back of a map of Cheung Chau that I have discovered this morning, crumpled up in my trouser pocket.

The closest you'll ever get.

What was *that* supposed to mean? Did Jade really think that I would derive pleasure from being crushed up against James on that stage? She always did make those distasteful homosexual jibes. It is to be regretted that her growth as a jazz musician has not developed hand in hand with any emotional maturity. Or was Jade's comment referring to her brother's own lack of emotional maturity: the act of singing with him being the only means of breaching the distance that he maintains between himself and those outsiders wishing to infiltrate his universe?

More probably, Jade was implying that it was my final opportunity to be near James before he made his inevitable escape, and that my chances of spending time with him on Cheung Chau Island were negligible. If this is what she meant, then she is mistaken. For this time I am in no doubt that James Kelly and I will meet and talk. I know this, because it is what James wants. For reasons best known to himself, he actually wants it even more than I do, and I cannot recall one instance in my dealings with James Kelly when he has not got what he wanted.

9.30 a.m. From the mezzanine floor of the Mandarin Oriental, I have followed the walkway leading down to the Outlying Islands Ferry Pier, paid my $7.50 for deluxe class, walked up through the air-conditioned area and out on to the sun deck. I am sitting on the front bench of the ferry, this time suitably attired for a sunny December day. I feel euphoric, for in less than one hour I will be disembarking on Cheung Chau Island.

10.35 a.m.
Turn right along the front and keep walking
till you reach the fire station.

The sights and smells of Cheung Chau are a welcome relief after the mayhem of Hong Kong Island. I cheerfully make my way past fish stalls and bobbing sampans to my right and open-fronted cafés to my left. Even the zigzagging bicycles fail to irritate me.

Turn left just after the fire station into a narrow
street. Take another left, past the dried squid stall and
the blind barber, then a final left and right, past the old
cinema. You have reached the 7 Up café. Wait here.
Carmen. xxx

One third of my vocal trio occupies the solitary table outside the café. He stands, offers his hand but remains tight-lipped.

'Delger?' We shake hands, but his face gives nothing away. 'Del? Delboy?'

'Delbert. Would you mind if we wait here for just three more minutes?'

He glances solemnly at his watch and we both sit in silence for the required length of time. 'My name is Delbert. Please follow me.'

'David Carpenter. What does Delger mean in Mongolian?'

'It's the name of a river. But my name is Delbert.'

'So you *are* from Mongolia, then?'

'No, I was born in Tsuen Wan, here in the New Territories.'

'So how do you know about Mongolian rivers?'

'Because I've travelled there many times: my father is Mongolian. But my name is not Delger. It's Delbert. '

'So who's Delger?'

'I have no idea, but you can call me Delboy. That's what Mister Kelly likes to call me. This way please.'

I follow him through a winding alley that opens onto a wider road. We stop outside the second doorway.

'We are here. The door is open. Please go through. Mister Kelly is waiting for you on the first floor.'

10.43 a.m. I am slowly mounting the wooden stairs, stepping in time to an instantly recognisable sound. The creak, creak, creak of the old red rocker had once accompanied James' ramblings as I sat outside his locked bedroom door, one New Year's Eve in Outlane. I am unsure as to whether the motive for my synchronised footsteps is to surprise him or to steady my nerves. Judging by the gradually increasing interval between each creak, it is evident that James is not only aware of my slow ascent, but is attempting to control my speed as though I were his remote-controlled toy. With three steps to go, both the rocking chair and I come to a standstill.

'Carpenter! It's almost 10.45. I'm out here on the balcony. Bring two Tsing Tao's from the kitchen fridge.'

The stone-floored living room is, as expected, sparse and meticulous, with every item set in its allocated place. The white-painted walls are bare apart from one photograph of Luke posing on his motorbike, a Winmau dartboard, and a framed sketch of James cradling baby Nicky. I collect the beers from a spotless kitchen and walk through an open door opposite that leads out on to the balcony. A long, slender object wrapped in gold cloth leans up against the outer wall. The bamboo shakuhachi lies across a blue metal table. Set each side of the table are two chairs, angled towards each other at forty-five degrees. The chair that awaits me is made of brown wicker, strewn with white cushions. The chair containing James is his grandmother's much-travelled red rocker. However, from where I'm standing, the only indication of its occupier is one jutting elbow and a rising plume of smoke. Clutching a beer in each hand, I take two further steps and am finally standing opposite James Kelly. But this time he is clearly not about to go anywhere.

Looking slightly podgy in just a white T-shirt, khaki shorts and navy-blue flip-flops, he is sprawled out on the rocker, his languorous demeanour somehow incongruous against the meticulous and austere surroundings. Without looking up, his left arm stretches out lazily towards me. He takes his beer and sets it down on the metal table next to the shakuhachi. A cigarette burns down in an ashtray on the floor. He continues to stare intently into the watch on his left wrist, until, finally, it conveys the information that causes him to break into a beaming smile. His head slowly lifts … and for the very first time James' watery blue eyes are looking directly into mine.

'Carpenter!'

'Hello James.'

He takes another glance at his watch, reaches down and stubs out the cigarette. 'We only have until 12.15 for me to answer your four questions. Let's begin.'

'And am I supposed to know what these four questions are?'

'Yes, because each question is based upon a person that you know. Shall I tell you in which order to ask them?'

I feel I'm being railroaded. In a bid to maintain equal footing, I move slowly to the balcony rail and indicate the building opposite.

'Is that CC's second property?'

'It's mine now. I own the ground-floor flat. Carmen's been

staying there but she'll be leaving on Monday. You're to be her second guest of the day.'

'Yes, I'm expected at one.'

'Keep looking down. Carmen's first guest is about to arrive. Shall we give her a wave?'

I turn abruptly and sit down on the wicker chair.

'I'd really rather not. I'm surprised that you smoke.'

'Why is that, Carpenter? Perhaps it's because we've never met. It's a pleasure to make your acquaintance.'

James' regal arm gesture annoys me.

'No offence James, but I hadn't given you much thought until you popped up on that pathetic quiz show.'

'But I was pretty cool, wasn't I?'

'If by cool you mean relaxed, yes, I did remark to Barrie how at ease you appeared. He put it down to the calming presence of your family in the front row.'

'That's very funny. My doctor put it down to a new prescription. Thanks for coming to my party last night. We made a superb singing group, didn't we?'

'I'd brought your birthday present to the club. But by the time I remembered it, you'd already left and I was slumped out on a sofa. Then I think I was sick in Benny's car. Belated happy birthday!'

James unwraps the set of Harrow darts and places one carefully on the table next to the shakuhachi.

'Perfect. I'll use this later to answer your third question. Oh look, Carpenter! The subject of question number one has just arrived across the road. She's staring up at us with a very pained expression.'

I keep my focus on James.

'It's *Jacqueline Stewart* that has a question for you, James, not me.'

'Excellent! Do you know her question?'

Yes. She'd like to know if you'd do anything to hurt her.'

James grins.

'Would she? Shall we invite her up?'

I simply cannot let this happen.

'I thought you weren't speaking to her.'

The grin fades.

'I will *never* speak to her again.'

James' sudden distraught expression causes me to relax. I take a brief glance over the balcony.

'I'm relieved to hear it and I did warn you. Whatever she's up to, she should be stopped.'

'Oh yes, she will be stopped. And you will help us, won't you, Carpenter.'

'Well, I'll certainly do what I can.'

Carmen is opening the door to let Jax in. The impact of James bringing his fist crashing down onto the table causes me to start and turn back towards him.

'We *hate* her. And you hate her as much as we do, don't you, Carpenter!'

'I wouldn't go that far. I'm just sorry I invited her to Ken's funeral in the first place. She hardly knew the man.'

'And why were *you* there, Carpenter?'

I blanch at James' knowing expression.

'You know very well why I was there. I came to see *you*. And you were expecting me. So why didn't you show up?'

'Jade said I could baby-sit Nicky. My nephew and I were having an excellent time until we were invaded by that lunatic. Why did you give Jax our address?'

'I didn't. Barrie gave it to her in the Waggon.'

James takes a large swig of beer and leans back in the rocker.

'Now ask me your first question.'

'I have a question about that afternoon.'

James laughs like an excited child.

'Yes, you *do*!'

'What game were you playing that led Jax to believe that you were a murderer?'

James claps his hands.

'That is the correct question. I'll go and fetch the book.'

James has settled back in the rocker. A large book now rests on his lap.

'Nicky and I were in the front room. He was tossing and turning in his cot as I blew him long notes on the shakuhachi. My hope was that its sound might send him off to sleep. Did I ever thank you for giving me such a wondrous present? It is always by my side as a comforter. But on that afternoon it wasn't casting its spell on my baby nephew. That's when I discovered this book that CC had left on the sofa before he set off for the funeral.'

James holds up *Spirit of the Shadow Warrior* for my inspection. From within its swirling dark orange cover, a collage of mysterious faces and Japanese weaponry conspire to lure vulnerable readers into its world of pretentious nonsense. To confirm my suspicions, he opens the book, holds it close to his face, and begins reciting a passage in the manner of a Dalek, intoning each syllable on the same pitch and with equal stress. I have no idea whether this meaningless delivery is meant to be humorous. Luckily, the book masks my unsmiling, and near-yawning mouth.

'... *Attaining the core essence of the ninja art begins with the paring away of inessentials to reach a base state of personal spiritual purity, and culminates in the ability to move freely without defilement between the polar realms of brightness and darkness, as necessitated by the scheme of totality.*'

James' enquiring eyes appear above the volume, awaiting my reaction. I can only shake my head.

'So who wrote this stuff?'

'The author is quoting from an ancient encyclopaedia about the art of the ninja. But can you understand it, Carpenter?'

My mind had wandered after the first phrase.

'Not one word. Can you?'

'Of course I can! And so must *you*, before you throw the dart that will answer question three. Nicky had finally gone off to sleep when the doorbell rang. She was scary, like a spectre, with black netting hanging down from her hat, hiding her face. I should have realised then that she's even more evil than Uncle Ken. She pecked my cheek as though we were old friends. Then she was hovering over Nicky and placed her strange hat on his tummy. As she turned round, I suddenly remembered who she was and could visualise her sitting in my dressing room at the Alexandra Palace. She'd been explaining numerology and drawing a sketch of me.'

'That was the drawing that I posted to you.'

'Yes, and for some reason, she now demanded to see that drawing, refusing to accept that I'd left it in Matsudo. She insisted that I'd hidden it somewhere in the house and started rummaging round the room.'

'She was off her head on acid.'

'All I knew was that she was crazy and I was feeling very agitated. That was until she stumbled upon CC's book and everything changed. Jax settled herself into the sofa and was now quietly leafing through the illustrations. Then she stumbled upon a picture that caused her upper body to jolt. She looked up, smiled, and formally declared that I was a ninja. It was as though she had uncovered my true identity and was bestowing an honorary title upon me.' James snaps out of his vision and grins. 'Naturally, I accepted.'

'You let her believe that you were a ninja? Wasn't that going to send her even crazier?'

'I didn't care. I had to gain control of this madwoman. Nicky had started to settle down, goo-gooing at his new plaything. At first I cautiously observed Jax from a safe distance as she studied other illustrations but soon summoned the courage to sit down beside her. Now we were flicking through the pages together. And there, suddenly before us, was the picture that had us both entranced. Look for yourself. It's on page 143.'

Apart from the long wooden pipe protruding from his mouth, the masked, leather-clad figure stalking through the undergrowth reminds me more of the British wrestler Doctor Death than a deadly assassin. I try to look impressed, inviting James to continue.

'I stepped over into her world and we glanced at each other as though we had become collaborators, perhaps even lovers. She showed no surprise when I got up, walked over to the shakuhachi that was propped up next to the sideboard, and ceremoniously raised it above my head. I then opened a drawer that contained my sets of darts and removed one from its case. I slid the dart down the bamboo tube, put it to my lips, and aimed at her forehead. Jax stood up. Her confusion filled me with pleasure. Once again, I raised the flute horizontally above my head and proclaimed, "This is how I deal with my enemies!" But then, as though acknowledging that we were both playing a children's game, she grinned at me. "But I'm not your enemy, am I, James?" In a silly, deep voice, I replied, "I had but one enemy, and he shall soon be laid out in Pole Moor cemetery." It was an exceedingly good game.'

James leans back into the rocker and gazes silently at me, awaiting my response.

'And was that it?'

'Yes, apart from the sex upstairs afterwards.' I choose not to respond to James' provocative smile. 'So, now you can ask me question number two. Ask me about the man from Mongolia.'

'Okay, James: who is Delger?'

'I will give you two answers: the first is nobody, and the second is Jade. There is no Delger, and Jade is Delger. The man that sang with us last night and brought you here this morning is our cleaner, Delbert. He is also part Mongolian, although he was born in Hong Kong.

'CC first brought me here to Cheung Chau on 18 December 1977, for a brief holiday. When we arrived in the flat, Delbert was actually out here sweeping this balcony. We'd just travelled from Japan and were both exhausted, so Delbert kindly cooked us a meal. There was a very bad atmosphere. CC was still frosty with me for the way I had behaved towards Master Onuma, so I was thankful to find someone else who wanted to chat. That afternoon, Delbert and I walked together along the harbour. I can still remember the Mongolian song he taught me. It was about a black horse. Shall I sing it to you?'

'I'd rather learn when Delbert introduced you to overtone singing.'

'Never! The very first time we discussed overtone singing was yesterday morning, when I asked him to join us on stage at the Fringe Club.'

'So, last night, when Jade invited the audience to spot the impostor—'

'That's right. Delbert was the impostor! He'd never even attempted to sing overtones before yesterday evening. He had no idea what he was doing. It's very funny, isn't it, Carpenter!'

'So what about Delger? When did *he* first appear?'

'Delger first appeared when Jade made him up. Ha ha!'

'Why would your sister do that?'

'Before I explain, you must answer *my* question. Answer me this: What do you know about overtones?'

I hear the irritation in my voice.

'Why can't you just answer *my* question?'

James' voice rises above my own.

'Because it is *impossible* to answer until you've told me everything you know about overtones.'

'Well, that won't take long. I know that each overtone

has a fixed mathematical relationship to the fundamental note and— '

James has waved me to a halt.

'No Carpenter, don't give me facts. What do you *really* know?'

I raise my hands in exasperation.

'Well, clearly, I know nothing. Please enlighten me.'

I instantly regret my sarcasm, having no wish to antagonise him. Fortunately, he has taken my words at face value.

'I will now reveal to you the secret of overtones. Children cannot exist without parents, but overtones can be both themselves *and* their parents. An overtone child can be at home with his parents. Yet in that same instant, he can also be playing alone in the garden.'

'I'm afraid that didn't reveal anything, James.'

'Then I'll say it another way. The overtone parent and child can be in two places at once. But one can also transform into the other. *Now* do you understand?'

'No. It might help if we move away from parents and children.'

'Then imagine an archer moving freely between himself and his target. But if he suddenly loses ground, then his arrow is wasted.' James looks at me expectantly. I shake my head. 'Carpenter, you've just *got* to understand or I'll not be able to answer question three. Then your dart will be wasted.'

'Look, James, why don't we save time by popping the dart back in its case, scrubbing question three and sticking with question two. Who is Delger?'

'Don't you see? Without overtones, there is no Delger. He only comes into being by way of the overtones that floated from Jade's soprano, through the walls of her bedroom and into mine.'

James has been silently rocking for two minutes. His eyes are defocused. When he speaks, it's as though he is merely voicing the continuation of an internal monologue.

'I tried humming long, low notes for hours on end, but to no avail. Then, six months later, during a dull June afternoon in Matsudo, they finally came dancing out my shakuhachi. That evening I wrote to Jade, asking her what I was hearing.'

'You also wrote to me. Did she explain?'

'No. She eventually wrote back in July, only to say that all her energy was taken up with being eight months pregnant. When CC and I returned to Yorkshire for December of that year, Jade was in no mood to answer questions. She spent the whole Christmas blubbing over her stupid father's death, changing nappies and screaming at Mum. In the end, she stormed off to Auntie Doris in Wakefield. By September she'd dumped Nicky on Doris and moved to Leeds to start her jazz course.'

'So she'd forgotten about your question.'

'Oh no. She wrote from Leeds, saying that she'd pinned a message up on the students' notice board. But it took a year before anyone responded.'

'And that person was Carmen.'

'Yes. And Carmen put her in touch with Dominic, who specialised in overtone singing. He'd studied the technique in Mongolia. But by the time that Jade finally got round to sending me everything I could ever wish to know about Mongolian throat singing, my mind was elsewhere. I had come to hate CC, hate Master Onuma and hate Kyudo. I no longer wished to remain in Japan and knew exactly where I wanted to go.'

'You wanted to move here, to Cheung Chau.'

'Not just to Cheung Chau ... I wanted to move into this flat, where there was a bedroom that CC had previously prepared for me, and where there was a man who had once been content to be my friend for nothing in return. Delbert is the one person that has never asked anything of me.' A momentary pause is my only evidence that his statement may be meant to hurt me. 'I knew that this flat was still unoccupied, and that CC no longer had any use for it. And by that time, I had become such an embarrassment to him that he would surely be relieved to see the back of me.'

'This all sounds very calculating.'

James springs to his feet and I'm left staring at the decelerating rocker as it slowly squeaks to a halt. For the first time, I feel intimidated by his close proximity and rising agitation.

'I was not planning anything. I *had* to leave! It was unbearable. *Everything* was unbearable. Only Jade and the big man could help me. You couldn't have helped me, could you! What could *you* have done?'

I try to appear calm as he peers down over the balcony. After an anxious glance at his watch, he turns and lights up another cigarette. He is again staring at me, awaiting my response.

'Did you speak to your father or sister about any of this?'

'I wrote down all my thoughts and posted them to Jade. I told her how wretched I had become, and the happier life that might be awaiting me, how I yearned to return to my paradise island and again walk by the harbour with Delbert, singing his Mongolian songs. My letter was rather melodramatic, but something needed to happen. A fortnight later I received this short note from her.'

James bends down to scoop up a folded sheet of paper from under the ashtray. He drops it onto my lap and slumps back into the rocker as though suddenly drained of energy.

My darling James,
You are about to receive the first in a series of letters and packages from YOUR NEW IMAGINARY FRIEND!
Here's all you need to know about him:
His name is Delger and he is a Mongolian khoomii singer, soon to be moving from England to Hong Kong. Carmen's friend, Dominic, has recommended him to you, and the exciting news is that Delger will be delighted to accept you as a student. In time, you will

be required to join him in Hong Kong, but for now he insists that you undertake a course of exercises that will acquaint you with the basic technique. You will shortly be receiving these written instructions, together with cassettes containing examples of khoomii singing.

Please inform CC of the situation as soon as possible. He will surely accommodate you!

With all my love, your amazingly brilliant sister,

Jade

'So I'd say that it was my sister who was calculating, wouldn't you?'

'I'd say that you were both acting dishonestly.'

'Yes, we were. She started sending letters, tapes, even a photo of a total stranger, signed: "Best wishes, Delger." Each evening I would play the cassettes at full volume and read my letters aloud to CC at every opportunity. I began refusing to attend the practice hall, and insisting that I had to join my new teacher in Hong Kong. CC finally conceded and phoned Mum to propose plans for my transportation. Yes, he would gladly chaperone me to my new home, help me settle in and even provide a second flat to house Delger. It took CC a few months to set up the move, and by the time he was finally accompanying me onto the plane, we were equally relieved. Jade needed to manufacture one final letter to inform us that Delger would be unable to meet CC during his brief stay, as he would be judging a throat singing competition in Tuva during that period. There was also just one occasion, some time after I had moved here, when Mum phoned me, asking if she could speak to Delger. I pretended to call him over, and then sung her a chorus from the song about the black horse.'

'You seem to derive great pleasure from deceiving people.'

'Yes, I do. I certainly enjoyed deceiving you last night.

Delbert's vocal efforts at the Fringe Club were for your benefit alone.'

'So I was the only person who believed Delbert to be Delger: the master khoomii singer from Mongolia?'

'Yes, apart from Mum and Barrie ... But Mum never minds what happens as long as I seem cheerful. And Barrie doesn't count. He's a fool. Everyone here knows Delbert. He cleans the club and is very popular. It was very funny to see him up there and enjoying himself so much.'

'So you got exactly what you wanted and will now presumably live here happily ever after.'

'I've lived here very happily for six years, but now it's time to move to my true home. There is only one place I've ever wished to live happily ever after, and that's in Barrie's house at Marsden Gate. This was promised to me from the start.'

'You want to live with Barrie and your mother?'

'Oh no. I want to live with Jade, Nicky and the big man. Mum and Barrie will move to Cheung Chau and live in the flat opposite.'

'That is totally unrealistic. Brenda tells me that Barrie dislikes Hong Kong.'

'But Mum loves it. CC has also offered Barrie a lucrative job as site manager for his company's new building project in Sha Tin. And Barrie's far too greedy to refuse.'

'But what makes you think you can just move people around just to suit you?'

'Because I've done it before – if it hadn't been for me removing the obstacle, Mum would never have moved into Marsden Gate with Barrie.'

'The obstacle being Ken, I suppose.'

'Ken is to be saved for question four. It's now time for question three.'

'Not yet. What do you mean, Marsden Gate was promised to you?'

'It was promised to me back in the days when they were still building the house. Whenever I visited Dad in the caravan, he gave me his word that one day the three of us would live there together. Now, with Nicky, there'll be four. Fetch some more beer. We only have another seventy minutes.'

11.05 a.m. Ten minutes ago James announced that he was taking a break and retired to his bedroom. Now he is once again slumped back in the rocker with a fresh cigarette and can of Tsing Tao.

'Question one was about Jax. Question two was about Delger. Question four will be about Ken. Who do you think question three is about?'

'You?'

'Yes, me! It's the question you have always wished to ask me.'

I shrug.

'I'll give you a clue by asking *you* a question. What do you *really* want from me?'

'You overestimate your importance. I want nothing from you. Had you asked me that question nine years ago, when my inflated ego mistakenly took you for a kindred spirit, the answer might have been friendship.'

'You were very lonely, Carpenter. I remember telling you so.'

'Perhaps I was isolated in those days, but I'm no longer that person. I've come here now more out of curiosity than friendship.'

James has adopted his serious, overly concentrated expression. He leans forward and rests his hand on mine.

'So what is it that you *really* want from me?'

I hastily withdraw my hand.

'If you're waiting for me to confess that I fancied you, fell in love with you or some such nonsense, then you're in for a disappointment. I've never really gone in for that sort of thing, and particularly not with men. But as you obviously dreamed up these four questions weeks ago, I expect you'd like me to ask whether you find me attractive. As I don't require an answer, we can save time by moving straight on to question four and Ken.'

James is suddenly looking very concerned. The chair begins to rock.

'I am not stupid. Do not speak to me as though I were an imbecile. I have no interest in such a trivial question. You know very well that there is a far more important question you wish to ask me. My answer will help you.'

How dare he patronise me! I stand up.

'I've really had enough of this. I'm having lunch with Carmen in an hour. So, if you have no objection, I'll take a look round the island for a while. Let's keep in touch.'

'I know very well what you want of me. You want to know how I do it. You have *always* wanted to know how I do it, so that *you* can do it. Please don't go Carpenter; let me show you.'

11.09 a.m. I am taking refuge in the bustling street scene opposite to counteract James' intense stare.

'Tell me that I'm right, Carpenter, that it all began with bull's eyes. You saw what I could do and yearned to do it for yourself. But you never have.'

'Incorrect. I hit the bull's eye on my third attempt.'

'But never since – I will guide you. There are two stages. But we can only proceed with the first stage on one condition: you must give me your word that, whatever happens, you'll also undergo the second stage, that you will do everything I ask of you.'

For some reason, I find his wide-eyed expression of anticipation rather comical and suppress a laugh by furrowing my brow. He begins to nod his head and I find myself imitating the action. He smiles, I smile and somehow I have entered the contract.

11.13 a.m. We are facing the dartboard. James has sculpted me into position: leading foot pointing forward, right foot angled to the side, big toe level with left heel.

'Swivel your hips. Your shoulders need to be at right angles to your left foot. Now take hold of the dart at its centre of gravity. Grip lightly with the tips of your thumb, forefinger and index finger. That's right – just below your fingernails. Stretch out your forearm as far as it will go. No, keep it vertical to your body. Good. Now your body is still. As you release, all motion will be confined to your forearm. There has to be a minimum of movement or nothing will work.' James positions himself behind me and gently cradles my left elbow with his hand. 'Think back to when you first saw me throw a dart. Tell me what you imagine I did at the moment of release.'

'I think you went somewhere else. You softened, phased out, drifted into another world.'

James lets go of my elbow and angrily snatches the dart from my left hand.

'No! Why won't you listen? It's the very opposite. When an overtone splits from its parent note, it is incapable of getting lost. *Why* can't it get lost?'

'Tell me again,'

'Because its parent will never abandon it! You just have to understand that they are both as nimble as ghosts, capable of slipping between two worlds. They can even exchange places with one another. However could they do this if one of them was half asleep?'

'I still don't know what you're talking about. Can't you just tell me what I'm supposed to do?'

'Just stay *totally* awake or this is never going to happen! We'll start again.'

James edges in closer behind me. I feel his breath on the back of my neck as he makes subtle adjustments to my elbow with his fingertips.

'I want you to really *see* the bull. Prepare to enter its eye. Travel to its inner ring and sit inside for a moment. Now travel back to yourself. You are moving freely from here to there and back again. This is because you are in both places. But you must keep fully awake. Now it's time to forget the target until stage two. Shut your eyes. Cock back your wrist. Release the dart. Perfect! But your eyes must remain closed until I've removed your dart from the board.'

11.20 a.m. We are seated back in our respective chairs but now my adrenalin is pumping.

'Did I hit the bull's eye?'

'I've told you! The target has no relevance at this stage. We must move on.'

'I've lost track. Would that be to stage two or question four?'

'Carpenter, I am not playing the game that you think I am. I can only guide you through stage two once you have asked the final question. Now ask it!'

'Very well, question four: what were your movements on the day that Ken died?'

'You must first appreciate that Uncle Ken was never kind to me. He was *never* kind, neither before nor after the arrival of the dartboard on my thirteenth birthday. But from that day he began to change. Mockery transformed into what outsiders mistook for encouragement, but insiders knew to be bullying. In turn, my feelings towards him turned from fearfulness into hatred. I prayed for him to die and was glad when he did.'

'But he recognised your gift.'

'*What* gift? Don't imagine that I was hitting triple 20s from the first day. Nobody's capable of that. It took many months of constant practice before his scornful comments lessened. I could see him gauging how far he could push me, noting which parts of my new life elated me and which parts terrified me.'

'What terrified you?'

'The chaos of new situations. At first, chaos seemed everywhere. But Ken knew how to clear the path for me so that I could play my game, otherwise I was of no use to him. But I also learned how to work Uncle Ken to *my* advantage.'

'So CC is right. You can fake your emotions to suit yourself.'

'No, I cannot fake terror, but I can calculate its effect on others. I gradually learned how to handle him in my own way. I didn't need Dad's constant warnings that Uncle Ken was just using me to further his career. Of course he was! I could see that for myself.'

'Just as you can *now* see Jacqueline Stewart stepping into Ken's shoes.'

'But we will not let this happen, will we, Carpenter! Evildoers must be stopped.'

'I hardly see Jax as evil. But Ken did further *your* career. Didn't you want to be successful?'

'Yes I did. I wanted to become famous.'

'So one part of you was quite content with how things were developing.'

'Yes, until Uncle Ken pushed me onto that TV show. That's another thing I will never forgive him for.'

'But you would never have met CC … or me, for that matter – not that I made any impact on your life.'

'You did make me feel important, but CC made me feel—'

'Perhaps he made you feel like you made *me* feel.'

'Loving CC showed me how much I was coming to loathe Uncle Ken. I would have done anything for CC in those first weeks. It was as though he had come to rescue me.'

'You *were* doing anything for him. You gave up darts, you travelled to the other side of the world.'

'Yes, and initially my new life was wonderful. But soon, the novelty of Kyudo began turning into long hours of drudgery to no purpose. To be admonished time and time again by the master was hard enough. But to be constantly reminded that there wasn't *meant* to be any purpose or outcome to this drudgery made things intolerable.'

'But wasn't CC supportive?'

'My greatest disappointment was to witness CC's wounded pride when I didn't come up to his expectations. But I'll always be grateful to him for helping me to escape. I still believe that he truly wanted to change my life for the better. He wished me no harm, nor did he set out to harm Uncle Ken. It was Ken that set out to harm CC by spreading those poisonous rumours.'

'To be fair, James, they're equally culpable. CC may never have intended to harm Ken, but he certainly set out to deceive him. In doing so, he caused him a *great* deal of harm. That's why Ken, being the man he was, went after him. But believe me, CC felt great remorse for his actions. He still does.'

'Oh yes, I remember. He wanted to "make reparation with Mister Bell".'

James' sneering impersonation seems out of character.

'Are you suggesting that CC was insincere? I know he had every intention of making amends as far back as the summer of that year. That's when he wrote asking if I could be of any help. That was just six months before Ken died.'

'By then it was far too late for his reparations. Every single one of us: CC, Dad, Jade, even you, had already played our parts in Uncle Ken's downfall, just as we're now all plotting Jax's downfall.'

'I'm not plotting anything. Nor did I have anything whatever to do with Ken's downfall. And why would Jade have wanted to destroy her father? Her eulogy at the church showed how much she loved him.'

Although James' tone is not angry, its hardened edge makes me uneasy.

'You knew that there was no exhibition match in Hong Kong and that I'd taken the dartboard down from my bedroom wall. So why didn't you inform him? And Jade knew that I had no intention of proceeding to the second round of the Embassy championships. Why didn't she tell her loving father, instead of helping me out through the side door?'

'So you're blameless.'

'I was, initially. My personal contribution began only *after* his vicious attempts to cause trouble. But I only made three anonymous phone calls in all ... four if I count the final one that went wrong.'

'So *you* were scaring Ken with those threatening phone calls!'

'Oh yes, and I scared him very much. My first three impersonations of sinister Chinese thugs were all excellent. Number one took place on the morning of Monday, 9 January 1978 from Mum's phone to Uncle Ken's office in Wakefield. Number two was three weeks later. I called from the hotel in Retford that you recommended to us. You will remember the date.'

'February 6th: the first day of the Embassy – you and Jade phoned me from the Old Bell Hotel with that that infantile story.'

'Dad and CC were there too, but they left Jade and I to read you our splendid tale of Robin Hood and the mysterious archer. After that call, Jade went off to get ready. But I'd enjoyed our story so much that I felt inspired to phone Uncle Ken at his posh Nottingham hotel. I devised an even more splendid tale that culminated in a poisoned dart embedded between his eyes.

'After my return to Matsudo, he quickly faded from my memory. I had no further contact with the foul man until six months later. In fact I might never have bothered to make call number three, had Mum not phoned me on the evening of August 15th to announce the birth of my nephew. She'd just come from the hospital. Jade was in excellent health, but distraught that her father hadn't bothered to put in an appearance. His shameful excuse was that he had to stay in the office to await an important call. So I decided that it would be a pity to disappoint him.

'My fourth and final call to Uncle Ken, which I made on the day of his death, went disastrously wrong. It was around 6.30 in the morning. CC had left me guarding the bags in the Heathrow arrivals lounge while he went off to arrange a car hire. Sitting there on a suitcase, I was feeling even worse than when you met me at departures the previous year. But this time I had a strategy that was guaranteed to make me feel better. The public phone was just above my head, the receiver almost within reach. I had no English money and so asked the operator to reverse the charges. Eventually, as I listened to Mum's sleepy voice accepting the call, I felt some sympathy for her. Then all at once I was overcome with fury towards the man I could picture snoring in her bed. I was unable to stop myself, even though I knew that the stupid voice I was adopting would fool no one. To anyone else, my phoney accent would have sounded like a comedy Chinese detective, but because Mum was expecting us to arrive at Heathrow that morning, she assumed that I really was Mister Lee. She asked if James was okay. I replied that he was fine, but that I urgently needed to speak with Mister Bell. I felt panicked by the rising sound of his heavy breathing and curses as he stumbled down the stairs. But still I couldn't bring myself to hang up. Whatever foolishness I began to blurt out, he was on to me before I had reached the end of my first stuttered sentence. I don't remember much of what he said, but his abrasive language transported me back to those terrible times before the dartboard arrived.'

James has begun to pace the room and seems unaware of my presence. He is keeping close to the walls as though hiding from someone.

'James, why don't we get some air? Let's take a walk along the harbour. You can teach me that Mongolian song about a horse. Tell me the rest later.'

I'm unsure whether he's heard me. He has stopped circling and now presses his back hard against the bedroom door.

'Unspeakable words like cretin and simpleton banged around in my head throughout the miserable car journey from London to Huddersfield. And all the while, CC made it worse with his constant ramblings about the damage he'd caused and how there was still time "to make reparation with Mister Bell". As we turned off the motorway, I instructed him to drive straight to Marsden Gate, explaining that I wished to speak with dad before heading home. By midday we were parked opposite the two caravans. CC waited in the car as I made my way along the path, totally undecided as to what I should tell the big man.

'I sat there on Dad's unmade bed, my mind totally blank. As I watched him pour boiling water into two dirty mugs, I could only think to ask: "Where's Barrie?" Dad's reply led to all that followed. His words were far more valuable than any advice that he might have offered. "Well, if Ken's still round your mother's place, at least Barrie won't be there shagging her. So I expect you'll find Barrie in the Waggon." That venom in Dad's voice told me just how much he loathed these men, but particularly Barrie, who still owed him money for the building work. As we drove the mile from Marsden Gate to Outlane, I remember CC commenting on my sudden chirpiness. He was right. I felt excited.

'Fortunately, it was Uncle Ken that came to the door, and for that moment I wasn't afraid of him. I recall the stench of his beery breath as he grabbed at my coat. But I still managed to inform him, in just one calm sentence, precisely what Mum had been up to, and where Barrie could be found. He relaxed his hold on me and stared out towards the car where CC was unpacking the boot. Mum knew something was up and came racing from the kitchen. He glared back at her and then set off across the road as though he were sleepwalking. Mum hurriedly followed me out to the car as I was gathering up my small brown suitcase and the leather holder that contained my bow, arrows and shakuhachi. She tried hugging me, but I ducked, pulled away from her and headed indoors. Jade was waiting at the foot of the staircase, playfully barring my way. I pushed past her and locked myself in my bedroom.

'I first needed to stop my brain from racing through a stream of unconnected and undecipherable images. To calm me down, I removed my shakuhachi from its case and was soon pacing the room to the accompaniment of long, low, wavering notes. As my breathing rate decreased, so each note lengthened. My mind began to clear. I strolled over to the window and observed Mum and CC standing by the car, engrossed in an animated conversation. Although I could hear no words, it was clear from CC's agitated arm gestures that he was declining her advice. She watched him cross the road, then draped a couple of suits over her arm and trudged back towards our gate as CC entered the Waggon.

'I so wanted Jade beside me. I even thought of calling out to her. But then I heard the front door slam and spotted her standing on our side of the road, facing the pub. By the time I was opening the bedroom window, she'd already turned right. This meant that she was heading towards Marsden Gate to fetch Dad. Without having realised, I'd set the shakuhachi down on the window ledge and was starting to open the small brown suitcase. But you must believe me Carpenter. I had no plan.'

Tentatively, I walk towards James. He doesn't move.

'Plan to do what, James?' I step a little nearer until I'm

within three feet. I resist the impulse to take his hand. 'Plan to do what?'

'I had no plan to play or to open the window. I had no plan to open the suitcase.' James turns towards his bedroom and twists the door handle. 'Please follow me.'

11.35 a.m The white walls of James' bedroom are bare, apart from a full-length mirror and a framed drawing of the Lo Shu turtle. A bulging holdall props open one door of an empty wardrobe. A small, brown suitcase lies unopened on the bed. James sits down beside it and rests a hand on the clip. He looks up at me and speaks softly.

'I opened the lid, removed all my clothes and changed into the costume contained in this suitcase. You will now do the same. But I will need to dress you.'

'You will *what*?'

'These are not ordinary clothes. They must be treated with the utmost respect and fastened in the traditional way. Please strip off. We now have less than fifteen minutes to redress the balance.'

My forced laugh is received with silent solemnity. I raise both hands waist-high, palms outward.

'Okay James, I've been willing to accommodate you up to this point. But I draw the line at whatever perverted rituals you indulge in with your Delgers and Delboys. So, if you don't mind, I'll cut my losses and leave question four and stage two, or whatever numbers we've reached, to my own imagination. This, as the hippies used to say, really is not my scene.'

James stands up to face me. His hands are on my shoulders. My arms relax.

'No, Carpenter, I don't suppose it is your scene. Jade and I have always known that. We'd never taken you for a person with great expectations. To say this to your face saddens me and is not meant to hurt you. You and I can always be friends.

But for now, as you rightly say, the line is drawn. Enjoy your lunch with Carmen, and the rest of your stay. Shall we hug, like we did that day in Nottingham? Do you remember, just as CC and I were leaving the club?' I nod and comply. 'Now I need to continue here alone.'

I leave the room.

I am slumped on the red rocker, my feet pumping against the metal table. The regularly incessant creak, creak, creak is hopefully penetrating James' bedroom wall, to let it be known that I am desecrating his sacred space. Surely it will have the desired effect and propel him from his room with unbounded fury. But what would it take for James Kelly to really notice me? Only when he has hoisted me high above his shoulders and is dangling me over the balcony, might he finally feel my physical weight, thus deducing that I am a separate entity.

This cannot go on. Why ever have I allowed myself to be continually bulldozed by a man ten years my junior and possessing inferior intelligence? Why have I fallen for the watery blue eyes, the boyish charm that lasts only as long as I comply with his demands? Why am I bothering to protect him from the likes of Jax, when my care and concern will never be reciprocated, my existence only acknowledged within the confines of his self-obsessed scheme of things?

11.47 a.m. So, what keeps me? Why am I now hovering by his bedroom door? It can only be his apparent distress that draws me back in, past the bulging holdall that props open the door to the empty wardrobe. He has begun to unpack the small brown suitcase, setting each article of clothing neatly on the duvet. I startle him from his abstraction.

'Your bedroom's empty. Are you moving out?'

He doesn't look up. His voice is subdued.

'Yes. I'll stay with Jade and the big man tonight after their final gig at city hall. Then the three of us will fly home in the morning. You can move in here if you like. Mum and Barrie are staying on too. They'll move in opposite when Carmen moves out on Monday.'

As I stroke the black cotton fabric folded on the bed, I picture Lawrence's bared shoulder as he prepares to release an arrow.

'I recognise these clothes from the Kyudo workshop.'

He glances up at me with the trace of a smile.

'Shall I tell you their names? That's a hakama.' I edge closer as his focus returns to the unfolding of each item. 'I don't know if these white socks have a name, but they should fit you.'

I'm sitting on the bed, removing my sandals.

'Is there a prescribed order?'

'Yes, the keikogi comes next.'

He holds up a white, short-sleeved, quilted jacket and presses it to his chest. I attempt to regain his attention.

'Should I take off my shirt?'

'It's very important …'

There is still little eye contact, and he is murmuring to himself, as though I'd already left.

'James, I can barely hear you.'

He clears his throat but his words are still hard to decipher.

'It's very important that its cords are tied so that the lapel overlaps from left to right.'

'Will you tie it for me?'

As he quietly intones the memorised instructions involving bowknots and horizontal loops, I am detecting a sudden bashfulness lying behind his total immersion in the task. As the final bow is tied, he turns back towards the bed and passes a grey-striped belt back to me.

'This is called an obi. You can fasten it yourself. Then you will need to remove your trousers and pants before putting on the hakama.'

He holds up what looks to be a black pleated skirt, but I

have passed the point of protest. Indeed, in contrast to James' growing awkwardness, I am warming to the act of being dressed, being taken care of.

James, now on his knees, with both hands round my waist, is muttering the memorised instructions like a mantra.

'Fasten the two front ties, draw them to the back, cross them behind, pass them through to the front.' He stands up, takes my hand, and leads me to the mirror. I involuntarily grin at my reflection, but his face remains sombre. 'From the moment that we return to the balcony, you must conduct yourself like a true warrior. Only ask questions that relate to the eight stages of shooting. I listed them once in a letter to you. Do you remember them?'

'That was almost ten years ago.'

'Were they not explained at the Kyudo workshop?'

'Yes, but Lawrence's demonstration was sabotaged by Jacqueline Stewart. James, please believe what I say about her. Take my warning seriously.'

'I have done so. Well, you are ready. It's time to return to the balcony.'

11.58 a.m. 'I will now guide you through the seven stages. By the time you reach stage eight, I'll have left the room. This eighth stage is called zanshin. It will make sense of all that has preceded it, and requires that you are left alone during these final moments. During zanshin, you will retain your position while quietly reflecting on the energy that remains. It is vital that you remember to do this. Now, hold out your right hand. You require this under-glove for protection. The mitsugake has just three fingers. The thumb groove will notch the bowstring. Take the bow in your left hand and let its upper tip rest on the floor. Continue listening to me but I advise you not to speak, as it will disrupt your focus.

Part 4: Overtones

Stage 1 – Ashibumi: stance

'Thirty minutes before Uncle Ken's death, I was already dressed in the very same clothes that you are now wearing. Less than five minutes before his death, I was withdrawing my bow and arrow from its holder. I returned to the open window and looked down on to the empty street, just as you are now doing. I swivelled my body to the right and firmly planted my feet at a 60-degree angle, as you will now do.'

Stage 2 – Dozukuri: balance

'I placed my left hand on my hip and lowered my gaze with the intention of bringing my energy down into my diaphragm, and so arriving at a balanced state. But how could I pass through dozukuri when my whole being was consumed with panic and fear? The task was impossible! Yet, foolishly, I still moved on to yugamae.'

Stage 3 – Yugamae: readying the bow

'I raised the bow to its central position and laid my gloved hand against the string, so that the arrow could notch on to it. Here is the arrow that I used that day.'

I turn my head to the left, but James is just out of my field of vision.

'You intended to fire it?'

'You must retain your position! I then swivelled my upper body to the left and lifted my gaze towards the target area.'

'Your target area that day was the door leading to the saloon bar.'

'That is correct, just as your target area is now the door to the ground-floor flat opposite.'

Stage 4 – Uchiokoshi: raising the bow

I raised the bow to its highest position. Now the arrow was above my head. Normally, the arrow would have remained horizontal, but here it was necessary to tilt it downwards. You will do likewise.'

Stage 5 – Hikiwake: drawing apart the bow

'I slowly drew the bow apart with an equal effort to the left and right. My left hand journeyed forward towards its target, as my right hand pulled the arrow slowly back towards my ear. I drew until I could feel the arrow touch my cheek, just as you now feel it on yours.'

Stage 6 – Kai: the full draw

'I continued to draw the bow to the point where there can be no more expansion, where the only possible conclusion is release. At this moment there has to be a unification of body and mind: a total letting go of any worldly thoughts or intentions towards the target area. But how could I have hoped to attain such a state of mind, knowing that within minutes, my loathsome target would be thundering up the stairs and banging on the door of my bedroom?

'The door from the saloon bar opened. But it was an elderly couple that emerged, just as Luke and Jade will emerge from the door opposite in less than one minute from now. The old woman glanced up and muttered something to her husband, before they moved off in the direction of town. No, Carpenter! You must remain perfectly still. Hold your position and wait!'

PART 4: OVERTONES

12.08 p.m. Luke and Jade have stepped out onto the street. I am struggling to retain my composure. A bead of sweat runs down my cheek. I have to speak.

'James, they're both staring up. They can see us. Jade's grinning at me.'

'Do not react. They will move off as soon as the door closes behind them. Maintain your focus. When an object reaches its full extension, there can only be one outcome: release. This is hanare. Kai leads to hanare, not from any volition, but by default. But as Uncle Ken stepped off the pavement on to New Hey Road, the tables turned. For that moment, *he* was now the arrow on the verge of hanare and I was his potential target. Realising that there was no longer any possibility that I might also move into hanare, I resorted to the behaviour of an infant: I shouted ... not words, more a scream. He halted and looked up. Bleary-eyed and confused, he couldn't quite put together the image that hovered above him, as I leaned out of the window in full costume. My bow was at full stretch, the arrow directed at his forehead. I adjusted my aim and gave out a louder scream. But it felt more like a young child's attempt to frighten an adult than the war cry of a warrior. Then he smiled: that same hurtful smile you just saw on the face of his daughter. He began to lift his arm, perhaps with the intention of raising an imaginary glass to toast my failure, or to wag his finger at the naughty boy. I doubt that the lorry driver had time to give this final, half-completed gesture a second thought. But Uncle Ken's toast to my failure has never left me.'

'Your failure?'

My attention has again been drawn to the opening door opposite.

'Yes, my failure to destroy him ... Carpenter, listen to me. Listen very carefully. It is now vital that you hold your focus. You are about to travel between here and there.'

This time it is two young women that emerge: one Chinese, the other Western. The first woman, with schoolgirl fringe and black eyes, has already turned and disappeared back into the house. The taller willowy woman with the crop of black, tightly curled hair has begun to cross the road. She stops, instinctively aware that she is being watched. She looks up towards the balcony. Although she knows both these men, they are somehow unfamiliar. The handsome, blond man stands immobile, seemingly self-contained. And yet his expressionless, watery blue eyes do not respond to her quizzical smile. Does he not recognise her? She transfers her gaze to the second man. She is struggling to match the familiarity of his pasty face and unkempt hair with the strangeness of his costume. But the costume, in itself, is not strange. Once, the blond man had worn it well. But how ridiculous it looks on this overweight, sweaty man. And how clumsily he clutches the slender curve of wood that casts a scar-like shadow across his podgy white face. In spite of the woman's sense of danger, she takes a small step forward in the hope of catching the words that her ex, blue-eyed lover speaks to his older companion.

'Carpenter, do *not* look around. Hold your position! You once believed that I was special, but my pathetic inaction that day is sufficient justification for you to believe otherwise. So this is *your* moment to become special. You must now enter the place that I was incapable of entering. I want you to breathe in all the disappointments: accept that you have no gift, that your dart missed the bull's eye by six inches, that Carmen likes you but loves my sister. Breathe in all past and present hatreds. Acknowledge that this woman has only ever seen you as a figure of fun. Recall how she stepped over you to reach me. Reflect on how she is inflicting the selfsame damage that Uncle Ken once inflicted. Breathe in all the hurt, Carpenter. Then release it without a trace of emotion or intention, good or bad. Only then can we become true friends.'

12.15 p.m I aim the arrow at Jax's head.

12.16 p.m. **Stage 7 – Hanare: release**

Printed in Great Britain
by Amazon

63906165R00200